The P and Anna

By

Janice Nye

ISBN: 978-1-326-36461-8

PublishNation, London
www.publishnation.co.uk

To my husband, without whose encouragement this would still be a stack of typed sheets in the attic.

Chapter 1
Back to Poly

"And so begins another academic year," thought Anna, as she went to pick up the keys to her room in the hall of residence from the administrative department.   The offices were in a large, rambling building with a tower, straight out of a fairy story, tall, slim and round, with a pointed roof, the rest of the building was adorned by large bay windows, leaded lights and an impressive porch.   It had, probably in the 19th century, been someone's posh town house, but it was hard to imagine a family living there, especially since someone in the 1960's had decided it was going to be an administrative building.   They had split the space up with little regard to how it had been arranged before, large rooms had been divided into small offices, with no thought to the ornate plaster work on the ceilings and walls. Doors were likewise added with no attempt to blend in with existing ones. It all gave it a rather bodged look, as though someone had wanted a modern office block and was having to make do, either because there wasn't the money or they hadn't been allowed to clear the site.

"Room 27," said the lady behind the desk, handing over the keys.   "Do you know where it is?"

"Yes.   Same room as I had last year," said Anna.

"Good.   Here's your dining card," she said handing that over as well. "Welcome back."

"Thank-you," Anna said with a smile and headed back to her car so that she could begin unloading it before the rain started.

The hall of residence was another 19th Century town house, though, not quite so grand, more of a brick block behind tall brick walls.   It seemed to sit with it's back to the road, all the fancy frontage was on the other side, Anna remembered walking round it once.   There was a stone flight of stairs leading to an enormous entrance and a fancy ironwork balcony on the first floor, which was now part of the fire escape, a rather rusty looking ladder was hanging from it, presumably capable of being extended to the ground should the need arise, but Anna thought she'd have to be desperate before she used it. In front of the hall the outline of a formal flower beds could still be seen through the weeds, though it would probably take a brave, or foolhardy, person to walk to the end of the garden. All of which gave the impression that, when you approached the hall from the road, you were using the servants entrance. Like the administrative building, it too had been badly divided up for it's new use as a hall of residence. Decorative cornices being chopped up by new walls all through the building. New and old were coated with magnolia emulsion, with no attempt to make anything of the decorative plaster work, hence the images were gradually blurring out of existence with every additional layer of paint.

Anna carried the first load of bags up to her room, opening the door she looked at a very familiar sight. The furniture, probably dating from the time the house became part of the educational establishment, consisted of a dark wood desk, with a faded top and two drawers on the left hand side on which stood a black metal reading light. The most peculiar of wardrobes, dark wood, with a drawer underneath and on the left hand side, at right angles to the front, a book case on top of a small cupboard, like someone had decided to combine a wardrobe, cupboard and bookshelf in one piece of furniture. There was the same hard wearing dark greyish brown carpet. It had been put down the previous year and everyone had complained about getting static shocks from taps and door handles and a multitude of other things for a few weeks afterwards. But, that was just part of the newness and it soon wore off. Then there was the single bed with a faded orange and brown striped bedspread which topped about five thick blankets, great for baking you during the night, all of which were on top of sheets that were so crisp you could see sparks flying the first night after they were changed, yet more static. Other halls had duvets, but the old bedding was being used up for this one and some of it was getting rather thin, Anna had put her foot through a sheet the previous year, but no one had said anything about it. The main lampshade in the room was dark green metal, a very wide cone which did nothing to shade the light bulb from below, the bin, in matching green metal, sat under the white porcelain hand basin which was on the wall between the desk and a rather plain, but functional mid-brown book shelf. The only other furniture in the room being a chest of drawers and an armless arm chair covered in a faded blue patterned fabric. The same room, same view, down a cobbled back alley, it was almost like she'd never been away. A quarter of and hour later, the car had been emptied and

2

it's contents piled in the centre of the room.

"Should I phone home to say I've got here," Anna thought looking round. "Have they noticed I've gone yet. Debatable. They got under my feet whilst I was loading the car, but they were too busy telling me how callous and unfeeling I was to notice what I was doing. Didn't even notice the mini packing in at the end of the road. They don't usually miss an opportunity like that to tell me what a heap of crap it is. Not that it was anything major. Just the fuel pump contacts sticking. Nothing I couldn't cope with, all it takes is a sharp clout with something hard and heavy to free them up a bit. Unfortunately, it's underneath the car, by the nearside back wheel, not the easiest thing to get at, so I stuck a piece of fish tank tubing to a breather hole and threaded it up into the boot. A quick squirt with some WD40 down the tube and the contacts were clean and the car running smoothly. A much more elegant and clean method than rolling around under the car and quicker. Which was lucky, I don't think I'd have got much help if I had needed it and there'd have been a long lecture on how unreliable it is. All in all, it's a good job I didn't have to go back home to wash my hands. It isn't like they'd come up with an alternative way of getting to the Poly. The only one I can think of would involve them bringing me here and that I can't see happening, not without a lot of fuss," Anna yawned and stretched. "I could do with a drink," she thought searching out her kettle and filling it with water.

The kettle was just coming to the boil and Anna had got her stereo working when she heard a familiar knock on the door. She opened the door to Susan.

"Thought so," she said. "I was just making a cup of coffee."

"That was good timing," she said with a smile.

"Timing. That's got nothing to do with it. I think you can smell the coffee or hear the kettle or something."

"How was your holiday?" asked Susan making herself at home on the only armchair.

"Holiday?" said Anna.

"Yes. You know, the time between the end of last term and now," she said looking round for biscuits.

"I know that. But it doesn't feel as if I've been away," said Anna putting the cup in front of her friend. "So whatever it was can't have been very interesting or I'd remember. What did you do?"

"Nothing special. Summer work. Temping. I even got out of going

3

on the family holiday," said Susan smiling at the memory.

"Didn't you want to go?" asked Anna.

"No.   They've never been any good.   Packed together in a small caravan for a fortnight. No privacy. Every decision a committee meeting. All 'what are we going to do today?', then we end up doing what they want to do. Endless discussions on what to eat. It wouldn't be so bad, but Mum bought the food and planned the meals ages ago. Years ago. We eat the same thing on the same day every year and argue over everything," said Susan with a sigh.

"Sounds familiar," said Anna. "How did you avoid it?"

"I had to work that fortnight and didn't tell them to the last minute," Susan smiled.

"Why?" asked Anna.

"If they'd had time they'd have told the agency about the family holiday."

"They wouldn't, would they?" asked Anna.   "Then again, mine would've," she thought.

"I wouldn't put it past them," said Susan.

"How'd they take it?" asked Anna.

"Badly.   Very badly, but there was nothing they could do.   I tried playing it dumb, pretending I hadn't realised the dates clashed.   It didn't wash," said Susan.

"Oh!" said Anna.

"Our holidays are very predictable.   Last two weeks in July.   Always. Just have to look at the calender to know what the dates are.   We spend the first half of July planning and packing everything we need.   The holiday finding out what we should have packed and hadn't and blaming everyone else for the omission. And when we get home Mum and Dad tell us what a wonderful time we've all had.   Like we'd need to be told that if we had had a wonderful time," said Susan.

"So this year they went without you?" said Anna.

"After a bit of persuasion.   Mum said it was a family holiday and that meant all of us.   I told them that the people I was working for were depending on me. I was standing in for someone on maternity leave, she'd told me how everything was done, if I then had to explain it all to someone else they might do things wrong and the person I was standing in for might find out and come in to check on things and get worked up," said Susan.

"Was all that true," mumbled Anna.

4

"The bit about the maternity leave, I just embroidered it a bit," said Susan. "Anyway, they went, without me and phoned up each day to say what a good time they were all having. According to them, they found the only sunny place in Britain."

"So, what did you do for a holiday?" asked Anna.

"Nothing. I was going to go abroad with some friends, but Mum made such a fuss, it didn't seem worth the effort," said Susan with a sigh.

"So, apart from work, what did you do?" asked Anna.

"Met a few old friends," said Susan yawning.

"That entertaining was it," Anna said with a grin.

"Nothing to do except drink," Susan sighed.

"You seemed pretty keen on that yourself last year," said Anna.

"Yes. Still am. But there has to be more to it. There was nothing to talk about, except how many of our school friends were married and either pregnant or towing a toddler," Susan groaned.

"I know what you mean. I met one girl I'd been to school with, struggling with two toddlers and a baby," said Anna.

"Three! She couldn't have been in the same year!" said a rather startled Susan.

"She was," Anna insisted.

"But," Susan started.

"She told me, right in the middle of a busy supermarket, about how she'd been sterilised."

"About time too," said Susan, hoping to avoid the gory details. "Sounds like a one woman population explosion."

"That was what I thought," said Anna.

"It's depressing though, seeing your friends pushing prams, talking nothing but babies. Nappies, feeds, whether it sleeps through the night, who it looks like and God knows what else," said Susan with a sigh.

"Didn't they have anything else to talk about?" asked Anna, wondering how to get her off the subject of babies.

"No," Susan said thoughtfully. "Absolutely nothing. I didn't realise anyone could talk that much about babies. Anyway, can you remember your holiday yet?"

"Little brother had his exams," said Anna.

"So," said Susan. "We've all had them."

"I came back in time for the last ones. All I can say is they didn't make that much fuss when I did my A levels," said Anna.

"How do you mean?" asked Susan.

"I wasn't allowed to have the radio on, it might distract him. Couldn't come home late, I might disturb his sleep," Anna started. "Not that I ever did," she thought glumly.

"Not keen on your brother?" asked Susan.

"The feeling's mutual, always has been. I even got told off for asking him to pass the salt at tea. He might have been thinking about his exams. Thinking about them! He didn't seem to be doing anything else about them," said Anna.

"Didn't you do that with your exams?" asked Susan.

"I tried, but it didn't work, they told me that the world doesn't stop just because I'm having exams and I shouldn't keep telling my brother to be quiet. The thing is he always gets his way, its not just at exam time," Anna exclaimed.

"How did he do?" asked Susan, hoping to change the subject slightly.

"Ploughed the lot," smiled Anna.

"You were suitably sympathetic?" asked Susan.

"It was all I could do not to laugh out loud," said Anna.

"And your parents?" Susan persisted

"Thought there'd been some kind of mistake. Wanted the papers remarked. They couldn't accept the idea of him being anything short of brilliant. I almost felt sorry for them," Anna admitted.

"What's this, mellowing in your old age?" asked Susan.

"I just don't like to see their illusions shattered like that. They had such plans. Now they've had to re-think the lot. That and trying to explain it all away, to the rest of the family, has kept them busy since August," said Anna. "They wouldn't want anyone to think this was his fault."

"What's he going to do now?" asked Susan.

"Re-sit his exams at the College of Further Education. It seems the school atmosphere didn't suit him," said Anna.

"I didn't get on all that well at school," Susan started.

"He just doesn't like work. Never has done. If it doesn't come easy he's not interested, he just won't make the effort. Still, that's his problem," said Anna.

"Aren't you worried?" asked Susan.

"No," said Anna.

"But?" Susan started.

"He's got Mum, Dad, the Grandparents, Aunts, Uncles, the neighbours,

Mum's friends at the WI and God knows who else to worry about him, he doesn't need me," said Anna.

"But?" Susan tried again.

"They'll worry to their hearts content and he'll go his own sweet way, as he always does. He won't listen to me that's for certain, never has done, so there's no point in me worrying," said Anna.

"I suppose not," said Susan.

"What about your brothers and sister?" asked Anna changing the subject.

"They're boring. They're older than me and see me as the problem," said Susan.

"All of them?" said Anna.

"Yes. They've all got babies too. They come and it's all they talk about and I have to play with the messy dribbling things. They even expect me to remember their names and sexes."

"Is that so difficult?" asked Anna.

They all look the same. Revolting," said Susan.

"You've had quite a summer of them haven't you," smiled Anna

"Yes. I've had a permanent headache from their screaming and there's nothing more disgusting than a toddlers full nappy," said Susan shuddering.

"How about Jackie discussing the cardiovascular cat over tea?" Anna suggested.

"A toddlers full nappy beats that hands down, though I wouldn't have thought so at the time," said Susan grimacing at the memory.

"Pharmacists! You'd think they could talk about something else over tea. It's enough to put you off your food," said Anna.

"Looking at tea's enough to do that," said Susan.

"True, but it's difficult eating with your eyes closed," said Anna.

"Tried have you?" asked Susan.

"I think it was stew, followed by some sort of electric green dessert," said Anna.

"You peeped!" said Susan.

"Only briefly. It nearly blinded me."

"Talking of tea," said Susan.

"We'd better go or we'll miss the good stuff," said Anna getting to her feet.

"Is there any?" Susan asked.

"I don't know, I've never arrived that early, but I live in hope," said

Anna. "Got your dining card?"

"Yes," said Susan glancing out of the window. "Oh hell, it's raining."

"What did you expect?" asked Anna.

"Brilliant sunshine, now that we're back and can't enjoy it," said Susan.

"Ah, but we could enjoy it, we've no work to do yet, also, students are arriving, unloading cars, this is timed to get them and all their stuff soaked, added to that it's tea time and we have to go outside to the refectory. The sun'll come next week, when we have started doing some work."

"True," said Susan as they got their coats and headed off to tea. They left the hall, turned right and walked to the end of the road, waited for the lights to change so they could cross the busy dual carriageway, then crossed the road opposite the one their hall was on and went into a gate. This led to another road at the end of which stood the refectory, mostly glass and wood it was constructed with a V shaped roof. Built around the late sixties or early seventies, it seemed to have been forgotten by all but the weather and a growing, but orderly line of students waiting patiently outside it for the doors to be opened and tea to be served.

"I wonder if they've mended the roof yet?" said Anna as the doors opened.

"Doesn't look like it," said Susan pointing to a puddle on the seat of one of the many orange plastic chairs.

"Typical," said Anna as the queue moved towards the counter. Showing their dinner passes they picked up trays and turned their gaze to the food on display. First to those on the metal serving shelf and then to the plates bellow.

"What's that?" asked Susan pointing to something which looked like a model railway tunnel flooded with gravy.

"Rabbit in gravy," said the canteen lady.

"I think I'll have salad please," said Susan.

"Which one?" asked the canteen lady.

"Cheese."

"Here you are," she said handing over a plate.

"Thank-you," said Susan.

"Can I have a cheese salad as well please?" asked Anna after looking in vain for one on the counter.

"Yes, I'll just get one," said the canteen lady. Two minutes she was back.

"There," she said handing over the plate.

"That's chicken, not cheese," said Anna blankly.

"Didn't you want chicken?" asked the canteen lady looking slightly perplexed.

"No. I," Anna started.

"I'll have it and you can have my cheese salad," said Susan grabbing the plate and dumping hers on Anna's tray.

"Right," smiled the canteen lady, turning to the next person in the queue.

"Nothings changed," thought Anna.

The choice of puddings was between a vivid pink substance in a glass bowl, rice pudding with black bits on top or chocolate sponge. Chocolate sponge seemed the best bet, without comment they both picked up a bowl of it.

"Which do you think is the chocolate custard?" asked Susan gazing at the custard trolley.

"The one on the right," said Anna thoughtfully. "It's got a skin, the other has a layer of oil."

"I don't know. The yellow custard hasn't got a skin," said Susan looking from tin to tin.

"More people have yellow custard, it hasn't had time to develop a skin," said Anna. "Also, I just saw one of the canteen ladies put it in."

"I think I'll have the white sauce," said Susan decidedly.

"Chicken," said Anna giggling.

"No, white sauce," smiled Susan, taking the ladle and pouring it over her pudding.

"You're sure?" asked Anna, pouring chocolate sauce over her pudding.

"Where would you like to sit?" asked Susan looking across the room at the disarray of pale grey tables and orange plastic chairs.

"As far from that blessed Battle Zone machine as possible. I was hoping they'd get rid of it whilst we were away. It's like eating on the Somme when that thing's going," said Anna scowling in the direction of the offending arcade machine.

"It wouldn't be so bad if it didn't play that stupid tune when someone wins," muttered Susan, as they picked their way through the tables.

"This looks O.K," she said stopping at a table fairly near the door, but not so close as to be in a draught. "The seats are dry," she added, almost as a bonus.

"What is that tune?" asked Anna as the machine assailed the air with it's victory cry.

9

"Oh. Some wally's national anthem," muttered Susan busy arranging her tea on the table, then dumping the tray on the other side out of her way. The computer generated racket subsided and Anna turned to arrange her tea on the table.

"No. I recognise it, it's the finale to the 1812 overture," said Anna.

"Whatever, it gets pretty repetitious very quickly," said Susan.

"I unplugged it last year when no one was looking. Took them a week to find out what was wrong. Hilda told me they got an engineer out to it, she wasn't impressed with him, it was half an hour before he noticed it wasn't plugged in," said Anna.

"I would have liked to have seen their faces when they found out what the problem was," grinned Susan. "How's the cheese?"

"Sweaty. And the chicken?"

"Greasy."

"They've got down to their usual standard depressingly fast," said Anna as the lettuce leaf fell of her fork. "They usually manage a couple of days of the almost edible before they get into the swing of things, least they did last year."

"Let's just hope it doesn't get any worse," said Susan watching Anna gazing at a fork full of desiccated grated carrot, disappointment and resignation writ large on her face.

"The idea doesn't bear thinking of," said Anna giving up and turning to the chocolate pudding.

"What shall we do this evening?" asked Susan also starting on her pudding.

"I don't know. What's on?"

"There's a band at Scunthorpe Building."

"What're they like?" asked Anna.

"Australian," said Susan after a moments thought.

"Not that lot that was here last year?" asked Anna.

"Borage? Don't think so. Why?" asked Susan.

"I could only hear out of one ear for a while after I saw them," said Anna.

"I heard they were a bit loud," muttered Susan clearing up the last of her chocolate pudding. "There's always a disco or the Poly bar," she suggested reluctantly putting down the empty bowl.

"Borage. I thought that was a herb. Still, we could see what the band's like," said Anna after a moments pause. "After all we can always leave if they're crap."

"That's settled then," said Susan.

"Yes," agreed Anna, finishing her pudding. "By the way, it defiantly was chocolate custard."

"Unless the gravy's sweet."

"You're disgusting," muttered Anna.

"I do my best," smiled Susan.

"Ah well, back to the unpacking," said Anna.

"I suppose so," sighed Susan, "I'll drop in when I've finished, then we can hit the town, or rather Scunthorpe Building."

Chapter 2
First day of the New Year

The dream was just getting interesting when it was shattered by the sound of the alarm clock. The last fragments dissolving as Anna groped round for the timepiece so she could stop the racket.

"Where am I?" she thought vainly trying to identify the ceiling. One moment it looked like the one at home, all white painted spiky Artex then the light changed and she thought she was at her Nana's home, with it's higher ceiling covered with anaglypta wallpaper. Sitting up she brought her eyes to focus on a white porcelain hand basin beneath which was a dark green metal waste paper bin.

"Poly," sighed Anna and dragged herself out of bed. Five minutes later, washed and dressed she went to wake Susan up. Knocking loudly on the door, she expected a long wait, but it was opened almost instantly.

"My God! Not only is the girl awake, but dressed as well," exclaimed Anna. "What magical transformation has taken place over the holidays."

"Come on in you facetious bugger. I've just got to clean my teeth and I'll be ready," said Susan with a grin.

"Hang on a mo. Spill the beans. How did you manage it?" asked Anna.

"I've got a new alarm clock."

"Well it must be pretty fantastic to wake you and not rouse the rest of the hall," said Anna.

"It's got a very piercing alarm. Do you want to hear it?"

"No. No. I'll take your word for it. It must be very piercing though, to get you up. You'd better be careful though, or you'll be full of holes by the end of the week," said Anna smiling.

"Was that supposed to be funny?" asked Susan.

"Best I can do, I'm in shock," laughed Anna.

"Do you think you could manage a little food before we potter over to Manchester Building to register?" asked Susan with a touch of mock sympathy in her voice.

"I could, but I thought we were going to the refectory for breakfast," said Anna.

"Come on," said Susan grabbing her coat and bag. "Let's see if breakfast's down to its usual standard."

Five minutes later, Anna tapped he slice of carbonised toast on the plate, it cracked in three, the toast not the plate.

"At least I don't have to cut it," she said looking dubiously at the fragments.

"Yes," said Susan busy trying to make some impression on her slice with a blunt dinner knife. "I think it'd be easier cutting the plate," she added and turned to her coffee.

Meanwhile Anna had managed to get some butter to stick to one of the fragments. She took a bite and a look of disgust spread over her face.

"That bad?" asked Susan.

"Butter's rancid," said Anna after swallowing hard.

"The coffee's disgusting too," added Susan putting down her cup.

"I thought that one was tea," said Anna.

"I wish they'd label those urns," said Susan looking into the cup. "At least you'd know what it was meant to be. Oh well. I suppose we'd better be off or they'll think we're not coming this year," she added after a quick glance at her watch.

"There's some wouldn't miss us," said Anna.

"If you will keep being sarcastic to Clare," said Susan.

"She makes it so easy, she's such an idiot."

"Come on," said Susan. "Shift."

Manchester Building, a 1960's red brick block, thronged with the usual first day chaos. It made Anna feel like an old hand wading into the crowd of bewildered students, sure of her destination. Two minutes later she was as bemused as the rest. Registration wasn't in their usual lecture room. It had been moved to a much larger lecture theatre so all three years could be fitted in, but there was nothing and no one to say where it was.

"They could've let us know," she said struggling against the crowd. "Or at least put a sign up."

"They could've, but when's that ever made any odds," said Susan looking round for a space to sit.

"I know but," Anna looked round despairingly.

"I know. You keep hoping," said Susan.

"Looks like we're here," said Anna looking into a room and trying not to look flustered.

"It does," agreed Susan heading towards some familiar people. Nine o'clock. They were neither late nor early. Twenty minutes later the lecturers arrived. The freshers fell silent, the rest carried on with their gossiping.

"Looks like they were gathering somewhere so they could all arrive together," said Anna.

"Does have that appearance," agreed Susan. "Wonder what bombshell they're going to drop on us this time."

"You mean, like last year when they changed the field trip from Rome to Berwick?" asked Anna.

"Yes, like that," said Susan.

"Could be anything," said Anna. "But may just be nothing."

"I don't like the way they look," said Susan thoughtfully.

"They'd all improve from a paper bag over their heads, or better still over the whole of them. But that could be said any day," said Anna.

"It's not that," said Susan. "They look sort of furtive, you know what I mean."

"Furt. Furt."

"Dimwit," said Susan, aiming a playful clout at Anna who ducked and Susan just hit clear air.

"Hello everyone," shouted Mr Jamerson, looking rather nervously round the room, the idea of gathering all three years in one room didn't seem like such a good one now when they were all in front of him. The sound of the gossiping ceased abruptly as everyone directed their gaze towards him. He adjusted the collar of his new shirt and the tie, which suddenly felt a bit on the tight side, straightened the jacket of his new dark blue suit, which he'd got because when his wife took the previous one to the dry cleaners for it's annual clean, they'd pointed out that the collar and cuffs were fraying and there was some staining that might be difficult to remove.

"Welcome to the beginning of the new year. Most of you will know me, but for the benefit of the new intake, I am Damien Jamerson and I am the head of the course," he paused for a moment, as if expecting a round of applause. None was forthcoming, so he proceeded. "I've gathered you all together so that we can sort out the registration forms and I can explain about the new syllabus." There was another pause, but this time he got a response, confused whispers which turned to angry exclamations of "What new syllabus."

"I'll explain about that later," he said quickly. "First we'd better sort out these registration forms, then you'll be able to collect your grants, assuming they've come yet. As most of the older students know they can sometimes be a day or two late. Anyway, we'll hand the forms out and when you've filled them in I'll sign them so hopefully there wont be any hold ups," he finished and started handing out the paperwork before anyone could ask any more questions.

"We deserve a degree for just filling this in," muttered Anna trying to explain what was needed to someone else.

After some twenty minutes the noise began to die down and the students sat back having completed the necessary documentation.

"If you're having any problems, I'm sure Mr Thomas here won't mind helping you," said Mr Jamerson. Ignoring the startled expression Mr Thomas turned on him he continued "Meanwhile, I'll check and sign the completed forms. Just bring them up here."

"Check every detail! It would've been quicker if he'd filled them in himself, after all they know all the information," muttered Susan impatiently, but eventually all the paperwork was done and even Mr Jamerson couldn't hold things up any longer.

"About the new syllabus," he said and the room turned its attention on him. "As some of you may have heard, last year, it was decided to update the course and to do this we employed the computer. All the information was put onto punch cards, the relevant keys were depressed and the cogs whirred into action."

"What was wrong with the old one?" asked someone on the other side of the room.

"Have you got any copies of the new syllabus?" asked someone else.

"We haven't got that organised yet, but we will get them to you as soon as we can. Till then we will make sure you know all that it is necessary for you to study. Now I think we may as well stop for a twenty minute tea break. The first years can meet back here, the rest of you know your usual rooms. Well. Good morning everyone. And I hope you all have a good year," said Mr Jamerson, departing quickly, followed, rather rapidly, by the other lecturers. For a moment there was silence, followed by a general hum as people gradually realised there was no reason to stay there and then,

15

by a general movement towards the common room. The second and third years leading the way, the first years bringing up the rear, not totally sure that they should leave the lecture theatre.

Just less than twenty minutes later the first years dashed off, leaving several half empty polystyrene beakers scattered on the tables. The rest left a few minutes later, unhurried, carrying their unfinished coffee and still talking about the changes and the chances of getting a copy of the new syllabus before the last exam. Speculation continued amongst the second years until Mr Thomas walked in, only ten minutes late.

"So, what's this new syllabus," they demanded almost in unison.

"Oh that's nothing to worry about," he said.

"That's all very well, but I didn't think you could change anything that major part way through a course," said Alison.

"It isn't exactly a new syllabus."

"What is it then?" interrupted Christine, Alison's friend. "Because Mr Jamerson said it was a new syllabus."

"What we've done is take the information about the course and input it into the computer," Mr Thomas started.

"We know that," interrupted Ian, carrying on with his self appointed role as form spokesperson. "It's about all we do know."

"From that information the computer has worked out a time table, sorted out book lists and organised the assignments. That sort of thing. Not really a new syllabus." continued Mr Thomas, "Just a better organised one."

"So why did Mr Jamerson say it was a new syllabus?" asked Alison, not wanting to drop the subject.

"It probably sounds better," said Mr Thomas, obviously uncomfortable at the barrage of questions.

"Why have you done it?" asked Susan.

"Well, because," he started looking round for inspiration. "Well, it will improve the coverage of the subject, optimise your studying by providing you with the best, most up to date sources of information," said Mr Thomas, looking pleased with himself at having thought of a phrase that sounded good to him at least. "That is the thing about computerisation and information technology. It will help to spread your work load more evenly throughout the year."

"There weren't any problems last year? Were there?" asked Anna.

"Ah, no. No. But things could have been better organised. I mean,

16

much as we try, it is difficult for us to know everything that has been written on every subject and we may miss something that could be important. Also, we are only human, we all tend to think our subject is the most important. The computer puts each subject into perspective. No one wants to spend too much time on a minor subject. It might affect the final results."

"Has that happened before?" asked Ian, glaring round the room, not wanting to be left out of the questioning.

"I don't think so," said Mr Thomas thoughtfully. "But it is a possibility that we would want to avoid. Anyway, you'll be wanting to see your time table," said Mr Thomas quickly fishing out some papers from his briefcase and handing them round.

"And here's a breakdown of what you will be studying for the next two weeks, along with the book list for the fifth and sixth weeks. Fifth and sixth weeks? Oh well, I'll get you the right book list for the next lesson, in the meantime you may as well keep these, you'll be better prepared for the lessons when they come. And now," he said handing over the last of the sheets. "We may as well break for dinner and you can get your grant cheques. Lectures will start again at, can I see your timetable? Thank you. Lectures start at 2pm in Howarth Building with Mr Jones. You do know where Howarth Building is don't you?" he asked at the puzzled faces staring at him. "It's the civil engineering block over by," he paused, no light was dawning in the students. "I'll get in touch with Mr Jones, if we meet here at quarter to two, I'll take you down to Howarth Building, either that or I'll find someone who knows where it is to take you there," he said and then dashed off.

"Vanity Fair? Sense and Sensibility? Pride and Prejudice?" said Anna.

"What are you wittering on about?" snapped Christine.

"It's the reading list for weeks five and six," said Anna.

"Typical, sounds more like a list for Creative Writing and English than for Environmental Science," said Ian.

"Let's hope it is our book list and not someone else's," said Alison.

"Why? If it was someone else's book list we could ditch it," said Anna.

"I wonder who's got our list," said Claire.

"God knows, but I wouldn't put it past them to get it totally wrong," said Susan.

"There's no one better at making a total cock-up of things than Mr. Jamerson," said Ian.

17

"Yes," said Mark. "Remember the end of year party he organised."

"Yes," said Anna. "Loads of whisky for the lecturers and no lager."

"Yes, couldn't even organise a booze up," said Susan.

Trying not to look eager the second years drifted back to their room in Manchester Building, by quarter to two they were all there waiting.

Fifteen minutes later.

"Mr Thomas is coming," said Christine dashing to a vacant seat.

"What are you doing here?   Shouldn't you be in Howarth Building with Mr Jones?" he said

"We've been waiting for you," said Alison.

"Why?"

"You told us to," said Clare.

"I did what?"

"Told us to meet you here at quarter to two and you'd take us over to Howarth Building," said Stewart.

"Did I?" said Mr Thomas. "I don't remember doing that."

"Well you did," said Ian.

Mr Thomas glanced at his watch.   "I've got a lecture and I should be there now, so I'd better go."

"How are we going to get to Howarth Building?" wailed Josie

"Walk," he said and dashed off.

"Thanks a bundle," muttered Anna.

"He's never bothered about being late for us," said Christine.

"Now what do we do?" asked Josie.

"Ask at the office," said Stewart.   "See if they know where it is."

So they dashed off to the office.

"It's down by the teacher training library, I think," said the secretary, looking up briefly from her typing, then putting on headphones and returning to her work.

"We could ask at the library," said Anna, as they obviously weren't going to get any more help from the secretary.   As no one could come up with a better idea, they headed for the library.

"That's next door," said the librarian.

They dashed next door.

"Is this Howarth Building?" they asked the Porter.

"No. No this is Wilkinson Building," he said.

For a moment no one said anything.

"Do you know where Howarth Building is?" asked Susan slowly.

"When you get out of the gate, turn right, cross the road, walk till you come to a road, cross that and Howarth Building is on the corner," he said smiling.

"Thank-you." they said and dashed off.

Howarth Building was exactly where he said it was, but Mr Jones was nowhere to be found.

"Now what?" wailed Josie, getting increasingly worked up.

"Not much we can do," said Alison. "We can't conjure him up out of thin air."

"May as well go back to Manchester Building," said Clare.

"But our lecture," said Josie.

"We've done our best," stated Stewart.

"It's quarter to three," said Anna. "We'd better get back before we miss the next one."

"So the wanderers return," said Mr Malcolm as they walked into their room. "Where have you all been? Mr Jones has been searching all over for you."

"We've been trying to find Howarth Building," said Ian.

"Very laudable I'm sure, but why this sudden desire to find Howarth Building when you're supposed to be having a lecture with Mr Jones?"

"Because that is where our lecture was," snapped Clare.

"No. It was in St. James's annexe," said Mr Malcolm.

"Mr Thomas said it was in Howarth Building," said Josie. "And it's here on our timetable."

"Did I hear my name mentioned?" asked Mr Thomas looking in at the door.

"Yes, they've just been explaining where they've been all afternoon," said Mr Malcolm.

"Not Howarth Building by any chance?" asked Mr Thomas.

"Yes," they chorused.

"That's where you told us to go," said Susan.

"And where the sheets you gave us earlier say we should have been," added Josie.

"There was a misprint on the timetable. Anyway, Mr Jones can take the lecture in here at four, so you won't lose out on anything and you'll know

19

where he is for the next week," said Mr Thomas.

"There aren't any more misprints are there?" asked Susan.

"Of course not. Anyway. Now that that's cleared up I'll leave you to Mr Malcolm, I don't want to take up any of his precious time," Mr Thomas finished and departed rapidly down the corridor.

"This is impossible," said Alison.

"There must be something we can do about this new syllabus," said Ian starting the discussion.

"That is, if it is a new syllabus," said Clare.

"We could do with some confirmation on that," said Anna. "Not all this 'aren't we clever using the computer' bit."

"And some advice on our rights, like, what they are and how we can get them," said Susan.

"And who's going to tell us that?" asked Christine.

"Good question," said Alison. "It's not exactly in anyone's interests to help us is it?"

"There's always the union," said Stewart. "It's supposed to be their job to protect our interests."

"Right then, if you go and talk to the Union President," said Clare.

"I think it might come better from one of you girls," Stewart said hesitantly.

"What do you mean?" asked Clare.

"He's chicken," giggled Susan. "He's frightened of our Poppy."

"Too right I am. Anyway, if one of you girls go she might be more helpful."

"Shall I go?" asked Susan.

"Yes," said everyone thankfully.

It was dinner time the next day before Susan had time to find the Union President. She was in their new offices in the admin building. Even the students on the stall advertising the students union, didn't know where their offices were, neither did the receptionist, she eventually found it's whereabouts from the lady cleaning the toilets.

"Have they actually changed the syllabus?" Poppy asked, sitting on the office desk, which was taking up most of the room, with her feet on the only chair Susan's side of the desk.

"I'm not sure," said Susan looking round for somewhere to sit but finding nothing.

"What do you mean, you're not sure?" asked Poppy looking pointedly at the office clock.

"Mr Jamerson said it was a new syllabus, devised by the computer from the course information. But Mr Thomas said it wasn't, that they'd only used the computer to organise things."

"I see your problem. Something's been changed, but you can't find out exactly what," said Poppy, checking her watch.

"Yes," said Susan, relieved that someone seemed to understand the nature of their plight.

"The problem we have is that that is a bit of a woolly complaint, if you see what I mean," said Poppy.

Susan looked downcast.

"Don't get me wrong, I would like to help," said Poppy.

Susan looked up hopefully.

"But we've got to work on facts. If you could say for certain that the syllabus has been changed and that they're not just using the computer to organise the work, then we might have a basis for action," Poppy added with a reassuring smile.

"The problem is finding that out," said Susan.

"I know what you mean, Jamerson and Thomas aren't the easiest of people to find, let alone get a straight answer from," said Poppy.

"True," came Susan's heartfelt reply. "Couldn't you find out for us?"

"Sorry. I don't think we're allowed to do that," said Poppy checking the clock on the wall and then her watch.

"Could you try," persisted Susan.

"It's best if you find out. Then we'll see what we can do. Anyway, I must be going now, there's a freshers do I have to attend," said Poppy escorting Susan the two steps to the door.

"Thanks for nothing," she thought, heading back to the common room in Manchester Building and a lunch of coffee and sandwiches.

"That bad," said Anna as Susan slumped down in the chair next to her.

"Worse," said Susan looking at the sandwiches.

"The union?" asked Anna.

"Won't help us without the facts," said Susan.

"There has to be something they can do," said Anna.

"Not without the facts. Which is something we haven't got and aren't

21

likely to have," said Susan glumly.

"Chris is in the union. Isn't he the Secretary or something. He might be able to help us," said Anna, playing with her coffee beaker and trying not to catch Susan's eye.

"If you want me to go asking that creep for anything," Susan started angrily.

"He's got a soft spot for you. Anyone can see that," said Anna quickly, remembering the way he kept following Susan around the previous year, even after she'd emptied his pint over him on several occasions.

"And I have one for him. A midden," snapped Susan.

"He's not that bad," said Anna, rather too quickly.

"You ask him then," said Susan.

"He'd be more likely to help you," said Anna, aiming the remains of her beaker at the nearby bin and missing.

"Not if I strangle the slimy toad first," said Susan. "Anyway, it's time someone else did something."

"Maybe someone else could ask him," said Anna.

"How about Josie?" suggested Susan.

"What have you got against her?" asked Anna, picking up the beaker and having another go at getting it in the bin.

"Nothing specific, anyway, I thought you said he wasn't that bad?" said Susan.

"She might not do it," said Anna.

"Oh she'd enjoy it," smiled Susan. "I never saw him without her being somewhere near."

"If you say so, but you can ask her," said Anna.

"Right," said Susan.

"Now we'd better get to our lectures," said Anna. "Do you know what we've got and where?"

"Hydrology in the usual room," Susan answered, after consulting her time table.

"The study of the water cycle," said Anna with a smile.

"An important subject," Susan replied, looking out of the window at the pouring rain.

"Very," agreed Anna. "Too much or too little water in any area of the world can be disastrous."

"It is important to understand flood plains and their place in the water cycle," added Susan.

"Along with the way in which pollution can get into the water table and how that may effect the local ecosystem," said Anna.

"Yes, it could be very interesting," said Susan.

An hour later the two walked out of the lecture.

"I think I know just about everything there is to know about the plumbing of your average semi-detached house," said Anna.

"Yes, I think I could make a fair fist of sorting out most problems common to domestic plumbing. I just don't see how that's going to help us with problems such as preserving the ecosystems of flood plains and the part they play in flood prevention," agreed Susan.

"Your guess is as good as mine, but if I don't get to a toilet soon I shall have a small flood problem of my own to worry about," said Anna.

The following day Susan and Anna went early to the nine o'clock lecture, so they could have a word with Josie before the tutor turned up. Josie wasn't there. Mr James, the tutor, arrived and was in full flow when she turned up looking furious, so furious that Mr James said nothing about her time keeping or the fact that she wasn't making any attempt to take notes, she was just scowling at Susan and muttering under her breath. Mr James ended the lecture fifteen minutes early and dashed off quickly.

"I hope you're proud of yourself," stormed Josie at Susan. "Thanks to you I've missed my breakfast."

"That wouldn't hurt you," thought Anna, looking at Josie.

"How the hell's that my fault?" Susan shouted.

"Because that scum bag you wanted me to talk to," shouted Josie.

"Chris?" suggested Susan.

"Yes. Chris. Your precious Chris. Not only didn't he have the courtesy to get me breakfast. He didn't even wake me up before he left. By the time I got to the refectory it was closed and I was late." Josie's words petered out as she realised quite what she had just said.

"You spent all night there?" asked Susan.

"I was trying to get him to help us," said Josie defensively.

"It took all night?" said Susan puzzled.

Josie said nothing, for a moment she was lost for words.

"Is he going to help us?" Susan asked, taking another tack.

"Of all the nerve," shouted Josie, looking round for something to throw at Susan.

"He's not going to help us," said Susan slowly.

"No. He's not," snapped Josie.

23

"You talked to him all night and still couldn't persuade him to help us," said Susan incredulously.

"Well," mumbled Josie, looking vaguely uncomfortable.

"What?" asked Susan as a few giggles began to break out from their fellow students.

"You said to persuade him," she muttered.

The penny finally dropped.

"Fool," muttered Susan. "I said talk to him."

"Well, if that's you're, attitude you can sort it out by yourself and much good may it do you," said Josie and stalked out of the room.

"So much for that," muttered Susan.

"I rang the exam board," said Anna.

"Good," said Susan. "What did they say."

"Same as the union. They want written proof and a copy of the new syllabus."

"How much do they want?" asked Clare. "I mean we could probably get together two weeks from each of the three years."

"That won't do, they want the lot," Anna said.

"I don't think that much exists," muttered Susan bitterly.

"What do you mean?" asked Christine.

"They'll have a months worth at most," said Susan.

"How can you be sure of that?" asked Stewart.

"Because if they had any more they'd have given it to us, come to think of it, they've probably given us as much as they've got," said Susan.

"It took them ages to give us the old syllabus, why do you think they're going to be any quicker with the new one," asked Alison.

"Because they want to prove how much more efficient everything is with this computer," said Susan, stating what was obvious to her, but not to anyone else.

"They wouldn't start the year if they didn't have the whole syllabus would they?" asked Christine. "I mean, I know they weren't that efficient at getting the syllabus to us last year, but that's just them, they wouldn't start the year without one."

"Of course not," snapped Stewart.

Susan shrugged her shoulders.

"You're just doing this to worry us," Ian added, deciding to join in the discussion.

"Can you prove me wrong?" asked Susan "I would really like it if you

24

could."

"Look. We're here. We've registered and had lectures," he said looking round for help from the other students.

"So?" said Susan.

"Well. They must be able to run the course," said Stewart.

"Do you remember Julie Carter?" asked Susan, changing tack.

"Who?" snapped Stewart caught off balance.

"Wasn't she on that course that didn't run last year?" asked Clare.

"Yes," said Susan.

"What!" Stewart looked round confused.

"There weren't enough of them to run the course. They were here for a couple of weeks, then, the course stopped and they all got sent home," said Anna.

"Well, she could probably get on another course," said Stewart.

"No. It was too late in the year. She re-sat her A levels to improve her grades," said Anna.

"You know a lot about her," said Stewart.

"She's back again this year, they've got enough to run the course," explained Anna. "Can't say I'd trust them, in her place, but that's her choice."

"You're just being alarmist," said Stewart.

"If we had the facts we'd know if there was cause for alarm," explained Susan patiently. "That's all that we want to do, find out the facts and whether there is cause for concern."

"Well I don't think there's anything to worry about," said Stewart stubbornly.

"Fine. You take it on trust," snapped Susan. "I'm going to find out the facts."

"They are lecturers, they know what they are doing," said Stewart flatly.

"Like Monday? Remember? We spent half the afternoon looking for Howarth Building and the lecture was in St. James's annex," said Susan, struggling to keep her temper.

"Everyone makes mistakes," he said dismissively.

"Then there's that book list we got, remember, Vanity Fair and all that, God knows whose course it was for, but it wasn't ours. Tuesday's lectures, the first was here, the next was two miles down the road and no time to get there and we've not finished the first week yet," said Susan.

"Like I said, everyone makes mistakes, there are bound to be a few

25

teething problems," said Stewart.

"Teething problems!   They know where all the buildings are, when they wrote the timetable they should've made sure it was physically possible to get to all of the lectures," Susan responded

"And then there's what they teach us when we get there," Anna butted in.

"What do you mean?" asked Stewart, turning to look at Anna.

"The hydrology lecture," Anna started.

"It's important to know how a house is plumbed," said Ian, trying to get in on the discussion.

"We're supposed to be studying the bigger picture, flood plains, glaciers, cloud seeding, that sort of thing," said Anna.   "It feels like we're being sidetracked from the main aim of the course."

"You're just paranoid," snapped Stewart.   "These are just a few teething troubles, the sort of problems associated with the implementation of a computerised system.   Once these mistakes are ironed out you'll see that you are just making a fuss over nothing."

"And if the new syllabus is the mistake," snapped Susan.

"I've had enough of this," Stewart shouted.   "I trust them and if you want to go stirring up shit you can do it without my help."

"That's fine by me," said Susan.   "I'm going to see Mr Jamerson and ask him exactly what is going on with this course.   I'm going to ask for a complete print out of this syllabus."

"You can do whatever you want," said Stewart.   "But I'm not going to support you."

"Neither am I," said Josie, picking up her bag and, like the rest of them, heading off somewhere for lunch.

"The impact of Napoleons Indian campaign on the cotton industry?" Anna mused,"I can see it's relevance at the time, but not now."   It was their first lecture after lunch.

"Did you say something?" asked Susan.

"The lecture we've just had, the stuff Mrs Grey was teaching us," Anna prompted her.

"Yes, what was she going on about?   All I heard was a load of references to fashion in Vanity Fair," said Susan.

"Weren't you paying attention?" asked Anna.

"Why should I, it wasn't in anyway relevant to what we are studying,"

26

said Susan.

"If you paid attention, you might find out if there was a relevance to our course, then you might have had more evidence that something is wrong," Anna explained.

"And was there any?"

"It shows that the book list we got on day one was ours, not someone else's," said Anna.

"And the relevance to our course?" Susan snapped.

"You've got me there," sighed Anna.

"Exactly. The lecture was rubbish. I gave it the attention it was due. None," Susan answered.

"Any more secrets you're keeping from me?" asked Anna, changing the subject, as they walked to the common room.

"Secrets? What secrets?" replied Susan startled.

"You never told me about a meeting with Mr Jamerson," muttered Anna.

"Oh that," Susan smiled.

"Yes. That," snapped Anna.

"The idea only just crossed my mind," Susan said.

"It sounded like it was all set up to me," said Anna doubtfully.

"Did it?" asked Susan, with a smile.

"Yes," said Anna flatly. "And it felt like you couldn't be bothered to tell me about it either," she thought.

"Did it sound impressive?" asked Susan giggling.

"Fairly," muttered Anna.

"Good. That supercilious pillock annoys me. So I haven't got his support. Big deal. What's his precious support ever done. You tell me that," shouted Susan as they walked into the common room. Everyone looked round to see what the fuss was about.

"You could say that about most of us," mumbled Anna trying to look unobtrusive, embarrassed by the way everyone in the room had turned to look at them.

"It's just his attitude, like he's the spokesman for us. If there's a problem it should be tackled now. It won't go away just because he doesn't choose to acknowledge it, it'll only get worse," said Susan, at a quieter volume.

"How are you going to get to see Mr Jamerson," asked Anna trying to change the subject slightly.

"I don't know," said Susan slowly. "You don't tend to see him around."

"Perhaps if you went through your personal tutor," suggested Anna.

"Mr Graham?" said Susan, looking at Anna as if she was an imbecile.

"Oh," muttered Anna.

"Quite," snapped Susan. "He might know everything about human geography, but beyond that he's hopeless. When you go to him with a problem you've got to keep reminding him who you are and what you've come about."

"Yes," Anna started.

"So what's the point in talking to him," Susan interrupted.

"Anyone else might get suspicious," Anna said.

"Suspicious. Suspicious of what? All I want to do is see Mr Jamerson to ask him about the syllabus. There's nothing wrong with that is there?" snapped Susan.

"No," mumbled Anna.

"When I see Mr Jamerson, they'll all know what I've come about. So what's the point in being secretive?" Susan asked.

"None," said Anna.

"Exactly," said Susan.

"I just thought, I mean, you may not get a sensible answer from him, but you won't get a straight answer from any of the others. At least he might tell you how to get to see Mr Jamerson, the others'd only hedge and tell you there wasn't any reason to bother him. That's all," said Anna.

"You've got a point there. It's just. He's such a dozy pillock. I don't know how he manages to get out of bed of a morning."

"I heard the problem was getting him into bed at night," said Anna, hoping Susan had calmed down a bit. "He gets so engrossed in his demographic research, he'd sit up all night if he was left. Just loses track of time."

"He's not totally there," said Susan.

"Good job he's got a job here," said Anna.

"Why?" said Susan, looking at Anna as if she was an idiot again.

"Can you imagine the chaos he could create if he was let lose on an unsuspecting world," said Anna.

"Oh God, yes, he creates enough problems here," giggled Susan.

"That reminds me, we've got him next," said Anna.

"If he remembers to turn up," said Susan.

"And comes to the right building." added Anna.

"Or at least the same one as us," said Susan.

28

"Complementary errors or something," said Anna. "Anyway, you could always try to talk to him afterwards. It is our last lecture of the day and with any luck he won't have any after us either."

"That's true. After all, there's no point making an appointment with him. He'd never remember it," said Susan.

"Hello," said Susan dumping her tea tray on the refectory table.

"I wouldn't sit there," said Anna looking up from her tea.

"Why not?" snapped Susan.

"You'll be under a leak," said Anna pointing to a puddle on the chair seat. "Take this seat," she added pointing to a chair on the other side of the table.

"Oh thanks," said Susan, moving over to the other side of the table and arranging her plates,

"Could you get rid of this," she added handing her the tray.

"Sure," said Anna handing it to someone who had just walked in. "I was beginning to think you weren't coming," she added.

"So was I," sighed Susan.

"What happened?" asked Anna.

"He said he had the new syllabus," said Susan.

"He did?" Anna asked sitting up.

"When we eventually located it. In his room, not his office. We turned his office upside down. It looked tidier when we'd finished. Anyway, then we tried his room and a very peculiar place that is," said Susan.

"How do you mean?" asked Anna.

"Difficult to explain. You can't hardly move for books, papers, magazines, they're piled everywhere," Susan started

"What's so surprising about that, he's always in the reference library, they'll all be related to birth's, marriages and deaths," said Anna.

"No, they weren't. But, anyway, we spent ages looking through them," said Susan, trying not to think about all the things they'd found.

"Till you found it," finished Anna.

"Yes and no," said Susan.

"Don't play games. Either you did or you didn't," said Anna.

"We found a syllabus," said Susan slowly.

"But?" asked Anna prompting her.

29

"It was dated 1964," said Susan.

"Oh God, I didn't think the course went back that far," said Anna.

"He unearthed it with an exclamation of "Here's the new syllabus", well, it did have draft copy stamped on it, but I don't think it was for this course, the course name was half a mile long, so it was probably an idea for a course which may or may not have become this one.   I don't think he knows what decade it is," said Susan.

"Did you manage to explain what you wanted?" asked Anna asked slowly.

"I'm not sure.   He did suggest that I talk to the head of the course, couldn't remember their name, but said if anyone would know it would be him or her.   He said he had heard that there were some women working in the Polytechnic, so he thought the head of the course might be one of them. Mr Jamerson's really made a big impression on him!" said Susan.

"He wouldn't know how to find Mr Jamerson then," said Anna.

"You've got it in one sunshine.   So, I'm back to square one," said Susan.

"You could try Mr Thomas.   He's supposed to be looking after our year," said Anna.

"I could, but I shouldn't think I'd get much more out of him," said Susan glumly.

"At least he knows what year it is," said Anna.

"And blooming cagey he is about it," said Susan.

"Shame we don't know someone who's good with computers," said Anna.

"Why?" Susan snapped.

"They could by-pass the lecturers and ask the computer for the syllabus," Anna suggested.

"It'd probably take an age to print out, then we'd have to play hunt the printer and it might be at that other Polytechnic, so we'd never find it," said Susan dismissively.

"A computer buff would be able to direct it to a specific printer, then again someone at the other Polytechnic might be able to get it for us, if only we knew someone there," said Anna.

"Speak for yourself," said Susan.   "I know someone there, quite a dish in fact."

"What does he do?" asked Anna.

"Computer Programming," said Susan.

"Perhaps he could help us then," Anna started.

30

"We can sort this out without dragging some man in to rescue us. Where are your feminist ideals?" snapped Susan.

"Oh sod it," thought Anna. "If you don't want to listen there's no point in arguing about it."

By the next day the idea had lodged in Susan's mind. It was logical and to make thing's easier Mr Thomas was teaching them, just before dinner. All Susan had to do was bide her time and catch him before he left. It was simple. She'd lull him into a false sense of security by not asking any awkward questions, or making any pointed remarks. Then, when the lecture was over she tackled him.

"Mr Thomas," she said, standing between him and the door.

"What!" he said startled. "Susan. Can I help you?"

"I hope so," Susan smiled sweetly. "It's about this new syllabus."

"Oh that," he said evasively. "It won't make any difference to you, so don't worry about it," he said.

"It must affect us, we're working by it?" said Susan.

"It's only to make things run more smoothly, make things easier for you," said Mr Thomas, looking longingly at the door.

"Can we have a copy of the syllabus?" asked Susan.

"What for?" he snapped.

"So I know what I'll be studying. What the exams are and when," Susan began.

"There's time enough to worry about those, the year's only just begun," said Mr Thomas.

"Maybe, but I'd like to know about it before the exams, I like to have my year planned so there are no unexpected assignments or anything," Susan persisted.

"You'll find out everything in plenty of time, don't worry about it. Anyway, much as I'd like to talk, I've got to go now," said Mr Thomas.

"Could I see Mr Jamerson about the syllabus," Susan persisted.

"Look," interrupted Mr Thomas. "I don't know why you're making such a fuss about this, but I haven't got the time to discuss it now."

"Later?" asked Susan hopefully.

"Yes. Later. Now I must go," said Mr Thomas.

"When?" asked Susan, but Mr Thomas had got past her and was

disappearing down the corridor as fast as he could, without actually running, so there was no response.

"Don't think you're going to put me off that easily," she thought furiously. "Because, if you can't give me a straight answer, then you're hiding something and I intend to find out what."

Chapter 3
Mr Thomas wishes to talk to Susan in his office.

It was Friday morning, Anna was walking slowly to lectures after eating a solitary breakfast.

"This is stupid," she thought checking her watch for the umpteenth time. "However, if I time it right I should arrive at the same time as the lecturer," thought Anna. "Then Susan'll have to wait till later to carry on this stupid argument. I know it's just putting it off, but, I was just trying to help. There was no need to be like that. None at all."

As the lecture room door came in view Anna's thoughts were distracted by the sight of Mr Thomas. He was standing by the door, which was odd as he wasn't timetabled to teach, though that didn't mean much and he was usually late when he did teach. It looked as though he was waiting for someone, but trying to look inconspicuous about it. Not easy at the best of times, but he was jogging on the spot, having the occasional bout of shadow boxing and to top it off he was wearing a bright red track suit which had been made for a much slimmer person. Also, the most energetic thing he was known for doing was trotting across the road to the pub and propping up the bar. All this activity, however, came to an end as soon as he saw Susan.

"Susan! Just the person I've been looking for," he exclaimed, as if he didn't know she'd be there.

"Well you've found me," smiled Susan. "What on earth are you doing in that revolting track suit?"

"Jogging of course," said Mr Thomas, struggling to catch his breath.

"When did you take that up?" asked Susan.

"I've been jogging for years," said Mr Thomas, slightly defensively.

"Really?" said Susan almost laughing.

"And what's so funny about that?" snapped Mr Thomas.

"Nothing," said Susan rather startled.

"Nothing, but?" snapped Mr Thomas a bit more in control of his breathing.

"You're face has gone the same colour as the track suit."

"Yes. Well. Anyway," said a flustered Mr Thomas. "I wanted to talk to you."

"Makes a change," said Susan. "What do you want to talk about?" she added before he could say something.

"Well. You don't seem to be getting on well with the new syllabus," said Mr Thomas gingerly.

"Not getting on well with it," started Susan angrily.

"I think we should discuss this in my office," he said quickly, trying to avoid any more of a scene in the corridor.

"What is there to discuss?" asked Susan. "We've nearly come to the end of the two weeks of new syllabus you gave us on the first day and there's no sign of any more turning up. What we've been taught so far doesn't seem to bear any relevance to the course. For a start off, I don't see how 19th Century fire guards and their design has anything to do with environmental science. Come to that, none of this 19th century stuff we've been studying is going to help us solve the worlds current environmental problems. We are wasting time, we should go back to the old syllabus before any more harm is done."

"If we don't learn from the past we can't solve the problems of the future," Mr Thomas started and stopped when he ran out of breath.

"We need to identify the problems before we can start finding their cause and solving them," Susan countered.

"I think we ought to talk in my office," said Mr Thomas, now fully in control of his breathing and trying to sound authoritative.

"Do you? Well, I'm sorry, but I've got a lecture now," said Susan, having just noticed the lecturer slipping into the lecture room.

"This has precedence," said Mr Thomas.

"What?" Susan exclaimed.

"You seem to be unhappy with the course. We are beginning to think that it might be better for you and all concerned, if we let you go," said Mr Thomas, his voice sounding very loud in the hushed corridor. For a moment everything seemed to stop. Then the noise and bustle resumed with vigour, everyone trying to pretend that nothing had happened. Susan looked stunned, for once she was short of a reply.

"If you'll come this way," said Mr Thomas edging her in the direction of

34

his office.

The mornings lectures finished at twelve and Anna rushed off in search of Susan. First stop was the common room, but a quick glance showed she wasn't there. Anna was just about to leave when she caught sight of Bert at his almost perpetual task of clearing up the rubbish which most of the students seemed incapable of putting in the bin.

"Perhaps he's seen her," she thought and was just about to ask when he spoke.

"What was all that with your friend Susan?" he asked.

"All what?" asked Anna before she had time to think.

"Bout half nine. In the car park, out there. Mr Thomas was shouting at her and ordering her into his car. I've never seen her so upset and she looked so happy when she came in this morning. What happened?"

"I don't know. Mr Thomas was waiting for her outside the lecture room at nine this morning. He wanted to talk to her in his office. About her leaving the course," mumbled Anna.

"What!" said Bert pausing in his efforts to get plastic beaker fragments out from under a chair.

"She's not been happy since they introduced the new syllabus," Anna subsided into silence.

"She told me what she thought of that," said Bert.

"That doesn't surprise me. She never stops talking about it," said Anna.

"Don't you think it's wrong?" Bert asked.

"Yes. But," Anna started.

"But?"

"There's nothing we can do. No one will listen. They're just not interested," she said.

"Oh."

"Do you know where he was taking her?" asked Anna.

"No," said Bert. "Though he did ask her which hall she was in. Why?"

"I just want to see her. See if there's anything I can do. Anyway, I'd best be off, the next lecture's at one," said Anna.

"Give her our best wishes," said Bert as she headed back to the door.

"Something's wrong. Something's very wrong," she muttered.

35

Ignoring the surprised expressions of her fellow students, Anna ran back to the hall, raced up the two flights of stairs to Susan's room and then leant on the wall whilst she got her breath back.

"It's very quiet in there," she thought gazing at the door. "Perhaps a quick peek through the keyhole."

A small noise took Anna's attention just before the door to the next room opened and Mary, the cleaner walked out.

"Have you seen Susan?" she asked.

"Have I seen Susan? have I just," she answered. "I don't know how a body can make so much noise."

"What?" asked Anna, stunned.

"All that shouting and banging on the door. I'm surprised it's not broken. He said she was upset, but her behaviour. Well it was quite ridiculous. We told him he couldn't leave her here. Not like that. All that noise. Quite disturbing."

"What's happened to Susan?" Anna interrupted. "That doesn't sound like Susan," she thought. "Susan's always so calm, in control, well, until recently."

"Well we had to restrain her, till the Doctor came."

"Restrain her?" asked Anna horrified.

"She might have hurt herself. The way she was thrashing about. As it is she's torn that sheet to shreds. It'll be no use for anything now."

"Why did they fetch a Doctor? What did he do?" asked Anna.

"Gave her a sedative. Had to, she was hysterical. It was doing her no good what-so-ever. I know it didn't do me any good, what with my nerves."

"Is she still in her room?" Anna asked, looking at the door.

"No. They took her away."

"Where to?" asked Anna.

"I don't know. I was just glad to see her go. All that fuss. God knows what it was all about. Something of nothing I shouldn't wonder. You know what these young girls are like."

"I should do, I am one myself," thought Anna, heading off, totally deflated.

"Mind where you're going," said Mrs Smithers-Jones as Anna narrowly missed colliding with her by the front door.

"Sorry," said Anna automatically apologising to the hall warden.

"I should think so. You could have knocked me over," she said sounding vaguely ruffled.

"Yes," thought Anna. "And a flea could trip up an elephant."

"Do you know where Susan is?" asked Anna quickly, before she got a lecture on looking where she was going.

"No. I haven't seen her since breakfast," said Mrs Smithers-Jones heading quickly for her office.

"Now that is odd," thought Anna. "You can't usually sneeze round here without her knowing."

"I was told she'd come back here," said Anna following her. "But she's not in her room."

"Are you sure she's come back. She doesn't usually come back during the day."

"Yes," said Anna positively.

"Well I haven't seen her," said Mrs Smithers-Jones. "Don't you have a lecture at one?" she added.

"Yes," said Anna glancing at the clock. "Oh God. Is that the time," she muttered and ran out of the hall, wondering how on earth the housekeeper at her hall of residence knew when her lectures were when even she didn't.

Anna arrived at the lecture out of breath and red in the face, but on time, much to the surprise of her fellow students. Anna running at all was a miracle. Twice in one day and one of those for a lecture by Mr Thomas, didn't happen. But she had her reasons, there were a few questions she had for Mr Thomas, assuming that he turned up, which she doubted very much he would.

The class waited patiently. Anna got her breath back. No one said anything, but after half an hour both she and her fellow students were getting fed up of waiting.

"By the time he gets here it'll be time for him to go again," muttered Ian.

"We'll never get through the syllabus at this rate," said Christine.

"Well we all know whose fault that is," said Josie.

"He should give us an extra lecture for the amount of time he's missed," said Clare.

"You can tell him that when he gets here," snapped Alison.

"If he comes," said Anna.

"Of course he'll come," said Stewart. "Someone would've said if he wasn't coming."

"Why wouldn't he come?" snapped Josie.

"Oh, weren't you here this morning when he dragged Susan off to her hall of residence and then had her sedated?" snapped Anna.

"Excuse me," said a voice from the door. "Are you waiting for Mr Thomas?"

"Yes," chorused the whole class.

"Mr Thomas can't come," she said.

"Great. You could've told us earlier," said Stewart. "We've been waiting over half an hour for him to turn up."

"Yes. You could have," echoed Josie. "We do have better things to do than hang around in a lecture room."

"Why can't he come?" asked Anna.

"Yes. Why?" asked Stewart scowling at Anna.

"He had to sub for Mr Jamerson at a seminar this afternoon."

"I suppose that can't be helped," said Stewart. "Will he reschedule this lecture?"

"Yes. He'll let you know about that when he's organised it."

"Where's Mr Jamerson?" asked Anna.

"At a conference in London."

"When will he be back?" asked Anna.

"Friday or Saturday, or Monday, it depends on how long it goes on."

"What's that got to do with our lecture?" asked Stewart.

"Nothing. But I would have thought they'd know about all this well in advance and they could've organised things better." said Anna.

"True," muttered Stewart.

"I think the conference was postponed from last weekend or was it last month, anyway, it was a last minute thing, the hotel got a cancellation and they were able to reschedule."

"Why do you want to know when he'll be back?" asked Josie, totally ignoring the girl from the office.

"So I can ask him about Susan," said Anna patiently.

"Why?" asked Josie.

"I want to know what's happened to her," said Anna.

"Really? I'm just glad to see the back of her. Perhaps now we can get on with some work," said Josie.

"Self first," said Anna quietly. "Sod anyone else."

38

"You were just as fed up with her as the rest of us," snapped Josie. "But now she's gone."

"And so has that twit with the message," groaned Anna.

"Hard luck. You'll just have to find Mr Jamerson when he comes back on Monday. If you can be bothered that is," said Josie.

"Go boil your head," shouted Anna storming out of the room. Josie was just a little too close to the mark.

It didn't take long for Anna to calm down, when she did she was standing outside the Faculty Office.

"What the hell am I doing here," she thought and was just about to leave when she noticed the Faculty Secretary approaching, then again it would have been very hard to miss her, a very large woman swaying gracefully down the corridor, all her attention on not spilling the contents of a polystyrene beaker. She didn't seem to see the people ducking out of her way.

"Hello," she smiled, noticing Anna propping up the Faculty Office door. "I don't suppose you could give me a hand with the door could you?" she asked.

"Yes. Sure. What do you want me to do?" asked Anna.

"I'll turn the key. You turn the handle and we'll both push. Thanks. Prop it open with that stone would you," she said nodding to a concrete lump. "The lock's playing up, the door slammed shut on me yesterday, it took three hours to persuade the caretaker to come round and unlock it. Hence the stone, but that's my problem, what's yours."

"I was trying to find out what's happened to Susan Lake. She's not been happy with the new syllabus. Mr Thomas wanted to talk to her this morning. I wondered where she was," muttered Anna.

"Have you asked Mr Thomas?"

"He's standing in on a seminar for Mr Jamerson," said Anna.

"Oh yes. I'll make enquiries and get back to you. What's your name?"

"Anna. Anna Walker."

"And you are enquiring about Susan Lake. Right. I'll see what I can do," she said, making a note on a scrap of paper.

"Would it be possible for me to make an appointment to see Mr Jamerson?" asked Anna.

"You're not fobbing me off that easily," she thought.

"I can't make appointments for him. He'll be back on Monday. Speak to him then," she said picking up the polystyrene beaker and giving Anna a

39

look that said.

"Are you still here?"

"Thank-you," muttered Anna, resisting the urge to slam the door shut on the way out, anyway, there was a lump of concrete in the way. "Thank-you for nothing," she thought returning to the lecture room. "Is this a conspiracy or just their normal stone-walling," she wondered walking through the door.

"So you've come back have you?" said Josie, almost as though she'd been waiting for her return.

"How pathetic," thought Anna. "How mind blowingly pathetic."

"No," she said. "This is an optical illusion."

"Typical. Think you're so clever don't you," snapped Josie.

"Compared with you so's a cow pat," thought Anna. "Go back to sleep why don't you," she said.

"What's wrong, can't you come up with another of our so called clever answers," said Josie.

"You're not worth the mental effort," said Anna.

"Really, well, if you're going to be like that. You're not worth the effort of talking to either. So there," said Josie turning away from Anna.

"So there," thought Anna. "How childish can you get. God. All this, it's just so laughable. Except. There must be some way of finding out what's happening. Mrs Smithers-Jones isn't likely to be any more forthcoming, but its not fair to worry Susan's Mum and Dad. So, it looks like I'll have to tackle Mrs Smithers-Jones again, at least I won't have to wait till Monday to find her."

Anna went straight to the refectory after lectures, not that she was putting off seeing Mrs Smithers-Jones. Well, not much. It was just that auto-pilot had brought her there and she thought she may as well get something to eat whilst she still felt up to facing the food.

"Have you got anything without meat?" asked Anna, looking at the various plates under the canteen lights.

"There's chicken salad."

"That's got meat in," said Anna. "Or at least it should have," she thought.

"I think I might have some cobblers," said the canteen lady walking into the depths of the kitchen.

"Really," thought Anna. "I'm not sure I want to know that."

"There," said the canteen lady, returning a couple of minutes later. "One vegetable cobbler."

"Thank-you," said Anna looking at a greyish mass with orange bits in it, topped with what looked like scone mix, plonked on the centre of the plate.

"What the hell's that," she thought, not daring to ask because the answer might be worse, she took it to the vegetable counter to choose between baked beans and chips to accompany it and choose rice pudding to follow.

It was a solitary meal, beyond the odd absent-minded glance to see if Susan was coming, she spent it trying to think of another way round the problem and failed.

"Right. This is getting me nowhere," thought Anna, draining the last of her tea, or coffee. "It's time to stop procrastinating and talk to Mrs Smithers-Jones. There's no alternative. At least she should be easy to find. She's difficult enough to avoid most days."

First Anna tried her office, just opposite the entrance to the hall, it was a small area partitioned off with wood and glass screens and had a clear view of anyone entering or leaving. Usually she kept the door open, so there was no chance of anyone nipping past unseen, but now, the light was out and the door firmly locked. Then she went to Patterson Building, a rather uninspiring, 1960's red brick student block, probably built on the space occupied by an outbuilding of some sort, something they couldn't manage to convert and could demolish without too much of an argument. It was said that Mrs Smithers-Jones lived there with her husband, presumably Mr Smithers-Jones. Anna assumed it must be some kind of Poly flat, like the one the Dean lived in on the ground floor of her hall. So she entered the building and started knocking on a door with the name Mrs Smithers-Jones written next to it, on the assumption that this was the place. Then again it could have been an empty broom cupboard for all the response she got to her knocking.

"There's no one in," said a voice from behind, which made her leap almost out of her skin.

"Oh," she said, rapidly trying to gather her wits and remember what she was doing there.

"I was coming to that conclusion," she said. "Do you know where Mrs Smithers-Jones is?" Anna asked, turning to face a scruffy looking boy.

"No," he said grinning at her.

"Do you know when she'll be back?" Anna tried.

"No," came his reply.

"Thanks a bundle," thought Anna.

"Is there anyway of leaving a message for her?" she asked.

"Not that I know of," he said.

"Not much use are you," said Anna.

"I've not had any complaints," he said his grin broadening.

"That does surprise me," said Anna looking him up and down and making her way out of the building as quickly as possible. The sound of laughter followed her.

Outside the rain had started and the wind had blown up from nowhere. Pulling her coat round her Anna bent her head to the wind and made a dash for her own hall of residence.

"Good job I'm not paranoid or I might think there was some sort of conspiracy going on," thought Anna shaking the rain out of her hair. "I'll catch up with her at eleven, when she comes to throw the visitors out. That'll be soon enough."

"Half past eleven," thought Anna standing up slowly from her seat in the corridor. "I get the impression Mrs Smithers-Jones isn't turning up tonight. The plot thickens. But there's not much I can do now. Tomorrow. Tomorrow I'll use another tack. Susan's tactic, I'll ask anyone and everyone till I get some answers."

The cold grey light of the next morning cast doubt on Anna's resolution. The tactic hadn't worked for Susan. She was gone. Missing. And probably still hadn't got any answers, or if she had no one knew.

"Perhaps caution is advised," thought Anna. "I don't want to go missing too," she shook her head. "That's a bit on the melodramatic side," she told herself. "Next you'll be picturing the course sending you to Coventry."

Wandering into the lecture room Anna was greeted by silence. The students avoided her eyes and talked loudly to each other, making a point of ignoring her.

"Hell, this is just so petty," thought Anna sitting down at her usual table and getting out her file. Glancing up she caught sight of two of Josie's friends moving away from the table in front of her.

42

"Josie Whitaker. You will regret this days work. I'm going to make sure of that," thought Anna carefully ignoring their behaviour and turning her attention to the timetable.

"I may as well find out what lecture it is we are waiting for today," she thought turning to the timetable amendment sheet, "God this is pathetic," she muttered after she'd read the sheet for the fifth time.

"What the hell is this lecture," said Anna, speaking out loud before she could stop herself.

"Your guess is as good as ours," said Christine.

"Well well, so someone's speaking to me," thought Anna.

"If you read your timetable you'd know," said Stewart. "It is very simple."

"Very simple," echoed Josie. "Can't you follow it."

"If I can't. It's certain you won't stand a chance," thought Anna.

"Simple is it," said Anna smiling. "So what's the first lecture."

"I don't know, but we're in the right room for it, as far as I can tell" said Christine. "And that's all I care about. I'm pissed off with hanging round for hours in the wrong room."

"So am I," said Ian.

"Half the lectures weren't in the rooms the timetable said they were in last week," said Alison.

"That means half of them were in the right rooms," said Josie.

"I didn't think they got it right that often," said Clare.

"What's this," said Mr Marks standing at the door. "Rebellion?"

"No," said Stewart scowling round at the rest of the class, as if expecting them all to fall into line.

"Who the hell does he think he is, class spokesperson," thought Anna.

"Some of our lectures are changing today," started Christine.

"Yes," said Stewart hurriedly intervening before Christine said too much. "We were just speculating on what was replacing them."

"And where they would be," finished Ian, whilst Stewart ducked quickly to avoid being hit by a ring file which Christine had thrown in his direction.

"Children," he said looking round the room and returning the file to Christine.

"If you've quite finished arguing I have a copy of your new timetable," he said handing the sheets to Clare. "When you've finished handing that round we can get on with some work," he said as the sound of paper shuffling died down. "Now, if everyone's here?"

43

"Yes," said Josie. "We're all here."

"Except for Susan," said Anna.

"Susan. Yes, well, we all know about Susan," said Mr Marks.

"No we don't," said Anna.

"Yes we do. She was taken out because she wasn't getting on with the course and she was disrupting it for everyone else," said Stewart.

"We don't know that. Not for certain. We don't know if she's left the course or what. I would like to know the official version of what's happened, rather than listen to gossip and speculation. I would also like to know what's happened to Susan, even if no one else does," said Anna.

"That's great. Do the bleeding hearts act, you're the only one who gives a damn. All we're bothered about are our degrees which is a damn sight more than she was," said Josie.

"Where is she?" Anna asked Mr Marks, pointedly ignoring Josie comments.

"I'm afraid I can't tell you that at the moment," said Mr Marks.

"Why not?" asked Anna.

"There are things to be organised. But, when it's settled, I'm sure you'll all be told," he said.

"Where is she now?" asked Anna, trying to get an answer.

"Look. We've wasted ten minutes of this lecture already. Can we get on with it," said Josie.

"Yes. There's a lot of work to get through, thanks to her," said Stewart.

"Where's Susan?" asked Anna.

"Shut up can't you," snapped Claire.

"When my questions answered," said Anna.

"She's gone home, for the time being, whilst she thinks things out," said Mr Marks.

"Happy now?" asked Josie. "Can we get on with some work."

"God. Someone strangle her and put us all out of our misery," thought Anna.

"I suppose so," said Anna.

"Thank God," muttered Stewart.

"No. I'm not happy. Not in the least," thought Anna. "But at least I know what to do. I'll ring Susan this evening. I've got her number in my address book. I'll have to get plenty of change. I could go to the bank at dinner time. I should think two pounds worth of ten pence coins should be enough. I could write, but it's not so immediate and if she didn't answer,

44

I'd never know if the letter got to her. She might not want to talk to me. At least if I ring I'll know."

"I'll see you here next week," said Mr Marks picking up his bag.

"What! Finished already!" thought Anna looking at her watch. "Oh well, at least he's not leaving early," she added, glancing at her notes. "Sir Walter Scott and the Antarctic? I think they've got the wrong Scott there. Let's see what the book list says, "Lochinvar", "Wandering Willies Tale", they have got to be joking, "Ivanhoe" and "Clyde Built, a history of ship building on the river Clyde". I'll have to read my notes and see what this was all about. It might even have been something interesting. Meanwhile, I'd better have a look at this time table, if I don't work out where the lectures are, this bunch of dim wits aren't going to tell me," glancing across the amended timetable sheet she couldn't help giggling to herself. "Well, going by previous events, this should provide plenty of scope for cock-ups. I can tell Susan about them when I ring her, assuming I can find the phone number. As long as it is in my address book it should be OK. I know exactly where it is. I can picture it in the top drawer of my desk."

It was after tea before Anna got back to her room, the desk drawer held many things. Too many things. None of them was the address book.

"Shut damn you," Anna muttered under her breath as the contents jammed the drawer. "This is ridiculous, it all fitted in there before I opened the drawer," she gave an extra shove, something gave and the drawer shut.

"I'll tidy that out later," she thought and turned to the next drawer.

Half an hour later she had gone through the desk, the bookshelves, chest of drawers and the wardrobe.

"Oh come on. This just isn't funny," she said sitting on the floor looking at the untidy mess her bookshelf had become. "I've looked everywhere. There's nowhere else. And I know I didn't leave it at home. I was writing a letter just the other day. I looked in it for the address. So where is it?" Anna's eyes wandered round the room, they came back to the bookshelf and rested on a mug.

"A cup of coffee. Sounds like a good idea to me. There might even be a chocolate digestive biscuit in the tin. I think there was one left," Anna

45

crawled on all fours over to the kettle and stopped.

"Typical," she muttered. "I mean it should've been the first place I looked. Between the bin and the kettle. Of course. The most logical place in the world to keep an address book. Why on earth did I even think of looking anywhere else," Anna picked up the book and thumbed through it.

"Here it is," she muttered standing up and grabbing the plastic bag of coins she got from the bank. "I knew I had the number. Now lets just hope the phone is free."

It wasn't.

"This is going to be a long job," she groaned and went to wait in the common room. After ten minutes she went back to the phone.

"Is she going to be long," thought Anna trying to read the girls mind.

"Do you want to use the phone?" the girl on the phone asked, whilst still listening to the person on the other end of the line.

"Yes," said Anna, half hoping she'd use it as an excuse to hang up.

"I wont not be long," she said. "Will you be in the common room?"

"Yes," said Anna, resigned to a long wait.

"Right, I'll let you know when I'm finished," she said pushing in another ten pence and turning her back on Anna. Returning to the common room she spent another twenty minutes waiting, then returned to the phone to find someone else using it.

"Thank-you very much," she thought and stomped back to the common room.

It was two hours before she finally got the phone to herself, or as much to herself as she could in a busy corridor.

"Good it's ringing," she thought. "Let's hope someone's in. Who should I ask for?"

"Hello," said a voice. "Susan's Mum," she guessed.

"Ah. Hello. I'm Anna, a friend of Susan's from the Poly," said Anna.

"Oh. Yes."

"Could I speak to Susan please?" Anna asked.

"No. She's not speaking to anyone."

"Oh," said Anna, her mind in a whirl. "I was just wondering when will she be coming back to the Poly?"

"She's not going back there ever."

"Why not?" asked Anna.

"She's had a nervous breakdown or something. It was thought that

46

taking her away from the Polytechnic would help. I can't see that going back would do her any good at all."

"Oh. But what's she going to do?" asked Anna.

"I don't know. No one does. We'll think about that later. When she's feeling better."

"Is there anything I can do to help her?" Anna asked.

"Stay out of her life."

"What!" said Anna startled.

"Stay out of her life. I don't want anybody or anything reminding her of that place. If you really want to help her, just leave her be, forget about her and let her forget. Don't ring and don't bother writing, she won't get your letters, I'll see to that."

"Oh," said Anna.

"Thank-you for phoning. Good-bye," she said and hung up.

"Good-bye," said Anna to the dead phone.

"Hello," said a voice behind her.

"What!" said Anna almost falling off the stool.

"Have you finished with the phone?" asked the girl.

"Yes," said Anna putting down the receiver and getting down from the stool.

"Do you have any change?" she asked.

"Yes. How much do you need?" asked Anna.

"I don't suppose you've got a pounds worth have you?" she asked.

"Sure," said Anna fishing in her pocket for the coins.

"Prepared for a long call were you?" she said.

"I was," said Anna counting out the coins.

"The phone is working OK isn't it?" she asked.

"Yes," said Anna.

"That's all right then," said the girl, with a smile.

"I suppose so," said Anna walking slowly away.

"This was not what I expected," she thought. "Of all the ways it could've gone. I didn't picture this."

"Hello Anna," said Christine as Anna nearly walked straight into her.

"Oh. Hello," said Anna. "Sorry I didn't see you there."

"No you didn't. You were miles away," said Christine.

"Yes. Sorry," said Anna again, automatically.

"What are you doing this evening?" asked Christine.

"Don't know. Nothing much. Why?" asked Anna.

47

"I was just going over to see Alison and some of the others. We're going out for a drink. Why don't you join us," said Christine.

"Thanks, but I don't think I'm flavour of the month at the moment. I might put a bit of a damper on things," said Anna.

"Then again, we might cheer you up a bit. You look as if you could do with it," said Christine.

"Well, if you're sure," said Anna.

"Yes," said Christine, not in the least bit sure.

"OK, but there's just one condition," said Anna.

"What?" asked Christine, hesitantly.

"No shop talk," said Anna.

"That goes without saying," said Christine trying not to look relieved.

The day dawned, not exactly bright and fresh. It had been a good night. Things had been a bit strained at first, but it didn't last. They'd gossiped and giggled about a million and one things, all of no consequence, none of which Anna could remember and then gone to their usual haunt for a dance. A strange place, you could walk past it in the daytime and not notice anything was there at all, but in the evenings when the neon sign was lit and the doors open wide, the warmth and the sound of the music leaking out onto the street sort of invited you to go inside. That and they did let students in for free some nights.

"There ought to be warnings about those cushions," thought Anna as she climbed stiffly out of bed. "They looked so thick and luxuriant. As if you could drown in them. The light must have been deceptive. That's the only explanation. There couldn't have had more than half an inch of foam. On plywood. With concrete underneath. I didn't think I'd stand again after I'd sat down, well, probably more flopped down. They'd have just thought I was drunk. I wonder if they have to leaver people out of those seats when they close up. Do they have a line of ambulances there to take them to the hospital to work out if they are paralytic or paralysed. Ouch my head. How can they keep that up. I'd hate to think what their livers are like. Oh God, why did I think of that?"

"You look awful," said Anna to her reflection in the mirror.

"This isn't getting us anywhere," she thought. "It's time to get ready for breakfast and another lecture packed day, what fun. Breakfast. Oh hell.

The food wouldn't be so bad. Well, no, it is pretty revolting at the best of times. But its that blasted space invaders machine. And that insistent bloody tune. What time is it?" she muttered picking up her alarm clock.

"Eight-thirty. Sod it. I'll have coffee and biscuits here. At least I'll know what I'm eating," she thought opening the biscuit tin.

"On second thoughts," she added putting the lid quickly back, "I'll just have the coffee," she bent to pick up the kettle and stopped.

"I think I'll skip breakfast," she groaned quietly, "I'll head for lectures. Whilst I still can. Maybe the fresh air will revive me."

Christine and Alison were already in the class room, looking extremely bright and cheerful.

"How the hell do they do it," thought Anna carefully lowering herself into her seat. "They make me feel tired just to look at them. I bet they even had breakfast. Oh God," she groaned. "That was stupid. Why did I think of that. I'd better think of something else. Like what? The lecture. Lets take a look at the latest version of the timetable. Sewage with Mr Wells. This just isn't my day. Mr Thomas is after that, I've got a few questions to ask him, then I'll give up. I just hope Mr Wells is late. Oh hell here he is. On time. Why does he have to look so jolly and talk so loud."

Mr Wells went into great detail, with diagrams and graphs, about sludge digestion, sedimentation, the back flushing of filter beds and many other things.

"God. He does like his sewage doesn't he," she thought and instantly regretted it.

The hour passed slowly, at least it did for Anna. When Mr Wells left most of the students dashed off to get a coffee, to drink whilst waiting for Mr Thomas, secure in the idea they'd probably have finished their drink before he arrived. Anna decided to skip that rather dubious pleasure.

"Oh no," thought Anna, catching a whiff of hot plastic and coffee from the beaker of a retuning student. "I'll never drink another mouthful of that revolting stuff again. How can they. It smells foul. I just hope no one starts playing with their beaker. I've never understood this fascination for breaking them up into little bits."

Ian drained his beaker and started to open it out like a sunflower.

49

"Oh God." groaned Anna. "Haven't I suffered enough. I'll drink slower next time. I will, I really will."

"Good morning," said Mr Thomas. "How is everyone this bright and sunny morning. All present and ready to work?"

"Yes. We're all here," said Josie.

"Except for Susan," added Anna.

"Can't you drop that," snapped Stewart. "Susan is gone. Live with it."

"Why, where to and for how long though we don't know," said Anna. "Not officially," she thought. "And I would like to hear their official take on the situation."

"Yes Susan has gone," said Mr Thomas. "She's had a nervous breakdown."

"At least they're keeping to the same story," thought Anna. "Though I still don't believe it."

"It is a great shame," said Mr Thomas.

"You've changed your tune," she thought.

"She was a talented student. It is a matter for regret that we couldn't do anything to prevent this from happening. But we didn't realise there was anything wrong till it was too late to do anything with her still here. Perhaps now she's away from whatever it is here that brought on the crisis, it can be resolved and maybe, sometime in the future she can finish her degree."

"You liar," thought Anna.

"Anyway, she's left the course. It was for her own good. I'm sure we all send her our best wishes for a speedy recovery," he paused for a moment. "Now we'd better get on with some work, you are behind in your schedule."

"Thanks to Susan," said Stewart.

"Yes. Thanks to her," echoed Josie.

"Nothing to do with the lectures always starting late, when they do start at all," thought Anna as Mr Thomas handed round the reading list. "Susan's gone. 'You only live twice' heads the recommended reading list and they just accept it all like a bunch of sheep."

Chapter 4
The Field Trip

Anna was back at the hall of residence, heading to her room after tea and walking past the telephone when it started to ring.

"Hello," said Anna picking up the receiver.

"Hello. Is Anna Walker there?" came a familiar voice.

"Good God, Mum's phoned me," she thought.

"Yes. It's me Mum. To what do I owe this honour?" she said.

"And you can cut that out. I don't know what's got into you these days," said Anna's Mum.

"Why have you rung?" asked Anna.

"And can't I ring my daughter if I want to?" her Mum asked.

"Of course you can," said Anna.

"I wanted to make sure you knew about your Great Aunt Elspeth's visit," said Mum.

"I was just going to ring you about that," said Anna.

"I thought I brought you up not to interrupt. I hope your manners improve before this weekend, I'll never hear the end of it if you upset Aunt Elspeth," said Mum.

"Neither will I," thought Anna.

"Well. You were going to say something, spit it out, or has the cat got your tongue," said Mum.

"I've got a field trip this weekend," said Anna.

"Don't talk nonsense, you haven't mentioned this before. Aunt Elspeth's coming this weekend and I expect to see you here," said Mum.

"They only told us about it this afternoon. It was supposed to be in October," Anna started.

"I thought that was cancelled," said Mum.

"It's OK for you to interrupt," thought Anna.

"No, it was postponed. Today they told us it was going to be the last weekend in November, which is this weekend. This is the first chance I've had to ring you," Anna explained.

51

"That's as maybe," said Mum. "You can't go. Aunt Elspeth's coming."

"I can't not go! It's an essential part of the course," Anna replied.

"I've got to go now. I'll see you on Friday," said Mum.

"Mum!" Anna exclaimed.

"Oh and bring a nice dress," Mum added. "I don't want Aunt Elspeth criticising me for what you wear."

"Mum," shouted Anna as the phone went dead. "Well I've told you," she muttered at the receiver. "If you don't choose to listen that's your problem. Bring a nice dress. How old does she think I am. Five! No, she'd have told me which nice dress to wear. That pretty pink dress with the lace collar. There was always a pretty pink dress. I hate pink. Well, she'll just have to see Great Aunt Elspeth without me. They can talk about me behind my back properly. Without me there. Great Aunt Elspeth, she didn't approve of me doing a degree in the first place. She'd really like to be the cause of me being chucked off the course. "Too much education is bad for a girl. She'll never get a husband like that," that's what she said. Much she knows about getting husbands. Ninety-eight years old and she hasn't got one yet and I can't see any turning up now, not unless they're after her money. Oh well, they should have got the idea by Sunday afternoon or Monday morning. There's going to be one hell of a row then, but there would be anyway. I'd be bound to do or say something wrong, just being there would probably remind her that she disapproves of me for something. Lets face it, whatever I do I'm in the wrong, so there's no point blowing the course in an attempt to avert a row, there's going to be one whatever. Not going home this weekend will put it off till later, so that's what I'll do and they can suck on that. The weekend can't come quick enough."

"If they think I'm going to ring them, they've got another thing coming," she thought angrily a million times or more that week, or at least every time she passed a telephone.

"They have spoken and they expect me to come trotting home like a good little doggy. Well I'm just not doing it," she kept telling herself.

By Friday though, she was getting worried. Friday, the day before the field trip, the day she should arrive home, sometime between six and seven in the evening.

"What are they playing at," she began to wonder. "What are they up to.

52

I can't see them just sitting back and doing nothing, so what will it be. How will their minds work," Anna deliberated through the day and over the evening meal. "They expect me to arrive sometime between six and seven, like a good little girl. By eight they might suspect something. Then what? Mum might ring the hall and check I've gone. And give me a right earful if I haven't. Then again, she might ring before eight, on the principle that if I'm here I shouldn't be. Whatever, if I'm not in to answer the phone she can't nag me. So where shall I go. The pub? Not by myself, there's nothing sadder than someone drinking alone in a pub and I don't exactly feel like company. Just somewhere warm and dark where I can hide away from everyone. The pictures. Of course. Wonder what's on. Something decent I hope. Then again, something totally useless could be good for a laugh," she thought heading off to the cinema before she changed her mind.

"It's already started," said the woman at the ticket box.

"Can I still get in?" asked Anna.

"Yes. Its just some people don't like coming in after the film's started in case they've missed something."

"I should think I'll be able to pick up the plot," said Anna glancing at the pictures from the film.

"I don't think there is much of a story to it, anyway, as I said, its up to you," said the woman, handing over the ticket.

"Thank-you," said Anna and headed for the doors, pushed her way through the heavy velvet curtains and stood for a moment in what seemed to be total darkness. Then she noticed the picture on the screen and the usherette holding her hand out for the ticket.

"Oh sorry," she muttered and handed it over. Without a word the usherette tore the ticket in two, handed half back to Anna and guided her through the darkness to an empty seat.

Anna settled back into the plush seat to enjoy the film or what was left of it. A sci-fi film. Somewhere in the depths of the universe a space ship was busy doing the meet and greet and collecting information about anything and everything they happened to come across. In the midst of their wanderings they come across something rather odd.

"They would wouldn't they," thought Anna. "The universe is full of them, that's why they went out there."

A manufactured object, but not man-made. They brought it on board to have a closer look at it.

"Good job its only small," thought Anna. "Or they'd have problems getting it in the ship, I suppose they could don space suits and go out to look at it, but that would be difficult to film."

They then stood around gawping at it, like a bunch of Muppets. It was a smooth cylinder of lilac coloured machined metal. No protuberances, indentations or obvious entrances, such as windows or doors, it did not hold their attention for long. They tried to open it up to see what was inside. Unfortunately there was no obvious way in and the lilac metal was too dense for them to scan through it and too hard for any of their cutting or drilling equipment to make any sort of impression on it. They soon tire of their new toy and leave it, still in the loading bay with it, with one man guarding it.

"No prizes for guessing what happens next," thought Anna as the guard wanders aimlessly round the thing. "It's amazing how stupid these people from the future are. You'd think they'd learn something from all the sci-fi films that have ever been made."

After if has been left untouched for a short time the object starts doing some information gathering of its own. It opens up and bits start coming out of it. The guard goes over to have a look.

"Dim wit," mutters Anna. "Did he argue over the contract. If he had any sense he'd report the developments and get the hell out of there, for all he knows it might be emitting poisonous gas or some sort of biological agent, he has no idea as to its intentions."

The thing grabs the guard and starts investigating him. Like the ships scientists, it examines the external appearance, then turns to study the internal structure. After examining all possible openings for a way in, the object decides to use drills and cutting equipment to gain access to the internal workings. It has more success than the humans in this and has a thorough, if messy, exploration of the guards workings.

It then tries to put the guard back together again. This is where the problems start, the tubing just won't all fit back in and the guard is no longer functioning. The object tries hard, trying to get all the bits back in, resealing the incision, everything short of picking him up and shaking him, but to no avail. After a while it gets bored and goes off in search of other toys to play with. Its curiosity not entirely satisfied by dismantling the guard.

"Perhaps it reckons it knows where it went wrong dismantling the first guard and wants to test the theory," thought Anna.

It takes a while for the alarm to be raised. The object spends a lot of time wandering down long empty corridors.

"That space ship must be enormous," thought Anna as the object proceeded further into the vessel. "They could've saved a fortune on building and fuel by missing out on all this unnecessary space."

The alarm is finally raised by someone, which the object has partially dismantled, staggering onto the bridge, gasping out a garbled explanation and dying.

"It's either suppressed laughter at the over acting or else the thought of having to clean up his own mess that did for him," thought Anna giggling.

From that point on they forget about investigating the object. Forget that they brought it on board. It has become a menace to all mankind, not just those on the ship and must be destroyed. Then there follows a few uncoordinated efforts to get rid of it in which they loose a few minor players.

"If it was Star Trek they'd have been wearing red tops," thought Anna as a couple more get zapped by the thing. "It's funny how these creatures never manage to kill anyone in command, after all they should be easy to spot and killing them would create chaos," Anna mused.

The crew withdrew for a committee meeting.

"What's the captain there for if he can't make a decision," thought Anna impatiently whilst they have a discussion as to what to do. After a lot of hand wringing they come up with a plan.

"My God. Wonders will never cease. You'd think they'd have a book with standard procedures for instances like that," thought Anna.

A simple plan.

"It would have to be," she thought.

The object was to be led into a room which could be opened into space. The door to the room was then to be made space tight, the port to space opened and the object flushed out.

"And that's going to do what? Destroy it? The things been floating round in space for ages? Drop it a hint that it's not welcome so that it goes off in a huff?"

A robot is to lead the object into the appropriate room, they choose a robot because it will be destroyed when the hatch is opened.

"All the self-sacrificing crew members presumably having already sacrificed themselves," Anna thought. "Presumably the robot thinks that this is the only way to save the crew."

Then once the ship is far enough from the thing, the idea is to turn their guns on it and atomise it.

"Strange how these peaceful space ships are always so heavily armed," thought Anna.

After which they stand round congratulating themselves on saving civilisation.

"Who says they saved civilisation. What proof did they have that civilisation was in any danger. They don't know anything about it, so how can they assess what sort of threat it posed? Also they don't know how many of them there are. It may be a one off, or it many be one of millions," Anna thought as the closing titles drifted across the screen. "And those millions may have learnt something about humans from that one. It could have had some sort of communication with them, or where ever it was it came from. They could be planning revenge."

The curtains close on the film, as the space ship carries on its merry way gathering information.

"I like the way they always end the film before the clean up job. Boy has that crew, what's left of it, got its work cut out, they've got to clean up all that mess created by partially dismembered crew members wandering the ship bleeding everywhere. There's a room that's been opened up to space, anything loose will have flown out and what's left will probably have been damaged. They've got that to sort out and then there's all the extra work to do to cover for the reduced crew numbers. Their clergy person'll be on time and a half with all the funerals, how many coffins do they carry on board. And then, that robot they lost will take some replacing. I shouldn't think the robot sales person drops in every other week, probably have to go to some space port or something, what with them pushing forward the frontiers of known space and all that. I shouldn't think it'll be cheap either, someone's going to have quite a job explaining that lot away. Still, they've only got themselves to blame for it. Bunch of dick heads. Anyone with half a brain could see what would happen," thought Anna making her way to the nearest exit. It was a one way door, she pushed her way through it and walked into a cold dimly lit corridor, like an underpass with a carpet. The sounds of the cinema disappeared when the door swung shut silently behind her, she jumped at the sudden end to the sound.

"Creepy," thought Anna and walked quickly to the other end of the corridor, but stopped short of the double doors, as there was a chain through both the handles and a padlock hanging from it.

"I don't believe it," she muttered, automatically trying the doors, they were locked.

"I'll just have to go back to the other door and hope someone opens it," she thought rapidly retracing her steps, but trying not to run she didn't want herself to know that she was beginning to panic. As she approached the door it opened and she heaved a sigh of relief.

"Could you hold the door open," she said loudly.

"What?" said the person coming through the door.

"Hold the door. You can't get out this way. The doors at the end of the corridor are locked," said Anna.

"Oh," he said holding open the door.

"Thank-you," she said squeezing past him.

"You're not from round here are you?" he said walking beside her back down the aisle looking for an alternative exit, one that lead to the outside.

"No," said Anna.

"It's the accent," he said.

"If I had a penny for every time I've heard that," thought Anna.

"Are you at the Poly?" he asked when she didn't reply.

"Yes," she said.

"Educated eh. What would you have done if I hadn't come?" he asked.

"Oh the same as anyone else, under the circumstances," said Anna.

"And what would that be?" he persisted.

"Panic," she said with a smile.

"Not try to open the door?"

"It was a one-way door. If you panic you'll usually attract someone's attention, then they can open the door. Simple really," said Anna.

"What if it didn't work," he asked.

"Someone else might make the same mistake. Like you," she said.

"I see," he smiled.

"And what would you have done?" asked Anna, beginning to get annoyed with all the questions.

"See if anyone came," he said

"And if they didn't?" asked Anna.

"Smash the door down," he answered with a grin.

"Unlike you, I'm not exactly built for that sort of activity," said Anna as they finally emerged from the cinema. The cold night air made her give an involuntary shiver.

57

"You OK," he asked.

"Yes thank-you. Why?" she asked.

"You shivered," he said.

"It's cold out here," Anna said.

"Cold. Its not cold," he laughed.

"OK, so I'm a sissy. But it was rather warm in the cinema and you do get used to the temperature."

"I don't know why they have it so hot," he said.

"I don't know either, but its the same with all cinema's. Gives you a shock when you get out," said Anna.

"Not if you take your jacket off whilst you're in there."

"OK. Dimwit that I am, I sat with my coat on and I've brought this on myself," she said in a bad mood and not wanting to stand talking in the street. Much to her surprise he started laughing and the sound was so infectious she was soon laughing along with him.

"I was just going to the pub. Would you like to join me," he asked.

"Oh. I don't know. I ought to get back," said Anna.

"Don't tell me. You've got a thesis on quantum physics to write and you went to the pictures to get some data."

"I don't think I could spell that, let alone write about it. No, I've got a field trip this weekend and I've got to catch the bus early tomorrow morning," she said.

"Where are you going?"

"I knew there was something I meant to ask."

"Do you mean you don't know where you're going?" he asked.

"Daft I know. I think it was the Gents toilets that distracted me," said Anna after a moments consideration.

"You've lost me there," he said.

"Part of the field trip involves a visit to an extremely fine example of a Victorian Gentleman's Public Convenience."

"You're visiting a Gent's bog!"

"Yes," said Anna moving away from the cinema door, out of the way of other people leaving.

"Is it still in use or has it been put in a museum," he asked starting to walk down the road.

"Well," said Anna following him down the road. "They said it was a working convenience. Which rather implies that it is in use."

"You'll get chucked out, won't you?"

"I would have thought so. But they seem to think that we'll be able to walk in, look at the cast iron cisterns, the porcelain urinals and whatever else is in there," she said.

"Like Victorian Johnny machines?" he asked.

"That only accept pre-decimal coins."

"But seriously, what sort of idiot thinks you'll be allowed to do this?" he asked.

"The sort that tells us about a field trip and doesn't say where we are going to. It probably hasn't crossed their minds and won't till we're being escorted out. I can just see the headlines."

"Shouldn't you tell them?" he asked.

"No. It's a long story, but the last one who tried pointing out their stupidities had to leave," said Anna.

"For pointing out how daft they are!"

"Yes. You see, they've computerised our course."

"Pardon!"

"They've got the computer to organise the timetable, what's to be studied and when, the assignments, field trips, exams, recommended reading, you name it, it sorts it. Or that's the theory at any rate," said Anna.

"And the computer organised this field trip?"

"I suppose so," said Anna as they came to a halt outside a pub.

"Would you like to join me for a drink?" he asked, looking at the pub sign and then at Anna.

"Well. I can't stay long."

"That's OK," he said pausing as he opened the door. "By the way, what's your name?"

"Anna. Anna Walker. What's yours?"

"Phil. Phil Parker."

"Good evening Phil, pleased to meet you."

"Pleasure's mutual," said Phil with a large grin and a bow.

"You're pleased to meet you as well," Anna giggled.

"Are you going in, or have I got to hold this door open all night? there's ten people gone in whilst we've been standing here gossiping," he said as someone walked through the door, the first since he'd opened it. Anna laughed and wandered into the pub with Phil following close behind.

"What would you like?" asked Phil.

"What?" asked Anna, who hadn't heard a word he'd said.

"To drink."

59

"Half of lager and lime, please," said Anna.

"Anna!" came a voice from by her elbow.

"Hello?" said Anna looking round sharply.

"Your Mum's been phoning you," said one of the girls from the hall of residence. "She said you were going home, she was worried because you hadn't turned up."

"Oh right. Thanks for telling me," said Anna.

"I was right," she thought. "Mum's rung the hall to check up on me."

"She's been ringing every five minutes," said the girl rather taken aback by Anna's lack of concern. "Sound's quite frantic."

"She would do," said Anna, the words slipping out before she could stop them.

"Mum. She should be on the stage," Anna thought, the expressions of Phil and the girl said that an explanation was expected.

"Great Aunt Elspeth's visiting this weekend, Mum told me to come home. I've got a field trip this weekend, I told her I couldn't come. She choose not to listen, that's all," said Anna.

"But. She's very upset," said the girl looking slightly nonplussed.

"Upset! Furious more like. She snapped her fingers and for once I didn't come running," said Anna.

"Oh," said the girl. "I thought you'd want to know," she added, edging off back into the crowd.

"Thanks for telling me," said Anna smiling.

"Patronising little cow," she thought. "You just wanted to see me panic."

"There's a phone at the end of the corridor over there," said Phil, handing her her drink.

"Thanks, but," Anna started.

"If your Mum's worried," Phil started.

"It'd be the first time," said Anna.

"What's special about Aunt Elspeth?" he asked taking another tack.

"Nothing really. She's in the country for six months visiting the relatives. This weekend she's visiting us," said Anna.

"And you'd rather see a Victorian bog?" asked Phil.

"You don't know my relatives, anyway, that's not the point," said Anna.

"Isn't it?"

"No. There are certain field trips you have to go on and get good marks for your reports, in order to pass the year," Anna explained.

60

"And this is one?"

"I don't know," said Anna. "That's the point. No one knows."

"What?"

"Its because the course was computerised, the computer hasn't finished organising everything yet, it hasn't decided which bits are essential, not that I've ever known them do anything like this which wasn't, but they say everything's going to be different with the computer organising things, so, you can't tell."

"That's crazy."

"I know, that's what Susan kept telling them," said Anna.

"Susan?" Phil asked.

"The one who had to leave," Anna explained.

"Did you tell your Mum this?"

"I tried, but she wouldn't listen. She likes to organise things, tell people what to do. She never consults and she definitely doesn't listens to anything anyone else says," said Anna.

"But, for the sake of your degree."

"She never wanted me to do a degree. Neither did Great Aunty Elspeth for that matter. Thought it was a complete waste of time," said Anna.

"Oh," said Phil.

"Hell, I sound just like Susan, paranoid," she thought.

"Anyway," she said hurriedly. "I've burdened you with enough of my problems. Thank-you for the drink. I'd better go. It's going to be a busy day tomorrow. I could do with plenty of sleep."

"Don't dash off like that," said Phil. "Whatever I said I didn't mean to offend you."

"Sorry," said Anna. "It's just, nothings going right and I really ought to get back."

"Can I walk you back to where ever it is you are staying?"

"You don't have to," said Anna.

"I want to."

"Why?" asked Anna.

"I'd hate to think of some poor unfortunate asking you the time and getting his head bitten off," said Phil smiling.

"Am I that bad?" asked Anna.

"No. Worse."

"Thanks a bundle."

"Pleasure I'm sure. Now where's this place you live?" he said guiding

61

her towards the door.

"Wakefield Building," said Anna smiling.

"Where?"

"On Westmorland Road."

"Not that boring newish building that looks like a stack of shoe boxes?" he asked.

"No. The Victorian heap next door," said Anna.

"The one that looks like a fortress hiding behind an enormous brick wall?"

"That's it," said Anna.

"I've often wondered what that looks like on the inside," said Phil hopefully.

"Are you asking to be invited in?" asked Anna.

"It's up to you. But it is an interesting building," Phil smiled.

"Well, if you behave yourself I might give you a guided tour of such delights as the laundry, the kitchen, the common room, the signing-in book."

"Signing-in book?" said Phil surprised.

"To be accurate there are two, one for residents, one for guests," said Anna.

"You have to sign a book when you go in and out of the building?" asked Phil.

"Well, you sign it in the morning, then put a tick next to your name when you go out and cross it out when you come in."

"And the guests have to sign in and out as well?"

"Yes. Its in case of fire. Makes it easier to identify the bodies."

"Thanks," muttered Phil.

"Oh and there's a weekend book as well."

"The weekends have to sign in and out?"

"It's for people who are going away for the weekend, they have to say where they're going and when they'll be back."

"To eliminate them from the body count."

"I suppose so," said Anna.

"Where will you tell them you're going to?"

"When?"

"Tomorrow. The field trip to the unknown. Remember," said Phil

"Oh shit!"

"Exactly," said Phil. "What will you put in the book."

"God knows, but that's not the problem now," said Anna gazing at the hall of residence.

"What is?" he asked.

"See that window, to the left of the door, second floor, with the light on."

"The one with the middle-aged man pacing the floor?" asked Phil.

"Yes. That's my room," said Anna.

"Who's he," asked Phil.

"My Dad."

"Doesn't look very happy," said Phil.

"You're a great comfort," said Anna.

"Maybe he'll see reason," Phil suggested.

"And change the habit of a life time, anyway, even if he understood, Mum never would and he'd catch it in the neck if she thought I'd talked him out of bringing me home," said Anna.

"So, what'll you do?" Phil asked.

"I don't know. Maybe he'll go home. I could wait and see. He can't sit there all night. They have strict rules on guests."

"The light's gone out. Maybe he's leaving."

"We'd better hide. Quick down here," said Anna nipping down a side street opposite the hall.

"What now?" asked Phil.

"I don't want to get caught. He'll only take me back home and I won't get any choice in the matter," said Anna.

"I guessed that, but why here?" asked Phil.

"We can see the entrance to the car park, over there, next to the hall. If Dad leaves we'll see him and I'll know if it's safe to go back to the hall. I don't want to spend all night standing out here."

"And he'll see us in the beam from his headlights," Phil added. "And pick you up."

"Oh hell," said Anna as a car started up in the car park. "Where can we hide," she muttered looking round frantically. She turned back to face the hall. Phil put his arms round Anna and picked her up.

"What the hell do you think you're playing at?" she hissed at him.

"Can you still see the exit to the car park?" Phil asked.

"Yes, but what's the big idea?" Anna asked.

"Your Dad'll see a courting couple down a back alley. He's not going to look close enough to identify you," said Phil.

63

"I hope you're right.   He'd half kill me if he saw me here," said Anna.

"What for, hiding from him or smooching in a back alley?" Phil asked laughing.

"The car's coming," said Anna.

"Is it him?"

"Not sure.   It's dark," said Anna and the driver obligingly turned his headlights on.

"Is that enough light?" asked Phil, sounding like he'd arranged it.

"Bit too much," muttered Anna.

"Do you recognise the car?" said Phil trying to sound a little more serious.

"Yes.   That's Dad," said Anna, watching as the car turned right and drove off in the direction of the family home.   "It's all right, you can put me down now," she added.   Phil sighed and placed Anna carefully back on the ground.

"What next?" he asked.

"I suppose we'd better go in and see what we can find out," she said after pausing a moment for thought.

"Like what?"

"I don't know.   He might have left a message or something.   Families, who'd have them."

"They're there when you need them," said Phil.

"Not my lot," muttered Anna fishing out her keys.   "Well, are you ready, this is Wakefield Building," she said unlocking the door.   "Would you like to come in?"

"Don't mind if I do," said Phil, following her into the building.

"Ah Anna.   It's a shame you weren't here a couple of minutes ago," said Mrs Smithers-Jones pouncing on her as soon as she walked through the door.

"Oh why?" said Anna trying to look as if she knew nothing.

"Your Father came to collect you.   I would have thought you could have been here rather than gallivanting round the town with," she glanced pointedly at Phil.

"He didn't have to come, I'm perfectly capable of driving myself home as you know, in any case, I've got a field trip tomorrow," said Anna.   "But you knew that as well," she thought.

"You could have told him.   It would have saved him the journey and the worry," she said flustered.

"I did," said Anna.

"Oh," she said. "Well I hope you're at least going to ring him to tell him what you are doing."

"Why?" asked Anna.

"He was very worried about you and it'll save him driving over tomorrow," said Mrs Smithers-Jones.

"What?" Anna said stunned.

"You weren't here, so he said he'd come back tomorrow morning, about eight, eight-thirty," said Mrs Smithers-Jones triumphantly.

"I'll give him time to get home before I ring," said Anna.

"Oh. Right," she said, deflated.

"Good-night," said Anna.

"Is your friend leaving?"

"He'll be out by one," said Anna with a smile.

"I'll be checking," she said throwing a last scowl at Phil and then stalking out of the front door.

"Who the hell was that," said Phil turning his gaze away from the front door to Anna.

"Mrs Smithers-Jones. The hall warden."

"How on earth can you put up with that?" he asked.

"Before I came here someone told me that people in Poly's tend to be more Motherly than those at Universities," said Anna.

"They've got an odd idea on Motherly that's all I can say."

"I don't know," said Anna signing herself in. "She's like my Mother, except you can reason with her."

"What's this about one o'clock?" he asked

"Guests are permitted between twelve noon and 1am on Fridays and Saturdays, twelve noon and 11pm the rest on the week."

"And I thought students had all the fun," said Phil.

"On our grants? You must be joking. Anyway, would you like a cup of coffee?"

"So long as I'm not keeping you up too late."

"Not losing your nerve are you. Mrs Smithers-Jones hasn't frightened you has she?" asked Anna smiling.

"No. It's just. Your field trip."

"I'm packed and ready to go tomorrow and I reckon about half an hour for a cup of coffee, then I'm kicking you out."

"That's nice, I'm to get thrown out onto the streets am I."

"Yes. Well, do you want a cup and a chance to see the luxuries of a student room or don't you?"

"Put that way, how could I possibly refuse," smiled Phil.

"Right. You'd better sign the visitors book," said Anna pointing to the table.

"Is there a space for comments?"

"Only in the repairs book," said Anna.

"What, not another book, there's half a rain forest down here," said Phil grinning.

"Hello Anna," came a voice from the basement steps, Anna and Phil both looked round to see a girl in a T-shirt cradling a mug of coffee in her hands.

"She knows my name. I ought to know hers," thought Anna.

"Your Dad's been here," she said.

"I know," said Anna. "Mrs Smithers-Jones told me all about it."

"Fine," said the girl and padded off to the common room.

"Are you coming?" asked Anna.

"But," he mumbled gazing in the direction of the common room.

"We can have coffee in there if you'd prefer," said Anna.

"No. No," he said. "Do we have to go down there for coffee?" he asked pointing to the basement stairs.

"No. I've got a kettle of my own," said Anna.

"Oh. All mod cons," he said leaning against the post at the bottom of the stairs. He didn't stay there for long though.

"It moved!" he exclaimed.

"What did?" asked Anna.

"The post. It moved, I swear it did," he said looking at the post as if it had tried to eat him.

"Well its old. Serves you right for leaning on it."

"Thanks. Are these stairs safe?"

"As far as I know," said Anna.

"And the building?"

"Some say its tinder dry and it wouldn't take much for it to go up in smoke," said Anna.

"I'm not surprised, its sweltering in here."

"And some of the wiring hums."

"Hence the visitors book."

"Exactly," said Anna.

66

"Nice."

"This is my room," said Anna unlocking the door.

"I've seen better furniture on the dump," said Phil standing in the middle and looking round the room.

"We get the dumps rejects."

"I thought students had modern furniture and duvets," he said puzzled.

"I think they try to set everything in context," said Anna thoughtfully. "The modern furniture goes to the modern halls."

"Hence this," he said looking round.

"Yes," said Anna.

"And the duvets?"

"We are the only hall that hasn't got them. They're rumoured to be coming next year. In the meantime, they're using up all the old linen on us. Everything's darned to hell and gone."

"So this is the Cinderella Hall," he said.

"Something like that, we even have to rent our own television. How do you like your coffee?"

"Black."

"You sure? I do have some real milk, its on the window sill keeping cold."

"That's what the milk bottles are doing out there, I did wonder. Do the students put them there or does the milkman deliver?"

"I believe he used to deliver, but he's not as young as he used to be," said Anna.

"He did!"

"No. Do you want milk?" asked Anna.

"No."

"With or without sugar?"

"Without."

"That sounds disgusting," said Anna.

"Depends on the coffee."

"How about this?" asked Anna holding up the jar.

"My favourite."

"Good," said Anna, making her coffee with milk and sugar.

"Biscuit?" she added, handing over the biscuit tin.

"Spoiling me are you."

"No, I just fancy one myself and it'd be rude to have one without offering one to you first," said Anna with a smile.

"And it would be impolite of me to turn you down because of my diet," said Phil.

"Are you on a diet?"

"No, but I might have been," said Phil.

Chapter 5
Heading off into the Unknown

The clatter of the alarm clock dragged Anna from a disturbing dream. She was running from something, she didn't know what, but it was catching up rather rapidly. It was quite a relief to wake up, even though it was still early and the sky was dark.

The building was silent, no one with any sense would be moving for several hours. It was the thought of being there when her Father arrived which dragged her from beneath the covers. She hadn't rung home. She thought about it after she'd said goodnight to Phil, at eleven-thirty, but it was only a passing thought which she had dismissed as useless.

"They wouldn't have listened," she thought sleepily getting together a breakfast of hot milky coffee and digestive biscuits. "And I'd have got an earful of how late it was, that I'd dragged them out of their beds. I wonder what Phil's doing," she thought stirring her coffee. As she bit into a biscuit the thought crossed her mind.

"I never asked him anything about himself. All that talk. He must think I'm a right egotist going on all the time about the course. What was the name of that pub? Not that I'd have the nerve to go in it by myself, but it would be nice to meet him again," she sighed. "Well, I'd best be off," she muttered. "Before Dad gets here," she added glancing at the clock.

"Polytechnic field trip," Anna wrote in the weekend book.

"The Poly should know where their field trips go. Mrs Smithers-Jones is bound to know, she knows everything. And I don't want to leave any clues for Dad to follow me," she thought.

Outside Manchester Building, that was where they had been told to wait for the bus. Anna arrived in plenty of time, before anyone else. She sat on a wall and waited, ignoring the curious glances of the occasional passer-by. She was just beginning to wonder if she was waiting in the wrong place when the other students from her course began to arrive.

The lecturers were ten minutes late, despite their threat to go without anyone who wasn't there by half past seven. Not that it mattered, the coach and it's driver were nowhere to be seen.

"This is ridiculous," muttered Mr Thomas, after waiting all of ten minutes. "I'm going to go and look for that coach. Wait here, I shouldn't be long," he added and headed off down the road.

A quarter of an hour later the bus turned up without Mr Thomas.

"What shall we do now?" Josie asked Mr Duffy, whilst the coach driver was busy opening up the hatches for the luggage to be stored.

"Put the luggage on the coach," said Mr Duffy, handing his bag over to the coach driver. The students followed his example and soon all the baggage was stowed away and the hatches secured.

"Can we get on the coach?" asked Clare.

"I'm not sure. Mr Thomas said we were to wait here," said Mr Duffy as the coach driver climbed into the driver's seat and he descended into indecision.

"Here, is on the bus," said Clare.

"Or where we're standing," said Stewart.

"Why don't we just go without him. That's what he said would happen to anyone who wasn't here when the coach arrived," said Alison.

"Yes," said Christine giggling. "The coach is here and he isn't."

"I don't think that would be very nice," said Mr Duffy.

"It's what he would have done if any of us had been late for the bus," said Alison.

"No he wouldn't," said Mr Duffy.

"That's what he said he'd do," said Alison.

"Yes it is," said Ian.

"He didn't mean it. He just wanted to make sure you all got here on time," said Mr Duffy, looking down the road in the hope of seeing Mr Thomas returning.

"Can't we at least get on the coach," said Clare. "It's cold out here and it'll take less time to get moving when he eventually does get back."

"He said to stay where we were," said Stewart. "That doesn't mean getting on the coach. It means staying where we are."

"And who the hell do you think you are to go laying down the law?" snapped Clare, but no one was listening, they were busy watching Mr Thomas, half walk, half run, panting up the road, his face bright red

70

reminding Anna of the last time she had seen Susan.

"What. Are you doing. Standing around. You should be. On the bus," he gasped

"We were following your instructions." answered Mr Duffy. "Are you all right, you don't look in the least bit well."

"Stop fussing. I'm just out of breath," he muttered. "Well," he snapped. "Are you going to stand there all day, or are you going to get everyone on the bus."

"Yes Mr Thomas," he muttered turning to the students.

"Would you mind getting on the coach," he murmured, but they were too busy getting on the coach to bother about anything he said. "Oh well," he muttered joining the general migration onto the coach. "Are you coming?" he asked Mr Thomas, who was leaning against the coach panting heavily, he glared at Mr Duffy, staggered onto the bus and dropped heavily into the first available seat, just behind the coach driver. The bus started up and the field trip began.

"Thank God for that," thought Anna watching through the window as they slowly left the town behind and the risk of her Dad spotting her decreased.

"Shame reading whilst I'm travelling makes me sick," she thought looking down the bus at the groups of chattering students. As she gazed out of the window the rain began to fall.

"Typical. Miserable weather to match a miserable day," she thought closing her eyes and drifting off to sleep.

Several hours later, Anna awoke, still sitting on the bus, but it was no longer moving. They were in a car park along with a lot of other coaches and lorries. Mr Thomas was standing up at the front saying something, Anna slowly brought her befuddled senses together enough to work out what he said.

"You can eat your sandwiches either here or at the picnic area," he said glancing out of the window at the rain. "But don't take your lunch into the cafeteria, they don't appreciate people bringing in their own food," he glanced at his watch and added, "I'll see you back here in an hour." Then disappeared off into the rain.

"Sandwiches. What sandwiches," thought Anna looking round confused. Mr Duffy handed her a parcel wrapped in cling film.

"Oh these!" she thought turning the parcel over in her hands and looking out of the window.

"Don't fancy getting soaked and if I lost track of the time, I doubt if this lot would either notice or mention it before they drove off," she muttered and slowly ate the cheese sandwich, the banana and the bag of crisps, re-wrapped the ham sandwich and put it on a vacant seat behind her. She closed her eyes and went back to sleep.

The coach came to a stop with a jolt outside the hotel. Anna was instantly awake. Outside was a row of terraced housing, two of which seemed to have been combined. The paintwork was the same colour and in the same state of neglect. There was a concrete area in front of the two buildings, covered with litter and sodden leaves.

"Daylight might help, but I doubt it," thought Anna.

"This is the hotel," said Mr Thomas. "There is one single room, for Mr Duffy, the rest of the rooms are for three, so if you'll divide yourself off into groups of three boys or three girls. Then we can get the rooms allocated and you can have your evening meal. Are there any questions?"

"What about you?" asked Christine. "Where are you staying?"

"There wasn't enough room for me here, so I'm staying somewhere else. Mr Duffy knows where I'll be if I'm needed," said Mr Thomas. Mr Duffy said nothing.

"There's only two of us," muttered Alison to Christine.

"I know, we need a third," she replied.

"Well I wouldn't want to share with Clare or any of her snobbish cronies," said Alison flatly.

"Too right," said Christine. "Well that cuts the choice down somewhat."

"Leaves Anna," said Alison.

"She's been very quiet of late," said Christine.

"Slept all the way here," said Alison.

"I didn't mean that," said Christine. "She's not been pointing out the cock-ups on the course lately. Hasn't argued with anyone."

"She never argued as much as Susan," said Alison.

"No one could argue that much," said Christine.

"We could ask her," said Alison. "She wasn't bad when we took her out drinking that night."

"True. Mind you, she didn't look too well the next day," said Christine.

"I don't think she's used to it. Not what we got her anyway," said Alison with a grin.

"No one could be used to that mixture," giggled Christine. "I did fell a bit guilty the next day, but she didn't say anything."

"So did I," Alison admitted.

"Come on lets ask her," said Christine getting up and moving over to Anna's part of the bus. "Hello Anna," she said rather hesitantly.

"Hello Christine, Alison," said Anna.

"We were wondering if," Alison started.

"I would make up the numbers?" asked Anna.

"Yes," said Christine looking somewhat uneasy.

"That about sums it up," mumbled Alison.

"At least they're not Clare's cronies," thought Anna. "Or Josie and they do talk to me."

"Don't mind if I do," said Anna with a smile.

"Good. Well that's settled that. Let's see if we can get a decent room," said Christine.

"If there is such a thing," said Anna looking at the façade of the hotel.

"It doesn't look very promising," agreed Alison.

"Well we want to get in on the division before Clare and that mob. We don't want to be left with the rubbish," said Christine. "So, we'd best get moving."

"Teachers pet. Probably has it sewn up already," replied Anna.

"True. Clare's bound to get the best room. She's such a creep," said Alison.

"She'll complain the loudest if she doesn't," said Anna.

"I'm surprised she isn't in the same hotel as Mr Thomas," said Alison.

"You've heard those rumours too," smiled Anna.

"More than that. I nearly tripped up over them in the park," said Alison giggling.

"They didn't see you did they?" asked Christine.

"No. They were too busy to notice me. Much too busy."

"If you've quite finished dividing off," said Mr Thomas. "I think it's time we went into the hotel. So, if you'll collect your things and follow me." His words were lost in chaos as everyone dashed to retrieve their bags, or tried to. After a moments hesitation Mr Thomas decided to make for the hotel and get out of the bedlam. He rang the door bell and waited. Five minutes later when the students were finally assembled on the forecourt, with their luggage the door bell was answered by a heavily built woman who's thick make up and dyed hair could not hide the fact that she was fifty years old if she was a day.

73

"You must be the students," she said.

"Yes," started Mr Thomas and Mr Duffy together.

"There is only one single room," she said looking from Mr Thomas to Mr Duffy.

"We know," said Mr Thomas.

"My colleague is staying at another establishment," added Mr Duffy.

"I see," she said turning sharply and heading up the stairs. "The rooms are this way. Shut the front door behind you," she paused at the top of the first flight of stairs unlocking a door she opened it she said. "This is the single room," Mr Duffy walked in and put down his bags. He walked out again, giving Mr Thomas a filthy look as he walked past.

"That good is it," thought Anna as they moved up to the second floor. There were four doors at the top of the stairs and a corridor that disappeared off round a corner. Three of the rooms went to the boys, the fourth went to Clare and two of her followers.

"Doesn't look like Clare's going to get much sympathy from that quarter thought Anna as Mr Thomas nipped quickly past Clare, his eyes fixed on the landlady who was busy making her way up yet another flight of stairs. At the top the landlady unlocked a door and started opening it, three of Clare's friends pushed their way from the back, past the landlady and into the room, knocking the handle out of her grasp as they did so.

"Well," she muttered as the third person took the key out of the lock and shut the door in her face. For a moment she stood looking stunned, then turned away and opened a second door, at right angles to the first. Josie and her friends pushed past her into that room, the last one grabbing the key from the lock and shutting the door behind her.

"Really," she added, turning away and almost jumped at the sight of Christine, Alison, Anna, Mr Thomas and Mr Duffy standing on the stairs.

"The other room's down here," she said heading off down a corridor, through a small arch on the left, up half a dozen steps, down a corridor under the eaves. A minute later the landlady stopped by another door, barely two feet from the top of a steep spiral staircase.

"I trust your students will treat my hotel with due respect," she said unlocking the door. "Tea is at seven o'clock, as is breakfast," she added and disappeared down the spiral staircase.

"Right. I'll pass that on to the rest of the students," said Mr Duffy heading down the corridor.

"I'll help you" said Mr Thomas following him.

74

"I suppose we may as well see what it's like," muttered Alison carefully edging her way past the top of the stairs and through the open door.

"I suppose so," said Christine following her into the room.

It certainly was an odd shape and the furniture was more shoved in any old way rather than arranged for use. The three single beds lay with the bed heads towards the lowest point of the eaves. The wardrobe was on the same wall as the door, it wouldn't have fitted anywhere else. Between that and the door was a large chest of drawers, the type with three mirrors on the top. The hand basin was tucked into a corner in front of a dormer window. The view, row upon row of wet slate roofs. Another mirror had been screwed to the wall to the left of the hand basin, the ones on the chest of drawers being useless due to age.

The three looked round.

"How much time have we got to kill before tea?" asked Alison.

"About half an hour," said Anna studying her watch. "Which bed would you like?" she asked, her eyes drawn back to the beds which rather dominated the centre of the room, late 60's or early 70's single divans made up with sheet's, blankets and pink candlewick bedspreads.

"Don't mind," said Christine. "They look equally uninspiring. How about you?"

"Not really bothered," said Anna.

"Alison?" asked Christine.

"Not bothered."

"Oh well," said Christine gazing at the beds. "I'll have the one in the middle and I think I'll move it away from the wall a bit."

"I'll have the one nearest the hand basin. In case I get thirsty in the night," said Alison, also pulling the bed away from the wall. Anna put the pillow at the foot of the remaining bed and lay down.

"You can't sleep like that," said Christine.

"I'll have to remake the bed a bit, but I see no reason why I shouldn't," said Anna.

"But," said Alison.

"There's no rules to say you can't," said Anna

"I suppose not," said Alison moving her pillow to the foot of the bed as Christine followed suit.

"We can put everything back as it was when we leave," said Anna yawning. "Tell me when it's six," she added closing her eyes.

"She's not gone to sleep again has she?" asked Christine after a few minutes silence.

"Don't know," said Alison. "But there's not much else to do is there."

"We could talk," said Christine after a moments contemplation.

"About what?" asked Alison gazing blankly out of the window.

"How the hell should I know," snapped Christine looking from Anna to Alison and back again.

"You're the one who wanted to talk," said Alison

"You're useless. Both of you," shouted Christine and flung herself down on the bed. Nobody took any notice. Anna continued to sleep and Alison stood daydreaming out of the window.

A couple of minutes before seven Anna stirred and checked her watch.

"I suppose we may as well head off to the dining room," she said to no one in particular.

"What!" said Alison jumping up at the sudden sound.

"And how are we going to find it?" snapped Christine sulkily.

"Find what?" asked Alison.

"The dining room, idiot," snapped Christine.

"Follow our noses," said Anna.

"OK," said Christine.

"Will someone please tell me what the hell you're talking about," shouted Alison.

"It's tea time," said Anna.

"But no one's said where the dining room is," added Christine.

"I can smell cooking," said Alison.

"So. We'll follow your nose," said Anna slowly standing up.

"Oh. Right," said Alison heading for the door, Anna got there first.

"Wait for me," yelled Christine leaping up and following.

Alison lead the way down the stairs to the basement where they found a dimly lit room very full of tables and dining chairs, all neatly laid out for tea.

"This looks to be the place," muttered Alison as they joined the group of students wandering aimlessly between the tables and getting black looks from the few residents that were there.

"Your tables are over here," said a bored looking girl who seemed to have appeared out of nowhere. She turned and walked to a group of tables each set for four. Everyone, even Mr Duffy, followed obediently in her wake. She waited patently as they all sat down.

"Tomato or chicken soup," she asked each person in turn, but when it came no one was entirely sure which they got. Anna hoped hers had been the tomato.

The next choice was

"Chicken or lamb."

"Do you have anything without meat?" asked Anna to a chorus of groans from her fellow students.

"We can do you a fried egg with some chips," said the girl after a moments thought.

"That'll be fine," said Anna wishing she could disappear into the wall behind her. The egg turned out to be well done, far more appetizing than the meat her fellow students were faced with. Pudding was tinned fruit salad and ice cream.

"What on earth do we do for the rest of the evening? "Christine asked as the last of the dishes was cleared away to the kitchen.

"Well, you could do worse than read all the background literature we provided for you," said Mr Duffy and was greeted by a chorus of groans.

"But then you've probably already done that," he added hurriedly, looking round and seeing most of the students nodding in agreement, he didn't see that most of them had their fingers crossed under the table.

"So, I suppose, you could all come with me to see what this pub, Mr Thomas recommended, is like."

"Sounds like a good idea," said Alison amidst a chorus of approval.

"That doesn't surprise me," thought Anna.

"Right. I'll be down by the front door in ten minutes. If you're not there we'll go without you," said Mr Duffy getting up quickly and leaving, but not before adding. "And I mean it."

"That's the most decisive thing I've ever heard him say," said Christine watching thoughtfully.

"Maybe," said Alison dismissively. "But we'd best get a move on or it'll be us he goes without."

"Yes," said Anna. "We've got more steps to climb than him," she added, heading for the stairs. "I only hope I can find my way back to that room," thought Anna taking the stairs two at a time and trying to ignore the sound of the wind and rain beating against the windows they passed.

Everyone was gathered in the hallway and they were just about to leave when the landlady turned up and walked through them all to the front door.

"Going out," she said sniffily.

"Yes," said Mr Duffy.

"Where to?" she asked standing by the front door and blocking the way.

"God I hope she doesn't expect to come too," muttered Clare.

"The Plough Inn," said Mr Duffy.

"That dump," she muttered. "Well I hope your coach is coming for you."

"No," said Mr Duffy. "We're going to walk."

"Walk!" she said. "In this weather!"

"Is it far?" he asked.

"A good four miles even if you don't get lost. And most do get lost round that way."

"Oh," he said looking out of the half glazed front door.

"Are you meeting anyone?" she asked.

"No," he said. "I don't suppose you know any pubs nearer?"

"One or two."

"Could you recommend any?" he asked cautiously.

"Well, the one round the corner is decent, as is the one at the end of the road."

"Thank-you for the advice," he said, fastening his coat. "Is everyone here?" he added, turning his back on her and addressing the students.

"Pleasure I'm sure," she muttered and stalked off in the direction of the dining room.

"Good riddance," muttered Josie.

"Meow," said Alison, much to Josie's disgust.

"Follow me," said Mr Duffy opening the front door and heading out into the rain. After a moments pause they all followed and found him standing at a road junction waiting for them. "I was beginning to think you'd got lost," he said, but his words where lost in the wind and rain and he was greeted by a row of blank expressions. He shrugged his shoulders and headed down the road hoping that the pub wasn't too far.

"The Green Man," the sign said, hanging from the wall of a stone end of terrace building.

"Must've been named after a zebra crossing," said Anna thoughtfully. Alison and Christine exchanged puzzled looks and followed the crowd, through a door at the corner of the building, into the lounge.

"It's a good job there weren't many here," said Anna as they stood by the bar waiting patiently as the barman leapt into a flurry of activity to serve them all.

"Yes it is," said Christine, looking round the room.

"There'd be standing room only," said Alison looking at the half dozen battered dark wood tables, the benches round the walls and the cluster of stools tripping people up as they crossed the centre of the room.

"Well.   What's everyone having?" asked Alison as the barman approached.

Anna hesitated.   "They can't pull any stunts with me here.   Wouldn't be in their interests, not with us having to share the same room," she thought. "Half of lager and lime," she said with a smile.   "Should be pretty innocuous," she thought.

"Same for me," said Christine.

"Three halves of lager and lime please," Alison said to the barman. Anna watched carefully as the drinks were served.

"There's a vacant table in the corner," said Christine.   "I'll sit there and save it for us," she added and disappeared off across the room.

"Fair enough," thought Anna.   "I'll wait here and carry my own drink. Not that I don't trust them, but I don't."

"Right," said Alison looking thoughtfully at the three glasses on the bar. "I'll take Christine's over for her," she added picking up two of the drinks. Anna picked hers up and followed her to the table.   They sat in silence. Not a group of three, but three individuals each avoiding the others eye. Drinking for the want of something to do.   Anna's eyes wandered round the room looking for inspiration.   They alighted on a lad playing the fruit machine without much luck.

"I wonder who created the fruit machine," she said absent mindedly.

"Don't know," said Christine blankly.

"Great," thought Anna.   "So much for that as a conversation starter.

"Neither do I," said Alison.   "But I should think if they got a penny for every one ever made they'd be pretty rich."

"I should think they'd get more than one penny," said Christine quickly.

"I know that.   I was just saying," Alison started to reply.

"If they only got one percent of the sale price of the machine it'd be more than one penny," Christine continued.

"It was just a turn of phrase," said Alison beginning to get agitated.

"Oh hell," thought Anna looking to the ceiling.

"Anyway, the person's probably dead now," Christine finished with a sigh and looked to the door.

"And I thought things couldn't get worse," thought Anna glancing at Alison "You can almost see the steam coming out of her ears." Then she saw the boy from the fruit machine leaning over the bar counter and taking a few bags of crisps. "Must know the owner," she thought returning her gaze to Alison and Christine.

"Well, he doubtless died rich and his family inherited a fortune and they're still coining it in," snapped Alison

"Assuming they inherited the patent and it didn't lapse on his death," said Christine

"I thought my family were the only ones like this," Anna mused looking at the two of them, Christine with her calm logic and Alison getting worked up about nothing. At the other side of the room Clare downed a gin and orange almost in one and one of her companions got up without a comment and bought another.

"Clare's fair knocking back the gin," Anna said.

"What!" said Christine sharply, Anna's comment coming out of the blue. Clare half drained the gin and orange that was put in front of her, then started tucking into a bag of pork scratchings.

"That's the second gin she's had in five minutes," said Anna nodding in Clare's direction.

"Wonder what she's like drunk?" speculated Alison.

"Don't know," said Christine thoughtfully. "I've never seen her drunk before."

"I've never seen her in a good mood either," said Alison.

"Looks like you stand a good chance of seeing her drunk," said Anna. "But I wouldn't hold out much hope for her being in a good mood. You could cut granite with that look."

"Could be interesting watching," grinned Alison, suddenly brighter.

"From a discreet distance," added Christine.

"Well of course," said Alison. "That goes without saying."

"I see," thought Anna. "I see a hell of a lot."

"She doesn't look too happy," Anna added thoughtfully.

"She never does," said Alison.

"I know, but she's usually angry, she's looking pretty miserable at the moment," muttered Anna.

"She's thwarted," said Alison looking pointedly at her empty glass.

"Is that painful?" asked Christine.

80

"Looks like it," said Anna"Same again?" she asked pointing to the glasses.

"Yes please," said Christine finishing hers off quickly.

"I thought you were never going to ask," smiled Alison.   "I don't suppose they have any peanuts do they?" she added gazing at a card, hanging on the wall, with packets of peanuts stapled to it, "Dry roasted would be nice."

"I think they're better for you," said Christine.

"They taste better," said Alison.

"I'll see," said Anna smiling.

"What the hell am I doing here," she thought propping up the bar waiting to be served.   The barman was getting another gin and orange and a bag of prawn cocktail crisps.   "Clare's going to regret this tomorrow," she thought, gazing into the mirror behind the bar.   "Though it may not be the worst of her problems."

"And what can I get for you?" asked the barman with a smile.

"Three halves of larger and lime."

"Coming up," he smiled.

"Oh and do you sell peanuts, dry roasted ones?" she asked smiling.

"Certainly," he said.

"Could I have three packets please," said Anna looking at the card of packets.

"One each should keep them happy," she thought.   "Am I appeasing them in the same way that Clare's being appeased.   How much did he say it was?   Oh well, I've got a five pound note.   It must be less than that," she smiled and handed it over.

"Thank-you," he smiled and went to the till at the far end of the bar.

"The next question is how to get this lot over there," she thought looking at the glasses and the packets, then glancing over at Alison and Christine, they were still deep in conversation.   "Doesn't look like they're going to help."

"Your change," said the barman.

"Thank-you" said Anna putting the money in her pocket.

"Would you like a tray?" he asked.

"Yes please," she smiled.   He smiled back and put the drinks and peanuts onto a tray that hadn't been there a minute before.

"Thank-you," smiled Anna and carried the tray over to Christine and Alison.

81

"And what's his name?" asked Christine.

"Whose?" asked Anna handing round the drinks and peanuts.

"The barman's. Who did you think," said Alison. "We saw you chatting up the only decent man in the place."

"I wouldn't say he was the only decent man," said Christine.

"I don't know what you mean," said Anna putting the empty glasses on the tray and returning them to the bar.

"Thank-you," smiled the barman.

"You've made a big impression there," said Christine giggling.

"And that's so funny is it," thought Anna. "Then again, these two would laugh at anything."

"I don't think so," she said. "I just saved him the job of having to collect the empties. After all, he's got his work cut out clearing up after Clare."

"She's fair going through the gin," muttered Christine.

"She may as well have a bottle and a straw," said Anna.

"I don't know how she can afford it," said Alison.

"She isn't," said Anna.

"So who is?" demanded Alison and Christine.

"Her friends paid for the first few, but the last two were bought by Mr Duffy," said Anna.

"I didn't see him go to the bar," said Christine.

"Neither did I," said Alison.

"No. But I saw him hand over some money to the last two people who went up to the bar," smiled Anna.

"That's stopped you looking so smug and changed the subject," thought Anna.

"But why would he buy Clare drinks?" Christine asked bemused.

"He might be intending on buying everyone a drink and just happened to start there," suggested Alison.

"Doesn't look like he's moving," said Christine.

"Maybe he feels sorry for her," said Anna.

"Sorry for her!" Christine and Alison turned to her.

"Mr Thomas was pointedly ignoring her and you've heard the rumours," Anna started.

"It did seem odd," said Christine.

"Looks like the love birds have had a tiff," giggled Alison.

"And Mr Duffy's providing her with a shoulder to cry on," added Anna.

82

"Shush. He's coming over," hissed Christine, picking up her packet of peanuts.

"Do you mind if I join you three," he asked pulling up a stool and sitting down.

"Much good it'd do if we did object," thought Anna as they sat their shaking their heads. "Now what small talk can he possibly think of," she pondered.

"Nice pub," he said after a moments pause. "They do a good pint of beer," he added nodding his head towards his glass.

"I'll take your word for that," said Alison and took a sip from her glass.

"The peanuts are good," said Christine offering the packet to Mr Duffy.

"Thank-you," he smiled taking a handful that all but emptied the packet. "Dry roasted. My favourite."

"Looks like it," thought Anna, quietly fishing out the last of her peanuts.

"Nice to see that the big businesses haven't got hold of it," said Anna looking round the pub.

"I was telling some of the others about a game I've come across," started Mr Duffy.

"Oh," murmured Christine.

"I start drawing six pictures, like this," he said pulling a pen and paper from his pocket. He divided the paper into six squares and drew a few lines in each.

"Then what?" asked Alison.

"Then you finish the pictures off," said Mr Duffy

"And what does that do?" asked Alison.

"How you complete the picture says something about the way your mind works," said Mr Duffy looking round them. "How about you Anna, would you like to finish the pictures?" he asked offering the pen and paper to her.

"No," she said, shaking her head.

"You can take your amateur psychology games, roll them up and stuff them where the sun don't shine," she thought smiling at him.

"Oh come on. Be a sport," he said still pushing the pen and paper towards her.

"Go on Anna," said Christine. "It'll be fun."

"You do it then," said Anna picking up her drink and leaning back against the wall.

"Oh well, if Anna doesn't want to join in," said Mr Duffy.

83

"Anna doesn't want some half arsed dickhead trying to analyse her," she thought not even bothering to acknowledge his comment or to meet his eye.

"Christine. You'll do it won't you," he said pushing the pen and paper towards her.

"Of course," said Christine taking the pen and paper. "How do I finish the pictures off?" she asked.

"However you feel they ought to be finished," smiled Mr Duffy.

"Oh hurry up," said Alison. "I want to have a go too."

"Of course. Here," he said pulling out some more paper and another pen from his pocket and starting off six more pictures.

"Came prepared didn't he," thought Anna.

"Finished," said Christine handing over her pictures. "Now what do they mean?" she asked.

"We'll wait till Alison's finished first, we wouldn't want to influence her judgement," said Mr Duffy looking closely at the sheet.

"And what do you think you see in that," thought Anna looking at the pictures, "I'm sure you can read whatever you want to into them."

"Whilst we're waiting would you all like a drink?" he asked, everyone nodded. "Right," he said looking round the table. "Lager and lime?"

"And peanuts," said Alison looking up from her drawing.

"Dry roasted?" smiled Christine.

"Of course," he said and left for the bar.

"God you make me sick," muttered Alison to Christine.

"What've I done?" asked Christine.

"Sucking up to Mr Duffy like that," Alison continued, finishing the last of the pictures.

"You're doing the stupid quiz too," Christine snapped.

"It's better than looking at his ugly mug or listen to him trying to make conversation," said Alison.

"I don't know," said Anna. "He's a bit stuck for subjects. It'd interesting watching him trying to find something to talk about."

"I hadn't thought of it that way," smirked Alison.

"You're rotten. Both of you. Rotten to the core. Can't you give him a chance," said Christine looking from Alison to Anna. Anna and Alison exchanged glances.

"No," they said smiling.

"I hope you choke on your peanuts," Christine hissed as Mr Duffy arrived with two of the drinks and the peanuts.

"You could've given him a hand," said Christine to Anna.

"So could you," smiled Anna.

"Neither of you gave me a hand," thought Anna watching as Mr Duffy brought the other drinks to the table, the barman obviously didn't deem him worth offering a tray to.

"You could have really sucked up to teacher, helping him with the drinks," said Alison putting down the pen and ducking as Christine aimed a clout at her.

"You'll get us thrown out if you behave like that," said Mr Duffy putting down his own drink and Alison's.

"Really," thought Anna. "The barman seems to find it amusing."

"So you've finished," said Mr Duffy picking up Alison's sheet. "Are you sure you don't want a go?" he asked Anna.

"I'm sure," she said.

"You never know what you might find out about yourself," he persisted.

"You can't tell me anything about myself that I don't already know," she thought picking up a packet of the peanuts he had brought. "And, if it's anything personal, I don't want these Muppets to know."

"No is no," she said.

Mr Duffy sighed and turned to Alison's sheet.

"Well. What do they tell you?" asked Christine.

"Each square represents a different aspect of your personality. How you complete the picture shows your response to it."

"You said that before," interrupted Alison.

"Let him get on with it," snapped Christine. "We're going to get nowhere fast if you keep sticking your oar in."

"All right. I won't say another word," said Alison.

"Right. You can carry on now," said Christine to Mr Duffy.

"Thank-you. I'm glad to hear it," he said, but his sarcasm was ignored.

"My lips are sealed," said Alison.

"Shut up, you aren't funny," said Christine.

"If you've quite finished?" asked Mr Duffy.

"Yes," they all said smiling.

"This one has to do with home and security. The rectangle at the centre bottom is seen as a front door. Christine, you've put a letter box and a door knob on the door and drawn two windows with curtains at the top left and right hand corners. Alison meanwhile has left the door blank, drawn four windows, each divided into four squares. It shows different aspects of

85

your personality, how you view home, in relation to life."

"How pathetic," thought Anna her attention moving from the table towards the bar where the lad who had been playing the fruit machine and pinching crisps, was now trying to get the jukebox to play something. After a couple of well aimed clouts, the machine started playing "A Horse With No Name", after which he returned to the fruit machine, pausing only to give the jukebox a quick clout when it came close to finishing the tune. The clout made it jump back to the beginning, he certainly wanted his money's worth. Luck was with him, with the fruit machine and the coins started flooding out, he pocketed his winnings and left. Anna's eyes following him through the door, staying on the door when it had swung shut behind him. The sound of a hand bell being vigorously shaken roused her from her day dream.

"Last orders," the barman shouted.

"Last orders," muttered Mr Duffy looking round in time to see the barman disappear into the public bar. It looked like he was going to have his hands full getting the last orders in there.

"Well, we may as well go before they chuck us out," he said with a sigh.

"Oh right," said Christine and Alison obediently draining the last of their drinks. Anna put her empty glass on the table. Mr Duffy stood up, looked round the room at the students, then left. There was a mass exodus as they all followed, afraid of being unable to find the hotel by themselves.

Chapter 6
A Sunday mornings visit to a gents public convenience on a suburban railway

"Mrs Noble kindly prepared some packed lunches for us," said Mr Duffy addressing the students gathered in the hall.   To be accurate, they were sitting on the stairs, leaning on walls and generally getting in the way of all the other guests.

"I think we may as well distribute them now since the coach doesn't seem to have arrived.   It might be a good idea if someone kept an eye out for it," said Mr Duffy.

"I can see the road," said Ian.

"Thanks," said Mr Duffy turning back to the students littering the hallway.   "In the meantime, we aren't the only ones staying here, so we shouldn't prevent other residents from using the stairs."

"Where can we move to?" asked Josie looking round the packed stairway.

"The bus is here," shouted Ian.

"Good," said Mr Duffy.   "We'll be off then.   Has everyone got their sandwiches.   We appear to have one packet left."

"Must be yours," said Anna.

"Oh yes," he said, looking at them as if they had just materialised in his hand.

"What about Mr Thomas's sandwiches," asked Clare.

"Ah.   I'm sure he'll organise his own," said Mr Duffy.   "Mrs Noble can't be expected to do any for him, he isn't staying here.   Anyway, we'd better get a move on, we don't want to keep the driver and Mr Thomas waiting do we?"

Outside the hotel chaos was gradually building up.   There had been no room for the coach to park by the kerb because of the many parked cars. So the driver had stopped in the middle of the road.

"So many cars," sighed Anna as the traffic built up at both ends of the bus. "Where are they all going to on a Sunday. And what effect do they think blowing their horns is going to have, other than make them unpopular with the residents. It won't move the bus. Not that there's anywhere for it to go to now."

Mr Duffy followed the last student onto the coach, paying no heed to the chaos and conducted a quick head count.

"Right we're all here Eric," he said to the driver. The coach door shut, just before an angry motorist tried to climb on board. Eric put the coach in gear and started moving slowly forward. For a moment there was silence as the drivers in front gazed in disbelief at the approaching vehicle and the impassive expression on the drivers face. Then they put their cars in reverse and scuttled out of his way, getting into the first parking space they came across and like the man who had tried to get on the coach, stared open mouthed as they sailed past into the first of many traffic jams. Sunday or no Sunday there was a lot of traffic on the road and it all seemed to be in front of them. Eric took the delays in his stride, but each hold up only served to wind Mr Thomas up.

The coach had barely stopped at the railway station car park when he was demanding to be let off. Without a glance to see if the students were following, he dashed off to the station.

"Seems desperate to get to this toilet," thought Anna watching him. Then suppressed a giggle as the meaning of her thoughts sank in.

"Yes. Well. We'd better get a move on," stammered Mr Duffy as the students filed past him, following in the wake of Mr Thomas.

Meanwhile Mr Thomas had arrived at the platform and was heading straight for an ornate coloured glass sign in the centre of a black wrought iron archway standing at the top of a flight of stairs. A wrought iron fence extended from the arch around the top of the staircase so that no one could fall down the hole. These were the gents, the ladies were nowhere to be seen.

Mr Thomas went straight down the stairs. After a moments hesitation the students followed. Halfway down they were greeted by a strong odour of fish. At the bottom was a tunnel stretching before them, the white tiles on the walls were covered in graffiti, the floor, strewn with litter, was extremely slippery. At the end, round a corner, was a double door, closed and padlocked. The sight of this stopped Mr Thomas in his tracks.

"What now?" asked Ian, the first of the students to catch up with him.

"Ahem," murmured Mr Thomas. "I'll go and see the Station Master.

88

Doubtless this is just an oversight. It shouldn't hold us up too long. Wait here, I'll be back shortly," he said looking round for some kind of response, but there was none, so he left, with many a scowl following him.

"How long does it take to find a Station Master," muttered Alison as she shuffled back from the bottom of the stairs for the umpteenth time.

"Give him half a chance," muttered Mr Duffy glancing towards the stairs.

"He's had a good ten minutes already," said Christine craning her neck to read some of the graffiti.

"You don't suppose he's forgotten us?" asked Josie.

"No," said Mr Duffy. "Give him a few minutes. If he's not back soon I'll go looking for him."

"And leave us in this stink," said Ian.

"Have you got any better ideas?" asked Mr Duffy. Ian shuffled off in silence to look up the stairs.

"Why don't we wait at the top of the stairs," suggested Anna. "There's no reason to stay down here."

"That's true," said Mr Duffy heading for the stairs, the students following him.

"That's better," thought Anna taking a deep breath and shivered as the chill edge of the wind struck home.

"Lets hope he doesn't keep us waiting too much longer," muttered Alison looking down the platform.

"What are you doing here?" demanded Mr Thomas ten minutes later.

"Waiting for you," said Ian.

"And why are you waiting here?" he asked. "You should be on the coach."

"You said to wait here," said Clare icily. "So here is where we waited."

"Oh. Well, lets get to the coach," said Mr Thomas.

"And the toilets?" persisted Clare.

"Oh. They're not open on Sundays. There's no call. We'll come back tomorrow," said Mr Thomas.

"Why? Don't the passengers need them on a Sunday?" asked Anna.

"Maybe they're not that desperate on a Sunday," sniggered Josie.

"Couldn't they be opened for us," said Clare standing her ground.

"No. They're very busy," said Mr Thomas. "They do have a railway to run."

"Too busy to go and open the toilets," Clare persisted.

"And, we are behind on our schedule. We ought to head for the safari park whilst things are still quiet," said Mr Thomas, not answering her question.

"Why are we going to a safari park?" asked Anna without thinking.

"I would have thought that was obvious," snapped Mr Thomas. "To observe the animals. Now, if we can head for the coach," he said stalking off to the car park, leaving the students and Mr Duffy to tag along behind.

"When will I learn to keep my big mouth shut," thought Anna climbing on the coach. "I should have left it to someone else to ask. They might have. Instead its just one more black mark against my name, which is something I could do without. Oh well, a safari park. I suppose it could be fun," thought Anna gazing through the window of the coach. "There must be something to them or people wouldn't flock to them in the summer. I just don't see the relevance. But there must be something."

"When are we going to get to this dump," demanded Clare interrupting the radio's 12 o'clock news summary.

"It is a safari park," started Mr Thomas.

"Should be there about half one," said Eric.

"Oh well," started Mr Duffy.

"What," snapped Mr Thomas.

"We may as well have our dinner now," said Mr Duffy. "It'll save time later."

"Where are the packed lunches?" asked Mr Thomas.

"I handed them out earlier, whilst we were waiting for the coach," said Mr Duffy.

"Where's mine?" demanded Mr Thomas.

"There didn't seem to be one for you," said Mr Duffy.

"You mean I haven't got any lunch!" snapped Mr Thomas.

"Mrs Noble must've assumed you were making your own arrangements," mumbled Mr Duffy.

"Can we start on our sandwiches now?" asked Clare.

"Yes," said Mr Thomas. "If you've got them you may as well eat them. Looks like I'll have to go without."

"Hard luck," said Clare.

"So I was right, the love birds have been bickering," whispered Alison.

"Mr Duffy wouldn't tell her where he was last night," whispered Christine. "I saw her asking him."

"Before or after we went to the pub?" asked Alison.

"Before."

"I'd have thought she'd know," said Anna.

"So would I," said Christine.

"I thought she was in a bad mood over something," said Alison.

"And when she's in a bad mood everyone knows about it," said Anna.

"And that tummy bug she got won't exactly sweeten her temper," said Christine.

"Tummy bug?" Anna asked.

"Spill the beans," said Alison.

"When I went to the toilet this morning there was someone in there being sick. I was debating whether or not to go in search of another one," said Christine.

"It's the only one I've found," said Alison.

"I found another, but the cistern was very precarious. I thought it was going to fall on my head when I flushed it," said Anna.

"Could've been nasty," said Alison.

"My thoughts precisely," said Anna. "Looked like cast iron."

"Heavy," said Alison.

"Do you want to know who was being sick or don't you?" interrupted Christine.

"Clare," said Alison.

"Yes," said Christine somewhat deflated.

"Probably all that gin she had yesterday," thought Anna, "But, they like a nice bit of gossip."

"Better watch what she eats," she said grinning.

"What?" asked Christine, whilst Alison looked puzzled.

"Large quantities of peculiar food. Like this stuff," said Anna looking a her sandwiches. "I think I'll donate these to Mr Thomas. I'd hate to think of him missing out on them."

"Nasty of you. But what will you eat?" asked Alison.

"An orange, a banana, a bag of crisps and maybe even this," she said, holding up a strange black lump wrapped in cling film.

"Go on then. It ought to confuse him," said Alison.

"Mr Thomas," said Anna.

"Yes Anna," said Mr Thomas.

"You can have my sandwiches if you like," said Anna.

"Well. If you don't want them," said Mr Thomas rather surprised.

"No," said Anna smiling sweetly.

"I can't identify what's in them," she thought. "And I'm not sure I'd want to."

"Oh. Well. I'd hate to see them going to waste," said Mr Thomas.

"So would I," said Anna passing them down the bus.

"That's got rid of them," she thought.

"Thank-you Anna," said Mr Thomas, as the sandwiches were finally handed to him. "It's nice to see that someone is concerned for my welfare."

Clare scowled as she scoffed her sandwiches. Mr Duffy said nothing.

"There's no need to make a performance out of it," thought Anna unzipping her banana.

"I wonder what that black stuff is?" said Christine cringing as her teeth squeaked on a gristly bit in the meat.

"Seems to have a lot of dried fruit in it," said Anna turning it over in her hand.

"Perhaps its some kind of emergency ration," suggested Alison, holding it up to the light.

"If you don't want it I'll have it," said Clare busily chewing on her portion of the stuff.

"Here," said Anna. "You can have it with pleasure."

"And mine," said Alison and Christine together, handing it over.

"Thanks," said Clare falling greedily on the packages. She heard a giggle and looked up.

"What are you two giggling about," she snapped.

"Nothing," they mumbled, going bright red and trying to stifle their laughter, but not succeeding. Clare scowled at them and turned back to the dried fruit.

"Cow," muttered Alison.

"I could kill you," said Christine ginning at Anna.

"Me?" smiled Anna.

"Unusual food. I ask you."

"At least we don't have to eat it. I wonder if it's got prunes in," Anna speculated.

"Why?" asked Christine.

"She won't have to worry about being regular," smiled Anna.

"Oh no," giggled Alison.

"Still giggling," came Clare's voice raised above the general chatter of the coach.

"What of it," muttered Christine looking out of the window. "Looks like we're almost there," she added, addressing the rest of the bus. "I can see the gates."

"At last," muttered Clare. "I thought we were going to stay on this blasted coach all day."

"This is a safari park," stated Mr Thomas. "We have to stay on the coach to see the animals."

"That's brilliant planning I must say. Cooped up in this crate all day," moaned Clare.

"There's probably somewhere for you to stretch your legs in the park," said Mr Duffy hopefully.

"There better had be," muttered Clare darkly.

"Bound to be," said Mr Thomas sounding more certain then he looked.

"You don't suppose that stuff's having effect already?" whispered Anna.

"What stuff?" asked Alison.

"The dried fruit," said Anna.

"Effect. You don't mean," Alison turned to Anna.

"Well, she's anxious to get off the coach and I've never noticed her keen on exercise before," smiled Anna.

"No. It can't work that quickly. She's only just eaten it," said Christine giggling.

"Why don't you share the joke with all of us, instead of just tittering away in the corner like that," came Clare's voice.

"Wind your neck in," shouted Alison.

"I think a little quiet would be in order," said Mr Thomas. "We are here to work."

Clare muttered something under her breath, but no one was paying any attention, they were too busy gazing out of the window at a fairly plain white wall topped with barbed wire and decorated with pictures of wild animals.

"The safari park does not appear to be open," said Eric leaning on the steering wheel and gazing down at the large entrance gates securely chained and padlocked.

"Are you sure this is the right gate?" asked Mr Thomas.

"Yes," said Eric pointing to a sign saying "Main Entrance."

"Perhaps we're early," suggested Mr Duffy.

"It's half past one," said Mr Thomas. "How can we be early."

"It was just a thought," muttered Mr Duffy.

"Looks to me like we're about three and a half months too early," said Eric pointing to a sign.

"Open March - October."

"Couldn't get in the toilets, the safari park is closed, this field trip's the most amusing cock-up we've had yet," thought Anna. "Hang on a minute, I think I saw a movement behind the gate."

"Where do you want me to go now?" asked Eric turning round to Mr Thomas.

"I don't know yet," said Mr Thomas. "I'll have to think about it for a minute."

"So much for getting a chance to stretch our legs," moaned Clare.

"When I want to know what you think I'll ask you," snapped Mr Thomas.

"Touchy," muttered Anna.

"There's someone coming," said Mr Duffy pointing to a small side gate to the left of the main gate.

"Yes. I know," snapped Mr Thomas at Mr Duffy. "There's no need to point out the obvious."

"Who is that man," thought Anna watching him whilst he hesitated for a moment by the side of the bus. He looked back at the gate, straightened himself up and knocked on the coach door. Eric pressed the button and the door opened.

"What are you doing?" said Mr Thomas looking up at the sound of the door. Eric nodded towards the door as the man stepped on board.

"Is there anything we can do to help you?" asked Mr Thomas.

"That's what I was going to ask you," he said hesitantly. "I mean, the park isn't open. We were just wondering if you were lost or something," his voice tailed off and he looked bleakly round the coach.

"Yes. We can see that the park is closed," said Mr Thomas icily. "That does not alter the fact that we made arrangements to view it today. And that is what we intend to do."

"You can't do that," said the man slowly shaking his head. "We're not open."

"I'm perfectly well aware of that fact," said Mr Thomas slowly. "But, as I said, we have made arrangements to view the park."

"We're not open," the man interrupted.

"God give me strength," muttered Mr Thomas.

"Do you have a superior?" asked Mr Duffy.

94

"Mr Armatage is in charge," said the man.

"Would it be possible to speak to him about this little misunderstanding?" asked Mr Duffy. Mr Thomas gave him an extremely sour sideways glance.

"Oh I don't know. I mean he's very busy," said the man.

"Mr Armatage had better shift himself over here. It is bad enough arriving and finding the gates locked. If we have to leave without looking round the park I shall be in touch with those in charge," snapped Mr Thomas.

"I'll get him," said the man and dashed off before Mr Thomas could say anything else.

"That'll be the last we see of him," said Clare gazing out of the coach.

"Have some faith," said Mr Duffy. "He said he would get Mr Armatage. We ought to give him a chance."

"Faith," muttered Mr Thomas. "What has faith got to do with it. If this Mr Armatage doesn't come I'll see to it that he's sacked."

Eric turned off the coach engine, the sound slowly died away and they sat in silence waiting and watching for someone to come.

"Looks like Clare was right for once," thought Anna getting bored watching the gate. "Hang on a minute though," she muttered to herself. "I'm sure I saw something move," she thought moving forward in her seat.

"What is it?" asked Alison.

"I'm not sure," said Anna slowly, as she began to make out the shape of a person in the undergrowth behind the small gate. "But I think Mr Armatage is coming."

"What!" said Alison, leaning across Christine to get to the window just in time to see the gates open and a man emerge.

"This should be interesting," Anna thought, smiling quietly to herself. The coach door opened and the man climbed on board.

"I am Mr Armatage. I believe you wish to speak to me," he said stiffly looking from Mr Duffy to Mr Thomas.

"Yes," said Mr Thomas. Mr Armatage concentrated his attention on him.

"We arranged to view the safari park today," said Mr Thomas.

"But the park is closed," he said.

"So your colleague told us several times," said Mr Thomas slowly. "That does not alter the fact that arrangements were made and we came here with the expectation of seeing the safari park, not sitting in front of a

95

pair of padlocked gates."

"Oh," said Mr Armatage. "Yes. I think I will have to speak to Mr Featherstone about this."

"Do so then," said Mr Thomas dismissively.

"Oh. Right then. I will," said Mr Armatage, hesitating a moment before he dashed back to the gate and security.

"So much for Mr Armatage," said Mr Thomas.

"He's probably in charge of the keepers or something," said Mr Duffy.

"So what gave that idiot on the gate the impression that he could sort anything out," snapped Mr Thomas.

"Maybe he is the immediate superior to the man on the gate and he came to see us before escalating things to a higher authority, just in case he could sort things out," suggested Mr Duffy.

"Fools. The place is run by mindless idiots," scowled Mr Thomas at Mr Duffy who turned to the window to watch for the approach of Mr Featherstone.

"And you Mr Thomas are the biggest fool around," thought Anna watching for the next arrival. "You should've gone through the schedule to see if it was in any way viable."

It took a lot of waiting, but eventually a man in a suit stepped out of the gate, following Mr Armatage. He pointed to the coach, said something and retreated back to the other side of the gate. Mr Featherstone watched the man leave and the turned his attention to the coach.

"Here comes Mr Featherstone," said Alison. Eric opened the coach door and the man entered.

"I have been told you have made arrangements to visit the safari park today," he said.

"Yes. That is so," said Mr Thomas.

"But as you can see. The park is closed," said Mr Featherstone, gesturing towards the gates.

"We are aware of that. We have been told it several times, in fact. Also, we could not have sat here for over an hour and not been aware of that. However, the fact remains, we made arrangements with the park to look round it today," Mr Thomas started.

"It would seem odd that anyone would arrange a visit for today," said Mr Featherstone.

"Here is the letter confirming the dates," said Mr Thomas fishing out a sheet of paper from a file, not bothering to comment on what Mr

96

Featherstone had just said.

"Everything's in order," said Mr Featherstone looking closely at the letter. "August," he muttered to himself.

"That is when the arrangements were made," said Mr Thomas.

"We had a problem with some bookings made then," said Mr Featherstone frowning deeply at the date.

"What sort of a problem," asked Mr Thomas.

"Like today, bookings were made for times that we weren't open," said Mr Featherstone.

"Why?" asked Mr Thomas.

"I don't know, one of the members of staff in the office, who has since left, did it and no one knows why," said Mr Featherstone.

"Well, if you know about the problem," started Mr Thomas.

"Most of the letters she sent were OK, it was just some of them that were affected, the thing is, the office copies had different dates to the ones that went out, so there was no way we could trace the bookings that were effected," said Mr Featherstone.

"Presumably this letter was one of them," said Mr Duffy.

"That's obvious," snapped Mr Thomas.

"So what are we going to do, this is one of the major items in our itinerary, this visit," said Mr Duffy.

"Well?" said Mr Thomas to Mr Featherstone.

"I can show you round. If that's what you want," said Mr Featherstone.

"Of course it is," snapped Mr Thomas.

"The only thing is the animals aren't at their most active at this time of year and we tend to do any major overhauls and building work now, so it doesn't inconvenience the public. Oh and of course the restaurant, shops and facilities aren't open."

"Typical," muttered Clare.

"Fair enough," said Mr Thomas, now can we get on with it.

"Oh right," said Mr Featherstone. "I'll just get the gate opened."

"Right," said Mr Thomas. Mr Featherstone hesitated for a moment, then left the coach and disappeared through the side gate and into the undergrowth.

"I wonder what the animals do in the winter," said Christine thoughtfully.

"Sit round in scarves and woolly mittens and decide what to get each other for Christmas," said Anna flippantly.

"I can picture it now," said Christine.

"Just a bit of a problem on how big a giraffes scarf would be," said Alison.

"They might have something like the neck of a polo necked jumper," said Christine.

"They're probably half asleep. A lot of animals hibernate in the winter. It may not be cold enough here for all the animals to hibernate, but they probably slow down a lot," said Anna thoughtfully. "Oh look, the gates are opening," she added just as Clare was about to start complaining about them giggling. "Thank goodness for that," she muttered and rested back in her seat. Mr Featherstone climbed on the coach, Eric shut the door and the coach progressed through the gates. Looking back Anna saw someone struggling to drag the unwieldy gates shut.

"Right. I want you all to keep a close look out for any animals. And I want a description of what they are doing," said Mr Thomas.

"Shame it isn't spring," giggled Alison.

"They don't all go mad in Spring," said Anna. "Sheep are at it this time of year, so that they can give birth in the spring."

"We're not likely to find many sheep amongst the lions," said Christine.

"I know that," said Anna. "But sheep can't be the only ones who time having their young in spring."

"Oh. I hadn't thought of that," muttered Christine turning to the windows to scour the park.

The coach proceeded slowly, Mr Featherstone pointed out the places the animals were normally to be found.

"So where are they?" asked Clare after fifteen minutes looking at an empty landscape.

"Some will be in the animal sheds, the rest are out there somewhere. Whilst the park is open we tend to feed the animals near the road, it brings them down for the visitors to see. This time of year there is no reason to do that. The animals get fed from more convenient points. Curiosity does bring some animals along to watch the visitors. But they won't expect to find any this time of the year, also, there's some building work going on at the far side of the park, they seem to find that fascinating," said Mr Featherstone.

"That must be unnerving for the builders," thought Anna.

"Great," muttered Clare.

"That's why the park's normally closed this time of year," said Mr

Featherstone.   Clare scowled at Mr Thomas and turned back to the window.   Mr Featherstone looked puzzled, but continued with his commentary of what animals should normally be clearly visible, along with any fact about them he could think of, relevant or otherwise, in a constant monotone.   It was just beginning to feel as though they had always been driving through the park listening to Mr Featherstone, when the bus stopped in the centre of a group of locked up buildings.

"This is the visitors centre.   When we're open it is a hive of activity," said Mr Featherstone.

"I'll take your word for it," said Clare.

"I'm sorry the visit was rather disappointing," he said looking sideways at the coach door.   Eric got the hint and opened it.   "Perhaps another visit could be organised when we're open."

"I'll be in touch," muttered Mr Thomas.

"Meanwhile, you can't miss the exit.   I'll send someone along to open the gate," Mr Featherstone finished and disappeared off in the direction of the largest of the closed buildings.

"So much for that," muttered Clare.

"Where to now?" asked Eric.

"Back to the hotel," said Mr Thomas.

It was late when the coach pulled up outside the hotel and the students piled out, they met Mrs Noble in the hall.   The sight of her stopped them in their tracks.   Mrs Noble was wearing a fake leopard skin coat over a very short tight black skirt and low cut polka dot blouse, her hair was piled high on her head and seemed to be tied in place by a translucent blue nylon headscarf, black stiletto's, fishnet stockings and yet another layer of make-up completed the picture.   She was heading for the door, but her attention was directed towards trying to stuff one last thing into an already overfull black patent leather clutch bag.

"Oh," she muttered, then catching sight of Mr Duffy getting off the coach she marched up to him.

"If you think I'm serving your dinner now you've got another think coming," she said.

"It's only half past seven," he said.

"Twenty five to eight," said Mrs Noble.   "Diner is served at seven and finished by seven-thirty. Now if you'll excuse me, this is my Bingo night and I don't want to be late."

"What are we going to eat?" asked Mr Duffy.

"I don't know I'm sure. You should have thought about that earlier," said Mrs Noble.

"We can't help the traffic," exclaimed Mr Thomas. "Be reasonable."

"Be reasonable! I get one night off a week and I'm not having it messed up by you," snapped Mrs Noble.

"But," stammered Mr Duffy.

"But nothing. And this place better not stink of take-away's when I get back," she added stalking off down the road.

"Now what are we going to do?" asked Mr Duffy.

"I don't know about you, but I'm going back to my hotel. They'll still be serving," said Mr Thomas.

"That sounds like a good idea. We'll come with you," said Mr Duffy.

"Ah. They only serve residents. There's a Chinese Restaurant near here. Eric could drop you off and you could walk back here afterwards."

"Right," said Mr Duffy turning to the students standing round in the hall. "Everyone back on the bus, Mr Thomas is treating us to a Chinese meal."

"What!" said Mr Thomas.

"It was your idea," said Mr Duffy. "You can't expect either me or the students to pay for it."

"But," stammered Mr Thomas.

"You can always claim it on expenses," said Mr Duffy.

"Thanks a bundle," said Mr Thomas.

Next day, at 6.30am, exactly, Anna's alarm clock went off.

"Oh hell," muttered Alison. "Tell me your clock's fast, I've only just got off to sleep."

Christine's alarm clock started ringing and she struck out a sleepy arm to silence it.

"Where the hell's that blasted clock," she muttered and fell out of bed as Alison's alarm clock joined in.

"They can't all be wrong," said Anna turning on the light.

"What did you do that for," said Christine. "I've got spots in front of

100

my eyes now."

"If we're going to get up we may as well see what we're doing," answered Anna making her way to the sink.

"You're heartless," muttered Alison dragging herself out of bed. "Christine. When are you going to stop that blasted racket," she added.

"My clock, I can't find it," wailed Christine. "My Gran bought it for me and I can't find it."

"Follow the sound, there's plenty of it." Alison snapped.

"But it's coming from everywhere," wailed Christine dashing aimlessly round the room.

"Just stand still and concentrate for a minute," said Alison.

"If you're so clever, you find it," snapped Christine.

"God they're hopeless," thought Anna.

"Top of the wardrobe, at the back," she said putting the towel back on the rail.

"What!" shouted Christine grabbing a chair and retrieving the clock.

"How did you know," she asked cradling the clock protectively and looking back at the wardrobe as if it had tried to attack her alarm clock, or at the very least tried to swallow the thing whole.

"You must have spent at least quarter of an hour last night explaining what the hell you were up to climbing all over the wardrobe hiding it, so that you couldn't just turn it off and go back to sleep," said Anna.

"Oh," said Christine.

"Could you turn that blasted thing off," snapped Alison.

"Oh yes," muttered Christine, turning the thing over in her hands, finally turning the alarm off, then almost jumping out of her skin and dropping the clock when someone knocked sharply on the door.

"Hello. Are you awake?" asked Mr Duffy.

"Yes," they chorused.

"Good. Breakfast is at seven. Don't be late."

"We won't," they shouted and Mr Duffy wandered off, the girls pulling faces at him from their side of the door.

"Wally," said Alison.

"More of a wet blanket really," said Anna thoughtfully.

"Well at least he's staying in the same hotel as us," said Christine.

"What's this. You've not gone soft on him have you? Quite monopolized him in the pub last night," said Alison ducking as a towel flew across the room at her.

"Anyway, we'll never get to breakfast like this," said Anna.

"And Mr Duffy would be upset, wouldn't he," said Alison.

"You are the limit," Christine fumed, glaring at Alison.

"What've I done?" asked Alison. "I only said you where monopolizing him at the pub, what's wrong are you really going soft on the prat?"

"How could you even think such a thing?" snapped Christine.

"Lets go to breakfast," said Anna getting bored and hungry.

"OK, but if you mention Mr Duffy again I'll, I'll."

"Start stuttering," finished Anna.

"You," shouted Christine storming out of the door. There was a loud clatter on the stairwell, a screech of pain and silence. Anna looked at Alison. Alison looked at Anna, then they dashed after Christine.

Christine was half-way down the spiral staircase trying to work out how to stand up without completing the decent. They were still pondering the problem when Mr Duffy arrived and helped her to her feet.

"Are you OK?" he asked, cautiously letting her go.

"Yes, I think so," she answered, carefully testing her ankles for any sign of weakness.

"You weren't rushing to breakfast were you?" Mr Duffy asked.

"No. No. Don't worry. There's no harm done," smiled Christine.

"Well. So long as you are all right. Personally I don't think it's safe having a door so close to such a steep staircase. You could've broken your neck."

"Not her. She's made of rubber," said Alison.

"She's just had a bad fall," snapped Mr Duffy. "Don't you have any sympathy for your friend."

"No. She should've looked where she was walking," said Alison after a moments thought.

"We're going to be late for breakfast if we stand here much longer," said Anna.

"Do you think you can make it down the rest of the stairs?" asked Mr Duffy of Christine.

"She can always fall the rest of the way," said Alison helpfully.

"I shall ignore that remark," said Mr Duffy stiffly.

"I think I'll be OK" said Christine gingerly trying a step.

"Well. Let me accompany you just in case," said Mr Duffy hovering round her.

"Shall we go," said Anna. "Or are we going to stand here all day," she

102

thought and led the way to breakfast.   "God give me strength," she muttered a vision of the whole day stretching before her.

Breakfast was down to standard and made even worse by the presence of Mr Duffy at their table.   After the meal was finished he stood up to address the students.

"The coach should be here at eight.   If you would gather in the hall."

"I don't want you blocking my hall again," said Mrs Noble.   "You'll have to wait somewhere else."

"Where would you suggest?" asked Mr Duffy.

"I suppose you could wait in the lounge," said Mrs Noble after a minutes thought.

"Most kind.   Where is it?" asked Mr Duffy.

"On the left hand side, as you come through the front door," started Mrs Noble.

"Thank-you.   You all heard that?   Good.   I'll see you there at eight," he said sitting down and turning to Christine.

"I'll have to go and sort out the packed lunches.   You will be all right won't you?" he asked anxiously.

"I'll be fine," said Christine with a smile.

"She'll have us to help her," said Alison smiling broadly.

"Yes," he muttered after a moments pause.

"See you at eight," said Alison coldly.

After a last glance at Christine he left.

"Do you have to be so rotten to him," snapped Christine.

"No.   But it's so easy," Alison smiled and Christine walked off.

"Touchy," muttered Alison following close behind.

"Isn't the silence nice," thought Anna, watching the second hand of the clock above the kitchen hatch ticking round.   "But I suppose I'd better go and see that they haven't throttled each other yet."

Chapter 7
Back to the Toilets

"You'd hardly think it was the same place," said Christine as Eric swung the bus into a rather tight parking space.

"It does look different with people here," said Alison.

"Lots of them. The car park's packed. I didn't think the coach would fit in," said Anna.

"It was a tight fit," said Christine looking out of the window. "Very tight."

"When I've got everyone's attention," said Mr Thomas.

"Berk," thought Anna, but looked in his direction as did everyone else.

"Good," he said. "We are on a bit of a tight schedule."

"Yes. And we all know whose fault that is," thought Anna.

"So without any further discussion I think we ought to proceed to the toilets."

"Didn't exactly hang around for discussions yesterday," muttered Alison as they made their way off the coach.

"Hurry up, for Christ's sake, we'll lose him," Christine said as Mr Thomas set off towards the station.

"Too late," said Anna.

"What!" said Christine trying to search the crowd for him.

"Doesn't matter," said Anna. "We know where he's gone. He'll just have to wait for us, all of us," she added looking at her fellow students.

Mr Thomas was waiting on the platform, his attempts at pacing the floor constantly being interrupted by the milling commuters.

"Right," he muttered herding them down the stairs.

"Who's going to say something," thought Anna looking round them. "The commuters on the platform? No. They're too busy trying to pretend we don't exist. After all, doing something might make them miss their trains. They're probably hoping we aren't going to catch the same train as them, because they are packed enough without us. The startled looking men leaving the toilets?Unlikely, they're just relieved not to be caught in there. That leaves those in the toilets, or more likely, those who want to go, but not in front of us. Whoever it is, I hope they're quick. The place stinks to high heaven and I, for one don't want to be in it any longer than I have to be."

"Now," said Mr Thomas, flinging open the double doors. "This is a fine example of a Victorian Gentleman's convenience. Look around you and you'll notice the urinals are incorporated into the tiling, the way the patterning on the tiles is echoed in the ornate castings of the cast iron cisterns and the design on the porcelain urinals is matched by that of the basins and the slab of marble that they are set into. Notice the way the plumbing is incorporated into the overall appearance. This room was created as a whole, it's impact seen from the view of a complete item. It is not just an assemblage of objects necessary because of their public health function. The pride of the Railway Company that brought it into being oozes from every urinal," said Mr Thomas, elaborately pointing out details with an umbrella.

"This is so embarrassing and I really don't want to think about things oozing from urinals!" thought Anna trying to avoid looking at any of the toilets occupants, the majority of whom were making as speedy a departure as humanly possible. Those approaching from the corridor made an about turn and returned to the platform, all that is with the exception of a man in a British Rail Uniform."

"Here comes trouble," muttered Alison.

"I presume you are in charge of this group," he said to Mr Thomas who was busy pointing out the channelling in the urinals.

"Yes," said Mr Thomas, moving to point out something else.

"I have been told to tell you and these young people to leave," he said.

"What!" said Mr Thomas spinning round to face him.

"There have been complaints."

"I am acquainting my students with a glorious example of Victoriana. Demonstrating to them the fact that no matter how humble the function the Victorians were more than happy to reflect the glory of their Empire in its edification."

"He doesn't look impressed," thought Anna, looking at the railwayman.

"If you wish to study the facilities I am sure the station master can arrange for them to be made available on a Sunday when they are not open to the public," he said.

"That isn't what we were told yesterday," said Mr Duffy.

"In the meantime I must tell you to leave," said the railwayman.

"But," Mr Thomas started.

"Before I feel compelled to get the Police to escort you from the premises," the Railwayman finished, barely noticing Mr Thomas's attempt to interrupt him.

"Oh," said Mr Thomas turning to the students. "I think we have got the ambiance of this glorious establishment."

"Is that what you call it?" thought Anna. "I'd call it stench and I can see why men are so much quicker using the facilities than women."

"We do have a tight schedule, so we'd better be moving on," Mr Thomas added to Mr Duffy.

"The gas installation?" asked Mr Duffy.

"Yes. Of course," snapped Mr Thomas and headed off back to the coach, the students and Mr Duffy following in his wake, leaving the Railwayman to follow at the rear, just in case they stopped somewhere else on the way to the coach.

"Gas installation? That sounds half way relevant," thought Anna. "How are they going to cock this up?"

An hour later the coach pulled up on a quiet tree lined suburban road.

"Either we're lost or its well hidden," thought Anna looking round the coach for some sort of gas installation. "Bloody well hidden."

"Now. If you'll get your things together. Eric will be back at four. That's right isn't it?" Mr Thomas asked Eric.

"Yes."

"Right. So don't leave anything like your sandwiches behind because you won't be able to nip out for them," he paused for a moment, but there was no response. "Right, well it looks like the gas board is already here, so we may as well go and join them," he added.

"Gas board? Where?" muttered Alison.

"I can't see anything?" said Christine spinning round in her seat.

"There's a gas van just in front of the coach," started Anna.

"So," snapped Alison and Christine.

"Pardon me for breathing," thought Anna.

"Well. Don't just sit there. Everyone off," said Mr Thomas.

"Oh well. Let's see what the twit's got us into this time," thought Anna following the rest off the coach and up the drive of the semi-detached house that the gas van was parked in front of.

"What the hell am I doing here," she thought as Mr Thomas rang the door bell. "I can't see anyone disguising a gas installation as a semi."

The front door was opened by a perplexed looking woman.

"Mark," she exclaimed, her expression changing to a broad smile as she recognised him and she kissed him enthusiastically on both cheeks.

"And this is your colleague," she added turning to a rather startled Mr Duffy.

"Mr Duffy," said Mr Thomas.

"Good morning," she said taking Mr Duffy firmly by the shoulders and kissing him as well.

"Good morning Mrs Ah," stammered Mr Duffy.

"Mrs Agnew," Mr Thomas added, by way of an introduction.

"Mrs Agnew. That is too too formal. You must call me Agatha."

"Thank-you. Agatha," said Mr Duffy.

"And what is your Christian name? I can't call you Mr Duffy, it is too much like going back to school do you not think," said Agatha.

"Ian," he said taking a deep breath. "My Christian name is Ian."

"A good name," she smiled with approval. "It suits you well. And these are your students," she added turning to the giggling group on the drive. "Ah, but I am a terrible hostess. Keeping you standing in the cold. Come in at once, you must have some coffee," she said standing aside, propping the door open in the process. "Go straight through to the kitchen, I've got some coffee on. I'll pour it out as soon as everyone's in," she said watching bemused as the students milled past her.

In the kitchen two gas men were busy installing a gas boiler despite Mr Agnew who was trying to help them.

"Hello Mark," smiled Mr Agnew. "It's a bit of a busy time at the moment. Did you know we're having gas central heating installed?"

"So this is the gas installation," thought Anna.

"Dear," said Agatha finally managing to get into the kitchen. "I thought we could all have coffee, in the living room, then Mark and Ian can introduce us to all their charming students."

"But," stammered Mr Agnew.

"I'm sure the gas men can manage perfectly well by themselves," interrupted Agatha and the gas men nodded in agreement.

"Well," he hesitated.

"We'll only be in the other room," she added. "You'll be on hand if they have any questions."

"All right," he said reluctantly.

"Right. If we start serving the coffee. Then those with can make their way to the living room and make way for the rest. I think that would be best," she said reaching for the first cup and hoping there were enough cups and coffee to go round.

"God this coffee's like liquid tar," thought Anna fighting down a mouthful and looking for somewhere to sit in the living room. "Looks like I'll have to sit on the floor."

"There's no need to hog the seats," said Mr Thomas clearing some space for Agatha and her husband to sit down.

"Now tell us all about this gas installation," said Mr Thomas smiling.

"Oh God. I was right. This is a bloody farce," thought Anna.

"Oh well," murmured Agatha. "What exactly do you want to know?"

"Whose big idea this whole bloody trip was," thought Anna.

"Well," said Mr Thomas thoughtfully. "What precipitated the decision to change your heating. The type of heating you've had up till now. What made you decide on gas central heating. That sort of thing," said Mr Thomas.

"Oh. Right. Well I'll do my best. You'll have to tell me if I wonder off the subject. I do tend to don't I dear," she looked at her husband.

"Um," he muttered gazing at the door.

"Yes. Well. We moved here thirty years ago. Didn't we dear."

"What was that?" he said shifting his gaze from the door to his wife.

"We moved in here thirty years ago, when we were newly married."

"Yes dear."

"There were coke fires in here and the dining room and gas fires in the two main bedrooms. The box room wasn't heated. There was a gas boiler in the bathroom for hot water, over the bath and another in the kitchen and a gas copper for boiling the clothes. I think they were installed when the house was built in the 1930's, by the time we moved in they were rather old, not that we minded of course," she glanced at her husband, but there was no response.

"Anyway, when we found out that Christopher, my eldest son, was on the way. There's a photograph of him on the mantelpiece, when he got his degree."

"And a right pratt he looks," thought Anna glancing at the mantelpiece.

108

"Well. When he was on the way we decided to sort out the heating and the hot water. Everything was so old and difficult to use." she glanced towards her husband.

"At that time the best deal was night store heaters with an immersion for the hot water. A lot of people were putting in oil fired central heating. But I didn't like the idea of it and then you have to have a great ugly oil tank in the garden."

"I thought my family were long winded, but God she takes the biscuit," Anna thought.

"But that was quite a few years ago," said Agatha.

"We know," Anna gazed at the ceiling. "I see you have an energetic spider population."

"When the night stores started packing in. We rang the electricity board to get them repaired, but we were told they were too old."

"I can't say as I blame them. I wouldn't fancy opening that thing up," Anna thought gazing at the ancient grey metal heater. "You never know what might be in there."

"They said they'd all pack in soon and we'd do better replacing them all at once rather than go for piecemeal replacement. They said the timings were different on the new ones. Or something"

"You'll have had one of the oldest tariffs with the longest economy times for this lot," thought Anna. "They've probably been wanting to shift you off that tariff for years and they saw this as the perfect opportunity."

"Anyway, it was soon after that we went to Aunt Matilda's daughter May's silver wedding anniversary do."

Mr Thomas looked puzzled, as did everyone else.

"May wasn't looking to well, rather heavy looking for her and so pale. I said so at the time didn't I dear."

"Yes," muttered Mr Agnew, his eyes fixed on the door.

"She wasn't well, couldn't eat, didn't want to dance, they had to rush her to hospital, she had terrible pains in her stomach which did rather put an end to the party."

"I should think it would," thought Anna.

"Some of us hung around to help, we tided up, put the food in the freezer, it was something to do whilst we waited for news. I got talking to one of my nephews, it was either David or Stephen,"

"Brian, it was Brian," said Mr Agnew

"Brian? Yes you're right dear, Brian, he'd just had gas central heating fitted and it hardly caused any mess at all and it was all so much cheaper to use and much more convenient. It all sounded so good we rang the gas board the next day, they said they'd come round the following day to advise us," said Agatha.

"God, you are a cold fish," thought Anna.

"We nearly forgot about the appointment, what with the news from the hospital about the twins."

"What twins!" Anna's ears pricked up.

"Aunt Matilda was reconciled to the idea of never being a grandmother and now two grandchildren, one of each. She was so happy. I was busy searching out baby clothes when the man from the gas board came to tell us about central heating. He was so helpful. And they're going to get rid of all the old heaters. Its got to be done very carefully, I didn't know, but it seems they have asbestos in them," she glanced at the heater as if it were about to eat her.

"Well, when we heard that we turned them off straight away, I haven't dared to have them on since and it is so difficult keeping the house warm with these electric bar heaters. We've had to buy quite a lot of them and it's still so cold. It will be a blessing when the gas central heating is in place. They put the radiators and all the piping round last week, today they are installing the boiler and then taking the night store heaters away."

"Stupid cow. Thirty years of use and now you're frightened to turn them on. That type is just like Granddad's, he told me they don't even have asbestos in, they were filled with sand. Though that'll make them hard enough to move, they'll weigh a ton," thought Anna gazing at the heater and smiling at the mental picture of the gas men trying to lift them. "I wonder if we'll see them moved. I wonder if we'll see anything," she thought looking at the door to the kitchen.

"Still, only a couple of days and we should have everything working, in the meantime, I don't think a cup of coffee would go amiss, it must be time for elevenses," she added, glancing at the clock and then took a second look.

"Half past one! I didn't think it was that late. You must be starving," said Agatha looking round the room and wondering if she was expected to feed them.

"We've all got packed lunches," said Mr Duffy, lifting up her plastic bag of sandwiches fruit and crisps.

"Aren't you the lucky ones," muttered Mr Thomas.

"Except for Mark," added Mr Duffy.

"Mark. You can't go without something to eat," said Agatha.

"It's all right," muttered Mr Thomas.

"No, I wouldn't dream of it, not in my house," said Agatha. "Your Mother would never forgive me."

"That's told you," thought Anna. "And it's told us how you knew about this gas installation."

"I will make you some sandwiches," Agatha declared.

"I'm going to check up on the gas men," muttered Mr Agnew and disappeared out of the room.

"So long as it isn't any trouble," said Mr Thomas.

"I'll be making some sandwiches for us anyway," said Agatha gazing after her husband. "A few more won't make any difference. And I can get the coffee going whilst I'm at it."

"Well, if you're sure," said Mr Thomas.

"Yes," she said walking out of the room.

"Four o'clock seems like a hell of a long way away," thought Anna. "Well at least she can't talk for the whole two and a half hours. She's got to stop whilst she's eating."

The day dragged slowly on till, at four o'clock the bus finally arrived and got them back to the guest house in time for tea.

"Just one more night without any privacy," thought Anna looking round the silent dinner table at Alison, Christine and Mr Duffy. "I think I might manage it. Just."

"Back to Poly tomorrow," said Mr Duffy.

"Yes," muttered Anna.

"Are you looking forward to it?" he asked.

"To the privacy," thought Anna.

"The Christmas dinner should be good," said Alison.

"Aren't you eager to get back to work?" he asked

"No," said Alison.

"Sewage first thing Wednesday morning," said Anna. "It's hard to build up the enthusiasm."

"Oh," he muttered subsiding into silence whilst Alison scowled at Christine.

"Life's a perpetual squabble for those two," thought Anna finishing the last of her banana fritters and ice cream.

"I think its time I outlined things for tomorrow," muttered Mr Duffy

111

glancing round the table at the empty bowls.

"I thought we were going back?" said Alison.

"Exactly.   We don't want to leave anyone behind do we," he said standing up.   "If everyone's listening," he started, glancing round the room till he felt sure he'd caught the eye of every student.   "As you know, we have a long journey ahead of us tomorrow, so we need to make an early start," Mr Duffy began.

"I'm sure I can hear the residents silently cheering," thought Anna, looking round the dining room at some of them, they had also paused in their eating, though they were trying not to look as though they were listening.

"It would help if you could all be down to breakfast for seven o'clock sharp and if you could be packed and ready to leave as soon as breakfast is over that would also be of assistance.   In the meantime, if you're short of something to do you can always start writing your reports whilst everything's still fresh in your minds."

"If that was a joke," muttered Alison.

"What was that," said Mr Duffy.

"When do these reports have to be in by?" she asked.

"Good question," thought Anna.   "This is the first I heard about handing anything in."

"A week tomorrow," he said.

"What!" screeched Clare.

"Hadn't Mr Thomas," he started looking round at the group, they were staring at him slowly shaking their heads.   "He wanted them marked and back before Christmas.   Just think of it this way, it'll be one thing less for you to do over the Christmas period."

"I'm sure you'll think of something else for us to do.   Just so we don't get bored," snapped Clare.

"Would we pull such a nasty trick on you?" asked Mr Duffy.

"Yes," she snapped.

"Um.   Well, if anyone needs me you know were to find me.   If not, I'll see you in the morning," said Mr Duffy making a quick exit.

"Well," said Alison to Christine and Anna.   "Shall we follow the example of our leader?"

"Pack and start writing our reports?" asked Christine.

"No," said Anna.

"Go to the pub," added Alison.

"But. What about the report?" said Christine.

"Christine. I'm surprised at you. Missing out on an opportunity to gawp a Mr Duffy," started Alison.

"I do not gawp," shouted Christine and everyone turned round to look.

"I could do with a drink," thought Anna.

"Shall we go," said Anna standing up.

"Where?" asked Christine.

"The pub down the road," said Anna.

"Are you sure?" asked Christine.

"It's the only pub we know round here," said Anna.

"And it's handy for him to stagger back from," added Alison.

"He doesn't stagger," snapped Christine.

"Does it matter," moaned Anna trying to usher them out of the room.

"You're always sniping at him. I wish you'd stop," snapped Christine.

"And change the habit of a lifetime," Alison answered glibly. "Anyway, can either of you give me one good reason why we should want to find him?"

"He's nice. It's interesting talking to him," started Christine.

"He might buy the drinks," said Anna.

"What are we standing here for," said Alison. "Lets get moving."

"Oh hell," moaned Alison as the alarm broke the silence.

"Tell me you set it wrong," groaned Christine. "Tell me its still the middle of the night. Please."

"Six thirty," said Anna killing the alarm.

"You're heartless," groaned Alison as her alarm clock went off. "There's a conspiracy against me," she muttered not moving a muscle to stop the alarm.

"No there isn't. You're just paranoid," snapped Christine. "And kill that bloody alarm before I kill you."

"Maybe you are paranoid," thought Anna. "But there is something odd going on, whether it's as thought out as a conspiracy is debatable," she climbed out of bed and turned the light on.

"What did you do that for," Alison groaned.

"So you can find your clock," said Anna as Christine's clock burst into life.

113

"Turn that bloody thing off," shouted Alison, wincing at the sound of her own voice.

"You're a fine one to talk," muttered Christine.

"God. You're as bad as each other," thought Anna glancing at the time as she packed her alarm clock.

"Quarter to seven. Don't you think its time to move if you want to be ready for breakfast by seven," she said.

"Don't talk to me about breakfast," moaned Alison.

"Serves you right for drinking so much," muttered Christine equally inactive.

"You weren't exactly teetotal yourself. Anyway, I had to be drunk to put up with you and Mr Duffy," Alison replied.

"And what do you mean by that," snapped Christine sitting up and turning on Alison.

"Hanging on his every word you were. It was sickening," snapped Alison.

"So is this," thought Anna glancing at her watch. "I wonder if they can dress in five minutes flat."

"You do realise it's five to seven don't you?" she asked.

"What!" said Christine, leaping for the hand basin, whilst Alison fell out of bed and started hunting for her clothes. They froze at the sound of a knock on the door.

"Who is it?" asked Anna.

"Me. Mr Duffy."

"What a surprise," thought Anna.

"Breakfast in five minutes," he said.

"We'll be there," said Anna. "Won't we?" she added looking at Alison and Christine frantically dashing round the room.

"Of course," said Alison.

"We won't be late," sang Christine.

"I'll see you at breakfast then," he said. "Be careful on the stairs," he added and shuffled off down the corridor.

"That's one thing I won't miss when we get back," muttered Alison.

"What!" snapped Christine.

"His ugly mug over breakfast."

"You," she shouted starting to throw things at Alison. Anna stood watching for a minute.

"If you're ready," Anna started.

114

"Ready?" said Christine.

"Breakfast," said Anna.

"Oh shit," she muttered and grabbed her shoes. Alison ducked and Christine crammed her feet in her shoes.

"I'm ready. What about you two," she said looking round.

"I've been ready for the past ten minutes," said Anna.

"OK, lets go," said Alison heading for the door, with Christine close behind.

"God give me strength," muttered Anna following in their wake.

Breakfast was subdued to say the least.

"They're not the only one's with hangovers," thought Anna looking round at the rest of the group busily not eating their breakfasts.

"The coach should be here at eight," said Mr Duffy looking round the tables. "If you could gather in the lounge, with all your luggage. Leave the rooms tidy, doors unlocked with the keys in the key holes. Don't leave anything behind, we're not coming back for anything. If you leave it. You've lost it," he finished and left before anyone could ask any questions.

"I wonder if Mrs Noble will do us a packed lunch."pondered Anna as they wandered back up the stairs.

"Such are the mysteries of life," said Alison.

"Packed lunches, or whether we'll get one?" asked Christine.

"Yes," said Alison arriving at their room.

"Thought so," said Christine, then glanced past Alison into the room. "Oh hell, it looks like a bomb hit it," she muttered.

"That's how we left it," said Anna squeezing past the two of them and started making her bed, putting the pillow back where it had originally been. "The sooner you start, the sooner we'll finish," she added and they leapt to life remaking their beds and packing their clothes.

"No arguments," thought Anna. "There must've been something in that breakfast."

"Right," said Christine gazing round the room looking very satisfied with herself. "Now for the lounge."

"Yes. Let's see if anyone else has arrived yet," said Alison.

They had. The lounge was packed.

"You're in my way," snapped an old man as a group of students wandered between him and the ancient television.

"Yes, you. I'm talking to you," he said to one of the group who had glanced in his direction.

"I'm watching the television and you're in my way," he shouted.

"We'd better shift," she said interrupting the conversation. "We're upsetting the Colonel," she added nodding in his direction.

They drifted off without even glancing in his direction.

"I should think so," he shouted, but his words were ignored.

Mr Duffy wandered into the room and stood in front of the television.

"Everyone here?" he asked looking round the room and having a quick head count.

"Are you in charge of this rabble?" asked the old man.

"The coach is here," shouted Ian from his look out post at the window.

"Right. Lets get moving," said Mr Duffy.

"I would like to complain to you about the inconsiderate behaviour of these louts," the Colonel persisted.

"We're just going," said Mr Duffy smiling.

"That's not good enough. I think I deserve an apology," he shouted.

"Sorry," said Mr Duffy as the last of the students filed out of the room.

"A proper apology," snapped the Colonel.

"Good morning," said Mr Duffy.

"Well really," said the old man. "I shall speak to Mrs Noble about your attitude."

"Fair enough," said Mr Duffy picking up his bag and leaving the hotel.

As the coach started down the road Mrs Noble and the old man came dashing out of the front door.

"I hope no one has left anything behind," said Mr Duffy politely waving to the landlady.

"God this place is a dump," muttered Christine as the coach approached the Poly.

"The dark doesn't do anything for it," said Alison glumly peering out of the windows.

"There's the Christmas dinner," said Anna. "That's usually good. At least we haven't missed that."

"Are you going to the Christmas dinner at Manchester Building too?" asked Alison.

"We weren't sure if you knew," stuttered Christine.

"And you didn't think to enlighten me," thought Anna.

116

"Yes," she said smiling. "Mrs Smithers-Jones said it would be such a shame to miss the Christmas dinner because of the field trip. So she arranged that I could go to this one instead."

"Oh," muttered Christine.

"Why don't we all go together," said Alison.

"Yes," said Christine eagerly jumping on the idea. "It would be a shame to eat alone."

"Yes it would," Anna admitted reluctantly.

"When will I be able to get rid of them," she thought.

"We can dump the bags back in the hall and meet Alison in Manchester Building in time for tea," continued Christine.

"Sure," thought Anna, nodding in agreement. "I can help you carry your bags back to Wakefield Hall, I don't know why you thought you'd need all that lot."

"You can never tell what you'll need," smiled Christine.

Standing in the queue for the Christmas dinner, waiting impatiently for the glass doors to be opened Anna gazed with amazement at the way it was all decked out. Streamers, tinsel, a Christmas tree and festive table cloths. The refectory by Wakefield Hall never looked like this.

The door opened and they followed the queue in.

"Yours is in the cafeteria downstairs," said the canteen lady when Christine and Anna handed over their tickets.

"What!" Christine and Anna looked puzzled.

"Your Christmas dinner is in the canteen downstairs," she repeated, handing back the tickets, "There's only room for the residents in here," she added.

"I'll eat down there with you," said Alison to Christine and Anna. "If that's all right," she added looking at the canteen lady and showing her dinner pass.

"There's room for you in here," she replied.

"I'll eat with my friends," repeated Alison.

"Fair enough," said the canteen lady, turning to the next person in the queue.

"I didn't know there were two canteens," said Anna.

"The other one's usually for breakfast and lunch," said Alison frowning.

Downstairs the canteen was deserted and bare of Christmas glitter. They went to the kitchen, only pausing for a moment at the door. Sitting on the side were three streaming Christmas dinners, one suitably vegetarian in appearance.

"So Mrs Smithers-Jones did remember," thought Anna picking up the vegetarian meal.

"These must be ours," she said.

"I suppose so," said Christine picking up a plate and looking round her. Nothing happened.

"Oh well. Lets go to the canteen and eat in some semblance of comfort," said Alison eager to get out of the kitchen, yet the sight of the dim empty canteen stopped them in their tracks.

"Where shall we sit?" murmured Alison.

"By the window," said Anna. "It's not so dark, or so far to carry the plates."

"Yes, they are hot," said Christine heading quickly towards a table.

"Happy Christmas," said Anna sitting herself down.

"Yes. Happy Christmas," said Alison looking nervously round her.

"Well, lets get stuck in," said Christine. "It'd be a shame to let the food go cold."

"True," said Anna. "A waste."

"Yes," echoed Alison and they began to eat.

"What next?" said Anna looking up from an empty plate.

"There must be some Christmas pudding," said Christine.

"It wouldn't be Christmas dinner without it," said Alison.

"In the kitchen?" said Anna.

"Seems reasonable," said Alison. Anna set off for the kitchen.

"Wait for us," shouted Christine as she and Alison rushed after her.

In the kitchen three bowls of streaming hot Christmas pudding and white sauce were on the side where the plates had been.

"There isn't even a skin on the custard," muttered Alison.

"Where did they come from?" asked Anna.

"Someone must have brought them down," said Christine.

"I know," said Anna. "But who and when? Because, I don't know about you, but I didn't hear anything or anybody."

"Neither did I," said Christine looking round nervously.

"Exactly," said Anna.

"Oh."

"The kitchens are probably connected, a lift or a staircase," snapped Alison. "Anyway, we may as well eat them whilst they're hot."

"True," said Anna smiling.

"This place is spooky enough without mystery canteen ladies," added Alison scowling at Anna.

"The light doesn't reach the edges of the room," said Christine following them back to the table.

"You find yourself peering to see if there are people lurking in the shadows," said Anna and a man walked out of the shadows over to the double fire doors barely ten foot from their table. He propped the doors opened and went out. A couple of minutes later he returned with some friends, they were all heavily laden.

"There's a band after the Christmas dinner," said Alison, answering the unspoken question.

"All we get is a meal," said Christine.

"And a mince pie," added Anna.

"Stuff the bloody mince pie," said Christine. "We don't get a party and a band."

"Not even a Christmas tree," sighed Anna.

"It wasn't exactly warm in here before," said Alison after a moments silence.

"No. And now its bloody freezing," said Christine.

"Only slightly warmer than our welcome," said Anna.

"Even the pudding's getting cold," said Alison.

"I feel like telling them where to stuff their pudding," muttered Christine.

"Me too. But I'd like to set it on fire first," said Anna.

"I'm pissed off with this," said Alison, poking half heartedly at the remains of the pudding with her spoon.

"Me too," said Christine.

"Let's go," said Anna dumping her spoon.

"Had we better take the dishes back to the kitchen?" asked Christine.

"After all the effort they've gone to to make us feel welcome," said Anna. "They can clean it up themselves."

"Yes," said Christine. "I'd have preferred to have just missed the whole thing than have this."

"Same here," said Anna.

"What now?" asked Christine.

119

"How about coming to my room for a coffee?" said Alison.

"Sounds like a good idea to me," said Christine.

"Me too," said Anna.

"Well a cup of coffee," she thought, "Then I'm out of here."

"Let's go then," said Alison heading for the door.

"Oh well, at least Wakefield Building does have something in its favour," thought Anna as they squashed into Alison's room. "At least there's room to swing a hamster there."

Alison filled the kettle from a hand basin hidden in what looked like a wardrobe.

"Makes you wonder what's hidden in the others," thought Anna looking at the line of identical doors.

"So where shall we go," asked Christine as Alison handed her a mug of coffee.

"I don't know," said Alison handing a mug to Anna.

"Come on Alison," said Christine. "Where've you hidden the biscuits?"

"I haven't hidden them. You scoffed the lot before we went on the field trip, remember," said Alison.

"I did not scoff them," said Christine.

"I had half a packet till you came round, there's none left now," said Alison. "I think the facts speak for themselves."

"You ate some too," said Christine. "Anyway, half a packet doesn't go very far."

"Not with you around," muttered Alison sitting down at her desk with her coffee.

"What was that?" asked Christine.

"We could go to the union pub for a drink," said Alison.

"I've got a headache," thought Anna. "And this coffee makes me feel sick."

"I don't want to go there," snapped Christine. "It'll be full of pharmacy students."

"No. Everyone'll be busy listening to the band," said Alison.

"Oh that's great. The place'll be like the Mary Celeste, only we'll be able to hear everyone else enjoying themselves and we won't be allowed to join in. Wonderful," snapped Christine.

"That's hardly my fault," snapped Alison.

"How the hell can I get out of this," thought Anna.

"There's the other union pub," Anna suggested finishing her coffee.

120

"That's full of art students," snapped Alison and Christine together.

"And a nice lot they are too," thought Anna. "Most of them anyway, the one's I don't like are the P.E. student teachers. If they've got a brain cell between the lot of them they're lucky."

"We could go to the leisure centre," said Alison.

"You can. I'm not," thought Anna.

"We could have a go at ice skating," said Christine.

"Yes. That should be good fun," agreed Alison.

"You can count me out," thought Anna.

"I think I'll just go back to Wakefield Hall," said Anna.

"What!" Christine and Alison looked up as though they'd forgotten she was there.

"I'm tired," she said.

"Tired of hearing you two squabbling," she thought.

"Oh. OK," they said.

"I'll see you tomorrow," she said negotiating her way past Alison's bags to the door.

"Bye," she added from the door, but they were already busy discussing skating and who was worst at it.

"Nice to feel wanted," Anna thought making her way out of the building, past the canteen which was reverberating to the sound of the band.

"The question is. Should I ring home when I get back to the hall. That's the burning issue, not which night spot to hit tonight. There'll be a row next time we speak, whenever. If I ring now it'll get it get it out of the way, also they might still be busy with Great Aunt Elspeth and so not able to talk. They won't be able to drop it on me whenever they feel like it. Or not ring for ages and make me feel guilty. The only thing for certain is that whatever I do is wrong," thought Anna, signing herself into the hall.

The phone began to ring.

"That can't be them, can it?" she thought picking up the receiver.

"Hello. Wakefield Hall," she said.

"Anna?" came her Mother's voice.

"Mum," she said,

"God her timing is so good," Anna thought.

"Where have you been. Your Father and I have been frantic trying to find you," shouted Mum.

"That'll be a new experience," thought Anna.

121

"I told you I was on a field trip this weekend. I've only just got back," explained Anna.

"Field trip? Your Great Aunt Elspeth came to see you, all the way from Canada."

"I thought she was in Australia?"

"Canada, Australia, what does it matter. She came a long way to see you and you were gallivanting off on some field trip," said Mum.

"She didn't come specifically to see me. She came to see the family," Anna interrupted again.

"What have I said about interrupting?"

"Don't."

"Exactly, anyway, she was especially looking forward to seeing you," said Mum.

"Like you'd know," thought Anna.

"I doubt it," Anna started

"She said so," said Mum, not letting Anna finish.

"I really believe that," thought Anna.

"Well, she'll be in the country for six months, I'm sure we'll manage to meet up sometime," said Anna.

"Well, if you're sure you can fit her in with your busy schedule," Mum started.

"If that's supposed to make me feel guilty, then it's failed," thought Anna.

"I'll find out her plans. I'm sure I'll be able to fit in with them sometime, even if its only at Christmas," said Anna.

"And how will you do that," snapped Mum.

"I'll write to her," said Anna.

"And where will you send this letter?" asked Mum sarcastically.

"To Uncle Cyril's," said Anna.

"She's not there," said Mum.

"No. But he's bound to have the latest update on her wanderings, so he'll know where to forward it to," said Anna.

"I see," said Mum.

"Yes. Pick the bones out of that one," thought Anna.

"I want you to know, your Father and I aren't in the least bit pleased with you," said Mum, taking another tack.

"Nothing new there then," thought Anna.

"Sorry," she said, but her Mother said nothing.

"I'm not putting up with this," thought Anna.

"Look. I've got to go. Someone else wants the phone," said Anna.

"I see," said Mum.

"Bye," said Anna as the line went dead.

"Oh well," thought Anna. "With luck and a passing wind that might have got the argument over with, but I doubt it very much. Knowing Mum, I won't hear the last of this, not for months, if ever."

Chapter 8
The Christmas Holidays

"And now for home and Christmas," thought Anna ten days later, settling herself into the drivers seat, her luggage, all that she thought she'd need over the holidays, was in the back, her room tidy, surfaces clear. "How long before Great Aunt Elspeth gets a name check, I wonder and the level of her disappointment in not seeing me?"

Two hours and an uneventful drive later Anna drew up outside her parents home. For a moment she sat listening to the silence, then a cold draught blew through the car. Shivering, Anna picked up her handbag and headed for the back door.

"Locked! That's odd. They must be out. Good job I've still got a key. Looks like they've left a message," thought Anna as she caught sight of a bright yellow patch on the fridge door.

Anna
Stopping at Julia's
    parents. Back Saturday.
Feed the dog.
Mum.

"Who the hell's Julia?" thought Anna.

P.S. Don't mess the drive
up with that car.

"That car! My car! You're still annoyed with me for learning to drive and getting myself a car so that I could go to Poly. You'd already said you weren't going to drive me that distance and I can imagine the fuss you'd make taking me to the railway station, so what did you expect me to do, not go to Poly. Probably, she didn't want me to go in the first place," muttered Anna opening the fridge door. "Half a pint of milk, half a dozen tins of dog food and another note, she muttered to herself, trying to asses the chances of sorting out something to eat.

Dog has half a tin twice a day.
(Breakfast and 5pm)Plus a
handful of biscuits. Let him
out at 10pm to do his business.

"That's the dog catered for, presumably I can fend for myself," thought Anna automatically shutting the fridge door before the dog could get in, not that he could do much without a tin-opener.

"Great guard dog you are," she said to the two brown eyes gazing soulfully at her.   "And you can take that look off your face.   I'm under instructions to feed you at five not before."

Paddy's head and tail sank to the floor, he turned and made his way slowly out of the room.

"There's no need for you to look so hard done by. At least they've left some food for you. That's more than they've done for me."

Paddy wasn't impressed.   He went to the front room safe in the knowledge that Anna wouldn't throw him out.

"What the hell's got into them.   They've never trusted me with the house before. Or Paddy. What they think I'd get up to I don't know. A drunken orgy. I'd be the only one there. No I wouldn't. I'd go to a better party. No, I wouldn't go to a party and definitely, not an orgy.

Still.   There's not much point standing here.   There's the car to unpack," thought Anna looking at the clock.

"It can wait till I've had something to eat."

Paddy wandered in as she started making a few sandwiches, but he didn't hang around, she wasn't opening any tins of dog food.

Taking a leaf out of Paddy's book she ate her sandwiches in comfort in the front room. Habit brought Paddy scrounging.

"You're too obvious," said Anna giving him a bit of her sandwiches. He wolfed it down and looked round for more.

"That's your lot. This is my lunch. You'll get no more," said Anna.

Paddy stood up and threw himself onto the hearth rug.

"You should be on the stage," muttered Anna finishing her sandwiches.

125

"And now to empty the car," she thought. "I may as well do my mucky washing before Mum gets back and makes a fuss about it."

Anna dumped her bag on her bed and looked round the room.

"God this room's a tip," she thought, her eye fell on the bed. "This hasn't been made, I'm sure I stripped it before I left. So why the mucky bed clothes. What's this?" she thought picking up a dark lump from the floor.

"Oh God. One of our Brian's smelly socks," she dropped it and sniffed her hand tentatively.

"I'll wash that in a minute," she thought pulling open the nearest drawer.

"Underpants," she pushed the drawer, but it wouldn't shut. She gave up and turned to the wardrobe.

"I see," she muttered seeing it full of Brain's clothes. The bookcase was empty of books, but packed with car magazines.

"The bastard," she muttered storming over to Brian's room. Opening the door she saw her clothes, those she'd left behind, dumped on the bed. Her books and papers in a heap on the floor along with a few old shoes.

"The swine. He's always wanted my room. Well if he thinks he's going to get away with this he's got another think coming," Anna fumed, she started taking the clothes from the cupboards and moving them back to his room.

"I didn't think he was into dresses," she muttered to Paddy when he came upstairs to see what was going on. "Especially not that shade of Barbie pink, wouldn't go with his eyes," she added, looking at one of the dresses. Paddy gave it a sniff and went back downstairs. "I'm not impressed with it either, not that there is that much of it. Couldn't wear that on a cold night," she added dumping them on the bed, where her clothes had been."

Then she took the rest of the stuff that had been littered round her room. Changed the bed and returned her things to their proper place, neatly folded onto drawers and hung up in the wardrobe.

"That's better," she thought looking round her room, with all her things back where she had left them. "Though there doesn't seem to be quite as much here as there was when I left," she added, then headed downstairs to the kitchen, where Paddy was draped over his basket.

126

"You. Dog," Anna addressed Paddy, he looked up hopefully. "Yes. You. You're getting fat," Anna continued, he put his head down. "You need some exercise," she added getting his lead, his eyes followed her. "You are going for a walk," he didn't move. Anna clipped on the lead and pulled him out of his basket. He decided to co-operate and walk and walk they did for a good two hours.

"Back in time for din dins," said Anna as Paddy flopped down in his basket. He didn't look up as she opened the fridge door, but he nearly knocked her flying when she put his dinner bowl down. By the time she'd brewed herself a cup of tea he'd wolfed the lot down and was fast asleep in his basket twitching occasionally as he chased rabbits through his dreams.

"You wouldn't know what to do if you caught one," she thought taking the cup of tea to the front room where she could put her feet up and relax.

"Mushroom curry, that's what I'll get for tea," thought Anna. "I'll get myself a mushroom curry. That'll really annoy Mum, assuming she notices. I can go to that place just down the road that she doesn't like. Half six," she added looking at the clock in the kitchen, I think I'll get it now. Half an hour later she brought the curry home and ate it in the front room washed down with a can of lager. Carefully putting the rubbish in the kitchen bin so her Mother could see it. She stayed up late watching films she knew her parents wouldn't allow her to see.

The next day Anna sat relaxed, watching the television, but listening for the return of her parents. She had waited all day and evening was well advanced when she heard a car coming up the drive.

"So they've finally condescended to come home," she thought not moving a muscle.

"Don't stir yourself," said Mum walking into the front room. "We could've been burglars come to rob the place."

"Burglars would've been quieter. Anyway, I would've thought our faithful hound would see off any intruders," said Anna.

"What've you done with that animal. He's flaked out in his basket?" asked Mum.

"Took him for a walk. He could do with the exercise," said Anna.

"And what are you getting at?" snapped Mum.

"He's fat," said Anna.

127

"And you're an expert on canine health are you?" asked Mum.

Brain stormed in.

"What've you done to my room?" he shouted at Anna.

"Returned your things to it and put mine back in my room," said Anna.

"You had no right," Brain stormed.

"You had no right to move my things. You've ruined my white dress. There's black ink all over it and it's dried in," said Anna, looking at her Mother.

"Don't be petty," said Mum.

"Petty. My best dress. I'd hardly worn it," said Anna.

"Anyway, it was an accident. It could've happened to anyone," said Mum.

"No it couldn't. Only he could have an accident like that and anyway, what the hell was he doing in my room to have accidents with my things," asked Anna.

"He needs more room, now Julia's coming to live with us. We thought he could have your room," said Mum.

"And you couldn't wait till I got back to ask me. You just moved in didn't you," Anna shouted at Brain. "How long's it been, a month, two months?"

"It's not been that long," murmured Mum.

"I should think it'd take even him more than a couple of weeks to get a room into the pig pen I found it in," snapped Anna.

"Anyway," interrupted Mum. "I don't see why I should start asking you or anyone else what I do in my house."

"That's good coming from someone who's always setting up housework rotas," snapped Anna. "You'd better make a note of that Julia," she added acknowledging the presence of the girl in the doorway. "You'll end up on the rota. Little brother here won't. He doesn't even know what a duster looks like, let alone what it's for."

"That's enough," snapped Mum. "I don't need you to tell me how to run my home."

"And I don't need you carting my things round like so much jumble. Oh and by the way, there are some things missing," said Anna.

"The boy scouts wanted some jumble," said Mum.

"And you just gave my clothes away," said Anna.

"It was rubbish and there wasn't enough room," said Mum.

"How would you know," snapped Anna. "You just dumped them in there and shut the door. There was plenty of space for them in my room, where they were, in the wardrobe, in the drawers. All neat and tidy. Cared for, they weren't rubbish."

"That's your opinion," said Mum.

"Yes. That's my opinion. And those were my clothes. But that obviously doesn't count for anything here," said Anna.

"Anyway," interrupted Mum. "That doesn't alter the fact that you will just have to move everything back as it was."

"And why the hell should I do that," shouted Anna.

"That's enough of that language. I don't know where you picked it up, but I will not have you using it in my house," said Mum and icy note drifting into her voice.

"Right. I'll go to my room and you won't have to listen to me," said Anna.

"It's not your room any more. Its ours," said Brian. "So shift your junk out before I do."

"Go play on the motorway," said Anna.

"Brain and Julia are having that room," said Mum.

"And who is she anyway," snapped Anna.

"She is Brian's girlfriend and she's expecting his baby," said Mum.

"Another of his little accidents," said Anna before she could stop herself.

"That's just about your level isn't it," said Brian, as Julia started sobbing. "Now look what you've done," he snapped at Anna, turning to put a protective arm round Julia.

"How touching," thought Anna. "I could be sick."

"I'm tired. My back aches," she wailed. "I just wanted to relax and unwind before going to bed in our room. Not walk into a row with her," she glared at Anna. "And now I don't even know where I'm sleeping," she sniffed long, loud and disgustingly. "I thought pregnant women weren't supposed to be upset."

"Don't you listen to a word she says," said Brain to Julia.

"No one else does so why should you be any different," said Anna.

"That's right. Be your normal bitchy self-centred self," said Brian.

"How about telling him off for his language," said Anna to her Mum.

"Stop getting at Julia. It's not fair," said Mum.

"You're a great one to talk about fair. Pitch me out of my room whilst I'm away. What comes next? Pitch my out of the house so there's room for the baby when it comes?" stormed Anna. The expected denials didn't come. Anna looked round the room, her Mum looking uncomfortable and Brian and Julia looking smug.

"So that's it," she thought and stormed off to her room.

"You're moving out of that room tonight," Mum shouted after her. "So you'd better start now."

Anna flung herself down on the bed. The door opened behind her and Mum walked in.

"Don't I get any privacy," she thought.

"Are you going to move this junk or do I have to?" said Mum.

"I'll move it tomorrow," muttered Anna.

"Tonight I said and tonight I mean. And if you won't move it your brother and I will and it'll be on your head if any of your precious things get damaged," said Mum standing in the doorway.

"Doesn't look like I've much choice then," snapped Anna.

"I've lost and I'll soon be out on my ear," she thought.

"Well," said Mum.

"Well what?" asked Anna.

"When are you going to get started?" asked Mum.

"When you've gone," said Anna.

"I'm not having you watching over me," she thought.

"Right then. We're going to have a cup of tea. This lot better be moved by the time we're finished."

"Thanks," muttered Anna, carefully moving her things back to Brian's room and then dumping Brian's things on the floor in her old room, along with what she assumed where Julia's clothes. Half an hour later she heard a wail from her old room and Brian dashing up the stairs, followed by a heavy thumping on the door.

"You bitch," yelled Brian. "You could've put the stuff away."

"Why, you didn't put my stuff away," replied Anna, feeling safe behind the bolted bedroom door.

"My best party dress, it's ruined," Julia wailed from across the hallway.

"That pink thing?" asked Anna.

"Oh no. Not the pink dress, you look beautiful in that," said Brian.

"Yes. It's all creased and ruined," sobbed Julia.

"All it needs is a good ironing," said Anna.

"Not that you'd know how to do that," she thought. "It does look a stranger to the iron, then again, I can't see you fitting in it again for a while."

"You should take more care over other peoples things," shouted Brian.

"I gave them the level of care you gave my stuff, in fact I gave them more care because I didn't spill ink all over them," said Anna. "And that dress isn't ruined, all I did was place it on the floor with the rest of your stuff, it was a mess before I even touched it."

Julia gave a wail and started sobbing loudly.

"You bitch," shouted Brian hammering on the door again.

"Sod off and stop that girlfriend of yours making such an unholy racket, I'm sure it can't be good for the baby," said Anna, in the hope that he would just go away.

"You'll pay for this," said Brian, giving the door a last thump before going to comfort Julia and get some sort of order in their room.

"When you've paid for my white dress," thought Anna, but said nothing, gradually peace descended on the house as Brian calmed Julia's sobs.

"I'll help you put your things in the cupboards, if you like," Mum offered.

"It's OK, we can manage," said Brian.

"Really, you never have before," thought Anna, putting the last of her things in the drawers in Brian's old room. "I wonder if there's some sort of air-freshener I can get to tackle the overwhelming stench in this room. One of his socks must have escaped or something."

Anna decided that the best way to avoid a row was to avoid her brother as much as possible and when he couldn't be avoided, like meal times, not to talk to him. Not exactly peace, but a workable truce.

The living room was empty, apart from Anna sitting sketching.

"This is my home. Just as much as anyone else's," she thought. "One week back and it feels like an eternity," she thought looking up again at a sound from the other side of the door. "Now who is it," she thought as the door opened slowly to reveal Mum and the tinsel Christmas tree.

"It's nearly Christmas," said Mum. "I thought we ought to put the tree up."

"I thought I was the only one in here," thought Anna looking round the room to see if Julia was there.

"Well. Are you going to give me a hand," snapped Mum.

"Julia must be out," thought Anna. "Either that or it's too much like hard work for her."

"OK Mum," she said putting down her sketch pad and pencil. "Where shall we put it?"

"Put what?" asked Mum.

"The Christmas tree," said Anna. "What did you think I meant," she thought.

Mum gestured towards the small table in the corner of the room. "On there," she started to say, but her eyes fell on the cheese plant. A massive thing that had taken over not just the small table, but the corner of the room. She looked round the rest of the room and her eyes came to a halt at the coffee table by the window.

"On there," she said. "It'll make a change and it'll be nice to see it through the window when the lights are on. You move the ornaments and I'll get the decorations," she added and headed quickly for the door. Anna's eyes followed her out of the room and stayed on the closed door for a moment, then she turned to the task of clearing away the ornaments. Next she turned to the Christmas tree.

"May as well set it up," thought Anna. "I'll get no thanks for it. But I'll catch hell if I don't," she eased the branches carefully out and attached it to the base and was standing back admiring the old tree when Mum walked in almost buried under a pile of boxes. Anna dashed forward and helped unload them onto the chair to the left of the Christmas tree.

"I didn't realise we had so many decorations," Anna murmured with surprise.

"I got some new and there were Grannies baubles," Mum said.

"I thought we weren't going to use them," Anna said.

"There's no point having them if no one sees them. Anyway, I want this Christmas to be special. We've got to make Julia feel at home," said Mum.

"Really," said Anna. "That's more than I feel and this is my home," she thought.

"Can't you do something to make her feel welcome," started Mum.

"She's got my room, what more do you want," said Anna.

"Be nice to her. She finds you intimidating and she shouldn't be upset, not in her condition," said Mum.

"Be nice to her. She doesn't even talk to me. She passes any comments through a third person, even when there isn't one there. Could you tell her I do have a name. In case you've forgotten, it's Anna."

132

"You don't give the poor little girl a chance," said Mum.

"Little! Compared with what. A barrage balloon," asked Anna.

"There's no need to be so nasty. She can't help it," said Mum.

"When's it due?" asked Anna.

"I may as well know," she thought. "Find out the chance of it arriving over Christmas."

"Not for another four or five months," said Mum.

"What's she expecting. A baby elephant!" asked Anna, the words were out before she could stop them.

"Don't you ever say anything like that in front of Julia," snapped Mum.

"Don't worry," said Anna. "She doesn't listen to anything I say anyway."

"Just be nice to her," Mum pleaded.

"Oh good. The Christmas lights work," said Anna as she turned the switch and the lights in the box gleamed out.

"Anna!"

"Sounds like Brian and 'little' Julia returning," said Anna as the back door slammed shut.

"Anna!" snapped Mum, when Brian walked in, Julia waddling in his wake. She kissed Mum and flopped down on Anna's chair.

"It was murder in town," she said. "My feet are killing me," she kicked off her shoes and looked up at the tree. "You're doing a wonderful job," she said to Mum.

"I was hoping to have it done by the time you got back," said Mum.

"Well. Now we're here we can help you. There's no point working alone," said Julia with a smile.

"It'll be nice to have some help," said Mum.

"Thank-you Mother," muttered Anna picking up her sketch book.

"You're sitting on my pencil," said Anna to Julia.

"I wondered what it was," said Julia fishing out the pencil and handing it to Brian. Anna snatched it from her hand.

"That's mine. And you're not having it," she thought glaring at Brian. Julia looked surprised.

"I hope your girl friend hasn't broken it," she said and Julia started crying.

"Oh God," Anna thought and left the living room for the privacy of her bedroom. "She should be on the stage," she thought, when she heard Mum comforting Julia. She also heard her brother on the stairs behind her.

133

"What's this little brother. Come to defend the fair Julia?" she said, turning and looking down at him from the top of the stairs.

"I won't have you upsetting her like this," he shouted.

"Go away," she said. "Go and look after your little precious. I'm in no mood for your tantrums."Brain dashed up the stairs and lashed out at Anna, but she had already ducked into her room and slammed the door shut pulling the bolt closed.

"You wait till I get my hands on you," he shouted shaking the door handle and hitting the door.

"You lay one finger on me little brother and you'll regret it," she muttered under her breath watching the door and hoping the bolt would hold.

"Come on down Brian," Julia's voice floated up the stairs. "Come and help us with the decorations. They're so pretty. Come and see."The door handle stopped jerking.

"I won't have her talking to you like that," said Brian, but the thump thump on the stairs showed he was going downstairs to help with the decorations.

"Don't waste your time on her," said Julia. "She's not worth it."

"Happy days," thought Anna picking up her pencil and sketch pad, which she had flung on the bed and returned to the sketch she had been working on earlier. A computer monitor hanging from a dead tree, the screen smashed. Piled on the ground were other pieces of obsolete computer hardware, smashed and broken.

A hesitant knock on the door distracted Anna from her sketch book.

"Who's there?" she asked.

"It's me," said Mum. "Are you coming down for tea?"

"Is it safe? Or is little brother going to beat me up?" asked Anna.

"You know he wouldn't hit you," said Mum.

"Does he know this," thought Anna.

"Anyway," said Mum. "It serves you right for winding him up. You know how sensitive he is."

"Him!" said Anna.

"Julia's feeling insecure. And he feels defensive of her. You've got to make allowances for them," said Mum.

"I've got to make allowances.   It's always me that has to make allowances," thought Anna.

"Are you coming down to tea?" asked Mum.

"And to apologise to them," said Anna.

"That would be nice," said Mum.

"I thought so," thought Anna smiling.

"But they're out," continued Mum.   "They've gone to see Julia's Mother. She wanted to see Brian."

"I thought she'd already seen him, when you had that big conference," said Anna.

"No.   No that was Julia's father and Step-Mother," said Mum.

"Oh," muttered Anna.

"Are you coming down to tea?" asked Mum after a long silence.

"In a couple of minutes," said Anna slowly.

"Everyone's out so you remember me," she thought.

"I'll be downstairs," said Mum reluctantly leaving the door.

"I'll just finish this drawing," she thought, ten minutes later she headed downstairs.

"You took your time," snapped Mum as Anna walked into the dining room.   "I was just about to send out a search party."

"Where's Dad?" asked Anna.

"At the office Christmas do," said Mum pouring out a mug of tea.

"Thank-you," said Anna.   "At least I don't have to make it this time," she thought.   "And it isn't stewed, so I would've had to if I'd come down when she called."

"Is that all you have to say," snapped Mum.

"Yes," said Anna after a moments thought.

"You were never easy to understand," said Mum.

"And Julia is," asked Anna.

"At least I know where I am with her," said Mum.

"Do you," thought Anna.   "I doubt that very much indeed."

"So what do you want.   Me to be like her," asked Anna.

"Four months gone," she thought.

"You couldn't be, even if you wanted to," said Mum.

"I think I could manage, if I was of a mind to," thought Anna.

"So what do you want?" asked Anna.

"Just be nice to her," said Mum.

"That again," thought Anna.

135

"Like I said before, she won't even acknowledge my existence," said Anna.

"You don't have to be nasty to her," said Mum.

"She didn't have to take my room," said Anna.

"Surely you can see. Brian's room would have been far too small for the two of them," Mum started.

"I would've swapped," said Anna. "If I'd been asked."

"So why all the fuss," asked Mum.

"You didn't ask. You damaged my things, gave some of them away and moved my room. You just took it for granted that I wouldn't mind," said Anna.

"Took you for granted! That we could never do," said Mum.

"Oh yes," thought Anna. "Pull the other one its got bells on."

"It's how I feel. Not that that matters to anyone," said Anna.

"There's no predicting you," said Mum.

"So why didn't you just wait and ask me," said Anna, suddenly feeling drained. "You must have known I'd be upset."

"There's no point in going over old ground," said her Mum slowly.

"What are you hedging round," Anna thought. "I can hear the cogs, why don't your spit it out."

"So, what do you want to talk about?" asked Anna.

"There's a bit of a problem about Christmas," said Mum after a long pause.

Anna looked up from her now empty cup of tea waiting for details.

"Your a great help I must say," snapped Mum.

"What's the problem with Christmas?" asked Anna. "It comes once a year and we're usually approximately ready for it."

"Julia's Father and Step-Mother have invited us for Christmas," said Mum

"Does Nana know?" asked Anna.

"I don't know how to tell her. She's so looking forward to seeing you and talking about the Poly." Mum looked up.

"Like Great Aunt Elspeth," thought Anna. "No that's uncharitable. Nana would be interested."

"I could go to Nana's if you like and the rest of you can go to see Julia's folk," said Anna.

"You don't mind?" asked Mum

"No. Nana always puts on a good spread. It'll be fun," said Anna.

136

"And it won't be at George and Helen's," Mum interrupted.

"Whose?"

"Julia's people"

"God. Talk about walking on egg shells," thought Anna.

"Probably, but without me there you can all talk babies," said Anna. "And I won't have to listen," she thought.

"Aren't you in the least bit interested in becoming an Aunty?" asked Mum.

"Aunty Anna," thought Anna, testing the words in here mind. "Doesn't sound quite right."

"No," she said.

"I don't know," said Mum shaking her head slowly. "I just feel sorry for any kid that has you as a Mother."

"Thanks Mum," thought Anna. "I really didn't want to know that."

The front door slammed shut.

"Sounds like Julia and Brain," said Anna.

"And I can't make a quick get away," she thought.

"They're early," said Mum perplexed.

Brain led a sobbing Julia into the dining room.

"What now!" thought Anna. "She's going to dehydrate the amount of crying she does."

"What's wrong?" Mum asked of Brain.

"It was awful," sobbed Julia.

"Have a seat," said Anna standing up and offering her chair.

"Thank-you," sobbed Julia as Brain helped her sit down.

"Would you like a cup of tea?" asked Anna.

"Please," said Julia.

"What's got Julia in this state?" Mum asked Brain.

"Her Mother?" asked Anna, heading for the kitchen.

"Yes!" said Brian. "She kept telling Julia to have an abortion. Said the baby would ruin her life, like Julia ruined hers."

Julia's sobs re-started as she was reminded of what her Mother had said to her.

"How could she say such a thing," said Mum.

"As long as you want the baby," said Anna from the kitchen door.

"Of course we do," snapped Julia.

"That's all right then," said Anna. "Do you take milk and sugar?"

"Milk and one sugar," said Julia. "But what about my Mum?"

137

"Once the baby's born and she sees you coping, she'll probably come round to the idea," said Anna.

"Of course she will," said Mum. "What woman wouldn't want her grandchild?"

"So that's it," thought Anna. "You just want a grandchild," and left for the kitchen to make the tea.

"It worked," thought Anna, as she returned with a tray of tea mugs to find Julia calm. "It wouldn't have with me. Then again, that sort of reaction wouldn't have come as a surprise."

"Milk and one sugar," said Anna starting with Julia's mug.

"Thank-you," said Julia gazing into the tea. She took a mouthful.

"This is good," she said.

"Thank-you," said Anna. "Would you like a biscuit?"

"No thank-you. I don't want to put on too much weight," she said gazing down at the bump.

"Oh God. She heard," thought Anna.

"Sorry," she muttered.

"It's OK," smiled Julia sipping the tea.

"Is this peace in our time or just a temporary truce," thought Anna her fingers crossed.

Christmas day dawned with no prospect of snow.

"There's one thing with going to see people on Christmas day," thought Anna, getting ready to go to Nana's and waiting for the bathroom, whilst everyone else got ready to see Julia's parents. "You don't have Christmas dinner to prepare, nor do you have the prospect of all those left-overs to eat for the next few days.

"You're sure you don't mind going to Nana's?" asked Mum as Anna climbed into the mini after she'd loaded all the Christmas presents onto the back seat. As her Mum had said, everyone was going to be there, so she may as well take all their presents and they could all be collected.

"I suggested it," said Anna for the umpteenth time, organising the presents.

138

"God knows why," she thought. "But I suggested it."

"If you're sure."

"Yes Mum, I'm sure," said Anna.

"Sure I don't want to spend Christmas with Julia's family," thought Anna.

"I can always leave early if I get fed up," said Anna.

"They're not that bad," muttered Mum distracted.

"I'll see you later," said Anna putting on her seat belt. "Enjoy yourself."

"Oh yes we will. George and Helen are a very jolly couple," said Mum.

"Good. I'll see you later," said Anna starting the engine.

"I'd better go and get ready," said Mum. "Drive carefully," she added and walked back to the house.

"God. You really are looking forward to today," thought Anna.

"Why are journeys so much shorter when you don't want to get there," thought Anna as her Grandmother's house came into view. "Not that Nana's a problem, it's just the whole family on mass, can be a bit daunting to say the least. Which is probably why she does a buffet, you couldn't get this lot all round a dining table, not in an ordinary house, you'd need a stately home at least and even that wouldn't work, they wander in at all times of the day, I can't imagine them all agreeing on a time to eat or even arrive. A continuous buffet is the only way to feed our hoard. Oh well, here goes, fixed smile at the ready," she thought taking a deep breath and getting out of the car.

"Hello Anna," said Aunty Jean waving from the front door.

"Spotted already," thought Anna, "That breaks the previous record by at least three seconds."

"Where's your Mum and Dad and Brian and this girlfriend we've heard so much about."

"Julia's Dad and Step-Mother invited them all over last minute. They couldn't get out of it, not without upsetting Julia."

"Oh yes. And they wouldn't want to upset her. Not in her condition," said Aunty Jean.

"No," said Anna. "They don't mind upsetting me though," she thought.

139

"When's the baby due?"

"About four months," said Anna.   "I think that's about right," she thought.

"And how do you like the idea of being an Aunty then," asked Aunty Jean.

"I couldn't give a shit," thought Anna.

"Haven't thought about it.   Where's Nana?" asked Anna.

"In the kitchen I should think," said Aunty Jean.   "You know what she's like."

"Yes.   Dynamite wouldn't shift her from that kitchen.   I'll go and see her," said Anna heading off.

"It's true," thought Anna.   "Dynamite wouldn't shift her from the kitchen, then again, in her place I'd be doing the same."

Anna was half way across the living room when she was waylaid by Aunty Helen.

"What's this about your brother?" she asked catching hold of Anna's arm as she walked past.

"Pardon?" asked Anna.

"Is it true that your brothers girlfriend is, ah, well."

"Pregnant?   Yes.   The baby's due in about four months," said Anna, moving to one side to let someone pass, they walked between her and Aunty Helen, so she had to let go of Anna's arm.

"I think its disgraceful.   I mean.   I don't know how your Mother can put up with having her in the house."

"They get on fine," said Anna.   "Mum's looking forward to being a Grandmother."

"That's as maybe.   I think she's putting on a brave face.   This'll be the end of all their plans for your brother.   He'll have to get a job now to support his family.   Its such a waste."

"I wonder what plans these are," Anna thought.   "Rather pointless, whatever, he's always gone his own way."

"So what's he going to do now?" continued Aunty Helen.

"I don't know.   No one's told me," said Anna.

"Told you!   I wouldn't have thought you'd wait to be told.   I'd expect you to ask.   He is your brother!" she said shaking her head and tutting.

"Don't I just know it," thought Anna.

"I'm sure I'll find out when they get round to telling me," said Anna.

"That's very casual I must say.   Aren't you interested?" Aunty Helen

140

demanded.

"No," said Anna smiling. "It isn't as if they're going to ask my opinion or anything," she thought.

"Your poor Mother must be at her wits end over the two of you," said Aunty Helen and walked off to get herself some more turkey from the heavily stacked buffet table.

"Why the hell should Mum be at her wits end about me. I'm not pregnant," thought Anna continuing her journey to the kitchen.

"Anna," said Aunty Carol.

"Oh God," thought Anna. "Not again."

"How are you?" asked Anna smiling.

"Mustn't grumble," said Aunty Carol.

"And the gall stones?" asked Anna, hoping to divert her from the subject of Julia.

"They can fit me in at Easter, so long as they don't flare up again," said Aunty Carol.

"I'll keep my fingers crossed for you," said Anna.

"Thank-you."

"Do you know where Nana is. I haven't seen her yet," Anna asked, trying to avoid being asked the question.

"She'll be in the kitchen I should think. Where's this girlfriend of your brother's?" asked Aunty Carol gazing round the room.

"If she was here you wouldn't have to ask," thought Anna.

"They're not here. Julia's Dad and Step-Mother invited them round. They couldn't refuse," said Anna.

"How's she coping with pregnancy?" asked Aunty Carol.

"How in hell should I know," thought Anna.

"All right I suppose. She's sick a lot and can't stand the smell of cooking," said Anna, hoping she was saying the right things.

"That's only to be expected. How is she in herself?" Aunty Carol persisted.

"God knows," thought Anna. "She doesn't talk to me."

"Seems happy enough," smiled Anna.

"And how do you like the idea of being an Aunty? Got the knitting needles going nineteen to the dozen have you?" asked Aunty Carol.

"Knitting! I hadn't thought about it," Anna said startled.

"What! A good little knitter like you. I don't believe that. I can't imagine you missing out on the chance to knit something for your niece or

141

nephew. Do you have any idea on the sex?"

"They haven't said anything about what sex the baby is and I haven't thought about knitting anything," said Anna. "Come to think of it, I haven't seen Julia doing any knitting."

"Ah well, these young girls, they don't know how to knit."

"She's only two years younger than me," said Anna.

"You're different. There's not many Mothers teach their daughters to knit, not now-a-days."

"Thanks a bunch," thought Anna. "I'm a knitting throw back. Great."

"I'm sure there'll be plenty of people knitting baby clothes. Anyway, I must find Nana. Where did you say she was?" asked Anna.

"In the kitchen, propping up the sink as usual," said Aunty Carol. "I keep trying to get her out of there, but every time my back's turned she sneaks back in."

"See you later," said Anna dashing off before she got any more questions.

"There she is," thought Anna, smiling at the sight of Nana, elbow deep in washing water, her sister Maggie doing the drying.

"Typical," she thought. "If I have any image of Christmas, this has to be it."

"Hello," she said.

"Happy Christmas," said Nana looking up from the suds.

"Where's the rest of your family?" asked Aunty Maggie.

"How many times is that. Thirty billion," thought Anna.

"Julia's people invited them over, last minute, they couldn't say no," said Anna.

"Didn't they ask you?" asked Aunty Maggie.

"Yes. But they can talk babies without me there," said Anna.

"Don't you want to talk babies?" asked Aunty Maggie.

"No. I can't think of anything more boring," said Anna.

"I'm sure you don't mean that. I bet you just can't wait to do some baby sitting," said Aunty Maggie.

"You must be joking," said Anna.

"It isn't like my dear brother's going to trust me with any kid of theirs," she thought. "Not in the near future anyway."

"Leave the poor girl alone," said Nana. "Anna, have you had anything to eat yet."

"Back to the old favourite. Food and how to stuff it down my neck," thought Anna. "Still, it makes a change from Julia and her baby."

"No. I thought I'd find you first," said Anna.

"If you've quite finished wiping the pattern off that plate Mag, give it to Anna and she can get herself some food on it. I did some vegetarian stuff, but I'm not sure if there's any left. Everyone fell on it like a pack of vultures. Just to see what vegetarians eat. If I'd known they were going to be like that I'd have hidden some for you," said Nana.

"I'll see what's left," said Anna taking the plate and wandering back into the fray.

"You really should have some of this turkey," said Aunty Agatha. "It's very good, so succulent, I can never get mine to come out this well."

"No thanks," said Anna.

"You must."

"I don't eat meat," said Anna.

"But this isn't meat. It's turkey," Aunty Agatha persisted.

"Turkey is white meat," Anna started.

"No one would know. I wouldn't tell," Aunty Agatha interrupted.

"Wouldn't you just," thought Anna. "There's a pretty good chance you'll tell them even if I don't eat any of it."

"I'd know," said Anna, with a forced smile.

"I don't know how your poor Mother copes," said Aunty Agatha shaking her head.

"She's used to me I guess. Anyway, I'm away at the Polytechnic most of the year."

"I suppose you must be right. Anyway, it must be the least of her worries at the moment."

"Not Julia again," she thought.

"What?" asked Anna.

"I may as well play it dumb," thought Anna. "After all, that's what they think I am."

"This girlfriend of your brother's. What's her name?" asked Aunty Agatha.

"Julia," said Anna, supplying the name.

"Apart from the upheaval that's caused, she must be worried that the same will happen to you when you get to that age," said Aunty Agatha.

"I don't believe I'm hearing this," thought Anna.

"Since she's younger than me that's hardly likely," said Anna.

"No. She's the same age as your brother, two years older than you," said Aunty Agatha.

"Brian is two years younger than me," corrected Anna.

"I should know," thought Anna.

"No. He's older. I remember looking after him when your Mother was in hospital with you. He was such an angel to look after," said Aunty Agatha, smiling at the memory.

"Brian!" thought Anna.

"Are you sure you're not thinking of Lisa's Ian. Everyone looked after him when she was expecting May."

"Ian! He must be the bane of poor Lisa's life. He breaks everything. God knows what he'll be when he grows up," said Aunty Agatha.

"I think he intends to be a surgeon," said Anna.

"Well I hope he never operates on me. That's all I can say," said Aunty Agatha.

"I'm sure he'd take great care of you," said Anna.

"I wouldn't trust him to carve a turkey. Talking of turkey, you really should have some, its very good," said Aunty Agatha, piling some more on her plate.

"No thank-you. I'll get some salad. Don't want to be putting on too much weight over Christmas," said Anna with a smile.

"Not that there's much chance of that," thought Anna looking at the remains on the table.

"You. Put on weight. That'd be the day," said Aunty Agatha.

"I'll ask Nana where this vegetarian stuff is," said Anna edging quietly away.

"It was round here somewhere," said Aunty Agatha turning back to the table. "I can't see it. Anna? Where has that girl gone?"

"Haven't you got any food?" asked Nana looking at the still clean place.

"Aunty Agatha was trying to fill me up with turkey," said Anna.

"She means well," said Nana.

"I know," said Anna with a sigh.

"There's some salad in this bowl. If you'd like it," said Nana.

"I used to wonder why you stayed in here doing the washing," said Anna.

"It means I don't have to face it tomorrow," said Nana diplomatically.

"Nana," said Grace, Anna's three year old cousin, tugging at Nana's dress.

"What is it?" asked Nana.

144

"Want some orange," said Grace.

"Of course," said Nana drying a handy glass.

"I'll nip off," said Anna. "If that's OK"

"I will see you again, before you go back?" asked Nana.

"Of course," said Anna.

"Take care," said Nana.

"Yes," said Anna, as Grace, concentrating hard, carried her orange juice into the dining room. Aunty Agatha turned from the table. The two met. Grace let out a wail as her orange juice went flying.

"You stupid child," said Aunty Agatha, mopping at her dress. "Can't you look where you're going."

"If you can't why should she," thought Anna.

"My drink," wailed Grace.

"Here have this one," said Nana ready with a replacement.

"Don't want that one," she sobbed as they tried pushing the second glass on her.

"That's enough of that young lady," said Grace's Mum, grabbing the nearest arm, shaking her and aiming a swift clout to the back of the knees. Grace let out on unholy howl.

"I'm off," thought Anna making quickly for the mini. Grace, still screaming, was being pushed and threatened into her her parents car as Anna drove off.

"Family!" she thought. "Still, it could have been worse, Great Aunt Elspeth could have been there and I'd have had to explain why I went on the field trip rather than come home for her visitation. I don't know why Mum made such a fuss over that anyway, Uncle Cyril said she was moving back into the country because she was finding the winters far too cold. Funny, she's been living there over forty years and it's only now that she notices that it gets cold in the winter. Shows how observant she is."

Home was silent. Paddy was asleep in the kitchen.

"Great guard dog you are," she muttered making herself some sandwiches.

"So much for Christmas," she thought. "Wonder if there's anything good on the box."

145

Chapter 9
The New Year

Day followed identical day in a stupor of watching television, eating and sleeping late. It seemed as though it would go on for ever. Anna was slumped in front of some ancient black and white film when Mum, Dad, Brain and Julia wandered in. Anna glanced up for a second then turned back to the film.

"Just a minute," she thought and turned back to look at them, standing there all dressed up for a party.

"Where are you going?" she asked.

"Scruples," said Mum.

"Anything special?" asked Anna.

"Don't you know what day it is?" laughed Brian. "I thought you were supposed to be clever."

"Its New Years Eve," said Mum.

"So. You've never bothered about it before," said Anna.

"We always celebrate," said Julia. "As a family."

"We're your family now," said Brian giving her a hug.

"So we're going to celebrate. Don't stay up too late," said Mum. "We'll see you tomorrow. Well, lets be off," she added and herded the others out of the room.

"Sod off then," thought Anna as she watched them drive off down the road. "Don't come looking to me to baby sit, after all, I'm obviously not family. I wouldn't have gone with you anyway, even if you had asked me," she returned to the settee and the film. "Can't think of anything worse than spending the evening pretending to be happy with that lot, even this film's better than that and that is pathetic," she thought reaching for the TV magazine and looking through the channels to see what was on.

"A load of crap. Nothing but World War Two re-fought and drunken Scotsmen playing the bagpipes. God how I hate New Year's eve. There must be some booze in this dump," she thought looking through the bottles in the sideboard. Only one of the bottles had been opened.

146

"Martini," she muttered holding it up to the light. "Oh well, there's enough for one glass. I can toast the New Year in, even if I am on my own. I wonder if there's anything I can put in this. Like ice and lemonade," she thought, putting the bottle down and going to rummage in the kitchen.

"No ice. No lemonade. Only lime cordial," she stood by the open fridge door contemplating the situation. "Should make an interesting mixture," she thought, pouring some lime juice into a glass and taking it back to the living room and the bottle of Martini.

"There must be something half-way decent on the box," she thought, picking up the paper again. "If not now, then at least sometime tonight. God knows I don't want to go to bed before midnight. It just wouldn't feel right somehow."

As Big Ben struck 12 Anna was watching the familiar scene of Trafalgar Square. She raised her glass in a salute to the merry makers.

"Perhaps Martini and lime aren't such a good combination," she muttered after taking a mouthful. Walking into the kitchen she poured the rest of it down the sink. "This must be the worst New Year ever," she thought. "Oh well. I may as well go to bed. There's no point in staying up. I don't want to be down here when that lot get back."

The sound of a car pulling up into the drive dragged Anna back from a very pleasant dream.

"Two-thirty," she muttered and put her alarm clock back on the bedside table. The engine stopped and she heard the doors slam shut.

"God knows what possessed me to let you drive," shouted Dad.

"I thought it was Mum driving," Anna said to herself. "Less revs, she's fine till Dad gets in the car, then everything goes wrong."

"I think all that vodka and beer had something to do with you not driving," said Mum sharply.

"Your driving would be enough to sober anyone up. God knows what you've done to my gearbox."

"You and your precious bloody car," snapped Mum.

"They've had a good time," thought Anna.

"And what's wrong with me having the odd drink," shouted Dad. "It is the New Year after all."

"Well, that's the world told," thought Anna.

147

"At least I'm not pregnant," he added.

"Heaven forbid," thought Anna.

"She had half a glass of wine to toast the New Year. Compared with you that's the picture of sobriety," snapped Mum.

"A great example of maternal instinct you are," shouted Dad.

"And you're such a saint, letting the poor girl freeze out here on the street whilst you slag her off to all and sundry," Mum yelled back at him.

"Where are they?" he asked.

"In the kitchen," thought Anna. "Julia's even managed to put the kettle on. I heard her filling it. I didn't realise she knew how to."

"So this is where you've sneaked off to," he shouted, staggering into the kitchen and kicking the dog basket. Paddy started howling fit to bust.

"Now look what you've done," shouted Mum. "You've set the dog off."

"Makes him sound like an alarm clock," thought Anna.

"You'd better shut that bloody mutt up or I will. Permanently," said Dad. Paddy gave a whimper and scuttled across the kitchen floor. A minute later he was scratching pathetically at her bedroom door.

"Mug," thought Anna getting out of bed and opening her bedroom door, he dashed in and went straight under the desk and tried to look inconspicuous by burrowing into the wall.

"Dimwit," muttered Anna climbing back into bed.

"You lay one finger on that dog and I'll report you to the RSPCA," said Mum.

"He'd have to catch him first," said Brian. "I didn't realise Paddy had some greyhound in him."

"Anyone for tea?" asked Julia.

"I don't need tea to sober me up," said Dad. "And I'm surprised at you allowing her to drink in her condition," he added to Brian.

"Half a glass of wine diluted with mineral water is hardly drinking," said Julia.

"Good God, the girl's going to stand up for herself for once," thought Anna.

"Drink is drink," said Dad.

"I checked up with the midwife before I touched a drop. I'm not so stupid as to put my baby at risk," said Julia.

"Good on you," thought Anna.

"Your Mother and I are going to bed," said Dad to Brian. "I suggest you try to sober up your girlfriend."

"A cup of tea would be very nice Julia," said Mum.

"That's told him," thought Anna, the kitchen door slammed shut and Dad stumbled up the stairs, crashing into just about everything on the way.

"God he has had a skin-full," thought Anna.

"Nice cup of tea that," said Mum.

"You didn't need to," said Julia.

"If he thinks he can order me around he's got another think coming," said Mum. "I'll go to bed when I choose. And don't let him think he can boss you about either," said Mum nodding to Brian. "If they get away with it once, they'll always be trying it on. Anyway, I'd best see what the old fools up to," she said standing up, swaying slightly. "Oh and don't pay any heed to anything he said. He didn't mean it," she added and left the kitchen, walking with exaggerated care.

"Didn't mean it. Didn't he just," muttered Julia.

"Maybe you shouldn't have," started Brian.

"You as well," snapped Julia. "Everyone gets pissed and they frown at me for having a mouthful of wine to toast the New Year."

"Don't exaggerate," said Brian.

"Exaggerate! Me! No, its you and your Dad that's doing that. A mouthful of wine and you're painting me as an alcoholic," said Julia. "An unfit Mother."

"You wanted the kid. I would've thought it was the least you could do," Brian started.

"Hang on a minute. This was your idea as well. It takes two and don't you forget it," said Julia.

"What's this," thought Anna. "Little brother and Julia planned it!"

"Sorry. It's just. I feel like a spare part. I've done my bit and there's nothing more I can do. I can't even support you and,"Brian started.

"Don't be so daft. I couldn't cope without you," said Julia.

"Really?" asked Brian.

"Do you want proof," asked Julia. "You know what Mum was like and Dad didn't care what I did as long as I wasn't living in his house with his new wife and all her kids. It isn't like there'd be room for me anyway.

"You don't mind that I haven't got a job?" asked Brian.

"It's you that minds, not me and you're doing your best. Something will turn up. I'm sure," said Julia.

"And I thought my family were bad," thought Anna. "Then again, I'm not pregnant, God knows what they'd do then."

149

With the New Year started life seemed to fall into a pattern, Dad at work, Brain job hunting, Mum and Julia, together most of the day talking babies, Mum trying to teach Julia to knit. Anna kept out of harms way, studying in her room and painting and wishing the holiday was over so that she could go back to the Poly.

Barely a week into the year, a letter arrived for Brian in the morning post

"What is it?" asked Julia.

"Yes. What is it?" asked Mum.

"Don't know," he said.

"Open it up then. Don't keep us in suspense," said Anna.

"Oh. Right," said Brain opening the envelope and reading the letter.

"Well?" asked Julia impatiently.

"I've got an interview," he said.

"What for?" asked Mum.

"A job with the county council," said Brian.

"As what?" asked Mum.

"A trainee computer operator," said Brian.

"That sounds all right," said Mum.

"Worried he was going to work on the bins," thought Anna.

"When's the interview?" asked Julia.

"Oh," he said, scanning the letter quickly "Ten thirty Wednesday. Doesn't that clash with the clinic?"

"Yes. But it's all right. I can manage," said Julia quickly.

"I said I'd go with you," said Brian frowning.

"If you get this job I'm going to have to manage by myself aren't I?" she said. "Don't worry. I can cope."

"Any other time and I'd take you," said Mum. "But I've got a dental appointment, it was the first I could get. I've got to get this tooth seen to, you know how painful it is."

"Really, it's the first I've heard of it," thought Anna.

"Yes. Of course," said Julia.

"We'll never hear the end if it if she has to get there by bus," Anna told herself.

"I could take you," she said and everyone turned to look at her.

150

"Well I could," thought Anna.

"Thank-you," said Julia smiling warmly at Brain.

"Well that's settled that then," he said.

Standing by the mini on Wednesday morning Julia didn't look quite so happy.

"She should fit in," thought Anna, glancing from the car to Julia.

"How do I shut this door?" asked Julia, getting comfortable in the passenger seat.

"My poor suspension," thought Anna as the car groaned.

"Just slam it," said Anna. "Oh and don't forget you seat belt. I'll just fish the other half out for you."

"How do you fasten it?" she asked, turning the two halves over in her hands.

"Put the hook in here," said Anna giving a quick demonstration. "And put the flap flat down, like that."

"And this works?"

"Oh yes. It's a magnetic catch. Very strong when it's fastened properly," said Anna. "They wouldn't be fitted if they didn't work. Use your brain girl," thought Anna.

"It's more comfortable than the other sort. It doesn't pull so much," said Julia.

"No I don't suppose it does," said Anna thoughtfully. "What shall we do?"

"Pardon?" Julia looked puzzled.

"Shall I drop you off at the clinic and pick you up later, or do you want me to come in with you?" asked Anna.

"It would be good if you'd come in with me," said Julia. "I haven't been to this clinic before. I went to the one near Dad's and," she hesitated.

"That's OK, I'll come in with you. How long do you think they'll be?" asked Anna.

"I don't know. I mean, I was given an appointment, but whether they run to time and how long they take," said Julia with a shrug.

"What have I let myself in for," thought Anna, as they drove towards the maternity hospital. It was a large dark grey concrete slab of a building, five floors of it, on three sides of a car park. She turned in and started

151

driving round looking for a parking space.

"They said there was plenty of parking space," said Julia looking round.

"Unfortunately most of it's occupied," said Anna smiling. "Let's see of I can get close to the door, or at least within a mile of it."

"I just hope I don't meet anyone I know," she thought.

"It's such a big place," said Julia, looking round nervously. "Where do we go?"

"I was hoping you'd know that," thought Anna, parking the car near a door marked reception.

"Better ask at reception," she said, Julia looked puzzled. "It's through that door over there," she added locking the car and walking quickly in that direction.

"Are you OK?" she asked after a minute, glancing towards Julia. "You seem a bit out of breath."

"If you could walk a bit slower," panted Julia.

"Sorry. I didn't think. It can't be easy for you," Anna started.

"With a great lump," finished Julia.

"It can't make things easy," said Anna.

"No. But at least it's only temporary," said Julia.

"This time next year you'll be back to normal," said Anna, trying to sound positive.

"Assuming you're not pregnant again," she thought, holding open the heavy door.

"I suppose so. I'd better ask the receptionist where to go," said Julia looking at the counter beneath the reception sign.

"I suppose so," said Anna.

"Because I'm not asking," she thought.

"Right. I'll be back in a minute," said Julia, hesitating.

"Maternity's through that door," said the receptionist, pointing to a pair of doors to the right which opened onto a corridor. "Go down to the end of the corridor and speak to the woman on the desk."

"Thank-you," stammered Julia.

"Right," said Anna, pulling the door open. "I could get a job as a door opener," she thought.

"She knew!" said Julia in a stage whisper which echoed round the magnolia painted plaster wall of a very long corridor.

"I wonder how," thought Anna, holding open the door at the far end of the corridor. In a place where several corridors converged sat a lady at a

152

simple varnished wood desk behind which were a few filing cabinets.

"Have you got your appointment card?" the lady asked Julia.

"Yes. Yes," said Julia. "It's in my handbag," she added opening up a large bag and searching through the jumble of its contents. "It's in here somewhere," she muttered. "I saw it yesterday. Ah, there it is," she said with a sigh of relief fishing out a rather battered looking pink card and handing it over with an apologetic grin.

"Thank-you," said the woman, with a sniff, carefully straightening out the card. "If you would wait over there Miss Green, I'll call you when it's your turn."

"Thank-you," muttered Julia, blushing a vivid scarlet.

"You cow," thought Anna. "Don't make it easy for her to come to this dump will you."

"Would you like a magazine to read?" asked Julia as Anna bumped into a low table covered with them.

"Yes. It'll help to pass the time," she muttered rubbing her shin.

"I didn't know there were so many different magazines on parenting," said Julia.

"Neither did I," sighed Anna.

"Parenting. God what an ugly word," she thought flicking through the magazines. "Where are these smiling toddlers and glowingly pregnant women they photographed for these magazines, they're not here and that's for certain," she thought gazing round a room that seemed full of bulging harassed women, screaming babies and toddlers. "We'll be here all day if this lot has to go in before us," she thought.

"Isn't that a lovely dress," said Julia, pointing to a picture in one of the magazines. "I hope I have a baby girl."

"Yes. Very pretty," said Anna.

"I can't see a real baby in it though," she thought. "It wouldn't be the same once baby had thrown up on it a few times. How do you wash puke out of lace?"

"I want everything to be perfect for my baby when it comes," said Julia.

"How's the knitting coming on?" asked Anna.

"Oh that. I don't think I'll ever get the hang of it. The simplest pattern we could find. And I'm still making a mess of it," said Julia with a sigh.

"I thought Mum was helping you?" asked Anna.

"She is but," Julia started.

"Miss Green. The Doctor will see you now," said the lady at the desk.

153

"Right. I'll go," said Julia, turning an even brighter shade of red.

"Good luck," said Anna. "I'll wait here for you shall I?" asked Anna.

"Oh. Yes. See you soon," said Julia.

"Down there. First door on the right," said the lady. Julia walked off and left Anna feeling very conspicuous.

"Let's take a closer look at these magazines then. Is the argument between terry towelling and disposables still rife. Is breast still best. God how long's she going to be. I hope no one I know sees me. They might think I'm pregnant, then again they might realise I'm here with someone else because I couldn't possibly be, I don't know which would be worst. Hell this magazine's boring. No wonder your brain turns to jelly when you're pregnant if you've got this to read. You'd think they'd have something about making the world a cleaner, better place for the baby. Then again, if their readers are like Julia," Anna glanced up and saw a bewildered looking Julia coming out of the door.

"Have you finished here?" asked Anna, Julia jumped.

"You startled me. I didn't see you coming," said Julia.

"Sorry," said Anna. "I didn't mean to."

"It's all right."

"Have you finished here?" asked Anna again.

"Yes. For the time being at any rate," said Julia.

"Are you OK?" asked Anna, feeling worried.

"Yes. Fine," said Julia.

"And. The pregnancy. How's that progressing?" asked Anna.

"Fine. There's no problem."Julia started.

"But?" asked Anna.

"What?" asked Julia.

"Nothing. It's just. You sound worried," said Anna.

"Twins! I'm expecting twins," said Julia, looking even more bewildered.

"Oh," said Anna, holding open the door for Julia. "Mum's knitting needles'll catch fire from the extra work."

"But Brian," Julia started.

"Will just have to get used to the idea," said Anna. "Anyway, don't they say its twice the joy."

"Twice the work, twice the food, twice the clothes, twice everything," said Julia.

"We'd best get back," said Anna. "Hopefully Brian will be back and he can reassure her," she thought.

"If only we had a place of our own it wouldn't be so bad," said Julia.

"Maybe the perfect place'll turn up soon," said Anna. "I didn't know you were looking," she thought.

"I wouldn't mind an imperfect place, as long as we can afford it," said Julia.

"Have you tried the council?" asked Anna.

"I don't think we qualify. Anyway, there's probably a very long waiting list," said Julia.

"You could ask. The worst they can say is bog off, in which case you'll be no worse off," said Anna.

"I hadn't thought of it that way," said Julia.

"And a family with two babies. You should have a high priority," said Anna.

"But what do I do? Who do I ask?" asked Julia, walking slowly across the car park.

"Ring the council, the housing department, they'll know what to do," said Anna.

"You make it sound so easy," said Julia.

"It might be easy. But you won't find out if you don't try," said Anna.

"I'll try. When we get back," said Julia sitting heavily in the passenger seat of the mini.

"I'll believe that when I see it," thought Anna slamming shut the door and walking round the car. "How come car parks are always full, when you're looking for a parking space and half empty when you decide to leave," she thought taking a last look round the car park and getting into the drivers seat. "Anyway, this is their problem, there's nothing I can do about it. I just hope they don't expect me to vacate that cupboard of a room for these twins."

"Why don't you park in the drive?" asked Julia as Anna parked by the kerb in front of her parents home.

"Mum says the car leaks oil and makes a mess of the concrete," said Anna.

"Does it?" asked Julia.

"Old cars always leak," said Anna.

"I suppose Brian'll have to park here when we get a car," said Julia thoughtfully.

"I doubt it," muttered Anna. "Mummy's little blue eyed boy won't have a leaky old car and even if it does leak oil on the drive they'll still blame my car," thought Anna.

"What?" asked Julia.

"You look tired. Why don't you nip into the house? I've just got to sort out the boot and then I'll be in," said Anna.

"Right," she said looking at the door. Anna dashed round and opened it for her.

"I'll lock it," she added, Julia waddled off up the drive without another word.

"How can anyone be so stupid," thought Anna looking at the disappearing figure. "Then again, she did fall for my brother. Am I getting intolerant in my old age or what," thought Anna gazing down the road, "Still, I'd better get a move on. Someone might miss me. And pigs might fly," she thought locking up the car. "Not that anyone in their right minds would pinch it," she thought.

"Sit and stay," she muttered to the car and followed Julia into the house. Julia was standing in the hall, staring at the telephone mesmerized.

"Do you know the council's number?" she asked.

"I'll find it for you," said Anna. "Have I got to do everything," she thought.

"Here it is," she said pointing to the number. Julia picked up the receiver and started dialling.

"I'll make a cup of tea," said Anna dashing off to the kitchen, before Julia asked her to do the talking for her.

Anna was just pouring herself a cup of tea when Julia wandered into the kitchen.

"There's a woman going to come here to see me on Thursday. Brain as well. If he's not at work," said Julia.

"Oh," said Anna.

"She's going to asses us. See how many points we have," said Julia looking somewhat perplexed.

"Yes. I suppose they will have to asses you," said Anna.

"I know. But why here? I said I could go to the council buildings."

"It's so they can asses your home background," said Anna.

"What!" asked Julia.

"It's to see what sort of housing you're used to, how clean and tidy you

156

keep it. That sort of thing," said Anna.

"I thought she was just trying to be helpful," said Julia sounding slightly deflated.

"Don't worry. This place is always spotless. She's bound to get a good impression," Anna reassured her.

"Yes. But," said Julia looking bewildered.

"Sounds like Brian, back from his interview," said Anna trying to change the subject.

"What'll he say?" Julia looked anxious.

"Don't know," said Anna, with a sigh.

"Hello everyone. The worker has returned," said Brian standing by the kitchen door.

"So you got the job," said Anna.

"Of course. Is there any tea left," said Brian, as if they could've done anything else.

"I'll just look," said Julia.

"I've got some studying to do," said Anna leaving the kitchen.

"Good luck with the job," she added.

"Thanks," said Brian. "What's with her?" he asked Julia. "Not mellowing in her old age is she?"

"I don't know why you're always so nasty to her. You and your Mother. Anna's been very supportive to me today," said Julia.

"Was I?" thought Anna carrying her mug of tea carefully up the stairs. "The girl's a fool. But easily pleased, must be why she fell for our Brian."

The sun glinted through the gap in the curtains of Anna's room on her bags which where waiting for the journey to the Poly. But it was neither the sun nor her alarm clock which had woken Anna. It was the sound of Brian getting ready for work. His alarm clock was enough to waken the dead. But it made little impression on Brian. The ringing lasted for what seemed an age. There was a muttering as the alarm was silenced, a loud thud and then a lot of swearing.

"Kicking him out of bed does seem rather unsubtle. But effective. I can't see him putting up with it for long though," thought Anna. A thudding sound came from the direction of the stairs.

"I don't know how the stairs stand it. You'd think he was an elephant the amount of racket he kicks up, still I'd better get up and say 'bye to him, not that he'll appreciate it. But I can't leave without saying good-bye," she thought and dragged herself out of bed.

"Good God," exclaimed Brain spitting cornflakes across the table. "What dragged you up this early."

"I heard a baby elephant dashing round the house, so I thought I'd better investigate," said Anna popping two slices of bread in the toaster.

"You don't usually get up when we do," said Julia.

"Thanks. You were supposed to deny that I sound like an elephant," said Brian.

"But you do," said Julia. "A very nice baby elephant," she added smiling.

"Nice!" thought Anna.

"I'm going back to Poly today," she said watching the toaster.

"Good," said Brian.

"Nice to know I'll be missed," she thought.

"Does this mean you won't be able to give me a lift to the council this morning?" asked Julia.

"Of course it does," snapped Mum before Anna could speak.

"Could you give Julia a lift Mum?" asked Brain.

"No I could not. I don't see what you need a council house for," she shouted. "There's plenty of room for you here."

"No there isn't," said Julia evenly. "And there'll be even less when the twins are born."

"I thought the lady from the council was coming here?" said Anna.

"There was some sort of mix up with the appointments or something. She did explain, but I didn't understand. Anyway, she asked if I could go to the council offices for the meeting instead. I didn't think it would be a problem."

"When's the appointment?" asked Anna.

"Ten o'clock."

"I could drop you off there, on my way to the Poly, but you'll have to make your own way back," said Anna picking her toast out of the toaster.

"Thanks," said Julia. "I can catch the bus back."

"So you're behind this are you," said Mum.

"I don't see why they shouldn't have a home of their own," said Anna.

"No you don't. You just want your old room back. It doesn't bother you that there'll be no furniture or carpets in this 'Council House' and no

158

money to buy any. You don't care that my Grandson's will be living on bare boards do you," shouted Mum.

"Boy's are they?" Anna asked Julia.

"They could've told us at the scan, but I don't want to know till they're born, it would spoil the surprise," said Julia.

"I just know they are, a woman can tell these things," said Mum.

"Like you knew I was a boy," said Anna. "I get the impression they're going to be girls," thought Anna.

"You're changing the subject," muttered Mum.

"The subject. So where are these twins going to sleep? The house is full," said Anna standing in the kitchen door and looking round.

"I thought. Brian's old room," started Mum.

"My room," said Anna.

"You're at Poly most of the year," said Mum.

"And what am I supposed to do during the holidays? Hang on a hook in the hall?" shouted Anna. "I mean, summer's about three months."

"Don't be stupid," snapped Mum.

"I don't want to push Anna out of her room," said Julia.

"You didn't mind before," thought Anna.

"I'd best be off to work," said Brian. "Don't want to be late."

"Oh. Right. Have you got your sandwiches?" asked Mum.

"Yes Mum," said Brian.

"Good luck and take care," said Julia.

"See you this evening," he said, grabbing his sandwiches and making a dash for it.

"I'd best be off too," said Dad.

"God I didn't even see him come in," thought Anna, jumping out of his way.

"We'll discuss this later," said Mum tidying the dishes into the sink.

"I haven't finished with that," Anna said, grabbing her mug of tea. "And just in case you've forgotten, I'm going back to the Poly today."

"We'll let you know what's happening, when we decide," said Mum.

"Will this be before or after anything I leave here gets thrown out?" asked Anna.

"There's no need to be hysterical," said Mum.

"I wouldn't say I was being hysterical, it's just going by recent events, that's what's likely to happen," said Anna.

"There's no talking to you when you get like this," said Mum leaving.

159

"Like what? not agreeing with everything you say," said Anna to her Mum's disappearing back. "It isn't like you try talking."

"I won't let them chuck you out," said Julia.

"I can't see you stopping them," thought Anna.

"I'll get the mini loaded. Then we can head for the council offices. I hope this goes well," she said.

"Thanks. Do you want a hand with the loading?" asked Julia.

"No. It's OK. Thanks," said Anna.

"I'm not an invalid," said Julia.

"No you're not," said Anna. "Well, if you want to help."

"Yes," said Julia.

"You could hold the doors open for me," said Anna.

"OK" said Julia flatly.

"I wonder how Julia's got on," thought Anna drinking a cup of coffee and gazing round her Poly room at her bags, a few more then she had intended to bring, but their contents did seem likely to end up at a charity shop. The things she had left probably would, but she wasn't bothered about them. "If I ring now, I'll probably get her, not Mum and the phone here should be free," she added to herself, heading downstairs to the phone.

"Ah. Hello. Who is it?" Julia's voice came through the phone.

"It's me. Anna."

"Oh. Hello."

"I just thought I'd ring to say I got to the Poly OK,"said Anna.

"Oh. Right. Good," said Julia.

"Great conversationalist," thought Anna.

"How did you get on this morning?" asked Anna.

"Not too well," said Julia.

"What did they say?" asked Anna.

"They said they'd put our names on the list," said Julia hesitantly.

"But?" asked Anna, it sounded like there was a but in what she had to say.

"They didn't hold out much hope. We aren't homeless and Mum told the woman they're going to do a loft conversion," said Julia.

"Typical," thought Anna. "And she says I'm a schemer."

"Well, you're on the list anyway," said Anna. "Though what use that'll

160

be I don't know," she thought.

"They said I could try some of the housing associations," said Julia.

"That's true," said Anna. "Why didn't I think of that," she thought.

"I've been put on the list by a few of them, but," Julia started.

"You have been quick," thought Anna.

"But?" she asked. "They weren't hopeful. They've got their hands full finding places for people who have nowhere to live," said Julia.

"Sorry," said Anna.

"You can't help it," said Julia.

"At least you've tried," said Anna. "And something might turn up."

"Yes," said Julia flatly.

"Oh well. Take care and don't let Mum boss you," said Anna.

"I'll do my best," said Julia.

"Bye," said Anna.

"Bye," said Julia and the phone went dead.

"Hopeless. The girl's hopeless. Mum'll just take over and I'll have to find somewhere else to live come the summer. Perhaps a summer job abroad or something, a rented room in town, it isn't like anyone will miss me or I could see if the Polytechnic let rooms over the summer."

Chapter 10
Back to Work

The third day back at the Poly and everything was running smoothly. Mr Thomas was bringing a politics lecture to a close, just before noon.

"Oh and before you dash off," he said. "I have some assignments for each of you," he smiled as the announcement was greeted by a chorus of groans. "Each assignment is different, so don't bother comparing notes," he added handing out the computer print outs.

"This can't be right," said Anna looking at the book list on the bottom of the sheet.

"Of course it is," said Mr Thomas reading the sheet over her shoulder. "The computer is never wrong."

"You can't expect me to read these," Anna started.

"That's entirely up to you, but you'll find the assignment difficult to do if you don't," said Mr Thomas handing out the last of the computer listings.

"If that's how it is," thought Anna. "I'd better get them out of the library and see what I can make of this."

"A politics assignment. It would be logical to find the books in the politics section. But I don't think these are going to be in there," thought Anna studying the list in the library. "But where will they be," she looked round and caught sight of a vacant microfiche viewer.

"Right," she muttered.

"I'm bagging that before anyone else gets it," she thought. "And what looks like a complete set of author microfiche. This must be my lucky day. All I have to do now is find the books."

Half an hour later Anna had found all of the books, none of them in the politics section, filled in the appropriate forms and was waiting in the queue to get them stamped.

"Bit of an odd selection," she thought, turning them over in her hands.

162

"Spy, biography and literary criticism, but at least I've got all the ones from the list. A miracle in itself."

"This the lot?" asked the librarian.

"Yes," said Anna.

"Don't know why you bother reading this load of rubbish, or why the library wastes shelf space on them," said the librarian stamping the books.

"They're on the book list for my latest assignment," said Anna, looking at the books and feeling the need to justify herself.

"Well, it must be a pretty weird course. That's all I can say," said the librarian, finally handing over the books with a look that said she was contemplating washing her hands now that she'd handled them.

"Who asked you," thought Anna. "You don't even know your own subject. 'Northanger Abbey' in historical monuments, I ask you. As for 'The Plague and I' going in the medical section. Anyone with half a brain could tell it wasn't a serious medical book. The woman doesn't know what she's talking about," thought Anna, but after a few hours of studying them in her room she was inclined to agree with her.

"No index. No list of chapters and the chapter headings aren't exactly illuminating. Looks like I'm going to have to read the things from beginning to end. I could do without that. It'll take ages. I just hope they make more sense than those photocopies Mr Jefferies gave us. I know they're something about the ethics and work practices of some group of professionals associated with housing. But that's about all and I got that from the title, it was all in academic speak and half the pages had been folded down to A4, they should have been straightened out before they were copied. Oh well, the sooner I start," she thought, gathering a pad of paper and a pen. With a cup of coffee by her side and a half eaten biscuit in her hand she picked a book at random and started reading.

"More of a story than anything else," thought Anna turning over the first page.

"Intriguing," she thought a little while later, picking up her mug and taking a mouthful of coffee.

"God. That's revolting," said Anna pulling a face. "It shouldn't have got cold that quick. It's only been," she thought glancing at the clock. "What! Quarter past five. Hell I'd better get to tea. Just as everything's beginning to hot up. God knows how he's going to get out of that mess. He's so subtle and unobtrusive in his spying. He's been caught by the people he's supposed to be watching. Their reaction to him is odd to say

163

the least. He's come to put a stop to their plans for world domination. All on his own. You'd think they'd just bop him off and dispose of the body, feed him to their pet sharks, that'd do the trick. It's taken long enough to find the current site, by the sounds of it, it'll have taken a good few years to build, it doesn't exactly sound like a small place, so it'll take an equal length of time to find the new place and rebuild. So they've got good reason to protect their base, it would seem logical and them being such ruthless evil people, you'd think it would be easy for them to bop him off. Talking of murder. I'd better get to the refectory whilst there's still a chance, vague though it may be, of there being something half-way edible for tea. Not quite in the class of the meal this idiots enemies are sharing with him, but all that's on offer to me."

Anna finished the first book that day. A week later she had finished all six books.

"A pretty good read," she thought, putting the last book down on her desk. "Though the plot is beginning to get rather repetitive and his incompetence is wearing thin. Its amazing he's managed to stay alive, as a spy. However, having said that, I don't see what this has got to do with any sort of political theory. But then, I don't suppose he gives much thought to politics. Still, this isn't getting the assignment done. God knows. I'm no nearer working out what the hell should go in it, let alone how I'm going to write it. There are no facts to work on, only fantasy. God knows what the author was thinking of when he wrote this lot. The gas bill or the electric bill, has to be something like that. Maybe there's a book about him in the library. It might shed some light on the subject. I may as well give it a whirl, there's nothing to lose," Anna thought.

At the library Anna found a couple of biographies. Flicking through the pages she found that he had died, but that the character, the so called hero of the books hadn't died with him. Others had continued writing about his exploits.

"I'd better find a few of those books as well," thought Anna. "See how they compare. The political theory might be more obvious in them. What the hell, I'm desperate and it sounds plausible and it might be interesting to see what the hero does with another author."

Back at the hall, she made herself another cup of coffee and sat down to tackle the biography. A strange book. Very shadowy, with few solid facts. His parents seemed more like ghosts than real people. Their Christian names were never mentioned, neither was his Mother's maiden name. His childhood and education were equally hazy, though it was thought that he did have both a childhood and an education of sorts.

"If the author knew so little about him, why the hell did he bother writing his biography?" she thought making yet another cup of coffee. "Must have been a big gas bill, or something. Let's hope this'll keep me awake till I finished reading it."

As the night progressed Anna found out that the author had got himself involved in the secret services round about the time of the second world war. Though it wasn't clear exactly when or how, though it could have been something to do with the university he went to, but it might not have.

"I suppose that's where he got his ideas for the books," thought Anna. "The question is, is spying really like he describes it, or has he glamorized it, to make himself look good, or is he just perpetuating the common perception of what spying is like. It would be nice to have some solid facts, something more than vague hints, even if only the date of his retirement, or his birthday, date of his marriage, name of wife, children how many, if any, anything. Hell, we know more about the character than his creator," Anna shook her head.

"He took up writing in his retirement and by the looks of the list of titles, was quite prolific. It seems there was some question about whether he should be allowed to publish them. I suppose there would be, if he was using his knowledge from work, then again, preventing publication might give credibility to the stories and people in them. A difficult problem," thought Anna.

"He died. That basically is all they say on the subject. No how, when, where, how old he was, whether it was expected or what. Though they do put forward the rather bizarre notion that the author was the victim of his own hero. How he managed that I'd hate to think. It's mystery enough that the hero should want to kill the author. Most characters, if the author hasn't killed them, die with their creator. I suppose he did manage to escape that.

After the author's death other writers were brought in to keep the hero alive and forever young and to introduce more gadgets and an almost sci-fi element to the plot.

"I suppose, if he's managed all that the character could have assassinated his creator, though it is a bit far fetched," thought Anna setting down the book. It was 4 am.

"That's enough for today," she thought yawning. "I'll sleep on it. I might come up with something. There's one thing for certain, I'm not going to come up with anything now. And since it's not due in tomorrow, it can go hang for the time being."

It was after tea the next day, or rather the same day, before Anna managed to return to the assignment. There hadn't even been time to think about it, the day had been so hectic, half the lectures were new subjects and in different rooms, none of which seemed to agree with anything on the timetable, hence, the busy day. Sitting down at her desk, with a fresh cup of coffee, resting her feet on the armchair, Anna caught sight of the small stack of books under a pad of paper.

"Shit. I'd forgotten about that," she muttered. "How in hell's name do they expect me to find any serious political ideals in that bunch of spy novels. I mean, no one in their right minds would take them seriously. They're good for a laugh, popular fiction, nothing more," Anna thought, picking up the stack, she flicked idly through each book in turn and tossed them onto the armchair.

"Perhaps that's it. Perhaps that's what they want. This is the authors view of the popular opinion of the world of espionage, though, going by the biography, I wouldn't have thought he'd know much about ordinary people. Still, I suppose it's a self-fulfilling prophecy. If you picture a life style in a certain light often enough, it will become accepted as an accurate portrayal.

Sounds feasible. Well it does to me and that's good enough.

I suppose the lack of political theory and analysis, the extreme polarity of the plot and characters. There is the good side, represented by the hero and the bad side, headed and dictated to, by the arch villain. It's just how he thinks people view spies. They're just doing a job. They don't consider the politics, their job is to obey orders. If they started analysing the politics and theories behind what they're told to do they might not like it and it might affect their efficiency. It's an amoral job and so requires amoral people to carry it out. Either that or someone so committed to the politics of their masters that they obey everything without question.

Despite this, the author feels compelled to paint his character as the hero, saviour of democracy and all that being British stands for.

As for the gadgets. The number increases with each book, or so it seems and there is an increasing emphasis on them when other authors take over the task of writing. The gadgets sort of take over, substitutes for the skills and knowledge which the spy lacks, or the new authors think he would lack. The increased reliance on them could be explained in many ways, but is probably a reflection on societies increasing fascination with things. The proliferation of machines for doing any number of pointless tasks. The amazing thing is that the hero manages to use all the little objects he's given, also, they always work when needed. It's not so surprising with some of the earlier books, but the more electronics get involved, the greater the chance for them to break down, especially the way he treats them, he isn't exactly careful with anything."

"Right," thought Anna looking down at her notes. "Is there anything I've missed out? Class! The hero is depicted as upper class, well mannered, even when he shoots people, always stops at the best hotels, immaculately dressed, pain in the arse, charms everyone and always has a witty answer. He's not gone through your average comprehensive school education. Even his degree is in classics, though what use that is in his line of work I dread to think.

Right, now all I have to do is write that down in a logical manner, with references from the books. "Simple really. I don't think. Oh well, one more cup of coffee and I'll get on with it. I can write it up neatly tomorrow, when I'm half asleep. That way I won't decide it's a load of crap and ditch it."

"Due in a week on Wednesday. I've finished it in plenty of time for once," she thought, yawning and glancing at the clock.

"4 am again. I'll be shattered tomorrow."

It was Monday morning, the first one after Anna had handed in her assignment to Mr Thomas. Sunny, warm, almost like a summers day, but with an odd sense of unreality about the place.

Heading for her first lecture, turning the corner in the corridor, Anna felt as though she had gone back in time. Back to the last time she had seen Susan.

There was Mr Thomas, same track suit, it was still too small for him, its

167

bright red colour still matched his face as he kept up his attempts at jogging on the spot and shadow boxing.

"But Susan isn't here," the thought screamed through Anna's brain, followed rapidly by the thought. "I'm not taking her place". But her feet continued down the corridor towards the lecture room and Mr Thomas.

"Keep cool," she told herself. "Bluff it out. This could just be a figment of your imagination. But my worst nightmare's couldn't dream up that shade of red. And the track suit isn't much better. I've got to get out of here, but if I run they'll win. Keep cool, it's all you can do."

"Ah Anna!" said Mr Thomas, stopping his pathetic fitness freak act and putting on his "I didn't know you were there look", when she was barely six feet from the open door. "Just the person I've been looking for."

"Really and to what do I owe this honour," asked Anna.

"Was that me speaking," she thought. "I'd better be more careful."

"I want to talk to you about this," said Mr Thomas shaking a small bundle of papers at her.

"Where the hell did those come from," thought Anna. "Green ink. Looks like my assignment. I hope his sweaty mitts won't make the ink run. It's not indelible."

"Is that my assignment?" she asked. "Stall for time," Anna told herself.

"Yes. This is your assignment. The one you handed in on Wednesday."

"That interesting is it?" she said.

"Interesting is hardly the word I'd use. I think we ought to talk. In my office," said Mr Thomas.

"Go to your office!" she thought. "Not if I can help it."

"I've got a lecture," said Anna, looking longingly though the open door as the rest of the students filed in, none of the looking in her direction.

"My office. Now," snapped Mr Thomas. "We need to consider whether you are happy on this course or whether we should let you go."

"Shit," she muttered to herself. "It's going to require a lot of smooth talking to get out of this."

"Well then," said Anna smiling. "Lead on."

"Keep smiling, it'll confuse him and that doesn't take much," she thought.

"Oh. Right. This way," he said looking down the corridor.

"Well, that threw him to start off with," thought Anna. "Though God alone knows what he expected me to do, leg it in the opposite direction?

168

Tempting though that is, I don't see it achieving much."

"This room here," said Mr Thomas opening a door on the right.

"Oh. I wondered where you hid yourself," said Anna wandering in and looking round the office. The Venetian blinds were open, Mr Thomas impatiently pulled the cord to close them and then turned on the light, illuminating the clutter of books, papers, half dead spider plants, an ancient kettle and several mouldy mugs.

"Lets hope he doesn't offer me anything to drink," thought Anna. "Though I don't suppose there's much danger of that."

"I hope you have a good explanation for this," he said tossing the assignment on the desk. It was creased and the ink was smudged.

"The sod," thought Anna. "If I'd handed it in looking like that he wouldn't mark it. I took time and effort over that and he treats it like rubbish."

"Well, I'm waiting," said Mr Thomas.

"For what?" thought Anna, but said nothing.

"Did you have a brainstorm or something when you wrote this," he said poking at the work with his index finger.

"No," said Anna.

"Probably," she thought. "But I'm not saying that. I'm not giving you an excuse to chuck me off the course. You want to do that, you're going to have to find the reasons."

"So what's your excuse for handing this in?" asked Mr Thomas.

"Excuse! Do I need an excuse for handing in my work! I thought it was expected of me," thought Anna.

"I just answered the question to the best of my ability," she said.

"Do you honestly expect me to believe that, after reading this!" snapped Mr Thomas waving the assignment at her.

"No. I'm a congenital liar," she thought. "No one in their right mind would believe a word I say. Then again, I'm having enough problems believing this is happening."

"It's the truth," she said. "Best keep it simple, though it would never cross my mind that you might actually believe anything I said," she thought.

"It was a simple enough assignment. All you had to do was state the political theories given in the books in the book list," said Mr Thomas, talking to Anna as if she were a simpleton.

"There weren't any. They were prominent by their absence, so that's

169

what I wrote about," said Anna.

Shaking his head slowly he sat down behind the desk.

"He ought to be on the stage," thought Anna. "At least he'd be out of my way, or maybe films, though I can't imagine him being able to remember a whole script."

"Sit down Anna," he said waving towards a chair.

"You'd think he could manage to put the books on the bookshelf," she thought moving them off the chair so she could sit down.

"Do you have to have them pointed out to you. I would have thought they were pretty obvious," said Mr Thomas.

"If they're so obvious what are they," thought Anna, but she said nothing.

"The basic conflict in the books is the incompatibility of the Capitalist and Communist systems and the reality of this political incompatibility is the cold war. The character in the books is just one of the many people who participate in this conflict."

"I wouldn't have said so," said Anna. "Especially as the villain in at least one of them is an international criminal who considers himself above politics.

"Oh. And where would you say the conflict arises. That is assuming you actually admit that there is some conflict depicted in the book," Mr Thomas almost shouted at her.

"That's right," thought Anna. "Leap down my throat before I get a chance to say my piece."

"There don't seem to be any great difficulties between the Capitalist and Communist countries. They seemed to be muddling along all right. It's just when a third party comes along stirring things up that there's problems. The enemy tends to be either organised crime or some power mad idiot who wants to rule the world. There are quite a few of the books where the Communists play no part at all and even some where they join with the west to solve the problem."

"There you go trying to justify your misguided ideas," said Mr Thomas.

"There you go not listening to a word I have to say," thought Anna.

"Don't you understand the purposes of the secret services, in a capitalist country, is to prevent the spread of Communism. That's why they are there," said Mr Thomas.

"What a load of crap," thought Anna.

"Spies have been around for thousands of years," started Anna.

170

"I didn't ask your opinion," said Mr Thomas.

"So much for a discussion," thought Anna.

"I also thought your attitude to the spy was very condescending and you picked up on a lot of trivial points. This is a very risky profession and I don't think you have any right to trivialise it," said Mr Thomas.

"He knew the risks when he took the job. Or at least he ought to have," said Anna.

"Well of course he knows the risks," said Mr Thomas.

"I doubt that sometimes," said Anna.

"And what do you mean by that?" asked Mr Thomas.

"So you do want my opinion now do you," thought Anna.

"He's extremely trusting, especially where women are concerned, goes anywhere with them, believes anything they say," Anna started.

"And you expect him to doubt everyone?" asked Mr Thomas.

"A little more caution might save him from walking into quite so many traps. I thought only bad spies got caught, yet he's supposed to be one of the best. Also, when he gets caught, he's quite happy to eat or drink anything they give him, he never stops to wonder what they've put in it. Just gets angry when they drug his coffee," said Anna.

"How was he to know they'd sink to such a low down trick," said Mr Thomas.

"He's dealing with a power mad lunatic who wants to rule the world. Someone who kills inefficient employees. A sleeping potion was the least he could expect," said Anna.

"Really. And what do you think this power mad lunatic would have done," asked Mr Thomas.

"Is this a danger signal?" thought Anna. "What the hell am I supposed to say? God, if this wasn't so serious it'd be laughable," she looked at the ceiling. "Oh well, in for a penny, in for a pound."

"He wants to dominate the world, he has spent a lot of time, effort and money creating a base from which to do this and the spy is the only person standing in his way. He'd either kill him without a second thought, use him to provide counter information and keep the authorities off his back, or discredit him," said Anna.

"I see. And that presumably is what you would do," asked Mr Thomas.

"If I was a megalomaniac intent on world domination. But I'm not. Most people aren't. However, he seems to meet this type of person a lot in his line of business, its about time he learnt how to deal with them," said

Anna.

"Answer that one," she thought.

"And there's your obvious dislike of what you refer to as the 'gadgetry', which I would have thought were simply tools of the trade," said Mr Thomas changing the subject. "How do you expect him to carry out his work without any tools."

"You make it sound so reasonable, but it isn't," thought Anna.

"I don't object to him having a few tricks up his sleeve, it's only to be expected and they're bound to be increasingly sophisticated. What I object to is his dependence on them. If they broke down he'd be in the shit," she said.

"Oops. I shouldn't have said that," thought Anna.

"But they don't break down. So its reasonable for him to depend upon them," said Mr Thomas. "Your hostility to computers is the most alarming aspect of this," again he pointed at the assignment.

"So that's it," thought Anna.

"Computers, especially the earlier ones, are delicate pieces of equipment. If you don't treat them properly they pack in. Look at the number of technicians the Polytechnic employs just to keep our computer going and that doesn't get thrown about the way his equipment does," said Anna.

"Let's see how he takes that," she thought.

"There's no reasoning with you is there," said Mr Thomas. "You just won't accept that you're wrong."

"You haven't listened to a word I've said," she thought.

"No," said Anna. "Because I'm right."

"I think you need to think things out," said Mr Thomas.

"What's there to think about," thought Anna. "You're a pillock and this is stupid."

"Are you in Hall of Residence?"

"Yes," said Anna.

"Right. I'll take you back there now."

"You don't need to," said Anna.

"I'm going to," said Mr Thomas. "You need to think things out by yourself and I want to make sure you do that."

"I don't like the sound of that," thought Anna.

"We can have another talk later," said Mr Thomas.

"Not if I can help it," thought Anna.

172

"Where's your car?" asked Anna.

"What!"

"Or do you intend us to walk to Wakefield Hall."

"It's in the car park."

"It would be," thought Anna.

"Lead on," she smiled broadly as he bumped into the bookshelf and knocked a stack of papers off.

"What will Mrs Smithers-Jones say," thought Anna. "A non-resident turning up before noon. Wonder if she'll let him in."

Anna unlocked the front door of Wakefield Hall.

"No Mrs Smithers-Jones? Is that why she said she hadn't seen Susan?" thought Anna looking round the entrance hall.

"Are you going to stand here all day?" asked Mr Thomas.

"What!" said Anna.

"For a moment there I forgot about him," she thought. "Don't start laughing. Not now."

"Your room," said Mr Thomas.

"I'm going," said Anna. "You don't have to accompany me to the door."

"I think I do," said Mr Thomas.

"You would," thought Anna.

"Guests aren't allowed in until noon," she said.

"I'm not a guest. I work at the Poly. Now get a move on," snapped Mr Thomas.

"Tetchy," thought Anna. "Oh well, I'd better sign in and go to my room like a good little girl."

"What are you doing now," shouted Mr Thomas.

"Signing in," said Anna. "It's the rules."

"Let me see," he said walking over to the book.

"You could sign the visitors book," said Anna. "But you're not a guest."

"No one in their right minds would invite you in," she thought then he started flicking through the book.

"For Christ's sake, I didn't have time to write anything and I wouldn't use any of the back pages, no one looks at them," snapped Anna.

"Anyway, I don't know what I'd write," she thought.

173

"So. Where's this room of yours?" he said looking up.

"I'm surprised you don't know that. Or do you," thought Anna heading for the stairs and her room, Mr Thomas following.

"So what happens next," she thought, unlocking the door to her room. "I suppose I'd better not slam the door in his smug little mug. Though it is a temptation. I'll just let it go, it'll shut itself."

"I'll talk to you this evening," he said catching the door and holding it open. "Lunch will be brought to you, along with your evening meal. You need to think by yourself. I don't want your contemplation to be interrupted by anything or anyone."

"And who the hell do you think you are. God Almighty himself," thought Anna. "Just don't think for one second that you're going to get away with this. I'll get you for this. Don't know how, don't know when, but I will."

Mr Thomas left, the door closing behind him, then Anna heard the click as he locked it.

"What on earth does he hope to achieve by that," thought Anna. "Even if I didn't have a key he couldn't lock me in. Not with that lock. So why the hell did he bother. To intimidate. And where the hell did he get the key. Perhaps this is just his way of saying 'I've got a key, you can't lock me out'. Feasible. Very. Though if I half turn the key in the lock and leave it there he won't be able to do that."

Anna stood in the middle of the room looking round.

"Mr Thomas is right. I do need time to think. But this isn't the place to do it. I've got to get away from here, from them. Best play it cagey though. Someone might be watching. I'll leave it an hour before I do anything. If they're still watching then, they'll watch all day and I hope they get piles for their pains. An hour of acting normal might lull them into thinking they've won.

So I've got an hour to kill. I ought to look natural, just in case, it might be paranoid, but there's no point taking chances. A coffee, listen to the radio, the usual things.

And when I'm gone. What then. What will they say, how will they explain it away. They'll think of something, there's no doubt, some half-way feasible lie. The annoying thing is they'll get away with it and there's nothing I can do to stop them. Unless.

I could write a note. Anyone watching would think I was working, rewriting the assignment, that'd throw them, make them think I don't realise

174

the seriousness of the situation. I do. I just don't understand how its got to this state. It's ridiculous. Totally. But they don't see it that way," Anna sighed and started writing to Christine.

The hour was nearly over, she folded the note up and wrote Christine's name and on the front.

"Right. Now to go. I can stick it under her door on the way. And she won't be back till after tea. When they find I'm gone they might search her room to see if I have left a note or something. So that's scuppered that idea. Anyway, what excuse would I have for going all the way up there. There are plenty of toilets closer. Toilets. I could nip out the French windows in the bathroom across the way. Get out down the ladder from the balcony. It'll get me near the mini, good job I didn't drive to lectures this morning, all the bin lorries in the area seemed to have converged outside the car park, so it was less stress to walk. Now it means that my car is on hand for a quick get away.

I could stick the note under someone else's door."

She added Christine's room number to the note.

"They can pass it on later, the quiet girl in the room next to the bathroom. Well, that's thought that through. I suppose I may as well do it."

Anna looked at the door.

"There must be something I've forgotten. Think. I intend to get out of here and drive off, won't get far without keys and cash, better not take too much it might look suspicious," she rummaged in her bag and put a few things in her pockets.

"That's everything," she thought glancing round the room.

"Deep breath. Now leave."

The landing was empty, the hall in silence.

"Act natural. There's no reason why I can't go to the toilet. No reason at all. It is the nearest toilet. Be bold. Walk across the middle of the landing. Slip the note under the door and get to the bathroom.

It's going to look a bit odd, me climbing down the fire escape, in clear view of Watkins Hall. It wouldn't look suspicious if the fire alarm was going," she thought and smashed the glass in a nearby fire alarm with the heel of her shoe. With the bells ringing fit to bust Anna left the bathroom through the French windows and climbed quickly down the fire escape ladder.

"And now for the car, before anyone notices I'm gone," she thought.

175

After driving for many hours down unfamiliar roads and through strange towns the landscape began to look familiar. Buildings rang bells, though she couldn't quite place where they were. She was almost home before she realised what she'd done.

Parking outside her parents home she paused for a moment.

"This is going to take a bit of explaining," she thought. "Still, I'm sure they'll understand, well they'll back me even if they don't," Anna rang the door bell, it was answered by her Mother.

"So you've come back then. He said you might," said Mum.

"Oh," said Anna. "Couldn't have got that one more wrong. The Poly's been in touch! But who? Mr Thomas I suppose. What's that bastard told them," the thoughts rushed through Anna's head.

"Well, don't just stand there looking stupid. Come in," said Mum holding the door open for her. "You'd better have a good explanation. Mr Thomas thinks you've taken leave of your senses. It's the only explanation he can come up with. Says you've a bee in your bonnet about the computer," said Mum.

"Did you sort out that enormous gas bill?" asked Anna, her mind wandering off on a tangent.

"Yes. It was a computer error, the decimal point was in the wrong place. They were most apologetic. But that's not the point," said Mum opening the living room door and blocking Anna's path to anywhere else.

"Yes, that is the point, very much the point," thought Anna. "But you're not in the mood to see it."

"Your Father and I were very disappointed in you. I thought you wanted a degree. I thought that was why you went to that Polytechnic," said Mum.

"You don't understand," bleated Anna.

"Don't we just," said Dad, appearing as if from nowhere. "We understand that you went away to learn and now you think you know more than your lecturers."

"You don't like what you're taught. So you blame them. You have the nerve to tell them they don't know what they're doing. Who do you think you are?" shouted Mum.

"They changed the syllabus," Anna tried to explain.

"And you're having a tantrum over it," said Mum.

"They got the computer to design the new syllabus," Anna started.

"And what's wrong with that. Computers do a lot of things perfectly

176

well," said Mum.

"Except gas bills," thought Anna.

"But the syllabus it produced is rubbish," Anna tried again.

"There you go again. You know best," said Mum.

"I know crap when I'm taught it and that's what that syllabus is full of," snapped Anna.

"I will not have you using that kind of language in this house. I don't know where you learnt it but I'm sure you never heard your Father or I talking like that," said Mum.

"I've picked up a lot of language like that on my course, it's amazing how much shit we talk about. Look Mum. That syllabus is rubbish. It doesn't cover the right subjects and I'm sure they're not allowed to change things as much as they have. The lecturers are just going along with it all because that's the easiest thing for them to do and because they don't want to risk losing their jobs," said Anna.

"They know what they're doing. It's their job after all," said Mum.

"If they knew what they were doing they'd be asking a lot of questions about this so called syllabus that the computer is slowly creating," snapped Anna.

"And why should they do that?" said Mum.

"How many times must I tell you. Because the syllabus the computer produced bears no resemblance to the course they are supposed to be teaching us," said Anna.

"I will not have you talking to your Mother like that, I don't know what's got into you. I suppose its some fancy ideas your so-called friends have been indoctrinating you with. But whilst you're in my house you will keep a civil tongue in your head," said Dad.

"I have not been indoctrinated with anything. I know what I'm talking about. I don't need anyone to tell me what to think. I've got a brain of my own and I'm perfectly capable of using it," said Anna.

"That's what you think," said Dad.

"And I suppose you think I'm some sort of imbecile," Anna started.

"If you're not going to listen to what your Mother or I have to say then you may as well go to your room and think over what you've done. I've got better things to do with my time than stand here arguing with you and so has your Mother," said Dad.

"That's just fine by me," said Anna storming out of the room.

"I'd get more understanding out of a brick wall than I would out of you

177

two," she thought slamming the living room door and taking the stairs two at a time. "Why in hell's name did I bother coming back here," she muttered flinging herself down on her bed and scowling into the darkness at the ceiling. "Anyone with half a brain would've known they wouldn't listen to a word I have to say. They never have done before. So why should they change the habit of a life-time.

Who are they ringing now? Are they going to tell the family about the disgrace I've brought on them. Get their version in before anyone has a chance of hearing the truth. Or are they ringing the Poly?" the question wandered into her mind. "No. No they wouldn't do that. They'll nag me to ring, but they wouldn't. Perhaps its Julia ringing her Dad. Come to think of it I haven't seen either her or little brother and it's not like him to stay away at a time like this and miss the chance to gloat.

Oh sod him," she thought. "I'm knackered."

The sun shining through the undrawn curtains eventually disturbed Anna. Rolling over in her sleep, she fell out of bed.

"What the hell," she muttered, trying to find which way was up.

"Where on earth am I?"

Lying on her back on the floor light began to dawn.

"Why the hell did I come here? What's the time? Where's my watch? Seven-thirty. And it's still ticking. So its probably right. I'd better get up. Try and reduce the things they can get at me for. God I feel rough. Maybe a shower. Then I'll sort out something clean to wear," Anna thought, heading for the bathroom.

"Look what the cat's dragged in," said Brian.

"Little brother. You wouldn't win any prizes for originality would you," she thought.

"Aren't you going to be late for work," said Anna, trying to get rid of him.

"What!" he muttered looking at his watch and checking that it was still ticking.

"You sod. You did that on purpose," he shouted at her, but Anna wasn't listening, she was busy making a dash for the bathroom, with a bath towel, whilst it was still empty.

A quarter of an hour later, she walked into the kitchen almost revived and refreshed.

"Let's hope they're in a better mood today," she thought, crossing her fingers and mentally touching wood.

178

"So you decided to get up today," said Dad, not lifting his glance from the newspaper.

"Like that is it," she thought, looking round the room.

"What's for breakfast?" she asked.

"Whatever you can be bothered to make yourself," said Mum.

"We're not here to wait on you," added Dad.

"I think I'll get some more orange juice," said Julia gazing at her empty glass.

"You stay where you are. I'll get some," said Mum. "And what do you think you're doing with that toaster," she added glaring at Anna.

"Making toast," said Anna, watching the two slices of bread in the toaster do absolutely nothing.

"You're going to have a long wait," said Dad. "The element blew last week."

"Thanks for telling me," muttered Anna, fishing out the bread.

"And how long were you going to leave a dead toaster lying round the kitchen, plugged in and looking ready to toast?" she thought.

"What was that?" snapped Mum.

"Is there any tea in the pot?" she asked.

"Have a look and you'll find out," said Mum.

"Thanks Mum," she thought, putting the bread under the grill and taking a look in the teapot.

"Well, there's something in there. Probably stewed to hell and gone. But it's warm. I'll give it a whirl," she thought.

"You can always make some fresh," said Mum. "If you can stir yourself."

"Stuff you," thought Anna. "I'll make myself a cup of coffee if that's your attitude."

"If you're not having that tea. I'll have it," said Dad holding out his mug.

"Worse than I expected," thought Anna topping up the mug. She only just managed to stop the teapot lid dropping out as the tea bags fell forward with a thump.

"What's burning," muttered Dad and Anna rushed to rescue her toast. Burnt black, it reminded her of the Poly.

"They're doing this on purpose," she thought furiously scraping the toast into the sink.

"I hope you're going to clean that up when you're finished making a

179

mess of my clean sink," said Mum.

"It's not going anywhere near your sink.   It's landing on these mucky dishes," Anna said.

"Dishes don't wash themselves," Mum replied.

"The devil finds work for ideal hands, but Mum gets in there quicker," she thought.

"I rang your Mr Thomas at the Polytechnic last night to tell him you were here," said Mum.

"What!" said Anna, nearly dropping her toast in the sink.

"He was very worried when you went missing, he didn't know where you'd gone or what you'd done," said Mum.

"My heart bleeds for him," she thought, buttering her toast.

"He was relieved to hear that you'd got home safely," said Dad.

"I bet he was," she thought.   "He would've been in the shit good and proper if anything had happened."

"And what else did he have to say, after enquiring after my health?" asked Anna.

"You can't just accept that the man was worried about you, can you," snapped Mum.

"No.   What else did he have to say?" Anna repeated her question.

"He thinks you need a rest.   Away from the Poly atmosphere.   A little time to think things out," she stopped for a moment, obviously waiting for a comment.

"About what I expected," thought Anna.

"He said that you're easily influenced and that mad girl, what was her name?" asked Mum.

"Susan?"

"Yes.   That was it.   He said she influenced you against the new syllabus and that you've been unsettled ever since she had to go away," Mum finished.

"I didn't need Susan to tell me the new syllabus was a pile of unmitigated crap," Anna started.

"Anna!   I told you yesterday what I think of that kind of language and I will hot have it used in my house," shouted Mum.

"How long have I got?" asked Anna, realising that she was not going to get anywhere trying to argue her case.

"What?" asked Mum.

"To do this thinking," said Anna.

180

"He said to give it a week or so," said Mum.

"And then?" asked Anna.

"He thought, perhaps we could all talk and decide what's best for you. You need time to calm down. See sense. That girl was a bad influence," said Dad.

"I'm not an imbecile. I've got a mind of my own," said Anna.

"So why don't you start using it. God knows you were always a difficult child," said Mum.

"Difficult, me. How was I difficult. Come on. I'd like to know," asked Anna.

"You were always so quiet. Too quiet," said Mum.

"With Brian around it was difficult to be heard," said Anna.

"You never tried. You never talked to us," said Dad.

"I'm talking now, but you won't listen," said Anna.

"You're the one who isn't listening. You're making things very difficult for your Dad and I," said Mum.

"Me! And how am I doing that," said Anna.

"You just are. I could do without the worry of all this. I've got enough to cope with," said Mum.

"It isn't exactly doing my degree a great deal of good either," snapped Anna.

"You should have thought that about that earlier," said Dad.

"And just learn whatever rubbish the computer spews out?" asked Anna.

"You're the one who wants a degree," said Mum.

"It shouldn't be this way," Anna shouted.

"You are taking me to the clinic aren't you?" asked Julia of Mum.

"Yes. Oh God, is that the time. We'd better be off. Have you got everything you need?" asked Mum.

"Yes," said Julia.

"Right then. Let's get going. You too Anna," said Mum.

"What do you want me for?" asked Anna. "I'm sure you can find the clinic perfectly well by yourself."

"You're coming and that's the end of that," said Mum.

"But Mum," Anna started.

"And I don't want another word from you," said Mum pushing her out of the kitchen in the direction of the garage.

"So much for thinking things out quietly, by myself, or even finishing my breakfast," thought Anna. "Perhaps they're worried I might do a bunk again. Or else they don't want to miss the opportunity to get at me. I thought the Maternity Hospital was further away than this. God the sight of this dump would put anyone off having kids. Maybe they should put it on posters."

"Don't just sit there," snapped Mum. "Help Julia out."

"It's OK, I can manage," said Julia.

"No it isn't. Anna can help you," snapped Mum.

"How long can the old bat keep this up," thought Anna. "Forever and a day at least."

That set the pattern of life, every time Mum went out, Anna had to go as well. If there was housework to do, Anna had to do it, whilst her Mum watched and told her that she was doing it all wrong.

"When am I going to get this time to think," Anna thought on the fourth day home.

"We're going to do some shopping for the twins," Mum announced.

"I hope you find what you're looking for," Anna said

"Can't they leave me here for once," she thought.

"Three pairs of eyes will make the looking easier," said Mum.

"Is Brian coming?" Anna asked.

"No. You are," said Mum.

"Do I have to," she muttered, knowing she didn't have any choice.

"Yes. So get ready now and don't keep us waiting," said Mum with a fixed smile, Julia wasn't looking so happy about it either.

A quarter of an hour later Anna was waiting in the hallway.

"What the hell takes them so long," she muttered, scowling at the stairs. "God knows, I'm ready and I don't even want to go," she thought and started absently flicking through the letters on the letter rack.

"That writing looks familiar," she thought pausing at one envelope. "It's addressed to me," she noted, picking it out. "How come no one told me about it. Post mark, 10th December, that's odd."

"Are you ready Anna," Mum's voice came floating down the stairs.

"Yes," shouted Anna, stuffing the letter quickly into her coat pocket.

"Good. I don't want you keeping us waiting," said Mum.

"Maybe I should take ages getting ready. Then they'd leave without me," she thought.

"God you look a mess," said Mum coming down the stairs.

"Thanks," said Anna.

"Can't you dress better than that.   I'm almost ashamed to be seen out with you," said Mum.

"I can always stay at home," said Anna hopefully.

"I'm sure you could, but your coming with us and that's the end of that," said Mum.

There then followed three of the most tedious hours of shopping Anna had ever had to endure, at the end of which Julia was nearly falling asleep on her feet and Anna was weighed down with shopping bags.

Day five started early, very early.

"Don't get the idea that you can spend all day in bed," shouted Mum battering on Anna's door.

"Where on earth would I get that idea from," thought Anna, rubbing the sleep from her eyes.

"You'd better be down in ten minutes.   I want the sheets off that bed so I can wash them," shouted Mum.

"And what else have you got lined up for me today," she thought gazing at the ceiling.   "Oh yes, the ironing as soon as the clothes are dry."

"Are you moving in there," shouted Mum.

"It's only eight o'clock," shouted Anna.

"Yes.   Well we can't all spend the day in bed.   Some of us have things to do and I'm not having you disrupting my day," said Mum.

"I see.   You're up, so everyone else has to be up too," thought Anna.

"You've got ten minutes, then I'm stripping that bed.   So you'd better be out of it," said Mum.

"Or you'll tip me on the floor and walk all over me.   I know," thought Anna.   "It's a good job I didn't come home for a rest or they'd have me decorating the whole house."

"Anyone in the bathroom?" she shouted to the closed door.

"Of course there isn't," said Mum bustling past.   "Everyone else has been up for ages.   They're not lazy like you.   And since you're moving, you can strip your bed for me and bring down anything else that needs washing."

"The bathroom's empty.   My God.   Run the flag up Julia isn't in there," thought Anna, almost colliding with Julia as she was leaving.

"Sorry," she muttered squashing herself against the wall so Julia could get past.

"The bathroom. The only place no one follows you and it's almost permanently occupied. God why can't they just leave me alone," she thought gazing at herself in the mirror. "If I was them I'd leave me alone. Well alone."

"Are you going to be in there all day," shouted Mum.

"For Christ's sake. I've only just got in here," shouted Anna.

"I've told you what I think about that sort of language," said Mum.

"Yes," thought Anna. "It's all right for anyone except me."

"And there's no need to sulk," shouted Mum.

"Who's sulking? I'm just trying to clean my teeth in peace," said Anna.

"If you'd stirred yourself a bit earlier," Mum started.

"I'd have got in Dad and Brian's way as they were getting ready for work," said Anna.

"Instead you're getting in my way whilst I'm doing the washing," said Mum.

"That's it," thought Anna.

"Do you want the laundry bin?" she asked.

"It would make things easier for me. After all its hard to wash the contents, with me this side of the door and it the other," Mum started.

"Here," said Anna, opening the bathroom door, dumping it in the corridor and closing the door.

"Perhaps I can have some peace," she thought.

"There's no need to be like that," said Mum.

"I was only trying to help," she said.

"God knows why. Whatever I do is wrong," she thought looking back at the mirror.

"Humph," said Mum, busy emptying the laundry bin down the stairs. "Put this back when you've finished in there," she added slamming the laundry bin down by the door.

"It's not surprising Dad avoids this place like the plague. Stand still for thirty seconds and you have a list of jobs the length of your arm," thought Anna.

"Did you hear me," shouted Mum.

"Yes Mummy," shouted Anna and returned to her room to strip the bed and throw the bed linen down the stairs. Then, she followed it down,

184

kicking the laundry ahead of her as she went and gathering it all up when she got to the bottom.

"I've got to get away," thought Anna. "This is just impossible. And so is getting away. Unless I sneak out, like a thief in the dark. I suppose it's a possibility. I'll see how I feel tonight."

"When are you going to bring those sheets down?" Mum's voice rose up the stairs.

"Here they are," said Anna handing them over.

"Tonight. About two o'clock. When everyone's sound asleep, I'm out of here," thought Anna. "What's the betting its my turn to do the ironing."

"I hope you've made your bed," said Mum, dumping it all on the kitchen floor, the washing machine was already in action.

"No," said Anna watching as it began a spin.

"It won't make itself," snapped Mum.

"I guessed that," thought Anna.

"What are you doing?" asked Mum.

"Making a cup of tea. Do you want one," said Anna.

"And when do you plan to make your bed?" Mum asked

"Sometime before I go to sleep in it," thought Anna. "What's the big rush. You were belly aching for the sheets and now you won't need them for ages."

"After breakfast," she said smiling.

"I assume you don't want a cup of tea," she thought as Mum walked out of the kitchen, followed closely by Julia.

"Well, that's got rid of them. Don't know how, must be the soap I'm using. I'd better use it again, it has such a wonderful effect. Shame it won't last. Perhaps if I stop in my room after I've made my bed. They might forget about me. Unlikely, but there's no reason why I can't try it on."

An hour later Mum hammered on Anna's door.

"Haven't you finished making that bed yet," she shouted.

"Hell, I nearly jumped out of my skin," thought Anna quickly hiding a bag of clothes in the back of the wardrobe.

"I was just giving my room a bit of a tidy," said Anna, looking round, everything was in its place, as always.

185

"That wouldn't take long," said Mum.

"Sarcastic cow," thought Anna. "You drummed tidiness into me from an early age. Only little brother could get away with any mess."

"Well. When you've finished that mammoth task. You can come down and join Julia and me in the front room. We'd hate to think of you sulking away all by yourself," said Mum when Anna made no reply.

"I see. Come down inside five minutes or there's going to be one hell of a row," thought Anna.

"I'll be down in a couple of minutes," she said looking round the small room.

"If you think I'm going to jump just because you've commanded it, you can think again," Anna thought. "True I'm coming down because I've been told to, but I don't have to do it straight away."

"There'll be a cup of tea waiting for you when you come down. If you want one," said Mum.

"Yes. Thanks," said Anna.

"Right. I'll see you downstairs in a couple of minutes," said Mum.

"Probably before the kettles boiled," said Anna, putting her favourite pen in her handbag. Carefully standing the bottle of ink up in the bottom and leaning the bag against the desk.

"I suppose I'd better go down," she thought, looking round the room, though she didn't know quite what for.

"Oh well," she muttered. "It would be nice having a cup of tea made for me for once."

"So you've decided to join us have you," said Mum as Anna wandered into the front room. Julia looked up from her knitting and wished she hadn't. By the looks of it she had just unravelled a bit and was in the middle of picking up the stitches when Anna had walked in. She was looking speechless as a couple of stitches laddered their way down to the cast on edge.

"I couldn't resist the offer of a cuppa," said Anna smiling.

"If that happened to me I'd be furious," she thought. "Mind, I'd have been a bit more careful picking up the stitches. She's going to have to unravel the whole lot and start again. It's the only thing she can do."

"A cup of tea would be nice," said Julia still looking at the knitting.

"Anna. Be a good girl and put the kettle on," said Mum.

"Nice," thought Anna. "Offer me a cup of tea, then tell me to make it myself."

186

"I suppose you want one too," she said to her Mum.

"Yes. Of course," said Mum.

"Professional tea maker am I," she thought. "I wondered what my role in life was."

"I wonder what Mandy wants," said Anna.

"What?" said Mum as the door bell rang.

"That's her now," said Anna as Mum rushed off to the front door. Unfortunately she closed the door on her way, so Anna couldn't hear anything, however, she wasn't long in bringing back the news.

"Mandy's little boy isn't feeling too well," said Mum.

"So?" thought Anna.

"Nothing infectious?" asked Julia looking worried.

"We don't want any German measles bugs round here," thought Anna.

"He's got a touch of flu. Poor little soul. He's got such a terrible cough," said Mum.

"She should get a doctor," said Julia.

"She has. He just left," said Mum.

"Oh well. He'll be all right then," said Julia.

"Very touching, your faith in the medical profession," thought Anna.

"The doctor left a prescription," said Mum.

"Probably for the cough," said Julia pulling the needles out of her knitting and starting to unravel it.

"The problem is getting the prescription," said Mum.

Julia looked up from her knitting puzzled.

"Where's the problem in that?" thought Anna.

"She can't take him to the Chemists, he's not really well enough to go and she can't exactly leave him at home by himself," said Mum, explaining what seemed obvious to her, but not them.

"She doesn't want us to look after him does she?" asked Julia.

"No. He's too grizzly. The mood he's in she wouldn't impose him on anyone else," said Mum.

"So what does she want us to do?" asked Anna.

"Nip down to the Chemists and get the prescription for her," said Mum. "It won't take long and it might help soothe the poor dears cough."

"I could do with going to the Chemists," said Julia.

"Well we can all go then," said Mum.

"Once more no one bothers to ask me," thought Anna. "Well, I'm not going this time."

187

In the kitchen the washing machine went into the first of many spins.

"I can't leave the machine to run by itself," said Mum.

"I do need to go to the Chemist," said Julia.

"We can't wait till the machine finishes," said Mum. "Baby Philip needs his medicine now."

"I don't need to go do I?" said Anna. "I can watch the machine."

"That's true," said Julia. "Anna can watch the machine."

"I don't know," Mum looked uncertain.

"It's either that or leave the machine run by itself," said Julia.

"And you know what happened when Aunty Mary's machine overheated," added Anna, her fingers mentally crossed.

"We won't be gone long," said Julia.

"All right," said Mum.

"Isn't it nice to be trusted," thought Anna.

"If anything happens, just turn the machine off," Mum started.

"Don't worry," said Anna.

"God. You'd think it was some temperamental nuclear power station, liable to blow up at any second, rather than a pretty sedate domestic washing machine, which in the last four years hasn't even succeeded in over-sudding, let alone flooding the kitchen," thought Anna.

"Right," said Mum. "We won't be long."

"Don't tell me they're actually going to leave me alone in the house," thought Anna as the front door slammed shut. "My God. They are. I don't believe it. I've just got to see them go," she thought and dashed up to her room in time to watch them drive off down the road. "Why wait till two in the morning," Anna muttered, pulling the bag out from the bottom of the wardrobe and her sleeping bag from on top of it, then, picking up her handbag and grabbing her coat she made her way to the front door.

"Now all I have to do is get in the mini and go," Anna told herself. "Simple." Yet her hand hesitated on the door knob.

The sun shinning brightly on the concrete drive seemed set to dazzle her.

"Bet all the lace curtains in the neighbourhood are twitching like mad," she thought, keeping her eyes fixed on the mini, as if by doing so she could prevent anyone from stopping her. Not that they should have any reason to.

Opening the car door, she took the opportunity for a brief glance round the street.

188

"Nothing moving. Or so it seems. Knowing them though, the bush telegraph will already be spinning into action. The casual observer might think that Mrs Bainbridge is engrossed in tidying up her garden, but those leaves have been on the ground since the beginning of autumn, if she was that fastidious she'd have cleared them away ages ago."

She dumped her handbag and coat on the passenger seat. The bag from the wardrobe and her sleeping bag she threw on the back seat.

"So far so good," she muttered getting into the drivers seat.

"That's better," she thought with a sigh as she slammed the door shut, put on her seat belt and started the engine. She took the hand brake off and started down the road in the opposite direction to the one in which Mum and Julia had just gone.

"There's no point in looking for trouble," she thought, instinctively heading away from the shops and the part of town where she was likely to be seen by either her Mother's cronies, or worse still, her Grandmother's friends. It was difficult avoiding them.

"They could teach MI5, the CIA and the KGB a thing or ten about surveillance and information gathering. So unobtrusive, they all look the same, out to lunch, but they miss nothing. They may be old, but they're far from gaga."

Anna drove through a part of town she'd never gone through before, in the hope that she would not be seen by anyone she knew, or who knew her. Consequently she headed out of town in a direction she'd never gone before and was soon hopelessly lost, but she wasn't in the least bit bothered about that, all she wanted to do was get away.

As the sun began to set she found herself driving down a quiet tree lined country lane. A place where twilight had already arrived. Rounding a corner she almost halted in her tracks at the awesome sight of the sun slowly descending into the sea. She drove the rest of the way to the coast, pulled off the road and came to a halt.

"That's far enough," she thought, yawning and stretching. "I think I'll stretch my legs, get a bit of fresh air and have a better look at this sunset. Perhaps I could think things out a bit, try and work out how on earth things have got to this state."

An hour or so later, as a cold wind blew up from the sea. Anna shivered. "It's getting a bit nippy. And dark. I must need my head seeing to, standing here freezing."

Taking a last look in the direction of the sea, Anna went back to her car. Wrapping her coat round her, she turned the engine on in an attempt to get some warmth back into herself.

"So much for finding the answers," she thought. "I've just come up with more questions, the main one for the moment being what the hell do I do next."

The clock in the car read 2.00 am.

"I doubt if that's right," she thought. "God knows why I keep it, it doesn't work properly. Just tells whatever time it feels like. Mind you, it does feel like two in the morning. Perhaps this is a suitable time to go to sleep. Curl up in my sleeping bag on the back seat. That sounds quite appealing, but first I'd better lock the doors. Can't see me getting much sleep unless they are locked," thought Anna, checking the passenger side door.

"That's locked."

Then she turned to the driver's side door.

"Shit. That doesn't lock from the inside. I could lock it through the window. But it doesn't slide too well, I'll nearly rupture myself opening it, not to mention shutting it afterwards. This is going to take a bit of thinking."

Anna sat for a moment, looking from one door to the other.

"I know," she thought.

Unlocking the passenger door and climbing out of the drivers side door.

"Oh my God, its freezing," she muttered, as the wind from the sea caught her, slammed the door shut and locked it.

"I can't see a blasted thing," she muttered, her hand on the car she felt her way round to the passenger side door. The wind nearly snatched the door out of her hand when she opened it, leaping into the passenger seat she slammed the door shut behind her.

"Now all I have to do is lock this door and climb into my sleeping bag," she thought looking at the back seat. "It's on there somewhere. Just because I can't see it. Well here goes," she thought, locking the door and climbing into the back of the car. There was a brief battle getting her sleeping bag out of its bag, which wasn't grateful for her efforts, as it took over the whole of the back of the car even though there wasn't really anywhere to put it, let alone lay it out flat so that she could get into it.

"These bags have got to go somewhere else," she thought contemplating the back seat. "The front passenger seat." She pushed the sleeping bag to one side and started heaving the bags over the seat backs into place.

"Now to lay out the sleeping bag," she thought, expecting a further battle, but it capitulated, Anna scrambled into it and fell into an exhausted sleep.

Anna awoke to find the sleeping bag over her head. Panic ruled as she fought her way out of the smothering darkness.

"Thank God for that," she sighed, looking at the sleeping bag in the floor pan.

"Good morning world," she muttered. "God, do I feel rough or do I feel rough? I should think I feel rough," she thought stuffing the sleeping bag back into its bag. "Oh I could kill for some breakfast. Talk of breakfast, that was the last meal I ate yesterday. My stomach thinks my throats been cut." Looking round at the sea, the empty road and the deserted countryside.

"I'm not going to get any breakfast here, wherever here is. So, I'd better head off down the road to see what I can find."

An hour later Anna was sitting in a picnic area, eating sandwiches and drinking a cup of tea bought from a caravan. She'd been to the toilet, had a wash, brushed her hair and was feeling more human. It was whilst she was paying for her breakfast that she found the letter, the one that had been hidden at the back of the letter rack. Her breakfast finished, her mind went back to it.

"Let's have a look," she thought, fishing it out of her coat pocket. "The writing is definitely familiar. Where's the post mark say it's from? I don't know anyone who lives there. Least, I don't think I do. Well, that's the envelope examined, I'm not going to find out anything more till I open it. So, in for a penny in for a pound."

She opened the envelope. Inside was a small scrap of paper, roughly folded in four, it looked as though it had been torn from a book, she unfolded it carefully.

191

"It's from Susan!" she muttered.

Dear Anna,
I don't know if you'll get this. They've put me in a loony bin.
For my own good. That's what they say. They just want to
shut me up. Something has got to be done to stop them. I don't
know what. It's difficult to think here, so its down to you to
stop them before they do any more damage. Be careful, or they'll
put you in here too.
  Help me, please, you're my only hope of getting out of here.

  Susan.

Anna read the letter several times and looked at the post mark again.
  "They kept this from me. They did it on purpose. But why?" Anna
gazed out of the window and shook her head. "It doesn't matter, at least
they didn't destroy it and now I've got it. But what can I do. Susan's
relying on me, but what does she expect me to do!" Anna closed her eyes,
the half formulated idea of just disappearing, like so many people
disappear, would have to be shelved.
  "If Susan was here," thought Anna, turning over the envelope in her
hands and catching sight of the post mark. "She shouldn't be in a loony
bin. I've got to get her out of there," she thought fishing out the atlas from
one of the large side pockets in the back of the car. "Now, let's see if I can
find this place she's in. Then all I need to do is find out where I am and I
can get there."

Chapter 11
The Asylum

Night saw Anna, in her car, parked down a dark back alley near the psychiatric hospital. She had driven hard all day, but the journey was long and she had arrived too late to visit, but had found the building, a large place, at least four floors tall and very wide, the depth was impossible to judge in the dark.

"So much for the idea of the great escape," she thought walking down the nearly deserted pavements back to her car. "There's nothing I can do now, she could be anywhere in that place and I don't fancy another night in this crate," she unlocked the door and climbed in. "I'd best try and find a guest house or something," she decided and started up the engine.

After about half an hour she came across a small, rather tatty looking guest house. She parked the mini on the forecourt, turned the engine off and the silence closed in around her.

"I can't do this," she thought looking at the front door, then she looked round the inside of the car. "Do you really want to sleep in this again," she told herself. "The worst they can say is there's no room in the inn, then you'll be no worse off," she added and got out of the car.

It seemed an age before anyone answered the door bell.

"Hello," she said nervously to the lady who opened the door. "I'm looking for a room for the night."

"Is it just for you?" she asked.

"Yes. Just me," said Anna.

"I do have a single room. If you'd like to follow me," she said opening the door wide.

"Where is this room, on the roof!" thought Anna, a few minutes later and the lady started up the stairs to the forth floor. The room, when they found it, was in the attic, up another flight of stairs.

"Hell, I didn't think the building was this tall!" thought Anna.

"This is the room," said the lady, opening the door.

"What am I supposed to do?" thought Anna. "Go in and look round I

193

suppose, it would be logical.   Is this a room or a cupboard? I thought some of the rooms in the Poly were small but.   Oh well, its only for the one night and it looks clean."

"This'll be fine," she muttered.

"I hope that's the right thing to say," she thought.

"Good," said the lady.   "Here's the key.   If you come downstairs you can sign the book."

"Thank-you," said Anna.

"A bit like Poly," she thought starting down the stairs.

"We start serving breakfast at seven thirty.   The dining room is in the basement," said the lady.

"What more stairs," thought Anna.

"We do a full cooked breakfast," the lady continued.

"Talking of breakfast. I'm starving," thought Anna.

"Is there somewhere round here that I can get something to eat," Anna asked.

"There's a Chinese Restaurant just round the corner," said the lady. "Now, here's the book," she added, pointing to a large black book on a table in the hall.

Name, address and signature it asked for.

"Real name and address, or shall I make one up.   The real one, no one'll expect me to use it and by the time anyone traces me I'll be long gone."

"Thank-you," said the lady as Anna put the pen down.

"If you turn left out of the door, take the first road on the left, you'll be able to see the Chinese Restaurant."

"Thank-you," said Anna.

"God, I'm starving," she thought.   "I hope they don't have too long a queue."

An hour later Anna was back in the attic room, perched on the bed eating mushroom curry and chips.

"That fills one hell of a hole," she thought mopping up the last of the curry sauce with the remaining chips and opening up a can of Coke.

"That's good. Blissful. I feel tons better. I suppose I'd better get back to the question of Susan and what to do next," she thought.   "The building I saw was enormous, without any knowledge of the place, or where abouts in it she is, assuming she's in there in the first place, it is difficult to make any solid plans.   I can't find out any of this without going there.   I could visit her.   It would be the last place they'd expect me to go, so they probably won't have warned the staff. It is a risk, but, it's got to be done. Right, that's decided on, I'll go after breakfast. Then what? I'll just have to play it by ear," she thought yawning. "One thing, there's no point in tackling tomorrow knackered. I'd better get some sleep whilst I've got a bed to sleep on."

The alarm clock dragged her from a bad dream. She was trying desperately to get out of a building. But she didn't know the way. Running through endless corridors, everywhere she turned men in white coats kept telling her how tired she was and inviting her to rest, but the rooms they showed her turned into padded cells with barred windows high in the walls. All she could hear was Susan screaming for help. Shaking her head, as if to empty the dream out, she got dressed and headed down to the dining room.

Breakfast was both good and plentiful. When she told the lady she was a vegetarian there was no fuss, she produced a most substantial mushroom omelette which set Anna up beautifully for whatever the day could throw at her. At nine o'clock she parked her mini near to the asylum, but out of sight of the main entrance.

"Now to tackle the men in white coats," she said, taking a deep breath. "I shouldn't think its visiting time now, but at least I should find out when it is. All I have to do is look calm. Act as if it's an everyday occurrence. Visiting a friend in a loony bin. Sure I do it all the time. And remember, no laughing or calling it a loony bin or you'll never get out and no more talking to yourself, it's a bad habit and one likely to get you locked up."

Entering the door of the asylum, she walked up to a desk marked reception.

"This looks the place to ask," she thought. "Or it would be if there was someone here."

Press the button for attention, said the sign.

"OK." she muttered.

A couple of minutes later a rather flustered looking nurse emerged from the door.

"Is there anything I can do to help you?" she enquired.

"A friend of mine. Susan Lake. Is staying here. I wondered if it would be possible to see her?" asked Anna.

"Susan Lake. Certainly. I can take you along to see her now. I'm sure it would do her a power of good to see a familiar face," said the nurse.

"Good," muttered Anna, with a smile. "I didn't expect this," she thought.

"Before you see her, I'd better warn you, she is sedated, so don't expect too much from her," the nurse smiled.

"Sedated!" Anna said, before she could stop herself.

"It's for her own good. We thought she would have settled down by now, but she doesn't seem to be showing any signs of doing so," the nurse added, leading Anna into a big room full of arm chairs.

"There she is," said the nurse, but Anna didn't recognise any of the people sitting so still on a group of arm chairs.

The nurse walked up to one girl.

"Susan. A friend of yours has come to see you," she said, but there was no response.

"Would you like to take her into the garden for a walk?" the nurse asked Anna. "The early spring flowers are very pretty just now."

"Yes," said Anna. "That would be nice."

"Stand up Susan," said the nurse getting hold of Susan's arms and hoisting her to her feet. "If you go out of that door, turn right, the door ahead of you leads to the garden," she added.

"How the hell am I going to get her to go anywhere!" thought Anna staring at Susan.

"Don't worry, just take her by the arm and she'll follow wherever you go," the nurse added with a smile, almost as if she had read Anna's mind.

"Fair enough," thought Anna, taking Susan's arm and leading her out into the garden, the nurse disappeared before Anna had even got to the door.

"I don't know what I expected," she thought. "But this wasn't it. Why did she have to be sedated. I was hoping she could come up with some ideas, some suggestions as to what to do next," Anna looked at Susan. "But talking to her would be like talking to a shop dummy. The only difference is this one walks. She must have gone down hill a lot since she wrote the letter. Either that or she's more sedated. I can't see her being able to hold a pen let alone write with it, not in this state," Anna headed away from the building, out into the large garden in search of the pretty flowers and some inspiration.

"What's that noise," she thought, the sound of a distant ringing attracting

196

her attention. "Such large grounds. I didn't think we'd got so far from the buildings. There's smoke coming from that window. This isn't a fire is it," she thought as a siren started wailing in the distance. A gate near the two of them was flung open and a fire engine rushed through. The people standing by the gate ran behind the engine to help in anyway possible. Anna stood and watched them hurrying past and disappear towards the building.

"There doesn't seem to be anyone watching the gate," she thought. "I wonder if anyone would notice if we just walked out."

On her way past the gates Anna took off her coat and draped it round her friends shoulders in an attempt to hide the institutional clothing.

"That looks better," she thought, catching her arm and guiding her round a lamp post, "And there's the mini. No one seems to have noticed as yet, but there's no point in hanging around. Now to get you into the car," Anna said to Susan, holding on to her arm whilst she unlocked the drivers door. "Now to climb in and unlock the passenger door," she thought, letting go of her friend in order to do so."

"Right. I've done that," she thought and looked up to see Susan walk into a fence on the other side of the road.

"Oh bloody hell," she muttered dashing over to retrieve her. "Thank God there's no traffic, she could've been flattened."

Anna guided her back to the car and opened the passenger door.

"All you have to do is get in and sit down," she muttered, but there was no response, so Anna pushed her towards the seat. Susan fell the last foot or two. Anna picked up her feet and put them inside the car, slammed the door shut and dashed round to the drivers door and climbed in.

"Maybe I should've left her there," thought Anna looking at Susan. "The lights are on but no one's home. Let's hope whatever they gave her wears off and quickly."

The sound of a siren made Anna freeze, she saw an ambulance dash down a road at right angles to the one in which she was parked.

"I've got to get out of here," she thought grabbing Susan's seat belt and fastening it as tightly as possible. "Let's hope that'll keep her still, I don't want her trying to help me drive."

A second siren went past, Anna started the car up and glanced at Susan. "I could pretend she was asleep if it wasn't for those eyes. Perhaps sunglasses," she thought, fishing a pair out from the door pocket and carefully balanced them on Susan's face.

197

"Well, it's a bit of an improvement. Now she only looks pretentious," thought Anna, heading off, away from the sound of the sirens.

By mid-day she was beginning to flag, she saw a sign by the roadside, tea and sandwiches, all in the next lay-by. A couple of hundred yards further on, there was 'Kate's cafe', a caravan on the verge. Leaving Susan still belted into the car, Anna got some sandwiches and tea. She handed a sandwich to Susan, who did nothing.

"This is going to be harder than I thought," Anna took the sandwich off Susan and wrapped it up again. "I'd best move the car somewhere else, people are going to stare."

Five minutes later Anna parked the car in a lay-by and made a second attempt at feeding Susan.

"I hope you appreciate what I'm doing for you," she said to Susan. "Here," she added, putting a sandwich into her hand, bringing the hand up to Susan's mouth, she prized the mouth open and pushed a corner of the sandwich in. It was then that Susan got the hang of it and started eating.

"Thank God for that," thought Anna and started tucking into her own sandwiches. She only paused to put a second sandwich into Susan's hand.

"And now for the tea," thought Anna, picking up the polystyrene beaker. "Warm, but not too hot to hold. Now, if I just put her hand round it. That's it."

Susan put the beaker to her mouth and started drinking.

"Good. That's right. You're getting there," said Anna carefully watching until a puzzled look on Susan's face made her suspect that the tea was finished.

"Let's see what's wrong," said Anna trying to prize the beaker out of Susan's hand.

"It's empty," said Anna, showing the beaker to her. "It's all gone. You've drunken it." There was no response. Anna drank her own tea, it was cold.

Whilst she drank it a caravan drove past.

"That's a thought," she said. "We could rent a caravan for a few days whilst whatever they gave her wears off. Once she's back to normal we can think about what to do next. All we need to do is find a nice quiet camp site where we can rent a caravan cheaply. Money, money, money. I suppose I'd better get some out of the bank. I just hope it lasts for, good question. How long does it need to last. Oh well, I've not long put my grant cheque in and I haven't paid my hall fees. I'll just have to try and make it last as long as possible.   When it runs out.   I'll sort out that problem when it happens.   I can't worry about it now.   It's just too much and there are too many improbables.   Anyway, it might never happen, someone might find us and put us both in a loony bin.

First though, a petrol station.   I am rather low on petrol."

It was late evening, Anna was totally lost and had been for the last few hours.   She was driving down a quiet country road for two reasons, one being that a quiet camp site would be down a quiet road, not off a dual carriage way, the other being, they might be looking for her and Susan and for some reason a black mark one mini gets noticed.

Now the sky was darkening and Anna was beginning to resign herself to another night in the car.   She was trying to work out how to organise things when she saw the camp site sign pointing up a one lane track.

"May as well give it a whirl," she thought.   "It might be open and they may just have a caravan to rent, though it is unlikely, no one else has had, or at least they haven't admitted to having one which adds up to the same."

At the end of the road was on old farmhouse built into the slope of the hill.   The house at one end of the building, a barn at the other.   All very reassuring.   Anna drew up to the garden gate, the sound of ferocious barking near by made her jump.

"It's all noise.   If they were loose, they'd have eaten me by now," she tried telling herself as she walked up the garden path to the front door.   The door opened almost instantly.

"With those dogs, who needs a door bell," thought Anna.

"Hello," said the woman who opened the door.   She looked the image of the farmers wife, ageing now, but still emitting a warm friendly atmosphere, a welcome for any traveller.

"Hello," said Anna, for a moment lost for words.

"What can I do to help you?" asked the farmers wife.

"Oh.   My sister and I.   We were wondering if we could rent a caravan here for a few days," said Anna, wondering if perhaps a rephrasing of the question might produce a better result.

"Yes certainly.   I've got a small caravan, I cleaned it out this morning for the start of the season.   You'll be welcome to that.   If you'll drive round the back I'll show you.   Just follow the track round to the left, ignore the gate on your left, go right through the one up the hill and the caravan's on the far left. I'll be along with you in a couple of minutes."

"Oh. Right," said Anna and walked back to the car. A couple of minutes later she was standing by the caravan door with the friendly lady from the farmhouse.

"Doesn't your sister want to see it as well?" she asked unlocking the door.

"Oh, she's asleep at the moment and I wouldn't want to disturb her. She's been very tired lately. We thought a holiday would do her the world of good. I like to let her sleep as much as possible and not worry her about anything," said Anna.

"Oh dear. Are you sure it isn't something more serious than that, I mean some people think they're over tired and it turns out they have cancer of something or other?" said the farmers wife.

"I don't think so. She's just worked herself to a standstill. Studies too much. Always has her head in a book. I'm hoping that the rest will sort things out," said Anna.

"Wouldn't she be better off at home?" asked the farmers wife.

"Now what do I say," thought Anna.

"She's got enough books there to start a library. It'd be impossible to get her to rest. Anyway, Mum'd have a blue fit if she saw her like this and she's not been so well lately, I don't know what this would do to her," said Anna, saying the first thing that came into her head.

"What if your sister doesn't get better?" asked the farmers wife.

"I think I ought to give it a few days rest before I worry about that," said Anna.

"One lie leads to another and now I'm digging a hole deep enough to bury myself in," she thought. "I just hope she stops asking questions, I don't know how many more answers I can make up."

"Well, if you're sure," said the farmers wife. "If you need any help though. If there's anything I can do."

"Thank-you," said Anna. "I think we'll be all right, but it's nice of you to offer."

"Well, if you like the caravan," the farmers wife asked

"Oh yes. It's fine, thank-you," said Anna.

"I'll leave you two in peace to settle in," she said.

"Thank-you," said Anna.

"Oh. The toilets are in the block over there," she added and headed off back down the hill.

"Thank-you," said Anna looking down the hill at the distant out-building. For a moment things didn't look very clear, then she saw Susan starting to move in the car.

"Oh bloody hell," Anna muttered and dashed over to the mini before Susan could do anything like take the handbrake off.

"Anna," mumbled Susan.

"I'm here. You're OK," said Anna sliding into the drivers seat.

"It is you? You're not just saying it are you?" asked Susan.

"What have they done to you," thought Anna.

"Of course it's me. We're sitting in my mini," said Anna.

"It's dark! Why's it dark?" asked Susan, starting to panic.

"We're in my car and the interior light doesn't work," said Anna

"I want to go to the toilet," said Susan.

"Hang on a minute," said Anna, fishing out a roll of toilet paper. Which she'd bought earlier that day, when she stopped briefly for food. Toilets on camp sites seldom have toilet paper and she thought it was best to be prepared.

Anna locked the car and they stumbled down the hill to the distant out building. It had two doors, one marked Gentlemen, the other Ladies. Susan headed for the first door.

"Not that one," said Anna grabbing her arm and gently pointing her to the Ladies.

A fluorescent light illuminated two hand basins, each with only one tap, two mirrors and two toilet cubicles which were far from identical, the only similarity being the lack of toilet paper and the profusion of dead insects.

"You'll need some toilet paper," said Anna.

"I hope she can manage this for herself," she thought.

"Oh yes," said Susan, holding out her hand.

"Right," muttered Anna reeling out a few feet of paper. "I'll be in the next cubicle," she added to Susan's disappearing back.

"God knows what I'll do if you need me," she thought. "But I'll be in the next cubicle."

On leaving the toilet she found Susan wandering from one hand basin to the other and back again looking rather perplexed.

"There's no hot tap," she said. "How can I wash my hands if there's no hot tap."

"There's a hot tap in the caravan. You can wash your hands there," said

Anna, her fingers crossed behind her back.

"I want to wash my hands and there's no hot tap," Susan persisted.

"You can wash your hands in the caravan. There's a hot tap in there," said Anna.

"I just hope there's some hot water in it," thought Anna.

"Caravan?" asked Susan.

"It's up the hill. I thought we could stay there for a few days until your mind's a bit clearer," said Anna.

"And I can wash my hands?" asked Susan.

"In the caravan. Yes," said Anna.

"Where is it?" asked Susan.

"Come on. I'll show you," said Anna.

"Assuming I can find it," said Anna looking up the hill into the darkness.

It took a little time to find the caravan, it didn't help that Susan kept wandering off, she found the mini by walking into it and from there, once Anna got her bearings, it was easy to find the caravan and then the key hole. Soon Anna had the door unlocked and opened.

"It's dark in there," said Susan standing in the doorway.

"Not for much longer," said Anna, taking a deep breath and mentally crossing her fingers as she flicked the light switch and a rather dim bare electric light did it's best to illuminate the interior of the small static caravan.

"Thank God it didn't have gas mantles," thought Anna. "I hate the bloody things. They petrify me. They're so hit and miss."

"Can I wash my hands now?" asked Susan still standing in the doorway. Her question brought Anna back from her mental meanderings to the caravan and the consolidating light from a fluorescent tube which was illuminating a small round basin with a mixer tap curving over it.

"Sure. Make yourself at home. I'll fish the soap out of the car," she added.

"If I can find it in the dark. God knows where it is," she thought.

"In my handbag," the thought flashed across her brain, she pictured herself putting it there. It had made the bag difficult to close.

"The bag's on my shoulder. Here," she said handing it over. Susan took it and went over to the hand basin.

"The water's cold," she said washing her hands.

"Oh God," muttered Anna.

"I'll ask about heating it tomorrow," she said. "I'll get the things out of the car," she added before Susan noticed that there wasn't a towel to dry her hands on. Anna brought her bags in first, followed by the sleeping bags and lastly the food and a towel she'd picked up at a market they passed somewhere along the road.

"There's no towel," started Susan as Anna came in with the last load form the car.

"Here," said Anna, dumping the towel in her hands and turning to put the things away.

"Let's see what the cupboards are like," she thought opening the nearest one.

"Plates, cups, knives, forks, pans, that solves what we eat off. Next on. Blankets. I was wondering how we'd cope with only one sleeping bag. Next cupboard, empty, looks clean, the food can go in there, its all in tins and packets."

"Have we got a tin opener?" asked Susan.

"What?" snapped Anna, startled by the comment.

"Have we got a tin opener?" repeated Susan

"Yes. There's one on my penknife. Why?" asked Anna.

"Why what?" asked Susan. "Why am I holding this?" she added looking at the towel as if it was a space alien.

"Hand it here," said Anna, holding out her hand for the towel.

"What do you want?" asked Susan as Anna took the towel and put it by the side of the hand basin.

"What the hell do I do now!" she thought, looking at the ceiling for inspiration.

"I'm hungry," said Susan.

"Of course you are," Anna smiled. "You sit here and I'll get something sorted," she added guiding her friend to the seats at the far end of the caravan. "I'll just get the rest of the food from the car."

Anna dashed out, took a deep breath of night air and then opened the car and fished out a carrier bag from behind the drivers seat. She was only gone for a couple of minutes, but when she got back, Susan was standing in the middle of the caravan looking wildly round her.

"Anna, thank God, where were you? where are we? what's happening?" a barrage of questions came from Susan who was flailing her arms around in a rather alarming manner.

"It's alright," Anna said, putting the bag down and walking over to

203

comfort her friend. "I was just getting some food from the car."

"I'm hungry," said Susan, looking surprised, as if the idea hadn't crossed her mind before.

"You sit here and I'll sort out something to eat," Anna assured her friend, carefully guiding her back to the seat.

"They usually bring the food," said Susan.

"At that place you were in?" asked Anna.

"Yes. They said I was put there for my own good," Susan spoke slowly as if trying to organise her thoughts.

"We're not there any more," said Anna. "I took you away from there."

"Where are we?" asked Susan.

"In a caravan," said Anna.

"Wont they take me back?" asked Susan.

"They've got to find you first," said Anna.

"I'm hungry," said Susan again.

"I've got a tin of mushroom soup, we could have that with bread," Anna suggested.

"That would be nice," said Susan gazing out of the window into the dark. "Where are we?" she asked.

"On a farm," said Anna, emptying the tin of soup into a pan and putting it on the stove. She gave it a bit of a stir, then set to finding plates. Ten minutes later, she had buttered some bread and put it on the plates along with the bowls and was waiting for the soup to finish warming through.

"I'm hungry," said Susan, looking round the caravan. "Where are we?"

"I'm just serving," said Anna.

"What's for tea?" asked Susan.

"Mushroom soup," said Anna, putting the plate and bowl in front of Susan.

"What's this?" asked Susan.

"Mushroom soup," said Anna. "I just hope she snaps out of this soon," she thought, carefully fanning the soup in the hope that it wouldn't be too hot for her friend to eat.

"I'm hungry," said Susan.

"Then you'd better eat," said Anna. "But be careful, the soup's hot," she added.

"What should I do?" asked Susan with the spoon poised barely an inch in front of her mouth.

"Blow on it," said Anna going to fetch her soup.

204

"Oh dear," said Susan a second later. Anna turned back to see that the soup which had been on the spoon was now on the table. She mopped it up quickly.

"Don't blow that hard," said Anna. "The idea is too cool the soup so that you can eat it, not to decorate the table with it."

"Oh," said Susan, taking a little more care to blow on the next spoonful of soup and then putting it in her mouth and smiling at the achievement.

"Slowly does it," thought Anna setting her soup down next to Susan's and starting to eat. She just managed to stop Susan dumping a whole slice of bread into her soup.

"You should break that up," she said demonstrating with her slice of bread, then fishing a bit out with her spoon and eating it.

"Oh," said Susan, carefully copying her.

"That's right," smiled Anna. "I hope I don't have to talk her through too many meals like this or I might end up taking her back."

"I'm tired," said Susan looking at the empty plate and bowl.

"So am I," said Anna. "We've just got to organise the beds."

"Where are the beds?" asked Susan.

"Those two settees probably convert into a bed," muttered Anna. "Though they do look large enough to sleep on as they are."

Susan lay down on one of the settees, rested her head on a cushion and went straight to sleep.

"It's nice for some," thought Anna, fishing a sheet and a couple of blankets out from the cupboard and draping them over her friend. Then she rolled out her sleeping bag on the other settee.

"I'd better do the washing before I go to bed," she thought. "It's not nice waking up to a load of mucky dishes."

Anna was just putting away the last of them and looking round for somewhere to hang the tea towel, in the hope that it would be dry in the morning, when Susan rolled over in her sleep, fell off the settee and sat up declaring.

"I want to go to the toilet."

"We'd better go then," said Anna, drying her hands and picking up the roll of toilet paper.

"Where am I? Where is the toilet?" said Susan looking round her. "Why are you here Anna?"

"I am here," said Anna. "Because I took you out of that place you were in and brought you here, which is a caravan on a farm. The toilet is in the

205

toilet block which is just down the hill from here."

"I need to go to the toilet," said Susan.

"So do I," said Anna. "Let's head off down the hill together and go to the toilet," she added waving the toilet roll about in an attempt to prove her intent or something and opening the door of the caravan.

"It's dark out there," said Susan.

"There's a light here," said Anna, setting the paper down and lighting a hurricane lamp. "That should light our way to the toilet block," she added, hoping there was enough oil in the thing to last the journey.

"Good," said Susan, not sounding very reassured, but venturing out into the darkness.

"It's that building down there," said Anna, pointing down the hill at a small concrete block which had electric light spilling out from the windows. "We'll soon be there," she added, redirecting Susan who was heading off up the hill. "What are you like," she muttered to herself. Five minutes later, she finally got Susan into the toilet block.

"There are two toilets," said Susan.

"One for you, one for me," said Anna.

"But which do I use?" asked Susan, holding out her hand for some paper.

"The one on the left," said Anna, handing over probably more than enough toilet paper. Susan went into the cubical on the right and shut the door.

"OK, I'll use it," said Anna to no one in particular.

Susan came out of the cubicle whilst Anna was washing her hands.

"I can't use those sinks," she declared. "They don't have enough taps."

"There's a sink in the caravan," said Anna, shaking the water off her hands. "You can wash your hands in that."

"Good," said Susan, hesitantly. "Where's the caravan?"

"Follow me," said Anna, picking up the toilet roll and hurricane lamp, then heading for the door.

"Where are we?" asked Susan as they walked back up the hill.

"On a farm," said Anna, hoping that Susan wouldn't ask any more than that, because she didn't know.

"It's dark," said Susan looking round whilst Anna unlocked the caravan door.

"It's night," said Anna, pushing the door open and standing back whilst Susan went in.

"Should I be asleep?" she asked, looking round the caravan.

"It would be a good idea," said Anna, ushering her towards the settee's.

"Where do I sleep?"

"Here," said Anna pulling back the sheet and blankets.

"Right," said Susan climbing onto the settee and going to sleep. Anna draped the bed clothes back over her and climbed into her sleeping bag.

"Let's hope I can get some sleep now," she thought, drifting off into a dream where men in white coats hitched up the caravan and were driving it back. She jumped out of the door with Susan when they stopped at the traffic lights, she awoke with a bump when she fell off the settee. Looking up, she saw Susan peering down at her.

"Where are we?" Susan asked.

"Good question," thought Anna looking round her and trying to get out of the sleeping bag.

"We are in a caravan," she said busily trying to get her bearings and looking at the light coming in through the window. "How about some breakfast?" she added trying to find her watch to find out what time it was. "Nine o'clock," she muttered to herself.

"I'm hungry," said Susan

"Let's see what we've got," said Anna, staggering to her feet and trying to remember which cupboard she had put the food in. "Bread and jam, washed down by a cup of tea?"

"I'm hungry," said Susan again.

"I'll take that as a yes," said Anna to herself and set about making jam sandwiches and tea whilst Susan looked out of the window.

"It's still lights on, no one home," thought Anna gazing at her friend,"Let's hope that whatever they gave her wears of soon."

After breakfast Anna washed the dishes and looked through the food she'd bought rather hurriedly the day before.

"Should be able to manage a couple of days with this lot. Which would be useful as I don't know where the shops are and I don't think it would be a good idea to either leave her alone for long or take her with me," she thought looking at Susan gazing blankly out of the window.

"I need the toilet," Susan suddenly declared.

"Right," said Anna, grabbing the toilet paper. "Let's go," she added opening the caravan door quickly so that Susan didn't walk into it. Instead she fell down the two steps that lead up to the caravan door and rolled a few yards down the hill. Anna rushed after her and helped her stand up again.

"Who put those steps there?" snapped Susan.

"Probably the person who put the caravan here," said Anna. "They make it easier to get in and out."

"You could've told me about them," said Susan.

"I thought you knew they were there, you used them OK yesterday," Anna added, locking the door and pointing Susan in the direction of the toilet block.

"Where are we going," shouted Susan. Fortunately it was a very quiet camp site, the only other people were on the far side of the field and they either hadn't got up yet or had already gone out, it was difficult to tell which, but everything was fastened down and no one was around to ask any questions about Susan's behaviour, for which Anna was very grateful.

"You wanted to go to the toilet," said Anna waving the roll of toilet paper at her.

"Isn't there one in the caravan?" asked Susan.

"No," said Anna, pointing her towards the toilet block. "The toilets are in there."

"Did we use those yesterday?" asked Susan.

"Yes," said Anna.

"Isn't there anywhere else?" asked Susan looking round.

"You could go behind a bush," said Anna with a sigh.

Susan gave her a dirty look and headed towards the toilet block without any further comment. Anna followed her quickly down the hill.

Lunch time was similar to tea of the previous day, Anna did some soup and bread, Susan ate it without comment and then returned to sitting staring out of the window, occasionally dashing out to the toilet.

"This is so boring," thought Anna after she had washed up the lunchtime dishes and put them back in the cupboard. As darkness began to fall they had tea and biscuits and when the stars came out they had a tea of baked beans and fried eggs on fried bread, soon after Susan was fast asleep under her blankets. Anna washed the dishes and was just about to get into her sleeping bag, when, just like the day before Susan declared that she wanted to go to the toilet.

"It would make sense to go," thought Anna, getting the toilet roll and opening the caravan door.

"Mind the steps," she added as Susan made her way to the door.

"What sort of idiot do you take me for?" snapped Susan making a point of walking carefully down the stairs, then tripping up over some unevenness in the field. Anna looked to the sky, locked the caravan door and headed down the hill to the toilet block. Susan scrambled to her feet and followed.

The next day Anna awoke to the sound of Susan screaming, followed rapidly by a loud thump as she fell off the settee. Anna turned to see her friend fighting her way out of the sheets and blankets and standing up. She turned round quickly as if looking for someone.

"I'm not going back," she yelled down the length of the caravan. "You can't make me," she added.

"Who are you talking to?" asked Anna, rubbing her eyes and looking round.

"The men in white coats," said Susan. "They were here, I know they were."

"Well, they're not here now," said Anna climbing out of her sleeping bag and looking round the caravan to make sure. "And the door's still locked, with the key in it, so they couldn't have got through there," she added, trying to reassure her friend.

"But I saw them," said Susan, not sounding quite so sure of herself.

"You may have been having a dream. They can feel very realistic sometimes," said Anna.

"I'm not going back there," said Susan, beginning to get worked up again.

"No," said Anna. "You're not going back. I wont let them take you back."

"I need the toilet," said Susan.

"So do I," said Anna with a sigh, getting the toilet paper.

"This is going to be a long day," thought Anna, as Susan walked past her, through the caravan door and fell down the steps into the field.

However, as the second day drew to a close Susan seemed to be getting back to her old self.

"What's this stuff?" she asked looking at her tea and poking at the contents with a spoon.

"Risotto," said Anna, looking up from her bowl.

"That covers a multitude of sins," said Susan.

"I could have fed you on dog shit yesterday, you wouldn't have noticed" thought Anna.

"You can always do the cooking if you want to. I won't stand in your

209

way," said Anna.

"What's in it, apart from rice and baked beans?" asked Susan, still poking at it with her spoon.

"Not volunteering for the cooking, you are getting back to normal," thought Anna

"T.V.P. mince, tomato chutney, tinned mixed veg and yeast extract," said Anna.

"Shouldn't we be eating some fresh veg. I mean, this sort of stuff can't exactly be brilliant for the complexion," said Susan.

"There are some oranges in the cupboard," Anna started.

"And where did they come from?" asked Susan.

"Spain," said Anna.

"Oh. Well, I suppose that's OK. then," said Susan.

"We can always get some fresh veg tomorrow, if you like," Anna suggested.

"And after that, what shall we do?" asked Susan.

"How do you mean?" asked Anna.

"We can't just sit around here and do nothing," said Susan.

"Why not?" asked Anna.

"Because we can't, we don't have unlimited money and we'd get bored. In any case, they've messed up our lives, we owe it to our fellow students to make sure that they don't do it to anyone else," said Susan.

"Are you sure you're not just after revenge?" asked Anna.

"What's wrong with that, you've got to admit, it would be nice, to have the last laugh on those smug bastards."

"Yes," said Anna. "But how."

"Another problem is clothes," added Susan, wrinkling up her nose at the institutional dress she was still wearing. "You're not so badly off, as least you've got a change of clothes. All I've got is this and it's beginning to smell."

"Yes, that is a problem," said Anna.

"Are you saying I smell?" asked Susan.

"No," said Anna. "You are."

"That's alright then," said Susan, not looking entirely certain about it.

"The problem is how do we get some clothes," said Anna. "We can't exactly have a spending spree, we don't have the cash and that dress might raise some eyebrows."

"Shame we can't just get our stuff from the Poly," said Susan.

"What do you mean?" asked Anna.

"I don't know about you, but I never took anything out of my room. As far as I know my stuff's still there," said Susan.

"I didn't take anything either," said Anna. "I suppose we could go back and get all our things."

"What if we get caught?" asked Susan.

"We could get caught anywhere. The Poly has the charm of being the last place they'd expect us to be, we could sell some of our books and things to boost our finances and it would be a way of getting back at them," said Anna.

"Which brings us back to the question of how to stop them, how to tell the world what they're doing. The way they follow that computer, you'd think it was Ceasers' wife or something," said Susan.

"What!" said Anna. "You're not rambling again are you," she thought.

"Ceasers' wife was supposed to be above suspicion or something, to be followed without question, they never question anything the computer tells them," said Susan.

"A computer is only as good as its programmer," Anna began slowly.

"Exactly, that friend of mine on the computer programming course said garbage in, garbage out," said Susan.

"What?" asked Anna.

"A computer is just a load of switches, it does what the programme tells it, it doesn't think, it is dependant on the user to input the right data and use the right programme, assuming it works. Hence if you put garbage in you get garbage out," Susan explained.

"I wonder who programmed the Poly computer," said Anna

"Does it matter which bonehead puked up that abomination of a program they used," asked Susan.

"Not really, but a professional wouldn't make the same mistakes as an amateur," said Anna.

"I don't think there is such a thing as a professional programmer, if they were professional then the computers wouldn't make the mistakes they do," said Susan.

"It would be nice if the computer did the informing," said Anna thoughtfully.

"How do you mean?" asked Susan.

"I don't know, but a lot of information can be passed from computer to computer. Since the computer caused the problem, it would be nice if we

211

could use it to pass on the knowledge of what has been going on.   Use it to tell the newspapers and let them tell the world," said Anna.

"It would be nice," said Susan.   "But we don't have access to the computer."

"Do you have any other ideas?" asked Anna.

"No," said Susan.

"Neither do I," admitted Anna.   "Still, at least we have decided on something."

"What!" asked Susan.

"To go back to the Poly for our things," said Anna.

"Oh.   Right," said Susan, not sounding quite so sure of herself.

"We could go tomorrow," said Anna, onto a roll.

"Tomorrow!" said Susan startled.

"It's too late to do anything today," Anna started.

"Yes.   But tomorrow?" Susan asked.

"The longer we leave it, the more likely they are to move our things, or for our parents to come and collect them," said Anna.

"Yes, but," said Susan.

"And you were the one who said we couldn't stay here forever," said Anna.

"But tomorrow," said Susan slowly.

"Is Friday, when lots of students go home for the weekend, so there won't be many people there.   Also, like you said, there's nothing to gain by waiting," said Anna.

"Alright.   Tomorrow it is then," said Susan.

"Right," said Anna.   "I think I'll have an early night, if you don't mind. Tomorrow stands a pretty good chance of being very long and very busy."

"Do you know how to get back to the Poly from here?" asked Susan

"No," said Anna.

"Do you have an atlas?   I could work it out for us," asked Susan.

"Yes.   It's in the car, but it won't be much use," Anna started.

"Why not, I can read a map, I can work out a route easy," said Susan.

"You could do, only I don't know where we are," said Anna yawning.

"What!" Susan exclaimed.

"We were lost when we got here," said Anna.

"Didn't you ask where we were?" Susan demanded.

"No," said Anna.

"But," Susan started.

"It didn't seem that important at the time," said Anna.

"But," Susan started.

"We'll soon find out tomorrow when we get moving," said Anna.

"But," Susan repeated

"Good night," said Anna, climbing into her sleeping bag and pulling it up over her head.

"You're impossible," shouted Susan.

"Most likely," said Anna. "Sleep well."

Chapter 12
The first return to the Poly

Early next morning they packed their belongings into the mini and drove off to pay the farmers wife for the rent of the caravan.

"I hope you enjoyed your stay," she said.

"Yes thank-you," said Anna. "It's been very peaceful."

"Your sister seems a lot better," she said.

"She is. Much more like her old self. No need for Mum to worry now," said Anna smiling.

"So thoughtful, your Mum doesn't know how lucky she is," said the farmers wife.

"I don't know about that. But we'd better be off, we've a long way to go and my map reading leaves a lot to be desired. Anyway. Good bye and thank-you for letting us stay," said Anna smiling.

"It's been a pleasure. Have a good journey," said the farmers wife.

"Thank-you," said Anna climbing into the driving seat of the mini. "Bye."

"Sister!" said Susan as they were bumping down the narrow back lane, it seemed bumpier than when they arrived.

"It sounded better than spaced out loony friend," said Anna.

"And what was that about me being much better?" asked Susan.

"I told her you were overworked," said Anna.

"Why?" asked Anna.

"You wouldn't ask that if you'd seen yourself when we arrived. I had to explain it away somehow. And it was the first thing to come to mind," said Anna.

"Oh," said Susan. "Was I bad."

"Out to lunch wasn't in it. She could see there was something not quite right with you and she could hardly see you at all," said Anna.

"Sorry," said Susan.

"Doesn't matter. It was hardly your fault anyway," said Anna pulling up by a road sign.

"Why've you stopped?" asked Susan.

"To find these places in the atlas," said Anna.

"But we're at none of them," said Susan.

"No. But it tells us how far we are from each of them. From that we can work out where we are and then you can work out a route to the Poly," said Anna with a smile.

"I see. You're finding a job for me. Eh," said Susan.

"You wanted to do it last night. Anyway, is it left or right here?" said Anna.

"Hang on a minute. Give me a chance. I haven't found them in the index yet. Let alone which page they're all on."

"OK" said Anna. "Tell me when you know where we are."

"We're here," said Susan after ten minutes studying the atlas, turning it this way and that and using her fingers as book marks until they were almost tied in a bow.

"Are you sure?" asked Anna.

"Certain," said Susan. "I do have an "A" level in Geography."

"Fine, so which road do I head down?" asked Anna.

"You head back the way we came," said Susan.

"OK," said Anna, turning the car round in the road and heading back the way they had come.

It was early evening when they drove back into the town. The journey had taken much longer than Anna had thought it would, mainly because Susan directed her down minor roads and round towns. They stopped at a small village shop to get some sandwiches and drinks for lunch, though Susan wouldn't come out of the car, instead she managed to look very suspicious, wearing sunglasses and pretending to be asleep. Anna felt so embarrassed, she was glad to get away from the village. They pulled into the side of the road, a little while later to eat their lunch.

Anna didn't park on Poly land, the car might be recognised, but she parked nearby, in a badly lit, tree lined cul-de-sac. Silence gradually replaced the sound of the engine.

"I'm sure that thing's running on longer than it was," thought Anna. "I'll have to read about it in the car book sometime."

"Well, we're here," she said.

215

"Yes," said Susan, not sounding very certain.

"I hope this isn't some sort of relapse," thought Anna.

"Now to get to our rooms," she added, sounding more certain than she felt.

"Yes," said Susan.

"I've got my keys. Have you got yours?" said Anna.

"No. I think they must have taken them away from me, after all, I wouldn't have much use for them would I," said Susan.

"Oh," said Anna. "I should've thought of that."

"Sorry," said Susan.

"You might have mentioned it," said Anna.

"I didn't think," said Susan.

"We'll just have to find another key," said Anna, trying to sound positive.

"Won't that be risky," said Susan.

"So's coming here, but we need our things, so we'll just have to chance it. Anyway, like I said yesterday, it's the weekend most people are away. Its just it would've been easier and quicker if you'd had your key," said Anna.

"Sorry," said Susan again.

"Do you know where they keep the spare keys?" asked Anna.

"I should think Mrs Smithers-Jones has a set," said Susan.

"We'd stand a better chance of breaking into the Tower of London than getting a key from there. Weren't there some in Knaresborough Hall?" Anna asked.

"Yes. In that room where we pay our hall fees," said Susan.

"Right then, we'd better get over there," said Anna.

"How'll we get in?" asked Susan, looking vaguely horrified.

"Ring the door bell and say we've come to use their washing machine," said Anna.

"At this time of night!" said Susan.

"Alright, we've come to collect something we washed earlier," said Anna.

"Do you think it'll work?" asked Susan.

"How the hell should I know," thought Anna.

"They probably won't even question us, why should they?" she said.

"I don't know," said Susan.

"Lets go. We can't sit here all night," said Anna.

"But," Susan wailed.

"Come on," she said, climbing out of the car.

"It's bad enough being here," she thought. "Without having to debate everything."

Susan climbed out quickly and started trying to lock her door.

"Just shut the door and I'll lock it," said Anna, getting back into the car and reaching across to lock the passenger door. "It's just a question of knowing how."

They rang the door bell at Knaresborough Hall long and loud but there was no response.

"What shall we do?" asked Susan.

"There's a basement door round the back isn't there?" asked Anna.

"Yes. Leads straight into the laundry," said Susan.

"We'll try that then," said Anna.

"Isn't that breaking an entry or something," asked Susan.

"Not if the door's unlocked and it usually is," said Anna.

"What if someone finds us?" asked Susan.

"What if they do, we're students aren't we?" said Anna.

"If you were a bit quieter they might not," she thought.

"I don't know about this," said Susan, hesitating.

"Would you like to wait here?" asked Anna.

"No. Don't leave me here alone!" Susan started.

"Come on then," said Anna and headed off, round to the back of the building. Susan gave a quick glance around and followed.

"Good, its open," said Anna walking into the darkened building, Susan on her heels.

"Do you know where it is from here?" asked Anna.

"Just along the corridor, I think its the third on the right."

"I hope you're right," said Anna opening the door for the laundry and then stifling an exclamation of pain as she fell straight down a short flight of stairs onto a concrete floor.

"Down the stairs and along the corridor," amended Susan.

"That wasn't what you said," said Anna.

"I thought you knew about the steps," said Susan.

"I forgot," said Anna, rubbing a bruised elbow.

"So did I. Are you all right?" asked Susan.

"I'll live. Come on lets find this key," said Anna.

"I do hope no one heard you. You did fall rather noisily," Susan started,

217

but stopped when she saw the look on Anna's face.

"I'll try and fall quietly next time. Is this the door?" asked Anna.

"You should know as well as me," said Susan

"Yes, but I've got no sense of direction. You claim to have one," said Anna, rubbing her other elbow.

"Your sense of direction," began Susan.

"Shush," said Anna, there's someone in there.

"What!" squeaked Susan as Anna pushed her into a dark corner, the door opened and a woman walked quickly down the corridor.

"Oh no," muttered Susan shaking.

"Right. Get in," muttered Anna pushing her through the open door. Susan looked round the room frightened.

"Where are those keys?" asked Anna.

"On the hooks over there," said Susan pointing to a wall.

"Here's the board for our hall," muttered Anna. "Number 38 wasn't it?"

"My room number? Yes," said Susan. "Oh do hurry up, she'll be back any minute."

"Yes," mumbled Anna, busy moving the keys around.

"What are you doing?" asked Susan hovering round the door.

"Trying to hide the fact that your key's missing," said Anna.

"Oh."

"We may as well make things hard for them. If they see your key gone they'll suspect something," said Anna.

"Yes," said Susan.

"Right. Lets go," said Anna.

"Yes," said Susan, almost running out of the room.

"Back the way we came or out of the front door?" asked Anna.

"I don't know. Which ever you think," said Susan.

"The front door," said Anna.

"Are you sure? There might be people there," said Susan.

"Students. And two more wouldn't look odd. Creeping round the back might," said Anna.

"But. But we just did that," said Susan.

"That's because no one would answer the front door," said Anna.

"But."

"Let's go. There's too much to do to hang round here all night," said Anna.

"Like what?" asked Susan.

218

"Get into our rooms and get a few things. Like my toothbrush," said Anna.

"Yes. I didn't like to mention it, but your breath," said Susan.

"Thank-you for nothing," said Anna, smiling at the lady who had returned to the room they had just left and locked the door.

"Don't want anyone pinching anything," she said to them as she quickly left.

"No," said Anna to the disappearing figure.

"Isn't that what we've just done?" asked Susan.

"It could be seen in that light," said Anna.

"Because that's what it is," said Susan.

"If our hall is as quiet as this it'll be easy to get to our rooms," said Anna changing the subject.

"Won't that be burglary," started Susan.

"How could it be. We're only collecting what is ours. If they refuse us access to our property that would be breaking the law, I think," said Anna.

"Couldn't we just ask them for our stuff," started Susan.

"I can't believe you just asked that, you know what would happen, they'd just take you back there," said Anna.

"And put me in there as well, given half a chance," thought Anna.

"Oh. Yes," said Susan.

"And I don't want to talk to them. Not that they listen anyway," Anna added.

"No. You're right there, they don't listen," said Susan.

"Wakefield Hall," said Anna, standing by the door in the perimeter wall.

"Should we try the front door this time?" asked Susan looking unsure.

"Why not?" asked Anna.

"Well," Susan started.

"We've got a key," said Anna pulling out her key ring.

"Yes," sighed Susan.

"Your room or mine," said Anna as she closed the door behind them.

"Yours, it's nearest," said Susan.

"Right," said Anna turning to the signing in book.

"What are you doing?" snapped Susan.

"Checking to see if the girl in the room next to me is in," said Anna.

"Why?" asked Susan.

"She might hear us," said Anna.

"Or to be more precise, she might hear you," thought Anna.

219

"Oh! Yes. Well, is she?" asked Susan.

"Is she what?" asked Anna.

"In. You idiot," said Susan.

"No. She's signed the weekend book," said Anna.

"Right. Let's go," said Susan.

"OK," said Anna.

They headed for the stairs trying to look unobtrusive, but failed completely, however, there was no one to see them looking like two thieves, so it didn't matter.

Opening the door of her room, Anna's hand went instinctively for the light switch, but Susan grabbed her arm.

"Should we put the light on?" she hissed in the doorway.

"It's going to make things difficult if we don't," said Anna.

"But what if we're seen?"

"I'll draw the curtains. Then we'll just be shapes and most people won't associate the window on the outside with the room on the inside, so they won't suspect anything."

"Mm mm," Susan started mumbling.

"I'll draw the curtains. You put on the light when I tell you," said Anna.

"OK," said Susan.

The room wasn't big, but crossing it to the window proved harder than Anna expected, she kept bumping into things on the way.

"Hurry up," hissed Susan, standing in the dark by the closed door. Anna drew the curtains.

"Now," said Anna.

"Are you sure this is wise?" asked Susan.

"Would you prefer to stumble round in the dark?" asked Anna, who stood for a minute blinking in the bright light, then she looked round mentally taking in all her possessions.

"Everything seems to be as I left it," she said thoughtfully.

"Looks tidy enough," said Susan.

"Would you like a cup of coffee?" asked Anna.

"I could do with one," she thought.

"What!" said Susan.

"Coffee and biscuits. There's all the things to make coffee and I've got some biscuits in the tin. We may as well be comfortable," said Anna.

"The cleaners'll only eat them if we don't," she thought.

"But, I thought we were just going to get in and out quickly, not hang

220

around having a party."

"I thought we could spend the night here, perhaps the weekend and have a bath, we could both do with one, as you said. If we're quiet no one will notice us," said Anna.

"What!" snapped Susan.

"It's either that or sleep in the car, if you'd prefer that," said Anna.

"How many sugars do you take?" asked Susan.

"One," said Anna. "That's changed your tune," she thought.

"Are these mugs clean?" asked Susan.

"They were. You'd better wash them though, they could be full of dust," said Anna.

"Or the cleaners might have been using them," said Susan.

"Give them a thorough wash. I'll get some packing done," said Anna.

A quarter of an hour later, a suitcase had been crammed full of clothes and the two girls were sitting drinking coffee and eating biscuits again.

"Are you going to pack everything?" asked Susan.

"I've no intention of leaving anything for them," said Anna.

"How will we fit it all in the car?"

"I was just planning on taking clothes with us and selling the rest, we could use the money," said Anna. "Which is what I explained to you yesterday," she thought.

"The guitar as well?" asked Susan.

"No. I thought we could keep that, we could always try busking," said Anna, loath to part with something her mother was so dead set against having.

Susan looked sceptical.

"People would pay us to stop," Anna added.

"Are you sure we wouldn't just get arrested," asked Susan.

"Pessimist," said Anna.

"Realist," said Susan.

"I'll finish packing my clothes. There's not much more," she muttered and soon a bulging holdall was standing next to the well stuffed suitcase.

"Now we can go to your room and you can pack," she said.

"You don't suppose they've let my room to someone else do you? I mean, I'd hate to walk in on someone else's room," Susan flustered.

"As far as I know they haven't, but I suppose they may have got around to moving your things. They may have put them in the box room, though, I would have thought, if they'd moved them, they'd have arranged for your parents to collect them."

"We could try there first.   My parents might be collecting them later," said Susan.

"Alright," said Anna heading for the door.

"Couldn't we leave it till later," said Susan.   "There might be people around."

"We'd have to sit up half the night if we're going to wait till everyone's asleep and it seems pretty quiet now," said Anna.

"Well. Couldn't we wait just a bit longer," said Susan.

"All right. but not much longer, I might lose my nerve."

"Oh. Well, I suppose we could go now, it does seem quiet out there," said Susan.

"It would get it over with," said Anna.

"OK," said Susan.

"Right. Let's go," said Anna opening the door, she turned round to see that Susan hadn't moved a muscle.

"Are you coming," she said.

"Oh.   Yes," said Susan leaping off the chair and almost sending it flying.   Crossing the room she tripped up over the two bags and managed to walk into the wall just to the left of the door, she stepped back and fell backwards onto the bed.

Anna sighed, lifted her gaze to the ceiling and shook her head, holding the door open she said.   "After you."Mustering as much dignity as she could Susan made her way through the door and waited whilst Anna locked it.

The landing was a large square with all the rooms round the edge of it, lit only by the emergency lighting, it was full of shadows and seemed even larger than usual and much more alarming.   Every noise made them shrink into the shadows in fright.   They made their, way round the edge to the stairs.   The centre felt too open and visible.

The fire door proved difficult, it was hard to stop it banging shut behind them.

The stairs were another hazard.   It felt as if everyone could hear them and they were going to be found at any second.   Passing the television room was worse, as someone might be in there and they might choose that moment to come out and find them.   But the place was in silence, no one was moving and they got to the basement without any problems.

"Where's the box room?" asked Susan in a stage whisper.

"I thought you knew," said Anna.

"So did I, but now I'm here," said Susan, looking round at all the closed doors ringing the bottom of the stairwell.

"Well, we'll work by elimination," said Anna, walking slowly down the corridor. "Those with numbers on are peoples rooms. That's the kitchen, that's the laundry. We'll try this door," she said standing in front of an anonymous looking door.

"Are you sure?" asked Susan.

"No," said Anna.

"Do you think we ought to?" asked Susan.

"Yes," said Anna.

"But," Susan began, but Anna had started to open the door. Susan shrank back to the wall, as the door revealed that the room was in darkness. Anna searched the wall for a light switch. Turning it on, she walked into the brightly illuminated room. Susan hurriedly followed, closing the door behind her and looking round nervously, as if the hall warden was going to materialise out of nowhere. Then her eye caught sight of something familiar.

"That's my bag!" she exclaimed opening it. "They didn't take much care packing my clothes, they're all screwed up, they could've at least folded them."

"There's another bag here," said Anna.

"That's my stuff too," said Susan after a quick look. "And this is my stereo," she added looking at the table.

"Do you recognise the stuff in the boxes?" asked Anna. Susan knelt on the floor and searched through them.

"Most of my stuff is here."

"What's missing?"

"Mugs, coffee, sugar, tea, biscuits. And I bet I know where they are," said Susan storming out of the room.

"Where?" said Anna dashing behind her to the cleaners room.

"Thought so," said Susan, pointing out her possessions on the table. "Judith kept asking me where I got them. Well, they're mine and I'm having them back," she added picking up the nearest thing to her. Anna grabbed the rest.

"They had no right, no right what-so-ever," muttered Susan going back to the box room and putting them in one of the boxes.

"What shall we do now?" she asked.

223

"Well, I was thinking baths might be a good idea," said Anna.

"You have got to be kidding."

"One of the reasons we came here was to get a change of clothes and because we were beginning to smell.   This is a good place to have a bath. Plenty of hot water, a bathroom, we have towels, soap," said Anna.

"What if someone sees us," said Susan.

"At this time of night.   Everyone's either gone out for the evening or gone home for the weekend.   This'll be the best chance and there's a bathroom right next to my room," said Anna.

"OK.   You've convinced me.   What'll we do after that," said Susan.

"I don't know about you, but I could do with a good night's sleep," said Anna.

"Where?" said Susan.

"There's not much point in trying your room now is there," said Anna yawning.

"Not really.   They've shifted everything here, so they may have got someone else in already," agreed Susan.

"Then we may as well use my room," said Anna.

"Were will I sleep?" asked Susan.

"The floor," suggested Anna.

"That's going to be a bit hard," said Susan.

"Not as hard as my car," thought Anna.

"We could grab some cushions from the telly room," she said.

"Won't they be missed?" asked Susan.

"Not if we put them back before anyone else gets up," said Anna.

"When do you think that'll be?" asked Susan.

"About dinner time.   It's Saturday tomorrow remember," said Anna.

"Oh good, then we won't have to get up early," said Susan.

"It would be an idea to.   We've got a lot to do and we ought to do it before anyone notices we're here," said Anna.

"Like what?" asked Susan.

"Sell a few things, books, kettles, stereos.   How many cushions do you want?" asked Anna standing in the door of the television room.

"Three should be plenty," said Susan.

"Sheets and blankets?" asked Anna.

"Where would we get them?" said Susan.

"Linen cupboard," said Anna.

"It'll be locked," said Susan

224

"We can try the other door," said Anna.

"Eh?"

"The one from the telly room," said Anna.

"Oh yes," said Susan heading for the door.

Ten minutes later the cushions and bed linen were stowed in Anna's room and Susan was soaking in the bathroom next door. Whilst Anna had sidled over to one on the other side of the landing. A little over an hour later the two of them were settling down to sleep, Susan in the bed and Anna on the cushions.

"Nothing new. She always gets her way, giving in is easier than spending half the night arguing about it," thought Anna. "Or listen to her complaining about her aches and pains for the next few weeks."

Anna was awakened by the sun filtering through the curtains, flooding the room with light. Stretching, she tried to orientate her mind and work out where she was and what she was doing there. Rolling over, she fell off the cushions onto the floor, the short pile of the nylon carpet was like sandpaper on her bare arms. Standing up quickly she took in the bags, the boxes of books, Susan, fast asleep on the bed and the cushions where she had slept. Gradually things came back.

She washed, dressed and returned the cushions to the television room. It was only when she got back that Susan woke up.

"Back in the land of the living are you," said Anna folding up the sheets and putting them in the bottom of the wardrobe.

"What time is it?" asked Susan sleepily.

"Eight. According to my watch," said Anna, putting it to her ear. "But I don't know if it's right."

"Oh," said Susan.

"Anyway, its time we were up and doing," said Anna.

"Do I have to get up," Susan moaned.

"Yes," said Anna.

"Oh. Can't I stay here," said Susan.

"Sod you. I'm not arguing," thought Anna.

"I'll get something for breakfast," she said. "You'd better be up by the time I get back."

"Or I'll leave you here," she thought. "And you can argue it out with the powers that be."

From the shop at the end of the road Anna managed to buy bread buns, margarine and jam. Not exactly the most wholesome of breakfasts, but better than nothing. Returning she let herself into her room. Susan froze in her attempt to bring order to her hair and peered cautiously out from between the many strands which hung over her face.

"Couldn't you have knocked or something," she said sharply. "You nearly gave me heart failure."

"Who did you think I was?" asked Anna.

"I didn't think. I nearly jumped out of my skin. You could have given me a warning," snapped Susan.

"And draw attention to us," said Anna.

"What've you got for breakfast?" Susan asked changing the subject.

"Buns and jam," said Anna, putting them on the desk.

"Tea or coffee?" Susan asked.

"Coffee?" said Anna, in the hope that something would wake her up.

"Yes. That's fine by me," said Susan.

"Right. I'll put the kettle on. You get the cups ready. Have you got any plates and knives?" asked Anna.

"Here," said Susan, handing over two small plates that she'd accidentally brought over from the refectory.

"Given half a chance, she'll take anything," thought Anna.

"So what's the plan for the day," said Susan finishing her breakfast and looking round to see if she'd missed any.

"Like I said before, all this stuff won't fit in the car," said Anna. "We'll have to sell some of it, we need the money."

"You're not really planning to spend another night here are you?" asked Susan.

"It would be comfortable," Anna started, but Susan's frightened look stopped her. "However, it might be pushing our luck a bit" she added.

"It might," said Susan. "I think I'd like to get away from this place as soon as possible."

"That's fine coming from you," said Anna.

"And what do you mean by that?" asked Susan.

"You're the lazy tyke who didn't want to get up this morning," replied Anna.

"It was comfortable," said Susan looking at the bed.

"I know, it was my bed," said Anna.

226

"I'd been looking forward to sleeping in it myself," she thought.

"You could have slept in it. I would have slept on the floor. You didn't have to," Susan started.

"No. But I wouldn't have heard the end of it if you had. But this is getting us nowhere," thought Anna.

"We'd better get a move on," she said.

"Where shall we sleep tonight?" Susan asked.

"I don't know," said Anna.

"What sort of answer is that?" asked Susan.

"Truthful," said Anna.

"How can you take things so lightly," Susan snapped.

"Have you any suggestions?" Anna asked.

"No. You know I haven't," said Susan.

"Well, if we get a few things sold, we might be able to stop at a B and B or a Youth Hostel or something," said Anna.

"All right. Keep your hair on. How are we going to shift all this stuff then," asked Susan.

"I thought I'd go and get the car. If you move the stuff down to the box room. We could load up through the basement door," said Anna.

"That's right. You get the easy jobs," snapped Susan.

"Do you want to fetch the car?" asked Anna holding out the car keys.

"You know I can't drive," snapped Susan.

"Exactly," said Anna.

"Be quick," said Susan.

"See you soon," said Anna getting up to leave.

"Aren't you going to take something down with you." asked Susan.

"Oh yes," she muttered picking up a box of books.

"Don't strain yourself," said Susan to the closing door.

The walk to the car was quite refreshing, however, it didn't make Anna feel inclined to go back to the hall.

"God knows what's got into Susan today," she thought. "Still, if I don't go back now she'll think I'm being lazy and she'd be right."

"What took you so long," snapped Susan as soon as she walked into the box room. "I've nearly shifted all your stuff down here."

"What's left?" asked Anna.

"Just the clothes."

"They may as well stay there for the moment. Let's get this lot loaded into the car."

227

"Is that all the thanks I get for heaving this lot down here," asked Susan.

"Looks like it," said Anna, after a moments pause.

"Oh well, just so long as I know," said Susan. "What shall we use to prop open the basement door?"

"That box of books, it looks weighty enough," said Anna.

"You're too right. Politics is heavy going at the best of times," said Susan, moving the box into position.

"Yes. But it should fetch a good price," said Anna.

"I'd be tempted to pay someone to take them away," said Susan.

"They're not that bad," said Anna, adjusting the position of the box. "They're a good cure for insomnia."

"What do you do, hit yourself on the head with them?" asked Susan.

"Of course. Lets go before someone comes," said Anna.

"Oh. Yes," said Susan picking up the first thing to come to hand and almost running to the car.

"Hang on a minute," muttered Anna, grabbing a box and following. "I've got to unlock it first."

"Get a move on," hissed Susan.

"I'm doing my best," said Anna, fishing the keys out of her pocket.

"Sorry," said Susan.

"I should think so," thought Anna.

"Shall we sell the books first or the other stuff?" asked Anna.

"I don't know. I hadn't thought," said Susan, beginning to get flustered.

"I was thinking, the books first," Anna started.

"That's fine by me," said Susan as they loaded the last of the things into the car. "Let's get going," she added climbing into the passenger seat and slamming the door shut behind her.

Three hours later they arrived back at the hall with an empty car and not quite as much money as they had hoped for.

"It was daylight robbery," muttered Susan.

"I know, but we didn't have much option," said Anna.

"But it was worth more, much more," Susan started.

"It was worth what we could get for it, we couldn't fit it all in the car," said Anna, trying to be realistic.

"I know, but," said Susan.

"It was either sell it or leave it here. It can't be helped, at least we have some money. Now we may as well load up the clothes and get the hell out of here," said Anna.

"Where shall we start?" asked Susan.

"With your stuff in the box room. It's the nearest and unless someone's got up, the basement door should still be open. I put it on the catch," said Anna.

"You left the basement door unlocked?" said Susan.

"Yes," said Anna.

"Someone could've got in," said Susan shocked.

"Like us," said Anna holding the door open for Susan.

"The place could've been robbed," Susan explained.

"I don't think thieves make a habit of trying doors just to see of they're unlocked," said Anna.

"Yes. But."

"Anyway, if they wanted to rob the place they'd just have to ring the door bell long enough and someone'd let them in. It isn't exactly a high security place. Remember when they put the burglar chain on. I managed to undo that from the outside, just by putting my hand through the open door and anyway, we're less likely to be seen using this door," said Anna.

"You've convinced me," said Susan, putting the last of her bags in the back of the mini, "Good job you've only got two bags."

"Yes," said Anna looking at the car. "We wouldn't get much more in."

"Are you saying I have a lot of things?" asked Susan.

"No. You are," said Anna.

"Well, that's my prerogative," said Susan, not entirely convinced.

"Exactly," said Anna, locking the car door. "We don't want anything pinched."

"Not that the locks would stop anyone half way determined," she thought.

"I'll stay with the car if you want," offered Susan.

"They might think you were going to pinch one of their precious cars," said Anna nodding towards the neighbouring hall.

"I've lugged half your stuff into my car, the least you can do is bring half of mine down here with me," thought Anna.

"Do you think the rumours are true, what they did to that lad that scratched one of their cars?" asked Susan.

"I wouldn't put it past that bunch of head cases," said Anna.

229

"But burning his feet with cigarettes," she looked towards the neighbouring hall, then dashed after Anna, back into Wakefield Building and up the stairs to Anna's room.

"We should leave the keys," she said to Susan as she took a last look round the room.

"But where should we leave them?" said Susan. "I don't fancy putting these back where we got them from," she added looking at the keys to her room.

"In here," said Anna, detaching the hall keys from the rest of her key ring and putting them in the top drawer of the desk,Susan put hers in with them.

"Wonder when they'll find them?" Susan said.

"Either when they search the room to find out if I've left anything, when they clean it out in readiness for the next student or when the next student turns up," said Anna.

"Lets go," said Susan.

"Yes," said Anna picking up one of her bags. "Before anyone wakes up."

"Yes," said Susan, grabbing the other bag and making a dash for the door.

They were in the basement before Susan paused for breath.

"What's that noise?" she asked wide eyed.

"What noise?" said Anna catching up with her.

"A sort of squeaking, creaking noise, along with some heavy breathing," said Susan.

"Oh. It could be a sort of creaking, squeaking and heavy breathing type of noise I suppose. Can't say as I heard anything myself," said Anna.

"Oh."

"Let's get a move on, before we meet someone who knows we shouldn't be here," said Anna, too late, as a group of students walked out of the kitchen past them.

"I'm sure they recognised me. I'm sure I saw surprise and recognition in their faces," said Susan. "They're going to tell. We'll get caught."

"Don't panic," said Anna. "It'll take a while for the penny to drop, then they've got to find someone and tell them. It's Saturday, it'll take ages and we'll be long gone. And anyway, they might have something better to do," said Anna. "Calmly does it. You'll draw attention to us," muttered Anna.

"Calm. You want me to act calm!" said Susan beginning to panic.

230

"Shush," said Anna. "Damn. The locks been dropped," said Anna putting down her bag and unlocking the basement door. A noise to her right attracted her attention. Susan glanced in the directions of Anna's horrified gaze. For a moment four pairs of eyes exchanged looks of surprise and disbelief.

"Anna! Susan!" exclaimed Mr Thomas and Mrs Smithers-Jones jumping down from the table in the cleaners little cubby hole. "What are you doing here?"

Anna looked from the door to the table to one side of it, then to Susan. Susan nodded, slowly putting her bag on the floor, they quickly pushed the table in front of the door, then picked up their bags and fled through the basement door. Anna dropped the catch on the lock to try and slow down any pursuit and ran to the car. Throwing her bag on the back seat she opened the passenger door for Susan and started up the engine.

As Susan put her bag in the back, Anna saw Mr Thomas approaching rapidly across the car park.

"Quick. Get in," shouted Anna.

Susan slammed the door shut as Mr Thomas got to the car. He made a grab for the door handle, but Anna put the car into reverse and he missed, his hand hit the door frame and he paused for a moment to check for damage. She put the car into first gear and headed for the car park entrance.

"Keep an eye on him," said Anna as she checked the road for traffic.

"He's coming," said Susan. "Can't we get out of here?"

"Not at the. Yes," said Anna, as a gap appeared. She shot quickly into the road just as Mr Thomas made a grab for the drivers door handle.

"I could do without this," said Susan shaking as she put her seat belt on and finding one end of Anna's seat belt there as well, she fastening it for her.

"So could I," said Anna shaking. "Can you tell me what he's up to. I shouldn't think he'll just let us drive off."

"Oh no!" screamed Susan.

"What?" shouted Anna.

"He's getting into his car," said Susan.

"God. Can't these cars go any faster?" muttered Anna.

"I think we're following a hearse," said Susan, peering towards the front of the traffic queue.

"Just our luck. He's got out of the car park. Some burke's let him out.

231

He's two cars behind us. What does he think he's going to do, have some kind of a car chase," said Anna.

"What shall we do?" snapped Susan.

"Try and lose him," said Anna.

"In this old crate?" said Susan.

"Old crate! I like that," said Anna.

"Well it can't exactly out run that thing," said Susan pointing at Mr Thomas' new Capri, "Even I know that."

"Well it's just going to have to, unless, of course you want to have another nice little chat with him," said Anna taking a sharp left out of the cortège. Unfortunately Mr Thomas noticed and followed. The two cars between them continued on with the cortège.

"What did you do that for?" asked Susan.

Anna took a right down a cobbled back alley without slowing down.

"How good's your suspension?" asked Susan.

"Hopefully better than his. Anyway, it's a new car and he's probably not going to want to risk it," said Anna. See, he's slowing down somewhat," she added.

"Perhaps, but he's still behind us," said Susan.

At the end of the alley Anna turned left and then right straight down another cobbled lane.

"I think that's," started Susan.

"No it hasn't. I didn't think we'd lose him that quickly," said Anna coming to a busy road.

"Please give me a gap in the traffic," Anna prayed silently. A small gap appeared and Anna turned right, it closed up almost as soon as she had, leaving Mr Thomas fuming, watching them driving away down the road and round the corner.

"Do you think we've got rid of him now?" asked Susan.

"Difficult to tell. He might be just a few cars behind," said Anna.

"Oh," said Susan.

"I suppose we can always take a few turns whilst he's out of our sight. It should make it harder for him to find us," said Anna, beginning to like the chase.

"I think we must've lost him," said Susan, five minutes and many turns later.

"I think so. We haven't seen him since he got stuck at the junction," said Anna.

"We must be safe then," Susan said relaxing slightly.

"Yes," said Anna. "Touch wood," she thought.

"Do you know where we are?" asked Susan looking round at the grimy, gardenless terraced houses that back onto the cobbled road.

"Not exactly" said Anna.

"What do you mean. Not exactly?" asked Susan.

"I think the docks are down here somewhere," Anna started.

"Great. And do you know how to get back to the town centre so we can get out of here," asked Susan.

"I think so," said Anna turning left. "This should get us to that big road that comes in past the art college."

"I'll take your word for it," said Susan

"Yes. I recognise that junction. I was right," said Anna.

"You were in doubt?" asked Susan.

"Well. Oh God! Its him again," said Anna.

"What! Who?" asked Susan, looking round.

"Mr Thomas. And I think he's seen us. At least he's turned in our direction," said Anna.

"He's waving at us. I think he wants us to stop," said Susan.

"That wouldn't surprise me," said Anna.

"There's no need to be sarcastic," snapped Susan.

"Or for you to state the obvious," said Anna. "Unless, of course, you want to see him."

"What do you mean? I can see him now and that's too close," said Susan.

"My thoughts precisely," said Anna quickly turning right in front of another cortège.

"Have a care! I don't want to be blotted by a hearse," said Susan.

"That load of cars should hold him up for a while. The deceased looks popular, either that or they're holding up a lot of people. Makes no odds," said Anna.

"How could you be so calculating. Those people are upset and you're just using them as an obstacle to set in his way," said Susan.

"They probably didn't notice us. Anyway, if I didn't set obstacles in his way. If we raced down a straight empty road he'd have caught us inside twenty yards. If we want to get away from him there's no place for playing fair or being nice or anything," said Anna.

"But," Susan started.

233

"Do you think he was being nice having you locked up in that dump?" asked Anna.

"Well."

"Well what?" asked Anna.

"No he wasn't, not really," said Susan.

"He wasn't being nice at all," said Anna. "He was getting you out of the way and I'd like to know why."

"Because of the syllabus," said Susan.

"There's that, yes, but, the way he's reacted, it makes me wonder whether there's more to it," said Anna.

"How do you mean?" asked Susan.

"I don't know, its just a feeling. I didn't know Mr Thomas knew the hall warden," said Anna.

"Well they certainly looked well acquainted," said Susan.

"I wouldn't have thought she'd wear that sort of underwear. I'd have thought armour plating was more her style," said Anna stopping at a zebra crossing to let an old lady cross.

"Mr Thomas is braver than I would've given him credit for being," said Susan.

"Either that or she's got him petrified," said Anna. "Like a rabbit caught in the beam of a car's headlights."

"Yes, that sounds more likely. Bet they were embarrassed when they saw us," said Susan giggling.

"Can't have been at it for long though," said Anna thoughtfully.

"What do you mean?" asked Susan.

"They'd have heard us loading the car from the box room," said Anna.

"That's true," said Susan. "You did make quite a noise."

"Also, it would have taken Mr Thomas longer to get in a fit state to chase after us," added Anna.

"That might have slowed him down a bit," Susan said thoughtfully.

"We could blackmail them, but no one would believe us," said Anna.

"Shame we didn't have a camera," said Susan.

"It would've shattered the lens," said Anna, moving off again.

"There's no need to be nasty," said Susan.

"Who's being nasty," asked Anna.

"That's true. It was quite a shock to the system, so it's a good job they hadn't got far," said Susan.

"You can say that again. Anyway, we're nearly out of this dump. We

234

can forget all about it and them," said Anna.

"Where are we going?" asked Susan.

"Away," said Anna vaguely.

"What are we going to do now?" asked Susan.

"Don't know," said Anna.

"Shouldn't we have a plan?" asked Susan.

"I suppose so. My first thought was to put some distance between us and them," said Anna.

"You don't think he's still behind us?" asked Susan looking nervously out of the back window.

"I shouldn't think so, but we don't want to be somewhere where he might come across us by accident," said Anna.

"Then what?" asked Susan.

"I don't know. But I'm sure we'll think of something," said Anna as they passed a sign indicating the town boundary. "I hope that's the last I see of that festering hole."

"Same here," said Susan.

A few hours later, the car pulling up woke Susan from her sleep.

"What've you stopped for?" asked Susan sleepily.

"To read that road sign," said Anna.

"Oh. What does it say?" asked Susan.

"That the road closes in ten minutes time," said Anna.

"Why? And who's closing it?" asked Susan.

"It is closing because the tide comes in and that place over there becomes an island and you can only get there by boat and I don't suppose anyone is going to come and put a barrier across, they just expect you not to be stupid," said Anna stretching.

"We'd better go back then," said Susan.

"I don't know," said Anna.

"We don't want to get caught there till the tide turns do we?" said Susan.

"We might get caught on the island, but with any luck Mr Thomas, if he is following us, will get caught on the mainland," said Anna.

"I hadn't thought of that. What are we waiting for then, we don't want the tide to come in whilst were debating do we," said Susan.

"No," said Anna starting up the engine and heading off down the road.

"Hope my watch isn't slow," she thought, glancing seawards. "The sea seems far enough off. But you can never tell, it all depends on how fast it comes in."

A picture wandered into Anna's mind, she was five years old and they were at the seaside. She was paddling. Pushing her feet into the wet sandy sea bed, then pulling them out again and laughing at the feel of the suction on her feet. Seeing the water filling in her foot prints. So fascinating, she didn't see the tide turn. There was no warning. It just hit her. One minute the sea was ankle deep. Next there seemed to be miles of it above her head. Someone pulled her out and asked where her parents were. He woke them up by shouting. He told them exactly what he thought of them. All the noise woke little brother up and that set him off. The man left because he couldn't compete with her brother for volume of sound. She'd been told off, after he'd gone and the holiday ended. It was the last time they went to the seaside.

The land began to rise. They had reached the other side and Anna drove a little way up the hill. She pulled off the road at a spot where she could see clear across the causeway to the mainland.

"What've you stopped here for?" asked Susan.

"To see if Mr Thomas is following us. And to watch the tide come in," said Anna.

"It's turned," said Susan pointing to the incoming tide. They watched in silence as the sea approached the road, then swept over it. Covering it quickly and effortlessly. Soon it was lost from sight.

"Not a good place to break down," said Susan.

"Or to find out your watch is slow," said Anna.

"Eh?" mumbled Susan.

"It'd take a formula one racing car to outrun that tide," said Anna.

"I thought we could sort of splash through it," said Susan.

"Don't be daft. The ignition'd get soaked," said Anna. "Amongst a few other things," she thought.

"So?" asked Susan.

"It'd stall and take at least ten minutes to get it started again." explained Anna.

"Well, we'd probably float," said Susan as Anna started up the engine.

"Like a brick," said Anna. "Keep an eye out for somewhere to sleep would you."

"Can't we drive round for a bit and explore," asked Susan.

"I've been driving all day," said Anna.

"Not quite, it was noon before we set off."

"And it's seven o'clock now. That's seven hours," said Anna.

"We've had breaks," Susan started.

"I'm not arguing. We'll find somewhere to stop tonight, then if you want to explore you can go ahead and do it by yourself," said Anna.

"Oh," said Susan, subsiding into silence.

It was Anna who noticed the B and B sign with the vacancies card hiding in the window. She stopped in front of the house.

"What've we stopped here for?" snapped Susan, Anna pointed to the sign. "Oh."

"Shall we go in," said Anna.

"It's not very exiting looking is it," said Susan.

"No," said Anna.

"Couldn't we find somewhere more interesting," asked Susan.

"I suppose we could scour the island for somewhere that is exciting enough for you. But I have a strong suspicion we wouldn't find anywhere. In any case I have no intention of driving any further," said Anna.

"You're just being pig headed," snapped Susan.

"Yes. Now shall we go in?" asked Anna.

"Doesn't look like I've got much choice does it," said Susan.

"You could sleep in the car, but I shouldn't think that'd be very exciting either," said Anna, "It certainly isn't comfortable and with all our stuff in it there's far less room."

The passenger door slammed shut and Susan stood on the pavement, arms folded, the picture of impatience. Anna, laughing silently to herself, took her time over covering their things with the sleeping bag and locking up.

"As you're so tired. I'll do the talking," said Susan.

"Sure," smiled Anna. "You're the boss. Just make sure we get somewhere to stay."

"Don't act up and get us thrown out," Anna thought.

"Are you coming," said Susan.

"Lead on," Anna replied.

"Right," said Susan hesitating slightly and then making for the front door. There was no door bell, so she knocked, using the rather ostentatious door knocker, a brass lion's head which shone from over polishing. A mournful looking lion, but then, anyone would look sad with a brass ring that size stuck in their mouth.

Susan's hand was raised to knock again when the door opened.

"Oh," she said, flustered, tucking the offending hand behind her back.

"What do you want," said a rather blousey lady, in her late 60's, with dyed blond hair, which was showing a good inch of root and make-up which looked like it had been applied with a trowel.

"Oh. My sister and I, we're on holiday and we need somewhere to stop for the night," said Susan.

"We've got no vacancies," said the lady.

"But the sign in the window says," Susan started.

"I've been too busy to change it," said the lady.

"But," said Susan.

"We've no vacancies. You'll have to try somewhere else," she said and slammed the door in their faces.

"Thanks for nothing," muttered Anna heading back to the car.

"If they've no rooms," said Susan shrugging her shoulders.

"No room. No room for us," said Anna.

"How can you tell?" asked Susan.

"The sign," Anna started, climbing into the car.

"She hadn't had time to change it," said Susan.

"Rubbish. They don't like having vacancy signs up. They come down as soon as the place is full. She just didn't want to have us littering up her nice clean guest house," said Anna.

"God, you get cynical when you're tired," snapped Susan.

"I'll do the talking next time," said Anna

"Are you saying it was my fault we didn't get a room?" said Susan.

"No," said Anna. "But you didn't want to stay here," she thought.

It was nearly an hour later, they stopped at a hotel, which also had a thriving restaurant and Susan had gone in to ask for directions. Anna, who had nodded off in the drivers seat, was rudely awakened by Susan returning and opening the drivers door.

"I've got us a room," shouted Susan.

"What!" said Anna leaping up and looking round her.

"I've got us a room for the night," said Susan.

"Where?" asked Anna.

"Here," said Susan proudly.

"And how much is that going to cost us?" asked Anna looking at the dark shape of the building.

"Nothing," said Susan.

"I'm asleep," said Anna.

"No it's true. The girl who does the washing and helps serve the breakfasts has gone. There's a replacement coming tomorrow, but their stuck today," said Susan.

"So we're working for our bed," said Anna.

"Well at least its a bed and if we can do this a lot, the money will last longer," said Susan.

"OK" said Anna climbing out of the car. "Lead the way."

"And we get an evening meal and breakfast as well," said Susan eagerly leading her to the hotel. "We get to eat first. Then we do the washing," said Susan.

"I could do with something to eat. I'm just about all in," said Anna.

"Not too tired to do the washing?" asked Susan.

"I'll tell you after I've eaten," said Anna.

"You sit here, I'll get the food," said Susan ushering Anna to a quiet table by the door.

"Don't forget I'm a vegetarian," said Anna.

"I hope she heard me," thought Anna as Susan dashed off.

"Pizza," said Anna as Susan put a plate on the table in front of her.

"It's vegetarian," said Susan.

"Of course," thought Anna, digging in.

The sight of the kitchen made Anna and Susan stop in their tracks. Every available surface seemed to be buried under a mountain of dirty dishes.

"Do you want to wash or dry?" asked Anna looking round the room for the sink.

"You should look at things positively," said Susan.

"Fine. Do you want to wash or dry," Anna asked again.

"If you don't mind. I'll dry. The detergent's not good for my hands," said Susan.

"Fine," said Anna rolling up her sleeves and approaching the sink which she had spotted in the corner of the room. It was full of cold stagnant water, food coated plates and greasy lipstick smeared cups.

"Well there's some of those pink gloves," she thought and picked them up.

"Oh God. They're soft," she muttered dropping them onto an already over full bin.

"What do you mean. They're soft?" asked Susan.

"The rubber's perished," said Anna gritting her teeth and fishing down into the foul smelling water.

"What are you doing?" asked Susan.

"Trying to find the plug," said Anna.

"Why?" asked Susan.

"Can't wash anything in this," said Anna nodding towards the sink.

"Wouldn't it be easier if you emptied the dishes out first?" asked Susan.

"And without being rude, where would you suggest I put them," asked Anna. Susan looked round the room, a girl came in and dumped a tray of mucky crocks on the only available space.

"They're shouting for clean crockery. So you'd better get a shift on," she said.

"Where do we put the clean stuff?" asked Susan, the girl looked round.

"I'll get you a trolley," she said. "Back in a minute."

"All right. I'll admit its not perfect," said Susan.

"But at least we don't have to pay for it and its got to be more comfortable than sleeping in the mini," said Anna with a sigh, finally getting some hot water through, she gave the sink a liberal squirt with a very thin looking washing up liquid and set to work on the mountain of dishes.

Susan smiled.

"Where are the tea towels?" she asked of the girl returning with the trolley.

"That cupboard over there. And you'd better get using them quick. There's hardly any clean stuff left," she said dashing off as a loud voice yelled for her to serve a customer.

"You'd better dry as I wash, there doesn't seem to be anywhere to stack it whilst it drains," said Anna handing over the first of many plates.

"It could be worse. Couldn't it?" asked Susan drying the plate with a greyish tea towel.

"Yes. We could've seen this lot before we ate," said Anna.

240

"Thanks," said Susan.

"And we could've seen the kitchen," added Anna.

"Don't mention that," said Susan looking slightly green at the thought of it, every surface seemed to ooze grease. Anna smiled and handed over the third plate.

Climbing into the mini next morning Anna felt sticky, dirty and somewhat queasy. It had not been the most comfortable of nights, the room had been somewhere between the kitchen and the bins, it stank of fried food and everywhere looked coated with grease. It was also much too close to the boiler for comfort, they hadn't needed an alarm clock to wake them, the boiler ignited with such a bang, they thought for a moment that the thing had exploded.

Breakfast was something she didn't care to think about much either. The scrambled egg had a rather odd hue to it, difficult to describe, but odd. The butter on the toast was definitely rancid, she recognised the flavour from breakfasts at the Poly, whist the toast had a vaguely musty taste to it. It didn't help that they then spent the next few hours washing up the breakfast dishes.

"Don't know where they all come from," Anna muttered as she remembered the mountains of plates, the hotel didn't look big enough to hold that many guest's and the restaurant didn't open in the morning. Her skin still felt greasy after ten minutes of washing with the most uncooperative bar of soap she's ever come across, but they had left the place stacked with clean crockery and cutlery and Anna had tried to clean the sink, she really had tried, but some things just aren't possible.

Sitting in the drivers seat, trying to summon up the get up and go she was rudely brought back to the real world by the sound of Susan hammering on the passenger door.

"Don't smash it in," snapped Anna opening the door.

"Where the hell were you? Not in this world that's for certain," said Susan.

"I'm tired. All right. Don't I get a minutes peace," snapped Anna.

"What's eating you?" asked Susan.

"Probably something in the scrambled egg," said Anna, trying not to think about it too much.

241

"It did look a bit off," said Susan.

"Only a bit?"

"The bacon and sausages were fine," said Susan.

"Great. I'm a vegetarian," said Anna.

"That's your decision," said Susan.

"Yes it is," said Anna starting the car. "Have you by any chance thought about where we should go when we get back to the mainland."

"I was thinking. It might be an idea to stay here. For the time being. Till we decide what to do next," said Susan.

"Here?" asked Anna, looking back at the building, an old stone built farmhouse which had been extended on several occasions and not exactly sympathetically, since the 1960's until it was hard to find the original building, though not at all difficult to find the overflowing bins.

"Well, not in this dump," said Susan.

"I should hope not," said Anna.

"I meant somewhere on the island," said Susan.

"Why?" asked Anna.

"Well, we're safe here. Mr Thomas can't get us. But if we get off the island. He might be waiting for us," said Susan.

"If we can cross to the mainland, he can cross to the island and there's not many places to hide here," said Anna.

"I suppose we ought to leave," said Susan.

"But?" asked Anna.

"What if he's waiting for us."

"What if he's here. Looking for us. There is that risk, though I can't see him spending that much time looking for us, he has a job to do. We just caught him in an embarrassing situation," said Anna.

"With his trousers down," said Susan giggling.

"It gave us a head start, you've got to admit," said Anna, smiling.

"Thing is. With her!"said Susan.

"An odd combination. Maybe he likes being dominated," said Anna.

"Or beaten up," said Susan. "Anyway, where shall we go?"

"I don't know. I was hoping you'd come up with some ideas."

"Me! You should know better than that. It takes me all my time to decide whether I want tea or coffee," said Susan.

"Oh well, at least you can't say I didn't ask," said Anna.

"So where are we going then?" said Susan.

"Forward," said Anna, putting the car into reverse in order to get out of the parking space.

Chapter 13
A pause for thought

Forward they drove, across the causeway, onto the mainland and down the coast road, pausing only to buy sandwiches and lemonade at a shop in a small village. Half an hour later they pulled off the road and parked on a quiet stretch of beach for their lunch.

"Tasty sandwich that," said Anna holding out her hand for the bottle of lemonade.

"Yes they are," said Susan handing over the bottle. "Shame the lemonade's warm."

"Well, it's a warm day, for the time of year. You can't expect to keep it cold," said Anna, yawning, stretching and settling back in the drivers seat with her eyes closed.

"Back in the land of the living are you," said Susan as Anna rubbed the sleep out of her eyes.

"Five minutes kip and you make it sound as if I've slept the afternoon away," said Anna stretching.

"It's ten past four," said Susan glancing at her watch.

"Are you sure that's right?" asked Anna.

"It was at four. I checked with the radio," said Susan.

"Oh God," muttered Anna sinking back in her seat.

"Is that it?" said Susan.

"What do you mean?" asked Anna.

"Are we going to sit here all day or are we going to do something," said Susan.

"Like what?" asked Anna. "How about you deciding something for a change," she thought.

"Go somewhere else. Get something to eat. Find somewhere to stay the night. Little things like that," said Susan.

244

"In other words. Get shifting," said Anna.

"Yes," said Susan.

Anna started the engine and put the car into reverse, but it didn't move. She checked the handbrake.

"Well that's off," she thought and revved the engine a bit more.

"Shouldn't we be moving?" asked Susan.

"Yes," said Anna.

"Why aren't we?" asked Susan.

"I don't think the tyres are gripping the sand," said Anna.

"What?"

"Could you nip out and see what the front wheels are doing," said Anna.

"What!"

"Just do it," snapped Anna and a startled Susan leapt out of the car and ran round to the front.

"They're going round and round and flinging sand up," she said.

"Right," said Anna, turning the engine off.

"Why've you stopped the engine?" asked Susan.

"Because all we're doing is digging ourselves deeper into the sand," said Anna.

"What shall we do?" asked Susan.

"We could push it onto firmer ground," said Anna looking round for firmer ground.

"I would help, but with my back. I don't think I dare risk it," Susan started.

"Yeah. Funny how it always plays up when there's some work to do," thought Anna.

"Then we'd better go for help," said Anna.

"Do you think that's wise. Mr Thomas," Susan started.

"I can't shift it by myself. I would have thought with this load there'd be plenty of traction. But seems like there isn't. So we'll just have to try and find someone to help," said Anna.

"Can't we try a bit longer. We might succeed," Susan suggested.

"We might succeed in burying ourselves," said Anna. "We need to put something under the tyres, something for them to grip on to, so the car can get moving. The thing is, we haven't got anything suitable."

"Isn't there anything we can do?" said Susan, looking round wildly, as if an answer would spring up out of nowhere.

"Go and get some help," said Anna.

"But. Mr Thomas," Susan started.

"Has probably gone back to the Poly. He has a job. He can't spend all his time looking for us. He wouldn't have the first idea were to even start, so the chances of him finding us here are pretty slim to say the least. So, are you coming with me or do you want to stay with the car," said Anna.

"Which do you think'd be best?" asked Susan.

"Just one decision. That's all I ask," thought Anna.

"I don't know. It's entirely up to you. But if you stay with the car you can keep an eye on the stuff," she said.

"You're not going to leave me alone are you?" asked Susan.

"Then you'd better come with me," said Anna.

"But," Susan started.

"The choice is simple, you either stay here by yourself, or you come with me to find help," said Anna, getting more and more frustrated.

"Couldn't we wait here for someone to come," suggested Susan hopefully.

"How many people have you seen this afternoon?" asked Anna.

"None," Susan admitted.

"Exactly. Do you really expect that to change?" asked Anna.

"No," said Susan getting out of the car.

"Right. Well, there were some buildings being done up down the road. We might be able to find someone there to help us," said Anna locking the passenger door and then getting out of the car and locking her door.

"I see. Go and find a man to fix it eh," said Susan following down the road. "That doesn't exactly comply with feminist ideals does it."

"Assuming only men do up houses doesn't comply with feminist ideals either, neither does being unable to drive and therefore being dependent on others for transport. Admitting you need help getting your car moved is common sense. In this situation a man would do the same thing. Anyway, you weren't much help, so don't go preaching feminism to me. You're a damn sight more dependent than I am," said Anna.

"All right. Keep you hair on. I just thought I'd mention it. There's no need to get all aerated. Can't a body speak without getting their head bitten off?" said Susan. "Well can't they?" repeated Susan when Anna didn't answer.

"I'm thinking about it," said Anna.

"Let me know when you come to a decision won't you," said Susan.

"He looks familiar?" said Anna.

"Him. On the dump truck?" asked Susan. "Can't say as I've seen him before and I'd not forget that in a rush."

"That's a fine attitude to take. He's a human being, not a lump of meat. If he treated you like that you'd be furious and rightly so. You should judge someone by their personality and their actions, not their looks," said Anna.

"Yes," said Susan. He does move well."

"Your incorrigible," said Anna.

"Where are you going?" asked Susan, dashing after Anna.

"He might be able to help us with the mini," said Anna.

"That's true," said Susan smiling.

"I just wish I could put a name to the face. I feel sure I've met him before," said Anna.

"God. Your memory," said Susan.

"Just because I haven't got a one track mind like you," said Anna.

"You must have, to follow my train of thought," said Susan.

The man on the dump truck smiled broadly at Anna. Watching as they walked over in his direction, he turned off the engine so they didn't have to shout to make themselves heard.

"Hello Anna. And what brings you out here?" he asked.

"We parked the car on the beach back there and its got stuck," said Anna, still racking her brain to put a name to him.

"Yes. We tried to move it, but, I finally talked her into going for help," said Susan.

"You," Anna started.

"My name's Susan, by the way. It doesn't look as if Anna's going to introduce us, so what's your name."

"I'm Phil. You're not the Susan who disappeared just before Christmas are you. The one with the nervous breakdown."

"Yes. How did you know about that?" asked Susan.

"Anna told me. By the way, how did that field trip go?" he asked Anna.

"The pictures, he was at that stupid film," the thought clicked in Anna's mind.

"That was a complete fiasco from start to finish," she said.

"As bad as you thought it would be?" he asked.

"Worse. Much worse. The lecturers hadn't thought to contact British Rail. The toilets were locked on the Sunday, so they took us back on the Monday morning and it was full of commuters."

247

"Commuters."

"Nipping to the loo on their way to work," said Anna smiling at the memory of their surprised expressions.

"Oh no," laughed Phil.

"They complained about us," said Anna.

"I wouldn't have complained about you," said Phil.

"I think it was Mr Thomas getting in everyone's way, pointing out the ancient plumbing with an umbrella, going on about the design of the urinals and the way the pattern of the tiles was adapted to complement their design. He uses a rather large brolly to point things out.   Poor souls didn't know what he was going to point to next.   As it was he nearly caught a few people with it.   In his hands a brolly is quite a dangerous implement," Anna said laughing.

"I wish I'd been there to see it," Phil smiled.

"So do I," said Susan bitterly.

"It was rather comical.   Even when we got thrown out," Anna added with a laugh.

"Yes.   Well, I'm sure we could talk about this all day," interrupted Susan.   "But this isn't shifting the car is it."

"Of course.   The car.   We'll I'm sure we can pull it out with this," he said patting the dump truck.

"Where will we sit?" asked Susan.

"In there," he said pointing to the scoop.

"I'll get filthy in there," she said.

"You can wait here till we get back," said Anna, carefully climbing in and making herself reasonably comfortable.

"OK, but don't you dare forget me," said Susan, not looking at all certain about the whole thing.

"As if we could," said Phil, starting the engine and drowning out Susan's reply.

Not the most comfortable method of transport, but five minutes found them back at the mini.

"So this is your car," he said gazing at the thirteen year old mini.

"It gets me around.   Generally," said Anna defensively.

"You've got it well loaded.   Where are you two going?" asked Phil.

"We hadn't decided," said Anna.

"Some more odd stuff happening on your course?" asked Phil.

"Yes.   I thought I'd get away to think things out," said Anna.

248

"What about your parents?" asked Phil.

"I went to them first. They told Mr Thomas. It was odd, they listened to him, but not to me," said Anna.

"How did you end up with her?" asked Phil, looking down the road to where Susan was standing waiting for them.

"I found a letter from her at home. It arrived before Christmas, but they didn't tell me about it. She'd been put in an institution. I went to see her and we just walked out of the place," said Anna.

"No one tried to stop you?"

"I think they were busy putting the fire out. I went to visit her and the nurse suggested I took her for a walk in the gardens and then all this smoke started coming out of the windows. So, we just walked out of the gate they opened to let the fire engines in," said Anna.

"And all this?" he said looking at the car.

"We thought we'd get our stuff back from the Poly. Susan did look rather obvious in her institutional clothes and she was beginning to smell," said Anna.

"They didn't stop you?" he asked.

"They didn't notice we were there till we were just about to leave, so we had to leave a bit quicker than we intended, but we had everything we'd gone for," said Anna with a smile.

"They didn't chase you or anything did they?" asked Phil.

"They tried, but we outran them," said Anna patting the mini.

"What were they driving, a hearse?"

"No, but we did see quite a few of them about, he was driving a new Capri," said Anna.

"Then it must be quicker than it looks," said Phil looking at the mini. "What are you going to do next?" he asked.

"I'm not sure. We haven't thought that one out yet," said Anna.

"You can't spend all your life hiding."

"We know and we can't leave them to mess up other people's lives, the way they have ours. We've got to stop them. We just haven't worked out how," said Anna. "Did I just say that," she thought. "Then again, they must be stopped."

"And how will you do that whilst you're dashing about the country?" asked Phil.

"I don't know. But we'd better get the car shifted, Susan'll start worrying," said Anna.

"We've not been that long," he said fishing the rope out of the dumper.

"It doesn't take much. She's got no idea of time and she's paranoid about being sent back there. They had her drugged up to the eyeballs," said Anna.

"That's understandable," he said looking thoughtfully at the mini.

"It passed it's M.O.T. just before Christmas. Didn't need a re-test or anything," Anna mumbled.

"Looks solid enough," he said tying the rope to the rear subframe and attaching the other end to the dump truck.

"Do you want me to do anything?" asked Anna.

"Take the handbrake off?"

"Oh. Yes. Yes of course," she said fumbling for her keys. "I should've thought. I'll only be a minute."

"It's all right. There's no rush."

"There," she said slamming shut the door. "Is there anything else I can do."

"No," he said putting the dump truck into reverse.

Two minutes later the car was back on the road.

"Thank-you. Thank-you," Anna shouted above the sound of the dump truck, patting the car cautiously as he untied the rope.

"I was thinking," he said, standing in the road, holding one end of the rope. "The buildings I'm converting. I'm staying there whilst I'm working on them. No one minds. You and your friend, if you wanted. No one would mind. No one would know. You could stop here too. There's plenty of room and you could think out your plan of action. Well, its an idea anyway. You don't have to. It's just an idea."

"You're sure it'd be all right?" said Anna.

"Oh yes. There'd be no problems. Of course its still a bit rough," said Phil.

"It can't be as rough as sleeping in that," she added pointing to the mini.

"You've slept in there?" said Phil, looking at all the bags.

"It was before I collected Susan and most of the bags," said Anna.

"Anyway, they can't be far off completion," said Anna looking at the buildings.

"They're not far off. Just a couple of weeks, they'll be done and I'll be off somewhere else."

"We should've come up with something by then," said Anna. "And it'll be easier without all that driving. It's not the quietest of cars. Susan doesn't realise how tiring it is," said Anna.

"Doesn't she share the driving?"

"Can't drive. And with her lapses of concentration it wouldn't be a good idea. Anyway, the car can be temperamental."

"You don't trust her with it?" asked Phil.

"No. Anyway, we'd best go back and tell her."

"You go first and I'll follow. If it can outrun a Capri, it can go faster than a dump truck," said Phil.

"It has its moments, specially when the sun's shining. It can still leave a lot of cars standing at the lights," said Anna getting in the car and heading back down the road to Susan.

"God I'm knackered," thought Anna. "I shouldn't be, I've slept all afternoon.

How am I going to put this to Susan. I need this rest. I can't go any further. That's how I'll tell her if she argues. I'll give her an ultimatum," thought Anna, pulling off the road and driving into the courtyard in the centre of the buildings and out of sight of the road.

"What are you parking here for?" asked Susan dashing up to the mini.

"Phil said we could stay here for a few days," said Anna.

"Where will we sleep?" asked Susan, looking round the courtyard.

"The buildings on that side are ready for sale," said Anna, pointing to the ones on the right. "But those on this side aren't quite finished yet so we can sleep anywhere in them. He says there's plenty of room," said Anna.

"Oh. Well, I don't mind if you don't," said Susan.

"Good. That's settled that then," said Anna as the dump truck turned into the drive. "I'll tell Phil."

"Could you ask him where the toilets are whilst you're at it. I'm fair busting for a leak."

Meals, at first, were a bit of a haphazard affair. Anna was too tired to cook and spent most of her time sleeping. Susan wasn't much on cooking, she couldn't keep her mind on it. Hard boiled eggs tended to boil dry and explode, everything else was either burnt to a crisp or nearly raw. It didn't seem fair to expect Phil to organise the food as well as provide the accommodation, but he always seemed quite happy to nip down the road for a take-away.

251

A few days rest and Anna was feeling much better. An evening meal at half past nine which was a combination of half cooked and burnt food convinced her to take charge of the meals.

"I'm no chef," she thought. "But I can't do worse than this."

The next day she planned the meal, simple quick and easy, but tasty, her one good dish, the one that always went down well. Mushrooms and courgettes in white sauce on cracked wheat. Anna was especially pleased with her efforts.

"How's it coming on?" asked Phil leaning against the door.

"Nearly done," said Anna. "About five minutes and it'll be ready for serving."

"I got a bottle of wine," said Phil.

"That'll be nice," said Anna with a smile.

"I'll put it in the fridge. Give it time to cool a bit," said Phil.

"Do you know if there are any glasses?" she asked.

"Glasses?" said Phil.

"For the wine," said Anna.

"Wine glasses there aren't. But there are a few tumblers. I think they came free with petrol or something," said Phil.

"They'll do fine. The wine was a good idea of yours. It'll make the meal special," said Anna smiling.

"Well, when's this special meal going to be ready," said Susan bursting into the room. "I'm half starved."

"I don't know if we should feed you now," said Anna. "I was thinking of waiting till at least nine."

"What!" Susan exclaimed, as Phil hid his head in the wall cupboard, pretending to look for the tumblers. "I'll never last. I'll be fainting. It'd be cruel. And the food would be spoilt. It would be such a waste."

"Well we might let you eat now if you promise to do the dishes," said Anna thoughtfully.

"Yes. Of course. I'll do the dishes. You won't make me wait. It'd be cruel and the food smells so nice," said Susan ready to agree to anything.

Phil could suppress the laughter no longer, nearly dropping the tumblers, he lent against the wall laughing. Anna started giggling. Susan looked from Phil to Anna.

"You rotten lot. I've a good mind not to do the dishes for that," snapped Susan.

"Your face," laughed Anna. "It was a picture, but it would've served

252

you right if we had made you wait. You kept us waiting long enough for tea yesterday."

"Well, if it'd been left to you we'd have had nothing," snapped Susan.

"Shall we eat before it burns," suggested Phil holding three plates and a serving spoon.

"It would be a shame to spoil it," said Anna.

"OK. So I'm not brilliant in the kitchen," said Susan.

"How much do you want?" asked Anna.

"Oh. I don't know. Just dish it out. I'll eat what I'm given. You know me. I'm not fussy," said Susan.

"Right," said Anna lining up the three plates.

"There's more than I thought," said Anna, as the plates filled up and the pan didn't seem to empty. "Oh well, I can make something out if it tomorrow. The mushrooms didn't shrink as much as I expected."

"It looks lovely," said Phil fishing out the cutlery.

"Yes. So lets cut the talk and tuck in," said Susan grabbing the first plate and sitting herself at the kitchen table.

"You'll need these," said Phil handing over a knife and fork.

"They would help," said Susan.

"Quicker than using your fingers," said Anna bringing the two remaining plates over.

"Swap you a plate for a knife and fork," she said to Phil.

The meal was good. So was the wine. Anna and Phil finished it off whilst Susan made the coffee. It was her coffee percolator. No one had been prepared to give her more than fifty pence for it and she refused to be parted from it for that. Anna couldn't be bothered to argue the point.

"Have you had any thoughts about the future?" asked Phil gazing at the last drops of wine in his glass. "Not that I'm trying to get rid of you or anything," he added hastily. "I was just wondering."

"Haven't really given it much thought," said Anna.

"Neither have I," said Susan, bringing the coffee stuff in from the kitchen.

"You've been too busy sun-bathing," said Phil.

"True. But I looked so pale, anyone would think I'd just got out of an institution or something, also, at this time of year, you have to grab every bit of sun you can and it has been glorious this week."

"Perhaps," said Anna. "But Phil is right, we ought to be thinking about what we're going to do," said Anna.

253

"Why?" asked Susan

"Because we can't spend the rest of our lives here. Phil'll be finished in another week. And there's more to life than topping your sun tan up."

"Your only jealous cos you don't tan," said Susan.

"What happens. Do you go red and peel?" asked Phil with a grin.

"I go pink, my freckles multiply, then, in the evening the pink fades. The only way I'll ever get a tan is if my freckles join up," said Anna.

"I'll try not show you up," said Susan.

"Doesn't bother me in the slightest. Though I think we're getting side-tracked. The question is what are we going to do next," said Anna.

"Do we really have to do something," said Susan.

"Yes. We said we were going to do something about the course. Something to make them drop that syllabus. It's just a question of what," said Anna.

"Easier said than done," muttered Susan.

"At least you know what you want to do," said Phil.

"Great. I'd like to fly to the moon, but I know I'll never get there," snapped Susan

"You never know what the future might bring. Twenty or thirty years time they might be running package trips there," said Phil.

"You've been reading too many sci-fi books. That's your problem. Reality isn't like that. In reality someone can make a total mess of your life and if they've got the power, they can keep it hidden. They can bury the facts and steam roller anyone who argues with them," said Susan.

"That's what we need to do. Get the facts known," said Anna gazing into her glass of wine. "All we need is to bring them out into the open so that there's nothing they can do to hide what they've done."

"And how do you propose to do that," snapped Susan.

"The newspapers," Anna started.

"They aren't likely to listen to us," Susan interrupted her. "We haven't got any documentary evidence. They'd just ask us for proof and we haven't got any."

"So get the proof," said Phil.

"That's at the Poly and we can't exactly go back there again to get it," said Susan.

"It's all in the computer," said Anna.

"That bloody tin box. That's the source of all our problems," snapped Susan.

254

"Don't be daft. It's only a machine. It's the program that's caused the problems," said Anna.

"Same difference," snapped Susan.

"No it isn't. If we could get to the computer it could be programmed to send all the information to the newspapers. It would be such a big story they couldn't bury it then," said Anna.

"It might be possible to programme all that, if you were a computer genius, which neither of us is," said Susan.

"Or some sort of computer geek," said Phil

"Or a geek, or a wizard, it's all pie in the sky, isn't it?" shouted Susan, looking form Anna to Phil and then back to Anna. "Exactly," she added when no one said anything. "I know where all this is leading to, we've got to go back to the Poly and I don't fancy doing that or staying there long enough to programme that blasted computer. You're asking too much, much too much."

"What about that friend of yours, the one who's studying computer programming," said Anna. "Perhaps he'd help."

"You know a computer buff?" said Phil.

"Yes," said Susan. "But he's at a different Poly. What would work on his computer probably wouldn't work on ours. You know how temperamental these bloody things are."

"Wasn't there a land link between the computers in the two Polys?" said Anna.

"No one uses it any more," said Susan. "They were having problems with it, I think the project it was set up for was dropped, lack of funds or something."

"But the land line is still there," said Anna.

"And a right bloody nuisance it is too," snapped Susan.

"How come?" asked Phil.

"I don't know how, but sometimes when you were using the computer the land line would leap into action and you'd get something from the other computer. It could be a right pain," said Susan.

"Or you'd try and get a print out of what you'd done and none of the printers would respond, presumably there was one at the other Poly printing it out, whilst our printers would start printing stuff from them."

"How did you know it was from them?" asked Phil.

"The names of the people the letters were from, they weren't lecturers at our Poly, so I looked them up, they were at the other Poly. Also, I used to

255

find programs on my work space that I hadn't put there," said Anna.

"But why did it happen?" asked Phil.

"Gremlins in the machine," snapped Susan.

"Don't be daft," said Anna, gazing at her empty glass.

"All right clever clogs, you explain it," snapped Susan.

"Simple. Every area in a computer has an address. Some areas on our computer had the same address as areas on theirs. When the land line tripped into action the stuff went to the right address, but in the wrong computer. Logical," said Anna.

"Shame you can't use that land line to programme you computer from your friends Poly," said Phil.

"I don't see why we can't," said Anna. "Your friend wouldn't mind, would he?"

"Russell?" said Susan thoughtfully. "No, he wouldn't mind. We could go tomorrow and talk to him about it."

"That's settled that then," said Anna. "We have a plan of action."

"When's this coffee going to be ready?" asked Phil.

"Now," said Susan. "I'll pour it out."

"Then we'd better get our bags packed," said Anna.

"Can't we do that tomorrow?" asked Susan.

"Yes, can't you do that tomorrow?" Phil echoed.

"I might be able to, but if you leave it till tomorrow," said Anna, looking at Susan. "It'll be mid afternoon before we leave and we don't even know how far it is. I can't see this Russell being all that happy if we turn up on his doorstep in the middle of the night."

"OK. Point taken," said Susan. "I'll go and pack, as soon as I've finished my coffee and done the dishes."

"OK. I'll wash the dishes," said Anna.

"Why on earth did you do that?" asked Phil, as Susan went up the stairs to pack.

"Because I'd get a running commentary all through the dishes and she'd use it as an excuse not to pack her things till tomorrow, then I'd end up doing most of the packing whilst she stands there doing nothing except tell me that I'm doing it wrong. I know her all too well," said Anna.

"I'll dry if you wash," said Phil.

"Thanks," said Anna. "It would get things done quicker."

Chapter 14
Another Poly

The next day dawned bright and sunny, like all the days since they'd been there, Anna went downstairs to find Susan looking through the road atlas.

"I've found Russell's Polytechnic," she said with a grin. "I was going to plot a route there, but there's one problem," she added.

"What's that?" asked Phil wondering in, with a loaf of bread and some milk.

"I don't know where we are," she said.

"Bit fundamental that," said Anna. "Though it's not stopped us before."

"I can point that out on the map," said Phil. "But I'd like my breakfast first," he added, waving the bread and milk in the air.

"I'm sure we can manage that," said Anna with a grin.

After breakfast, Phil showed Susan where they were and then helped Anna load their bags back into the mini whilst Susan worked out a route.

"I've got it sorted," Susan declared, as Anna put the last of Susan's bags in the back of the mini.

"What a surprise," said Phil.

"Perfect timing," said Anna with a grin. "Just when all the work's done."

"What was that?" asked Susan, getting into the car.

"We were wondering if you'd like to go to the toilet before we go," said Anna.

"No. There's no point in hanging round. Lets hit the road," said Susan, closing the passenger door with a slam.

"Right," said Anna. "Well it was good of you to put us up," she said to Phil.

"No problems," he smiled. "It was interesting. When this is all over, if you're at a loose end or something, it would be nice to catch up," he added hesitantly. "Here's the office phone number, if you ring them they can always tell you where I am, they'll know where I'm going to next."

"Thanks," said Anna taking the business card he handed to her.

"Are you two going to be all day?" shouted Susan. "I thought the idea was to get an early start."

"Yes. We'd better go," said Anna putting the card in her pocket and getting into the car.

"Take care," said Phil and then closed the door. The engine burst into life and they headed off back down the road that they'd arrived on just a few days earlier.

"There's something about Polytechnic buildings that just shouts at you," thought Anna as they pulled up in front of what seemed to be a major building at Russell's Polytechnic.

"According to that sign its the administration building," said Susan.

"Right and that looks like a car park," said Anna.

"A load of stationary cars arranged in rows, generally reads as a car park, so?" asked Susan.

"We could park up and decide what to do rather than driving round in circles using up petrol and getting nowhere," said Anna turning into the car park.

"That makes sense," said Susan, looking round.

"So," said Anna with a sigh, turning the engine off, "Now that we're here how do you propose finding this Russell?"

"I don't know," said Susan. "I was rather hoping you'd come up with some ideas on that front," she added smiling rather sheepishly at Anna.

"God, do I have to do all the thinking," thought Anna. "My brain hurts with all this thinking, I'm just not used to it."

"We could ask at the administration building," she said. "After all we are in front of it," she added, gesturing towards the late 60's, early 70's office block.

"But what will we say? What should we ask them?" asked Susan looking and sounding flustered.

"Well we could say we are friends of the family, just passing through and thought it would be nice to meet up with him, Russell what-ever his name is. What is his surname?" Anna asked.

"I don't know his surname, they'll ask his surname and I don't know it," Susan started. "They might get suspicious and start asking questions. They might get on to the men in white coats."

"They will do if you get yourself worked up like this," thought Anna.

"Well, we could say we are thinking of doing computer studies next year and wondered where the building was that the lectures were in?" Anna suggested.

"They'd wonder why we didn't write to ask about the course," said Susan.

"We have, but as we were passing on our way to visit relatives, we thought we'd stop by and just have a look round," said Anna, her fingers mentally crossed, hoping that Susan thought the story would pass muster.

"It might work," she said hesitantly.

"Let me do the talking, just agree with anything I say and if it looks like they're getting suspicious we'll say we need to get something from the car and leg it," said Anna.

"OK, sounds like a plan, let's do it," Susan said, getting out of the car.

"Well, that's got her moving," thought Anna, leaning over to lock the passenger side door. "Better go with it before she runs out of steam," Anna looked round and saw Susan disappearing off in the direction of the administration building. "She certainly can shift it when she puts her mind to it," Anna thought dashing after her.

Susan came to a halt in front of the revolving door at the front of the building, the reception desk clearly visible through the glass wall.

"I never did like those doors," said Susan, "I'm never sure which way to push or anything."

"Can't say I'm keen on them either," said Anna, grabbing Susan by the arm and pulling her into the revolving door and out the other side. "That wasn't too bad was it?" she smiled, "Just a question of timing."

"Thanks," said Susan looking round stunned.

"Reception's there," Anna said pulling her towards the desk. "Good afternoon," she said, smiling at the Receptionist.

"Can I help you?" asked the Receptionist with a smile.

"I do hope so," Anna smiled, "We are thinking of studying computer science next year and as we were passing through, we were just wondering if we could see the building we'd be working in when we get here."

"That would be Somerville Building," said the Receptionist with a smile.

"Could you direct us there?" asked Anna.

"Certainly, there's a car park to the left of this building," she said, pointing in the direction of the car park the mini was in.

"That's where we parked our car," Anna smiled. "It is OK for us to park there isn't it?" she asked.

"Yes, it'll be fine there," smiled the Receptionist. "The car park is between the two buildings."

"That's great. Thank-you," smiled Anna and grabbing Susan by the arm pulled her back through the revolving doorway.

"That was easier than I thought it would be," said Anna once they were back out in the fresh air.

"Did you have to drag me through the door like that," snapped Susan.

"You didn't look like you were going to walk thought it under your own steam," said Anna. "And I thought it best to make as little fuss over it as possible so that it wouldn't register in anyone's memory."

"Why's that so important?" asked Susan.

"She's busy, within half an hour she'll probably have forgotten we've even been here," Anna smiled. "That way no one will ask any questions."

"You think of everything," said Susan.

"Someone has to," thought Anna, heading off across the car park.

"Wait for me," shouted Susan as she realised what Anna was doing.

"You didn't wait for me," thought Anna without a glance back.

"Do you have to walk so fast," grumbled Susan.

"We want to get there," said Anna pointing to Somerville Building, which was a slightly less impressive design, standing only two stories high, it looked to be of a similar age, but the paint on the windows was peeling and the drain pipes needed attention and had done for a while judging by the green stains on the walls.

"What do we do now," wailed Susan, after a quick look round to make sure no one was within hearing distance.

"Wait outside and see if you can spot him," Anna suggested, sitting down on a convenient low wall in front of the building.

"But, we could be here all day?" Susan moaned, sitting down next to her.

"I doubt it," said Anna. "It's nearly lunch time and there looks to be a lot of students heading for the door. So peel your eyes and get ready to spot this Russell fellow."

"There he is," said Susan pointing to a rather scruffy specimen tagging on the rear of the crowd.

"I thought you said he was a bit of a dish?" said Anna.

"You're just a philistine," muttered Susan. "Anyway, you were the one who was saying that you shouldn't judge people by their physical appearance."

"Susan? Susan Lake? Is that really you?" asked Russell walking up to Susan.

"Yes, it's me," smiled Susan.

"Well that solves the problem of attracting his attention," thought Anna.

"I dreamt about you last night," said Russell smiling. "Now here you are."

"Don't tell us about the dream, I really don't want to know," thought Anna.

"Yes. Here I am," said Susan smiling.

"How come you're here?" asked Russell.

"We came to see you," said Susan still smiling.

"Her face is going to crack if she keeps this up much longer," thought Anna.

"Why?" he asked. "Not that I mind you visiting or anything," he added quickly. "It's just so out of the blue."

"Sorry about that," said Susan. But, we've got a problem with the Poly computer and well, I thought of you," she paused looking sheepish.

"Hello, I'm Anna. We hoped you could help us," Anna said by way of a reminder that she was there as well.

"Am I right in supposing that this is something you don't want to ask your Poly's technicians about?" Russell asked Susan.

"You have it in one," said Anna rather annoyed by the fact that Russell hadn't even acknowledged her presence, let alone addressed any comments to her.

"So, what exactly is the nature of the problem?" Russell asked Susan.

"We don't want to go into a long winded discussion out here," Anna said to Susan. "We could also do with something to eat. Why don't you suggest we go somewhere to eat and talk about this."

"That sounds like a good idea," said Russell to Susan. "I know just the place, if you don't mind Italian."

"Lead on," said Anna.

"What do you think?" Russell asked Susan.

"Like Anna said, that sounds like a good idea, after all you know the area," Susan said with a warm smile.

"God I could puke," thought Anna. "Except my stomach's empty."

"So what is this computer problem?" asked Russell once they had got to the restaurant and the pizza's and garlic bread had been placed on the table.

"Well," Anna began, but stopped when she saw that Russell only had eyes for Susan. "You explain it," she said to Susan.

"Difficult to know where to start," Susan began.

"At the start of the year," said Anna. "At registration," she added helping herself to a slice of mushroom pizza.

"Yes, at registration for the beginning of the year," Susan said. "There was something very suspicious about the way the lecturers were behaving, almost like they were expecting trouble. Anyway, they told us that they'd computerised the course."

"In what way?" asked Russell.

"They were using the computer to optimise our study time, organise assignments, field trips, the time table, everything," said Susan.

"Was there a problem with that?" asked Russell.

"Wasn't there just," said Anna, but Russell paid no heed to what she had to say.

"Talk to yourself," thought Anna, picking up a piece of garlic bread.

"We are doing a degree in Environmental Science," said Susan slowly. "The work we were being asked to do bore no relevance to the course, the lecture rooms kept changing, as did the subjects we were being taught in them, we were given a new timetable nearly every week and even those weren't accurate."

"Didn't you try to talk to your tutors about this?" asked Russell.

"Yes, they got very defensive about things. Seemed to think that we were at fault for questioning it at all. Like we should embrace the new technology and just accept everything they told us," said Susan.

"Does sound like you didn't give it much of a chance," Russell, picking up his second piece of cheese and tomato pizza.

"Doesn't like mushrooms," thought Anna absently.

"Are you saying that we're nuts?" Susan demanded.

"No. No of course not," said Russell. "But if you'd listened to their explanation."

"They didn't explain anything," said Susan, starting to get agitated. "They said that if I didn't have faith in the computers then I had the problem and that was when they sent me off to, that place," her voice failed, the tears rolling down her face she turned to Anna. "You explain, I can't."

"What did they do to her?" Russell demanded of Anna.

262

"They put her away under the mental health act. Had her drugged up to the eyeballs and locked up," said Anna.

"All because she asked them questions?" asked Russell, finally talking to Anna.

"Questions they didn't want to answer," said Anna. "And they'd have done the same to me if I hadn't legged it," thought Anna, "but you aren't interested in that."

"Is that why you're here?" Russell asked.

"Yes," sobbed Susan. "There's something going on at that place that shouldn't be, they have to be stopped before they ruin anyone else's lives. We need to expose what they've done to the world, put it in the papers before they can stop us. Then they'd have to explain themselves."

"So you want me to go through your Polytechnic computer, find out what they've done and then patch it into the newspapers so that it gets published," Russell summed it all up.

"Yes," said Susan, smiling at him through her tears.

"It may take a few days, but I'm sure, for you Susan, I could do it," Russell smiled holding her hands and kissing them.

"God give me strength," thought Anna looking at them. The waiter came with the bill, Anna paid it because it didn't look like she stood any chance of attracting the attention of either Susan or Russell.

"If you've finished, I think they want us to leave," said Anna trying to get someone's attention.

"What's the time?" muttered Russell, looking at his watch. "I'll have to go back to lectures, but I must speak to you afterwards. Where are you staying?"

"Nowhere at the moment," said Susan, as they headed off out of the restaurant and back to Somerville Building.

"Right, well, there's an empty room on my floor. I should think you could crash there for a few days whilst I see what I can do. Look, I've got lectures for the next three hours, but if you meet me outside here after that, we can get you settled into the spare room," said Russell, pointing to Somerville Building.

"We'll be waiting," Susan smiled, stopping by the mini.

"Is that your car?" asked Russell, once again addressing everything to Susan.

"No, it's my car," said Anna.

"Right, well, I'll see you back here then, in three hours," said Russell to

Susan and then dashed off to his lectures.

"Talk about a charmless nerd," said Anna as they watched him heading back across the car park to Somerville Building.

"Do you have to be so rotten to him," asked Susan as they climbed back into the mini, the weather had turned, it was just starting to rain.

"I thought I was quite restrained," said Anna. "I didn't throttle the little snot."

"I don't know what he did to upset you," Susan began.

"Addressing everything to you and barely acknowledging my presence, how's that for starters," said Anna, slamming her door shut.

"It's just his way, he takes a while getting to know people," said Susan.

"Yes, well maybe he'd better learn that he won't get to know anyone if he doesn't acknowledge their existence," said Anna, closing her eyes in order to get some sleep and to end the conversation which was becoming tedious.

Just over three hours later Anna was awoken by the sound of tapping on the passenger side window of the mini.

"You're boyfriend's back," said Anna elbowing Susan in the ribs.

"What. Oh yes. Russell," mumbled Susan, opening the car door and smiling broadly.

"Hello," said Russell. "I've finished my lectures for the day."

"Good," smiled Susan.

"If you'd like to come to my hall of residence, we could sort out the empty room," said Russell looking hopefully at Susan.

"Is that invitation open to me as well?" Anna asked Susan, "Two can play at that game," she thought.

"Can Anna stay as well?" asked Susan, when Russell didn't answer Anna's question.

"Yes, I suppose so," said Russell to Susan.

"Great," thought Anna. "I'm here on sufferance."

"Well, shall we get there?" Anna snapped.

"Right," said Russell jumping. "If you give me a lift I can direct you?" he offered.

"Can you fit in the back?" Anna asked Susan.

"Sure," said Susan, looking at the luggage on the back seat.

264

"If you pass some of those over we can fit them into the front here," Russell said to Susan.   A couple of minutes later they'd made enough space in the back for them both to fit in.

"She doesn't need that much space," said Anna. "And you'll need somewhere to put your feet," she added, but her words were ignored and Russell climbed into the back of the car after Susan.

"Great," she thought, getting out to shut the passenger side door.   "I meant for him to sit in the front so that he could direct me, not for them both to sit in the back like I'm some sort of taxi driver."

"If you take a left down the hill after we leave the car park, then the third left followed by the forth right," started Russell.

"How about you direct me as we go, rather than give me a long list that I can forget or get in the wrong order," said Anna.

"Anna doesn't do remembering long lists," sighed Susan gazing at Russell.

"Oh right," said Russell.

"I thought it was left here?" said Anna at the exit to the car park.

"Left, down the hill," said Russell.   "Then third left."

"Can't do third left," said Anna.   "There's a no entry sign."

"What?   But I always go that way," said Russell.

"You wouldn't if you drove," said Anna.   "I'll try the next left, see if we can get to your hall that way."

It took half an hour driving round in ever increasing circles to get to the hall of residence and to park in one of the dozen parking spaces available for the residents.

"This must be fun at the start and end of the year," thought Anna, looking up at the 1960's brutalist tower block.   "Then again, I can't see it being a bundle of laughs living here at any time of the year."

"Will the car be safe here?" Anna asked and her question went totally ignored.

"Would you like to come up to my room?" Russell asked Susan.

"Yes," smiled Susan.

"Am I included in this invitation?" Anna asked Susan.

"Can Anna come as well?" Susan asked Russell.

"I suppose so," he said, his eyes never leaving Susan.

"Right then," said Anna locking the passenger door, getting out of the car and folding the seat forward so that Susan and Russell could get out. "Are you getting out?" she added.

265

"Of course," muttered Susan climbing out and turning to give Russell a hand.

"It's not the easiest of cars to get out of," said Russell with a laugh.

"Yes, well at least I have a car," thought Anna.

"Which floor are you on?" asked Anna looking up at the building again and turned to see Susan and Russell heading off towards a door into the hall. Anna quickly locked the car and dashed after them. "I don't want to be searching this dump for them," she thought.

"Hold the lift," she yelled to Susan, as she and Russell had got in a little bit ahead of her. Susan pressed the button to stop the lift moving whilst she rushed in.

"Don't forget me, I don't know where this room is," Anna hissed at Susan. "I don't even know which floor he's on."

"Sorry," Susan mouthed.

"You might be, but he isn't," thought Anna, glaring at his back. The lift doors opened.

"This is as far as the lift goes," said Russell. "My room is on the next floor, so we have to walk up one flight of stairs to get there."

"We would," thought Anna, following in their wake.

Russell flung open the fire door and said dramatically, "This is my floor."

"No it isn't, you don't own it," said someone walking past and heading downstairs.

"Ignore him," said Russell. "He's a right know it all."

"Takes one to know one," thought Anna.

"This is my room," said Russell unlocking a door on the right hand side of the corridor.

"This is nice," said Susan walking in and looking round. "Compact, great view," she added, stepping over the detritus on the floor.

"Mucky undies," thought Anna averting her gaze from the floor only to see more rubbish on every surface. "Obviously not used to cleaning up after himself.

"There's a double room we use for guests," said Russell. "No one's in it at the moment, if you'd like to see it?" he suggested to Susan.

"Yes. Let's see that," said Anna. "Quick, before the smell gets to us, God knows how your cleaners put up with this. I know ours would have a blue fit," thought Anna, getting out of Russell's room as quickly as she could.

266

"This is the guest room," said Russell opening the door of the room opposite. It seemed bleak and large in contrast, probably because of the lack of things on all the surfaces. The wall opposite the door was all window from about three foot to the ceiling, there was a large desk across the far end of the room, a chest of drawers by the door and a double bed on the other side of the door.

"We'd better get our sleeping bags and some things from the car," said Anna.

"Could you get them Anna?" asked Susan.

"No, you'll need to sort out what you want," said Anna. "If you think I'm carting your stuff up here," she thought. "You can get yourself another slave, because I'm not doing it."

"I'll help you," Russell smiled at Susan.

"Thank-you," she said smiling at him.

"You make me sick," thought Anna heading for the door.

"Come on," she said. "It's not going to come up here by its self."

"Be good if it did," said Susan.

"It would probably go to the wrong room," said Anna, holding the fire door open for Susan, Russell followed her through the door. "It is so tempting to slam the door in his face, but then, Susan would be upset and he probably wouldn't help with the computer."

Friday morning, their third morning as unofficial guests of the Poly, Anna and Susan were busy reading newspapers in the Poly library. They were bored of wondering round the town and felt less conspicuous in the library, which also gave them a chance of catching up with the world.

"Someone missing from a mental institution," a small story caught Anna's eye. "She went missing during a fire. At first it was thought that she might have perished in the fire, but no remains have been found, so they are working on the theory that she may have have wandered off in the commotion. The Police are still looking for her, but they say there is no danger to the general public."

"This is about Susan," she thought. "She's the missing girl. And it doesn't mention me. The penny didn't drop. The nurse must have forgotten about me. Susan should read this. There's Russell, he's looking worried, what's going on."

267

"Russell's looking worried," she said to Susan, who waved to attract his attention. He saw them and came over.

"Thank goodness I've found you," he said, putting his arms around Susan.

"What's wrong?" asked Susan.

Anna closed her newspaper and made a mental note to tell Susan about the story later.

"They've disconnected the land line," he said.

"What!" Susan exclaimed, sitting back down again with a thump.

"The technician's were saying we'd have fewer problems with data going astray now they've disconnected the land line," said Russell.

"What are we going to do?" wailed Susan, before Anna shushed her.

"Don't make so much noise," Anna said. "They'll chuck us out."

"Well the programming is mostly done," started Russell.

"Mostly isn't good enough," Susan snapped him.

"Don't push our luck," thought Anna.

"We could use a modem," suggested Russell.

"Oh yes. I can really see that. Ring up and ask if we can spread their computer files across the front pages of every national newspaper in the land. I'm sure they'd be only too delighted to link us up with their computer," snapped Susan.

"There's no need to be like that," snapped Anna to Susan. "After all, he doesn't have to help us," she added. "And he won't if you go at him like that," she thought to herself.

"I know. I'm sorry," said Susan quietening down a bit,"But I know what all this is leading up to. We're going to have to go back there aren't we?" she said, her words coming our in a rush and her eyes moving from Anna to Russell and stopping there.

"It looks that way," said Russell looking uncomfortable.

"I can't go back there, not again, can't you see that?" Susan looked at him with pleading in her eyes.

"I can always take Russell and you can wait here for us," said Anna.

"Can't you go by yourself?" Susan asked Anna.

"I'm not the computer expert," said Anna.

"Russell could tell you what to do," Susan started.

"And if it doesn't work on our computer, he'd know what to do, I wouldn't," said Anna. "And I get the impression we're only going to have one chance at this."

268

"He could go by himself," Susan suggested.

"I think that would be asking a bit much of him," hissed Anna. "Anyway, he doesn't know his way round the dump."

"OK," said Susan, squaring her shoulders. "If you can go, so can I."

"You don't trust me with that drip," thought Anna. "Personally I wouldn't touch him with a barge pole, well, not unless I could sharpen the end of it first."

"Well, that's settled that then," said Anna brightly. "We're all going."

"When should we go?" asked Susan, looking at Russell.

"As soon as possible," he said.

"My thoughts precisely," thought Anna.

"We can go any time, can't we Susan," she said.

"Oh. Yes," said Susan.

"It's just a question of when it's convenient for you," said Anna looking at Russell.

"I'm free for the rest of the day. We could go now," he said.

"That's fine by me," said Anna.

"Don't you think we ought to wait till later?" said Susan. "Everyone leaves early on a Friday, we don't want to bump into anyone."

"We could leave after lunch," said Anna, looking at a clock and noticing the time.

"As early as that," Susan looked alarmed.

"It's not the shortest of drives and we've got to allow for the car breaking down," said Anna.

"I suppose that is something to be taken into consideration," said Russell. "How old is it?"

"13 years old," said Anna.

"That ancient," said Russell. "I'm surprised it's still working."

"It's in perfectly good condition, passed its MOT just before Christmas," said Anna defensively, "Not that it's any of your business," she thought.

"I'll take your word for it. I don't know anything about cars," said Susan.

"Neither do I," said Russell. "I wouldn't know what an MOT proves anyway."

"It proves its safe to drive," said Anna.

"I'll take your word for that," said Russell.

"Well lets hope it doesn't breakdown," thought Anna. "Because it looks like I'll have to fix it if we do."

269

"What do you fancy for lunch then," she asked.

"We could get some sandwiches at the canteen," said Russell. "They should be open by now."

"Is it that time already?" asked Susan.

"Yes," said Russell. "I'm famished."

After dinner the sleeping bags were loaded in the car, just in case they were needed and they set off.

Six o'clock, on a cold windy evening, found them parked in a side street a couple of miles from the Poly.

"Can't we park a bit closer," moaned Susan. "It's an awful long way to walk."

"Do you want them to see the car," snapped Anna.

"I don't see that it matters," said Russell.

"It may be recognised and we don't want them suspecting anything," said Anna.

"But it's such a long way," muttered Susan.

"The exercise will do you good," said Anna.

"Thanks," muttered Susan.

"What shall we do for tea?" asked Russell.

"You could try our refectory," said Susan. "Then you can see what revolting food is really like."

"I don't think that would be a good idea," said Anna.

"Why not?" said Susan and Russell turning on Anna.

"We'd be recognised, our dinner tickets are now probably no longer valid," said Anna. "And anyway, you have to get a special dinner ticket for visitors."

"They'd probably need to be certified to eat there," thought Anna.

"Oh. But where can we eat?" said Susan.

"There's that Chinese restaurant just opposite the computer building. They do a good meal there, but it's never busy, so we're unlikely to be spotted and we can keep an eye on the building and go in when it looks quiet," said Anna.

"Sounds like a good idea," said Russell.

"Let's get a move on then," said Anna, ignoring the scowl on Susan's face.

270

The restaurant was empty, though a steady stream of people came in for takeaways.

"I suppose that's where they make most of their money," thought Anna.

The meal was good and it was tempting to get some wine to drink with it.

"Anna's driving and I need to keep my head clear, for the programming," said Russell when Susan suggested it.

"Oh," said Susan. "I suppose a coffee would be nice."

"Nice to be in on that decision," thought Anna.

"What time do they lock up for the night," asked Russell as they were sipping the last of the coffee and the bill appeared, as if by magic, in a saucer on the table.

"Nine o'clock," said Anna, watching as Russell pushed the saucer towards her.

"Then we ought to get a move on," he said as Anna took the hint and went to pay the bill.

"Are you sure?" asked Susan.

"We don't want to get locked in," he said to her.

"No. That's true. We'd better get going then," said Susan

"Yes," said Anna. "The sooner we start, the sooner we'll finish."

"And that can't be soon enough for me," she thought, putting her purse back into her handbag. "I'm tired of paying for that charmless nerd."

Entering through the side door, the building seemed excessively quiet. Every footstep echoed down the corridors, which seemed much longer than Anna remembered them.

"Is it my imagination or is someone watching us," thought Anna, looking round and trying to penetrate the darkness of the shadows with her eyes. But the shadows were too dense.

"Where's the computer room?" whispered Russell.

"Top floor," whispered Anna. "Up these stairs," she added heading off up, Susan and Russell followed after a moments hesitation. "There's a main room and a smaller one at the very top of the building. People usually forget about the smaller one."

"Not so loud," whispered Susan. "Someone might hear us."

"Where now," said Russell, slightly out of breath at the top of the stairs.

"Down the corridor and up one more flight," said Anna.

"Not more stairs," muttered Russell.

"You're out of condition," said Anna trying not to sound breathless.

271

"What's that noise?" hissed Susan.

"A printer," said Russell.

"Perhaps we ought to go," said Susan. "They might see us."

"Sounds like the main computer room," said Anna.

"Is there another computer room?" Russell asked Susan, who looked to Anna for an answer.

"There is a small room, on the next floor up," said Anna. "Like I've already told you, but you couldn't be arsed to listen to me could you," she thought.

"I thought we were on the top floor?" Russell said to Susan.

"The top full floor," said Anna. "But there's a flight of stairs at the far end of the corridor that leads to one little room which has a few terminals in it."

"I didn't know that," said Susan.

"Not many people do," said Anna. "That's why it's always possible to get on the computer there."

"That sounds like the room to use," Russell told Susan.

"If we go down a floor we can use the corridor down there to get to the other side of the building. They'll never see us then," Susan suggested.

"Couldn't we just sneak past the door," said Russell, "There doesn't seem to be anyone around," he added.

"It's probably just something being bashed out on the teleprinter," said Anna.

"I don't know," said Susan.

"It would get us there quicker," said Anna. "And I'd feel happier once we're there, she added. "Happier than standing in the middle of the corridor debating the matter," she thought looking round, trying not to let her imagination get the better of her.

"Let's get going then," said Susan, trying to decide which was the darkest side of the corridor. Anna walked quickly down the middle of the corridor, so that Susan and Russell had to run to catch up with her.

The small computer room was deserted. Russell had a choice of terminals and was soon hard at work. Susan sat down nearby looking adoringly.

"Oh God," thought Anna looking at her.

"I'll go outside and watch out for anyone coming," she said and went to sit at the top of the stairs, when no one said anything.

"Thank God she's gone," said Russell.

272

"She means well, but it is nice to be alone," Susan said gazing admiringly at Russell.

"I'm not so sure that she does mean well," said Russell.

"What do you mean?" asked Susan.

"Did she tell you about the newspaper report about someone missing from a mental institution?" he asked.

"What report?" asked Susan sharply.

"I thought not," said Russell. "The police are looking for you."

"Oh God no," said Susan sliding off the chair onto the ground.

"They weren't looking for anyone with you," he added. "So, if anything goes wrong she can blame it all on you and deny any knowledge of where you are and what you've done. She can drop you in it and just walk away."

"She wouldn't do that, she's always been there for me," stammered Susan.

"Are you sure of that, I mean the two of you are always bickering, are you sure she wouldn't leave you to take the blame as soon as all this is done?" he asked.

"What am I going to do?" Susan muttered, her head in her hands, she didn't see the look of satisfaction on Russell's face.

"When we've finished here, I'll find us somewhere safe to live, then we can dump her. I can keep you safe till they stop looking for you," said Russell.

"But what about Anna?" asked Susan.

"She's probably going to drop you in it as soon as it is convenient for her, so I don't know why you're worrying about her. We will just be getting in first," said Russell with a smile, pressing one last key which set the computer into action. "That's done it," he said. "Everything from Mr Thomas's area on the computer, plus all the storage space that was linked to it has been sent of to a newspaper which has direct input from their journalists, I know someone there who will pass this on to the major newspapers, give it a few days and this story will be unstoppable, Mr Thomas and his colleagues will get what's due to them," he said, his fingers mentally crossed behind his back as he hoped she didn't notice that the whole thing was dependent on someone in one newspaper being willing to pass a story on to another newspaper.

"You're so clever," said Susan. "We couldn't have done this without you."

273

"I know," he said with a smile. "Let's go and tell Anna what I've done," he added heading for the door to the computer room.

"It's done," Russell told Anna, as she stood up from the post at the top of the stairs. "The information has all been sent. There's nothing more to do, the story will be in the papers in the next few days and then some people will have a lot of questions to answer."

"So now we can get out of this dump," said Susan.

"And quickly," added Anna starting down the stairs, but a loud whoosh drowned out her words.

"What the hell!" exclaimed Russell.

"Sounds like the main computer room," said Anna dashing down the rest of the stairs. As she approached the main computer room a large sheet of flame shot out of the door. Anna skidded to a halt.

"Bloody hell," she muttered, "The teleprinter must have caught fire again," she added, heading back to the stairs, the sound of fire alarms adding to the din created by the fire spreading through the computer room.

"Did you do that?" Russell demanded, grabbing her arm as she dashed back to the stairs.

"Of course not," she snapped, shaking his hand off. "This is the last thing we need for a quiet exit."

"At least we don't have to raise the alarm," said Susan, from the stairs, as in the distance the sound of fire engines added to the confusion.

"True, but if they find us here," said Russell. "We're going to have some pretty difficult questions to answer."

"Oh," said Susan, increasing her pace down the stairs.

"How are we going to get out of here without being seen?" asked Russell.

"There's the basement door," said Anna. "If we're quick they shouldn't see us leaving."

"Where is it?" snapped Russell.

"Follow me," said Anna and ran down the stairs, one more flight down than they'd gone up.

"Here's the door," said Anna, ignoring the double doors to the right and making for what looked like a cupboard door.

"Let's hope the bloody things unlocked," she thought.

"Are you sure," said Russell looking doubtful.

"It's my Poly, I should know," thought Anna, but she said nothing merely opened the door and stepped out into the cool night air.

274

"Down here," said Anna leading the way down a flight of stairs to a car park.

"And where do we go from here?" asked Russell as they stood in the shadows at the edge of the car park, the whole area before them seemed brightly illuminated, too bright for them to venture into.

"If we stay in the shadows, work our way round the edge, there's an underpass over there," said Anna. "Then we can get well away from here."

"Sounds reasonable," said Russell, leading the way.

"Thank-you for nothing," thought Anna heading off for the underpass.

"That's a bit convenient," mouthed Russell to Susan.

The sound of an explosion came from the burning building, echoing round the underpass they had just dived into.

"What was that," muttered Anna, looking towards the mouth of the tunnel.

"I don't know," said Susan.

"Neither do I," said Russell. "But I don't want to stay here to find out."

"I wasn't suggesting that we did," said Anna. "I was just wondering what on earth they had in there to go off like that."

"Probably something in one of the labs," said Russell.

"There aren't any labs in that building," said Anna. "Not as far as I know. Not unless they've changed something in the last few weeks"

"Could be some of the cleaners they use for the printers, they can be pretty volatile," suggested Russell.

"Mr Thomas got them from somewhere, the cleaners said he was in charge of buying all the stuff they used, which always seemed a bit odd to me," said Anna.

"I think there's a lot of odd things we don't know about the Poly," said Susan shaking. "And I don't want to find out about them."

"I think we could do with a drink," said Russell putting his arm around Susan.

"Yes," said Anna taking a last look at the blazing building. "I noticed a pub near where we parked."

"Couldn't we go to one nearer?" asked Russell.

"Too much of a risk. We might be recognised," said Anna.

"And if we stand out as strangers we'll raise suspicions," said Susan.

"There's an off-licence over there," said Russell. "I'll get a bottle, we can drink it in the car."

"Sounds like a good idea," said Anna.

275

"Yes. If we get drunk we won't have to worry about staggering back to the car," said Susan.

"Exactly," said Anna.

"I don't think it's a good idea to drink and drive," said Russell.

"So you expected me to sit and watch whilst you two got sloshed and then drive all night to get you home," thought Anna.

"Who's driving?" she asked. "I have no intention of moving that car tonight. I've just had to run for my life from a burning building and only just got out just before it exploded. After a shock like that, I'm not sure it would be safe for me to drive."

"Oh," said Russell pausing for a moment.

"Well are you going to argue about it," thought Anna.

"I'll get a bottle," he said. "You'll be OK here won't you?" he asked Susan.

"She'll be fine," said Anna. "She can sit on the wall," she added as Susan sank down onto the wall, her legs refusing to support her any longer. "I can look after her," thought Anna. "I've been doing that for long enough."

Five minutes later he returned with a bottle of wine.

"We haven't got a corkscrew," he said by the way of an explanation as to the choice of drink, whilst he unscrewed the bottle top and helped Susan to some.

"I have," thought Anna in her mind picturing the penknife in her handbag and the corkscrew attachment. "You don't know everything."

"There that's brought the colour back to your cheeks," said Russell and took a swig of Blue Nun. "Do you think you can make it back to the car?"

"She'll have to," thought Anna. "We can't exactly get a taxi."

"I think so," said Susan, slowly standing up. "I'm feeling a lot better."

"You can lean on me," said Russell. "If Anna will lead the way," he added screwing the lid back on the wine bottle.

"Great," thought Anna.

"I'll just be a minute," she said.

"Where are you going?" asked Susan grabbing at Anna's arm.

"To the off-licence," she said. "I could do with a drink too."

"I forgot about you," muttered Russell, handing over the bottle.

"Much you did," thought Anna taking a long swig.

"Don't drink it all," said Russell just restraining himself from snatching the bottle back.

"Chance would be a fine thing," thought Anna handing the bottle back to Susan.

"To the car," she said, heading off into the dark. "Though quite how we're all going to sleep in it I don't know," she thought.

But back at the car Susan and Russell seemed to have worked that one out. They just climbed into the back and handed over Anna's sleeping bag.

"It's their decision," thought Anna. "But they're going to find it a bit cramped in there."

Chapter 15
The next day

In her dream Anna was relaxing in the sun.   Sitting comfortably on the front of a dump truck, not a cloud in the sky.   Her repose was rudely interrupted when a flock of squawking seagulls swooped down towards her. They never arrived, she surfaced from the dream first, yet the squawking continued.   For a moment she was confused, then she traced the sound to the back seat, to Susan and Russell who were in a bit of a tangle with the sleeping bag and would have fallen off the back seat into the floor pans if there had been enough room to do so.

"What on earth are you two doing down there?" she asked getting out of the car before their struggles pushed her into the steering wheel.

"What does it look like," shouted Susan, as Anna tried to smoother a laugh.   "Don't just stand there, give us a hand."

"You seem to be managing fine by yourself," she said as Susan fell back onto Russell.   "Careful, you're squashing the poor lad."

"I'd be OK if it wasn't for this sleeping bag," muttered Susan.   "It ties you up."

"OK.   I'll try to extract it," said Anna cautiously undoing the first sleeping bag zip she came to, then she pushed part of the sleeping bag onto the back seat out of their way.

"I think I can get out now," said Susan climbing over Russell to the driver's door and out leaving a trodden looking Russell in a heap on the floor.

"Serves you right," thought Anna with a smile.

He lay there for a moment and then dragged himself out of the car.

"If you could see yourselves," said Anna grinning.

"We can't possibly look worse than I feel," muttered Russell.

"Never mind," said Anna in mock sympathy.

"I've been trampled and my stomach thinks my throats been cut," he mumbled.

"Sorry," said Susan looking worried.

"Better see what we can find in the way of breakfast," said Anna.

"How do you mean?" asked Susan.

"There must be some shops round here," said Anna.

"Open at half past seven," muttered Russell, looking at his watch.

"Newsagents, petrol station shops, corner convenience shops," said Anna.

"There's a petrol station round the corner," said Susan. "I remember seeing it last night."

"Are you sure it was round that corner and not one of the half million other corners we went round last night," said Russell.

"Yes," said Susan. "I think so."

"Well we won't find out standing here," said Anna, locking the car and heading off down the road. Susan and Russell exchanged glances and then ran after her.

"There it is," said Susan. "I can see the shop windows," she pointed to a shop at the end of the street.

"That's a newsagents," said Russell.

"Are you sure?" asked Susan.

"Petrol stations have petrol pumps," he said .

"Well, no one's perfect," said Susan.

"How can you mistake a newsagents for a petrol station. I mean they look totally different. You can't get petrol at a newsagents can you," said Russell.

"OK. So it was a stupid mistake. There's no need to go on about it," said Susan.

"At least we'll be able to get a paper here," said Anna.

"What do you want a paper for," snapped Russell.

"None of your business," thought Anna.

"To read our story," she said.

"I told you it will be in the papers, but it's going to take a few days for it to percolate into the nationals, but it will get there. Don't you trust me," he snapped.

"Of course," said Anna. "About as much as I trust Mr Thomas," she thought. "It's just, with the place blowing up and all," she added.

"Everything was done by then. That wouldn't have had any effect," snapped Russell.

"With the place blowing up," Anna repeated herself. "I'd like to see what the local papers say about that, see if they have any ideas as to the

279

cause of the fire."

"Why, what are you afraid of?" snapped Russell.

"I'd rather not have the Police looking for me in respect to a fire, I would assume you two wouldn't either," said Anna looking from him to Susan who was busy looking in the shop window.

"I smell a rat, a dirty big one," Anna thought.

"They've got pasties," said Susan. "I could go a pasty for breakfast, what do you think?" she added looking at Russell.

"Yes, A pasty would be good," he said smiling at Susan.

"There's something not right about the way he smiles at her," thought Anna. "It gives me the creeps."

Back in the car Anna started looking through the local paper, whilst Russell tucked into his pasty.

"I don't know why you bothered," said Russell. "It isn't as if they are going to know anything about the cause of the fire, they'll still be damping it down."

"I want to know if there were any reports of people seen leaving the building or acting suspiciously near it," said Anna, not seeing the knowing look passing from Russell to Susan.

"If they were looking for anyone, they'd have found us by now," said Russell. "Don't you think it's about time we got away from here?"

"Yes," said Susan.

"Right," said Anna, finishing her breakfast. "I suppose we'd better take Russell back to his Poly now," she added.

"What will you do after that?" Russell asked Anna.

"Don't know. Have you any ideas Susan?" asked Anna. "So, he's finally talking to me," she thought. "What's he up to?"

"We don't have anywhere in particular to go, do we?" said Susan, looking at Russell for help.

"I suppose not," said Anna.

"We could find somewhere to stay near to Russell," said Susan.

"Rent a flat?" asked Anna.

"Something like that," said Susan.

"Sounds like a plan," said Anna. "We'll get Russell back to his Poly and see what we can organise."

280

"Oh dear," muttered Susan looking pleadingly at Russell.

"You've got to tell her," hissed Russell to Susan.

"Tell me what?" said Anna.

"What are you two cooking up?" she thought.

"I, I need the toilet," said Susan.

"I'm sure that wasn't it," thought Anna. "But I don't think I'm going to get a straight answer out of either of you just yet."

"So do I," said Russell.

"Well then we'd better find one before we head off back," said Anna. "I don't want you two wetting yourselves in my car."

"I could also do with going to the loo myself," she thought.

"We need some petrol, there may be some toilets at the petrol station, if not they should know where there are some," said Anna. "I don't suppose you feel like contributing to the cost?" she asked. "I've been paying for everything since we met," she thought. "And I'm rapidly running out of money."

"Oh. Right. Yes," said Russell.

"Have you got any money?" he asked Susan.

"Great," thought Anna. "Susan you're going to have a wonderful life with him."

"No," said Susan. "I didn't have any on me when I left that place."

"No and I've been looking after the cash since then," thought Anna.

"How about cash point cards?" he asked.

"They don't have much need for them in the loony bin," snapped Anna.

"But you must have had a bank account?" said Russell.

"Of course I did," snapped Susan.

"Do you know the account number?" asked Russell.

"No. It wouldn't help me, without a cheque guarantee card, a cheque book or some means of identity," muttered Susan. "And if I could prove who I was then the men in white suits would know where I was and would come looking for me. I'm not that stupid."

"This isn't going to help us pay for the petrol," said Anna. "I've only got five pounds left. Could you lend us some?" she asked, turning to Russell.

"Or don't you like spending your own money," thought Anna.

"Oh yes. Of course," said Russell.

"Would you like me to take you to a cash point machine, or would you prefer to use a cheque," asked Anna.

"If you stop at a bank," said Russell. "I'll get some cash out."

"Hurray," thought Anna. "I've actually managed to pry open your wallet," she parked on the kerb by the cash point, two minutes later he handed her ten pounds.

"I hope that'll help with the petrol," he said putting the ten pound note on the dashboard and climbing into the back of the car with Susan.

"Looks like it'll have to do," thought Anna pulling in at the first petrol station they came to and then heading back to Russell's Poly.

It took two hours to get back to Russell's Poly, once there Anna and Susan started looking for accommodation from one of the landlords on the Poly's list of approved lettings.

"They're all single rooms in student lets," said Susan glumly.

"And we're not students, not now," said Anna. "And I don't want to share a room with you, not with the likelihood of Russell popping round at all hours," she thought. "We need to look into private rented," she added.

"Don't they need a deposit, or references, or something," said Susan.

"I don't know. We'll just have to find out," said Anna.

"A friend of mine is in private rented," said Russell. "I'll see if I can talk to his landlord, he might have something. In the meantime, you two go back to the spare room on my floor and have a rest. You must be all in after yesterday," he added looking at Susan.

"Sounds like a plan," said Anna.

"Here's the key," he said to Susan. "I'll see you there later."

"When is he going to talk to me?" asked Anna as Russell headed off into the depths of the Poly.

"It's just his way," said Susan. "It's really rather sweet."

"In what way is that sweet?" asked Anna. "From where I'm standing its just plan bad manners."

"He's not good with people and he doesn't want me to think that he might be trying to chat you up. That's why it's sweet. To think, we only met at a party and he hasn't stopped thinking about me since then."Susan smiled.

"Someone's gaga round here, I'm just not sure who," thought Anna as they headed back to the car so they could return to the spare room in Russell's hall of residence.

It was nearly three o'clock by the time he got back.

"I've spoken to Tim's landlord, he's a really nice guy. He has a basement flat that has just become vacant, I went to see it and it looks

282

perfect," said Russell. "We can move in tomorrow."

"Sunday?" thought Anna. "Seems like an odd day to move in."

"Great," said Susan, looking lovingly at him.

"Shouldn't we look at it first," said Anna.

"Russell says it's fine and I trust him. Anyway, if we don't like it we can always find somewhere else," said Susan.

"Are there any documents to sign, deposits to pay, stuff like that?" asked Anna.

"Don't worry. I've sorted it all," said Russell, hurriedly.

"We need to get packed," said Susan looking round the room at her clothes which seemed to have seeped out of her bags onto the floor. Anna kept her things in their bags, ready to move whenever necessary.

"When can we move in?" Susan asked Russell.

"I've been promised the key first thing tomorrow. We can move in then, if Anna will help move the stuff over," said Russell looking at Anna.

"OK," said Anna. "He's up to something, I don't trust him when he talks to me and I trust him less when he looks at me whilst he's talking," she thought. "I don't know what, but there's something not right about this."

Next morning, Anna and Susan packed the mini whilst Russell went off to get the key to the flat. When he returned, half an hour later, the car was packed with Susan's stuff.

"I didn't realise she had this much, though I suppose with Russell in the car we can't put quite so much in," thought Anna as they all drove to the flat. "He can help with the unloading, got to be good for something," she thought as he climbed into the front passenger seat. "He's even going to sit beside me!"

"Let's see what this place looks like," said Anna with a smile.

"It's the basement of a Victorian terrace house. One of those tall posh one's," said Russell.

"Won't it be dark?" asked Susan.

"No. There's a flight of stairs down to it form the road and a window, you can see up to the pavement and the ground falls away at the back, so there's a door out onto a sunny garden."

"That sounds wonderful," said Susan smiling.

"Good," said Russell. "There it is, number 33," he pointed to a rather shabby looking house with peeling paint and a rusty fence.

"Great," thought Anna. "We can find somewhere else, or we can move on to another town when the love birds fall out."

"Let's get unpacking," she said as she pulled up in front of the house. "I'd like to see Russell do some work for a change," she thought.

With three of them working and the mini parked as close as possible to the front door, it didn't take long to unload Susan's stuff into the living room.

"Now for the Grand Tour," said Russell with a flourish.

"This is the living room," he said standing in the middle, pointing to two armchairs and a small coffee table, which were rather swamped by Susan's bags and baggage. "In here is the kitchen, he said opening a door which, Anna thought would lead to a cupboard under the stairs, but led to the smallest kitchen she had ever seen.

"That would be crowded with just me in," she thought, horrified.

"How sweet," murmured Susan.

"Is she drunk," thought Anna, "Or is this some sort of throw back to those drugs they had her on?"

"Then through here is the bathroom and the bedroom," added Russell, opening another door at right angles to the kitchen door, that led to a small corridor with two doors, one straight ahead and one to the left.

"So where's this back door?" thought Anna. "And the garden?"

"Can I see?" said Susan, wandering through the door.

"Of course," said Russell smiling.

The door on the left opened to reveal a shower room, rather than a bathroom and a very small one at that.

"It's all we'll need," Susan smiled.

"If you say so," thought Anna.

"Let's see what's through the other door," she said as Susan opened the remaining door.

"Perfect," Susan declared.

"One bedroomed," thought Anna. "And a double bed at that. I smell a rat and not one that's come here to live, no self respecting rat would do that."

"Let's go back and get my things now," said Anna. "Not that I intend to stop here for long," she thought.

"Yes. That would be a good idea," said Russell hurriedly glancing at

284

Susan.

"Yes. Lets do that," said Susan making for the stairs.

It didn't take long to pack Anna's stuff and, as they passed Russell's room, Anna noticed that it had a very empty look about it.

"Almost like he's moving out," thought Anna, as they headed down to the car.

"So where are you going now?" asked Russell, as the last thing was put onto the back seat.

"Talking to me again are you?" she thought. "You are up to something, you scheming so and so."

"To number 33," said Anna.

"It would be nice of you to give us a lift back, but where are you going after that?" asked Russell.

"I thought I was going to live there with Susan," said Anna. "But obviously you didn't," she thought.

"There really isn't room for the three of us there?" said Russell looking into the distance.

"You've got your room at the Polytechnic," said Anna, then the penny dropped. "You're moving in with Susan and you don't want me around," thought Anna. "But you were too gutless to say."

"We're in love," said Susan, as if that explained anything.

"We were wondering what you would do?" said Russell.

"I didn't know you cared," snapped Anna.

"I don't," said Russell. "But Susan was interested."

"Thanks," said Anna bitterly. "Of all the things that have happened this seems the most unreal," thought Anna looking at her mini.

"Now what do I do? Where do I go?" she thought settling herself in the drivers seat.

"Have you thought about going back to Phil?" asked Susan who looked suitably miserable.

"Why?" asked Anna.

"He was very concerned about you," said Susan.

"Which was more than you and Russell are," thought Anna.

"I think he fancies you," said Susan.

"Hasn't she gone yet," said Russell walking up to the mini.

"It's very tempting to run him over, it would be so easy," thought Anna. "But, I'd hate to damage the paintwork, he isn't worth it."

"Bye Susan. Good luck with him. You'll need it," said Anna.

285

"Thanks," said Susan to Anna.

"Did you have to say that," snapped Susan to Russell.

"I thought she'd have gone by now," he said.

"If you hadn't opened your big mouth we'd have got a lift back to number 33," said Susan.

"It isn't that far, anyway, I need to have one last check of my room and then hand the keys back," said Russell.

"You don't mind moving out of hall do you?" asked Susan.

"No. It was too restrictive and there were rumours that they were going to throw me out anyway," said Russell.

"I'm out of here. I mean, as far as they're concerned I've already left," thought Anna, shutting the car door and starting the engine and reversing out of the parking space. "I'll go before the sight of them makes me throw up," she turned left out of the car park and headed off down the road.

"I wonder if there's anything on the radio?" she thought, pressing the button.

"...Fire in the Polytechnic computer building is being investigated because just before the fire started information was sent from the computer which has led to the arrest of several of the lecturers for financial irregularities."

"What!" said Anna. "The pillock actually managed it."

"The Police are also looking into how the fire started. They want to hear from anyone who was anywhere near the building at the time and so may have seen something," the report continued.

Anna headed back up the road to tell Susan what she had just heard. Pulling up next to Russell, she opened the car door to tell him.

"Don't you know when you aren't wanted," Russell yelled at her.

"I just wanted to tell Susan," Anna started.

"Susan doesn't want anything to do with you. She wants to get on with her life and stop thinking about that place and what it did to her. You are a constant reminder of all that she's gone through," he shouted at her. "Just get out of her life. Go away. Now."

"Where is Susan?" asked Anna, looking round the pavement trying to see where her friend was, she'd only been gone a few minutes, yet Susan was nowhere to be seen.

"Go," yelled Russell, pulling the car door open and taking a swing at her, Anna ducked out of the way, lashing out at him with her elbow, she sent him flying across the pavement.

It was then that Anna saw Susan, rushing to the aid of her boyfriend.

"You bitch, can't you just leave us alone," Susan yelled at her, as Anna shut the car door. "Sod off, I don't want to see you ever again," she added kicking the car door.

"Well, if that's how you feel," thought Anna, putting the car into gear. "After all I've done for you. Sod it, I'm off," she headed off back down the road, laughing to herself as Russell tried to kick the car, missed and fell on his back in the middle of the road. Susan dashed to his side to comfort him and got pushed away whilst Russell got to his feet and shook his fist at the disappearing car.

"Heroin screws you up," a poster on a bus shelter announced.

"So do people," thought Anna taking one last look in the rear view mirror at Susan and Russell. "This sort of thing doesn't happen to a person like me, not in real life, it happens in films. Isn't this about the time they roll the credits and everything goes all tall and thin, with me driving into the distance, possibly, in search of Phil, leaving the audience to go home happily imagining the reunion but without having to actually go to the expense of making it. That makes the assumption that he's there or that I can find him. I could ring the phone number he gave me to check on his whereabouts. Then again I could just drive off into the unknown and see what I can find. The world is my oyster and all that crap.

I don't suppose the credits are flashing up on my boot lid. That could explain why I can't see them. There isn't FINIS superimposed on my number plate is there?

THE END

Printed in Great Britain
by Amazon

26827831R00165